DAKTOUM

CHRISTOPHER UPHAM

A NOVEL OF VIETNAM

For Edie
my inspiration!

Credits:

Design: Tom Joyce and Laura Duggan
Cover Art: MJ Davison
Published by: Cereus Press
ISBN:978-1-7351903-1-0
Printed in the USA

FOREWORD

Depending on where exactly you served and what your duty was, the American War in Viet Nam was many different wars. In the fifty years since the end of that war, thousands of books have been written that try to make sense of what was a horrific, moral collapse on the part of the United States and its allies. This large bibliography includes novels, memoirs, nonfiction studies, poetry, and drama. What separates *Daktoum* from the rest of these books is the author's precise focus on the middle ground of the war. This is the first novel that I'm aware of that narrates the tragedy that war is from the point of view of soldiers caught in this strange purgatory of basecamps, where human intrigues emerge in unexpected ways, the war always near enough to kill you. There was a front, a rear, and in between, there was this strange middle ground where many soldiers lived in relative comfort during the day and were rocketed or mortared during the night. These contrasts created a different kind of experience than those of line soldiers, and this middle ground could become an otherworldly place, defined by its own laws and sometimes ruled by officers deemed unfit to be in combat. Christopher Upham writes about this middle ground in the war with striking accuracy and with a passion that lifts his story out of the ordinary and into our lives.

What I like best about this book is the way that it rises above being simply another war story by relying on the war as a backdrop to human drama, in which a richly engaging tale of one man's struggle with trying to understand who he is, is revealed. I would say to my friends, "Hey, you need to read this book."

Bruce Weigl
Poet, writer, translator, and
winner of the Lannan Literary Award for Poetry

ACKNOWLEDGEMENTS

For early encouragements in writing this book, I'd like to thank Gloria Emerson, Tom Williams, Som Ranchan, and Ben Camardi, my agent at Harold Matson Company. I'm indebted to Maisie Cochran and Joaquin Lowe, my editors, and to Holly Payne for friendship and editorial guidance. Jan Suarez performed early manuscript work and my other sisters, Elaine, Ellice, Ellette, and Elizabeth were emotionally instrumental in allowing me to continue this work, as were Stephanie D'Arnall, S. Smith Patrick, and MJ Davison, who also designed the book cover. Isabelle Sorrell was a champion of this book. I'd also like to thank my long-time friend Diana Fuller for her belief in me, and Brett Hall and Louis B. Jones and all my friends and colleagues at the Community of Writers for long-standing encouragement. Laura Duggan at Nicasio Press provided publication help and design. Thanks to my great friends CB and Bruce Weigl for believing in me.

We used to wonder where the war lived, what it was that made it so vile. And now we know where it lives, that it is inside ourselves. For most people, it's the embarrassment, the need to make a choice, the choice that makes them go but feel remorse for not having been brave enough to stay at home, or which makes them stay at home but regret they can't share the way the others are going to die.

—Albert Camus

DAKTOUM

A novel by

Christopher Upham

1.

Scrappy, crew-cut Colonel John Lehr grinned at the blonde stewardess and stepped out of the plane onto an aluminum ramp, where the heat of Vietnam struck him like a rifle butt.

Saigon, he thought, thirteen years since my first posting.

A hundred combat soldiers stood on the hot tarmac, waiting to go home. Christ, Lehr thought, their eyes, like old men. They'd kill to get on this plane. They have killed.

Fighter jets roared overhead, and the colonel coughed as he stepped off the ramp. When the ache left his chest, Lehr glanced back.

At the top of the ramp, a handsome, young soldier shielded his eyes against the shattering light, his mouth gaping at the dirty yellow sky throbbing with planes and helicopters, rising and descending across the Bien Hoa runways.

Lehr watched the stone-faced veterans focused on the plane, and then the young replacement soldiers stepping down the ramp. Teenagers, Lehr thought. How many will make it back?

As the replacements exited the plane, Colonel Lehr—and his friend Colonel Eagleton—got into a car and sped over the oily concrete.

The olive sedan swept across the airbase through a gate with a fifty-caliber machine gun, where the driver rolled his eyes at a young guard, who nodded as the sedan lurched into the Saigon traffic.

Waves of bicycles, Pedi cabs and scooter buses crammed with peasants and chickens surrounded speeding U.S. Army trucks and Jeeps, while scooters and small motorcycles careened around old Citroen taxis through streams of black-clad Vietnamese continually crossing the road.

Lehr's old friend, Colonel Alexander Eagleton, grimaced.

"Saigon," Eagleton said. "The air is terrible."

Many of the water-stained storefronts and dusty, pastel houses were peppered with shrapnel scars.

Lehr stifled a laugh. "It's been like this since '56."

"Worse," Eagleton said. "A million refugees. Escalation."

Lehr lost his gaze into the dull sky, dreaming of 1962 Saigon—women steaming noodles in hot alleys, drinking Vietnamese sua da iced coffee, eating crisp croissants in cafes while Frenchmen in white linen conspired behind dark-green shutters in faded ochre villas where embassy girls sipped martinis under spinning fans, all those nights on the lush Cercle Sportif lawns with that French doctor sweating, breathless in tennis whites, her legs on fire, the compound air drunk with jasmine and frangipani. And always, slender Vietnamese schoolgirls laughing and swaying silk ao-dais, strolling home after Lycee beneath big flame trees, holding hands, or bicycling, their long, dark hair flowing behind. And only once in a while, late at night would you hear artillery, thundering out in the countryside like a distant dream.

"The Paris of the Orient," Eagleton murmured as Saigon streamed by. "Remember Evelyn and Phuong over at Ed's ... when he played that Viet Cong music?"

"Eagleton," Lehr said. "You're a goddamn romantic."

A young woman in high heels strutted the sidewalk, her hips rocking a red miniskirt as she sidestepped refugee families with all their belongings in cardboard boxes: rice pot, chopsticks and bowls, a green silk ao dai, creased sepia photographs of parents, children, the ancestors.

The car entered central Saigon.

The teeming street broadened into a graceful boulevard lined with Beaux-Artes buildings. The tall flame trees had been cut down, and the faded, once-immaculate villas were pockmarked with shrapnel. Barbed wire and broken glass crowned the tall compound walls and at every corner, exhausted soldiers manned machine guns in sandbagged towers.

Lehr inhaled the tropical rot seeping in through the air-conditioning.

"Definitely not the same," Eagleton said. "Who'd have ever thought Lansdale and his team would be the good old days? Remember his big house on Cong Ly? When he spoke, we had stars in our eyes."

"Things change," Lehr said. "Duty's the same."

Eagleton scoffed as Colonel Lehr took out a cigar.

"Pierce says the South Viets won't cut it," Eagleton said.

"Counterinsurgency requires patience," Lehr said, biting off the cigar end.

"An insurgency? The North Vietnamese Army?"

Lehr rolled down the window and spat out the cigar end.

"Windows closed, sir," the driver said. "Grenades."

"Roger. Nobody knows shit unless they're in the field," Lehr said, his voice trailing off. "Wait and see…"

The Ford stopped beside a faded yellow villa and scooters sped around them down the long boulevard running out to a distant green horizon shimmering beneath the dirty sky.

Helicopters boomed overhead, heading toward the Delta.

"Maybe I'll get lucky," Lehr said, lighting the cigar. "Land a combat assignment."

Eagleton raised his eyebrow and waved the smoke away.

"Lucky?"

*   *   *

At the top of the passenger ramp, Private First-Class Jack Halliday stepped into Vietnam, just another soldier in wrinkled khakis. Christ, he thought, it's hotter than Arizona. Not like the movies, nobody's shooting. Not yet. He wiped sweat from his stinging eyes. Exhaustion, humidity, and the deafening airbase overwhelmed Halliday, killing his fear.

Between the roaring runways, hundreds of soldiers crisscrossed gray tarmac, even little yellow Vietnamese guys in fatigues, some in cone hats and black pajamas. How the hell can you tell who the enemy is?

Aircraft shrieked through the haze, thundering toward the horizons. Small helicopters flitted and buzzed through the dense air as knifelike gunships howled, banking away. Dozens of Huey helicopters swarmed off the hot tarmac, rotors booming as they clattered away in a long, wavering line.

Beyond the runways, rows upon rows of battered, olive-colored planes and helicopters stretched forever.

*   *   *

When Jack Halliday's feet hit hot concrete, he promised himself, I'm coming back. With all my limbs.

A hundred soldiers waited for his plane.

Beneath faded boonie hats, two hundred watery eyes looked through Halliday with stark, dead, deeply tanned faces. No camaraderie, no good luck, not even recognition. The veterans' eyes were locked onto the silver jetliner.

The new soldiers trudged past the veterans and into a loose formation on the hot airfield.

A loudspeaker blared: "Flight 227 Bravo. Congratulations, gentlemen!"

The veterans grinned and rushed the plane. Not a word was spoken as the veterans streamed up the ramp into the replacements' airplane.

Halliday tried to forget all their fierce, desolate faces by dreaming of women. Is that what he would look like in a year?

*   *   *

The replacements dragged their duffel bags out of a big pile to a line of olive-colored school buses with their windows wrapped in mesh grenade screens.

Overhead, a giant helicopter howled with a small helicopter clutched to its belly. Thundering, the big helicopter lowered the smaller chopper on a cable toward waiting soldiers, whose fatigues whipped under the fierce blast.

"Jesus," Halliday whispered.

Fighter jets cracked afterburners on take-off, while on a parallel runway, fighters landed, screeching tires and popping white tail parachutes. On a parallel runway, squat cargo planes roared and shot up into the dirty sky.

As Halliday waited to board the bus, a silvery streak rocketed through the haze—his Boeing 707, and he wondered if he'd be on that plane a year from now.

Halliday banished the thought and hefted his duffel bags onto the bus.

*   *   *

After a brief twilight, darkness fell on the Long Bien Replacement Depot. Sweating, Halliday walked along a dim dirt street lined with windowless tropical barracks. Searchlights blasted dirt fields towards a faint tree line and darkness.

A flare popped.

Brilliant light swayed beneath a tiny parachute as a machine gun rattled and another rattled back, closer. A deep *thump*, a gentle rocketing overhead, and then an explosion, far away.

Halliday inhaled and tried to identify each sound. Radio voices drifted from a watchtower and faded into the beating of a helicopter. Eventually, the sounds felt as comfortable as a rattling truck fading into an Arizona night.

The searchlights' overglow fell on dusty camp streets, where shadowy wooden barracks resembled Old Tucson, the movie set town where Halliday's mother took him to see John Wayne filming *Rio Bravo* when she was the on-set nurse.

"Hey there, 'cruit! You!"

Three soldiers sat on a sandbag wall with their boots dangling down. A man's teeth and eyes flashed white.

"Yeah, you," he said to Halliday. "Got a cigarette?"

Halliday dug into his new jungle fatigues and flipped open a red Marlboro box.

"Thankyamuch."

The veteran sipped his beer and bent over Halliday's lighter.

"When'd y'all newbees get here?"

"Today," Halliday said.

"She-it. Ain't that bad," the man said with a giggle. "Come tomorrow, you only got three-hundred-sixty-four left."

The other replacement soldiers shifted.

"How many days do you have left?" Halliday asked.

"Me? She-it!" the man said. "I'm so short I can sit on a dime and swing my legs."

After he whooped, Halliday glanced down the dark barracks street. There was no one there.

"What's you M-O-S, 'cruit?"

"Combat engineer," Halliday replied.

"Oh yeah. Plenny a shit here in Viet-nam to blow up. Either we be blowing away Mister Charles, or he be blowing us away, there it is, man."

The soldier offered Halliday his beer. He drank and passed it on. The veteran dragged his cigarette hard and then flipped it tumbling, a red arc crossing the night.

"Gimme your lighter," the man said, producing a cigarette with a twisted end.

The veteran lit the joint and inhaled until his face shone. A second hit of marijuana made his pupils glow. He offered the joint around, but the three new men refused.

"Viet-fucking-nam," his voice loosened and became more guttural. "Can't hardly be-lieve it. Little old me, going back to the World. Goddamn. Even after eight-seven-five."

"What's 875?"

"Some fucked up shit. Army gives places, numbers. Place ain't worth nothing, if the Army can't even be bothered to think up a goddamn name—Firebase George the First Washington or motherfucking Nixon Jackass Mountain or Hill Abraham Lincoln or some shit."

"Where is this 875?"

"What the fuck it matter? Ain't no real place."

"Just trying to find out what's happening."

"*Happenin'? Shi-it. Happenin'* 'll find your sorry ass sooner than later, Ji-m, buh-lieve me."

"Where is it?"

"Why the fuck you wanna know, newbie?"

The veteran soldier slowly shook his head and exhaled.

"Sorry about that shit," he said. "Sometimes I'm a sorry-ass motherfucker. Nothing against you, man, just…"

"Just what?"

"Fucking tri-border."

"Tri-border?"

The veteran stared into the night and when he spoke his voice was hot with feeling.

"Up north. Border Cambodia, Laos—big jungle hills all run together like pigs in shit. Goddamn. 8-7-5. Thirteen thirty-eight. Six seven zero. Fuck those hills. Deep-assed valleys, mist never lifts, nasty-assed motherfucking jungle. Did six months 'fore I got jungle rot so bad they sent me down to Saigon. Tri-border, she-it. Devil himself don't even go up there. Ain't no little motherfuckers in cone hats dee-dee-ing through rice paddies with old carbines up there, no sir, no Viet Cong, no way, no-how. Trained N-V-A regulars, good uniforms, steel helmets, new A-Ks, B-40s, big-assed mortars, 1-2-2 Russian rockets. Stash always called that place 'you-are-in-the-deep-shit-now mountains.'"

He laughed.

"Fucking tigers, giant trees, motherfucking snakes, rats, monkeys, big old ants. Goddamn mosquitoes—national fucking bird of Vietnam, tiny little fuckers. Old Ho Chi Minh built himself a regular old gook freeway up in the tri-border, got off-ramps, tollbooths, rest stops, gas stations—all that shit. You know, *their* gooks, the gooks that fight, not *our* gooks, the ones who dress up in sunglasses and starched jungles an' drive girls around in new Jeeps. You never catch *our* gooks up there in the tri-border, no sir, never happen, G.I."

"Why is it so nasty?" the guy beside Halliday asked.

"Cause I fucking say so," he said. "Up there, N-V-A hung a dead G.I. upside-motherfucking-down from a big ole banyan. Sergeant Stash and Jimmy-o went bullshit, their main man—L-T Sears—jewels all spilling on the ground. Stash and Big O motherfucking lost it."

The man sucked on the joint hard.

"Lost it? How?" the new soldier asked.

The veteran turned around.

"You just dying your sorryass 'cruit life to *know* every fucking little thing, ain't you?"

The new soldier puffed up his chest.

"What's wrong with wanting to know."

"Know? Shit 'cruit. *Know?* You still got the stink of American lipstick on you, boy, you still pissing stateside water and shitting Mac-Donald's hamburgers. *Know?* I give you *know.* OK. All afternoon we taking fire from this nasty broke-down motherfucking little ville, bunch of our guys all fucked up—dead, medevacked, heat exhaustion. After artillery has a go at the ville, we head in. Just old men, women, children, no fighters, no weapons, no rice, nothing 'cept a mother and baby who won't stop crying, driving Sergeant Stash and Jimmy O bullshit crazy, so Stash and O start in—not like to get even, just to shut them the fuck up in the goddamn heat, all this gook screaming turning into something else—two of them ripping everything the fuck up. You know what *that's* like, don'tcha, Mr. Know? *You a big* man, ain't you, all gouging eyes and ears in your football huddle. Well, this here's the *real* deep shit, Jim, make you a fucking be-liev-er, all that blood from those tiny blue veins, Mr. Newby *wanna know*. Like you could *ever* in your sorry-ass motherfucking 'cruit lifetime even *hope* to *know*. I *forgot*. You already *know*, you a *bad man* back in your silly-assed high school quarterback, hand-job civilian world."

The veteran stared at his hands. The night grew quiet.

"Shit," he said. "There I go again."

He inhaled and exhaled.

"I ain't *done* it. But I fucking *seen* it and didn't do nothin' or say nothin'. That's way too much for this young trooper, you bic? That answer your fucking question?"

His voice trailed off. Somewhere far away in the night, the beating of a helicopter slowly became silence.

"We got them gooks back good," the man said. "Stroke of luck, karma, or some weird shit. Choppers they caught a whole motherfucking N-V-A battalion in an open field, their silly-assed officers done screwed the pooch. Air Force bring napalm down on 'em, a big old heap of hurt. Fried 'em up—crispy goddamn critters—N-V-A running all crazy—hundreds of 'em burning like fireflies. Afterwards, it rained two, three days with all them N-V-A dead in the mud where they fell. Their gook buddies never even come back to haul 'em off home to mamasan, so's their souls don't scream from being dead and all lost in a strange land. So all them dead N-V-A rotted, real quick like happens in the jungle. Door gunner showed me once, flying by. All them N-V-A just lumps in the mud and door gunner he say: 'Sun goes down? You don't want to be flying around here. Wind makes an awful bad-assed sound from those trees, like folks was out there dying.'"

The soldier's chin slipped to his chest.

All at once, he snapped up, took a last hit, grinned, slowly rolled his red eyes across the three new men, and pinched out the joint. He slipped the roach in his pocket and grabbed his M-16.

"Last guard duty," he said. "Sin loi, motherfuckers. Sorry about my rap—but your man asked. Anyway, don't mean nothing. Nothing means nothing over here."

The veteran snapped a round in his chamber, clicked the safety, and turned away.

"See y'all 'cruits later," he called over his shoulder. "*Good* luck."

He turned around, and then he walked right back and stuck his face close to the replacement who wanted to know.

"Hey 'cruit?" he said. "That story? I souvenir you. Just 'til you get your own. There it *is* man. There it fucking *is*."

He grinned, waved his weapon, and shuffled away.

Light from a barracks door flashed his lanky form into a black cut-out that slid forward and slowly wavered away into a guard tower silhouetted beneath the harsh perimeter lights.

"He's bullshitting," said the cocky soldier.

"Yeah," Halliday and the other man agreed.

"Completely," the soldier went on, his voice cracking. "That baby killer shit don't happen over here."

The three quickly looked away, forced grins, nodded, and split up. Each young man walked alone down the dim dirt streets back to their long wooden barracks.

Halliday wandered through dark rows of twisting and groaning young men and found his metal bunk. He undressed, slipped beneath the mosquito net, and lay on top of the sheets sweating. Halliday thought about the man and his story as he listened to the soldiers' labored breathing, the artillery, helicopters, and small arms fire popping in the distance. Just before he fell asleep, Halliday remembered that the soldier hadn't returned his new Zippo lighter.

2.

Colonel John Lehr hung by his feet in leather straps on a wooden exercise ladder doing sit-ups. Red-faced Lehr perspired freely, puffing as Colonel Eagleton appeared, upside-down.

"Is this what Log command considers recreation?"

"Keeps the ticker going," Lehr panted.

Colonel Lehr gripped the top rung with a muscled arm and then lowered himself to the floor with surprising agility for a forty-two-year-old man. Taking an olive gym towel from Eagleton, Lehr wiped his flushed face.

"How's Christina?" Eagleton said.

"I should cut her out of my will," Lehr said. "I know when I'm not loved."

Eagleton shook his head and grinned.

"What the hell are you doing making personal calls during duty hours, Colonel?"

"I'm concerned," Eagleton said.

"Goddamned contractors, stealing us blind," Lehr scoffed. "They should band together with our Vietnamese, start their own cutthroat country. Serve them both right. Chickenshit birds of a feather."

"Tact never was your strong suit," Eagleton said.

"If I was tact*ful*, I'd be a Joint Chief by now," Lehr said. "I just care more about tac*tics*. What's on your mind, Colonel?"

"I'm O-I-C of field grade assignments," Eagleton said. "Still interested in a command?"

"Just give me a shot, Eagleton."

Lehr hoisted onto a leather side horse and rubbed his neck with the towel.

"Thieving contractors are not exactly my idea of mission."

"*Mission?*" Eagleton said. "It's not 1964, and you're not an advisor in Tam Linh."

Lehr jumped off the side horse.

"I hate goddamn paper wars," Lehr said.

Lehr arched his sweaty towel across the room and into a cloth basket near the door.

"If a command comes up, just let me know, all right?"

"Wait and see?" Eagleton said, cracking a smile.

Lehr grinned. Back in 1964, the ambassador always used those words to avoid decisions.

Five laughing young officers pushed through the gym door and went silent when they spotted the two colonels.

"That's what's wrong with this war," Lehr said, frowning. "No balls."

*   *   *

A week later, Jack Halliday rode an Army convoy through the jungle to the Central Highlands town of Nhu Canh Du. Halliday felt good—he hadn't panicked on his first convoy. The Vietnamese along the road had ignored the dusty, long line of trucks, except for the young women in shiny pastel blouses sitting on a ramshackle porch who waved and called to the soldiers with sweet, high, laughing voices.

The convoy crossed a swift river over a gray iron bridge and drove up a low rise past an old French military camp flying the yellow South Vietnamese flag with its three blood-red stripes.

The driver peeled off the convoy and wheeled the big truck under a wooden arch with twin red castles that read: "99th Engineers – When The Going Gets Tough, the Tough Get Going – Normandy-Pusan-Vietnam." The truck entered the small camp and skidded to a stop before a row of dusty tents.

"Daktoum, 99th camp," the driver said. "Suck it up."

Halliday tossed down his duffle bags and jumped out, and the truck sped away in a cloud of red dust. He faced a big canvas tent with a torn screen door.

A tremendous explosion shook the ground.

Halliday dove behind a wall of sandbags.

Two sweating soldiers in olive t-shirts ran out of the tent and studied a nearby dirt field surrounded by barbed wire, where three soldiers slowly picked themselves off the ground.

A low scream haunted the stifling air.

The older soldier ran to the field, where black smoke drifted away. He quickly returned and whispered to the other. After the screaming stopped, the two men grimaced and frowned, and the older soldier went back in the tent.

The other soldier—a fleshy, red-haired youth who smelled like licorice—turned and scowled at Halliday crouched behind the sandbagged wall.

"You a 99th replacement?" the soldier demanded with a slight lisp.

"Yeah. What happened?"

"Some stupid fucker blew himself up clearing a French minefield. Get the fuck up, go get your fucking 201 file, and leave your personal shit outside."

The soldier grinned and went into the tent.

Halliday fished out the file from his duffle bag, scraped open the rickety screen door, and went inside.

The sweltering canvas room held desks, olive file cabinets, grimy clipboards, a small refrigerator, and a bulletin board with faded mimeographed notices. The red-haired soldier grabbed Halliday's file and sat at a messy desk with a blue desk fan.

"Combat engineer, Merton?" a voice yelled from behind a plywood partition.

"Yep," the clerk replied, fitting paper into a typewriter. "Two years college. So maybe he can fucking read and write."

"Send him in."

Inside, a sallow man in a T-shirt with a blond mustache and black circles around his eyes sat at a desk that took up half the small room, which smelled of sweat, damp canvas, and cigarettes. A big fan blew dust at a screened window.

A black plastic sign on the desk read: LT. JAMES MACELROY, CE, ADJUTANT.

"PFC Halliday reporting as ordered, sir."

Halliday saluted, and the lieutenant made a lopsided grin.

"Sit down, Halliday—don't salute in a combat zone. If the gooks see you, they'll shoot me. Unless that's your intent."

"No sir."

"I was joking."

"Yes sir."

Halliday sat down with a puff of red dust.

"Jesus, you're filthy. Convoy?"

"Yes, sir."

The lieutenant studied Halliday's file.

"This hotter than Arizona?"

"Yes sir."

"So, were you in a ... fraternity at...?"

"Northern Arizona, yes sir."

"What house?"

"Sigma Chi."

The lieutenant grinned.

"No shit. In hoc, brother. Fresno State."

The lieutenant shook his hand in the not-so-secret grip.

"Merton," the lieutenant yelled. "Two Cokes."

A refrigerator door opened and slammed. The clerk pushed through the tent flap, handed a cold Coke to the lieutenant, and slammed the other down in front of Halliday.

"Newcomb still need a driver?" the lieutenant said.

"That's the word, sir," the clerk said and exited.

"Think you can drive and keep a colonel happy?"

"Sure, yes, sir," Halliday nodded, only knowing that he didn't want to clear minefields.

"Good," the lieutenant said, leaning back in his chair. "Then you're the colonel's driver."

Halliday popped the can, and brown fizz sprayed everywhere.

3.

Three weeks later, Jack Halliday parked the colonel's jeep beside a canvas tent in the small 99th Engineers' camp overlooking Nhu Canh Du. He sat under the shade of a tent flap and waited for a radio call.

All around Halliday, dusty engineer soldiers fed bonfires with half-destroyed hootch buildings and watchtowers. Nearby, a bulldozer unearthed big redwood timbers from underground bunkers and pushed the large beams into big fires burning colorless under the harsh light.

The three thousand men of 3rd Brigade of the 73rd Infantry were pulling out—the first military unit in Vietnam to go home. On orders from Saigon to temporarily take over their huge firebase at Daktoum, two miles down the road, the 99th was destroying their small camp.

An endless convoy of the 73rd Infantry had turned Highway 14 into a tunnel of dust, where lines of Jeeps, armored personnel carriers, and tanks rumbled along with troop trucks, overflowing with drunken soldiers.

Halliday heard dogs barking and turned to a pack of camp dogs circling a grimy, French, stucco building. The dogs kicked up dust, hell bent on catching the 99th's pet monkey.

Matted with red soil, the monkey raced in and out of the circling pack, taunting the dogs. Just as a dog opened his jaws, the monkey shot ahead into the running circle, pounced on and sank his sharp teeth into another canine's neck, producing a loud yelp. Then the monkey sped back into the dust cloud of dogs racing around the building before once again biting yet another canine and provoking an endless chase.

Halliday chuckled.

An ambulance Jeep, with a stretcher sticking out the back, bounced out of the convoy dust, pulled into the burning camp, and stopped beside Halliday's Jeep.

A tall, black soldier leaned out of the open Jeep.

"Hey man. You seen a yellow dog?"

Halliday pointed at the yelping pack circling the old French headquarters.

The medic studied the dogs and shook his head. He shut off his Jeep, climbed out, and joined Halliday squatting in the shade beneath a sagging tent flap.

"Doc ain't gonna believe this shit."

Halliday nodded and held up a soft drink as the medic sat down.

"Soda?"

"Sure, man."

Halliday went to his Jeep, dug into an ammo box beaded with water, and pulled out a cold can.

"*Ice?*" the medic said. "How the hell … oh, you're the colonel's driver."

"You know," Halliday said. "You look like …"

The medic lifted his chin and crinkled his eyes.

"Yeah, 'we all look alike', right?" the black medic said with a challenging smile.

"No, no. We rode up on the convoy together. Halliday."

"Oh, you *that* 'cruit—when C Company's dump trucks hit those mines. Ben."

Ben offered his fist, and Halliday eagerly tapped it, like he learned from the crew when he sang Motown songs in boot camp—the first blacks he had ever known.

"Where you from?" Ben asked Halliday.

"Tucson, Arizona."

"Oh, cowboy?"

"No. Where you from?"

"Anaheim—and not the ghetto. California, suburban. Drafted?"

Halliday nodded.

"Couldn't see goin' to Canada," Ben said. "Too cold."

"Me neither."

They sipped their sodas.

Under the smoke, the dust, and the big, pale fires, bulldozers clanked, leveling the 99th's ruined camp.

"Man," Ben said. "So, our Infantry's di-di-mauing back to the World and leaving us at Daktoum. The gooks are up there, digging in Rocket Ridge pre-paring to kick our ass. And all Doc's worried about is his dog. Sergeant Clancy damn near shit."

Ben pointed at a yellow dog circling the French building.

"Doc's dog, chasing the monkey. Un-fucking-real."

Across the ruined camp, an olive-green bulldozer knocked over a guard tower.

"Fuck you, tower!" a soldier screamed as the wooden tower toppled over with an explosion of red dust.

Just beyond the engineer camp's barbed wire, three Vietnamese men squatted on the dust-filled road, waiting for the wood and the metal they knew the engineers would leave. Shrieks and sporadic gunfire from the infantry convoy rose over the whine of engines.

A bare-chested engineer poked into a fire and screamed a rebel yell. He raised a blackened snake on his rifle bayonet, shook it overhead, and danced around the fire, whooping. He tossed the burned snake back into the fire. Shots rang out from the convoy.

"Roasting *snakes*," Ben said, "Army hauls us ten thousand miles here to burn down our hootches and hunt for dogs chased by monkeys. She-it."

Sprinting around the French headquarters, the monkey jumped up on a yellow dog and sank his teeth into the yelping canine's neck.

"That yours?" Halliday asked.

Ben nodded.

An open Jeep bounced out of the infantry convoy and wheeled through the engineer gate.

"OO-wee," Ben said. "Here come King Shit himself."

A burly black man wearing Hollywood wraparound sunglasses and starched fatigues pointed at Ben from the passenger seat of the bouncing Jeep.

Medical Staff Sergeant Elwood Jason Clancy directed the driver, Jamison—a baby-faced soldier known as "The Colorado Kid"—to stop. As the dust settled, Clancy glared at Ben.

"Specialist Benjamin. You better be telling me that you have found the captain's dog," Clancy demanded, sweeping his hand across the burning camp. "In case you ain't noticed, Specialist, the 99th Engineers are moving out."

Sitting in the shade, Ben calmly sipped his Coke as the stocky sergeant shifted under the hot sun.

"We ain't actually 'moving *out*,' are we, Sergeant Clancy?" Ben said, pointing at the convoy dust. "We're just *moving*. Not like those infantry going back to the World."

"If you ain't found Doc's dog, Specialist," Clancy asked. "Then why you sitting on your dead ass drinking you a Coke?"

"Who said I didn't find the dog, Sergeant?"

"Then where is he, Specialist?"

"Right over there," Ben said easily.

Clancy turned to the circle of dogs, frowned, and turned back.

"Then how come you ain't got him yet?"

"I am not possessed of the proper military expertise."

"Specialist Benjamin, you saying what I think you are?"

"I am a highly-trained medical specialist," Ben said. "Nothing in my service contract calls for me to engage with wild animals. My body is currently the property of the United States Army Medical Corps, and I will not betray my country by doing something for which I have absolutely no aptitude. Do you think Sam trained me for twelve months as a medic on the taxpayer's dime just to get rabies and be sent home? I don't think so. So, as soon as Doc's dog gets tired of that monkey chewing on his ass, I'll grab him and get on with the 'moving out'."

Clancy bustled out of the Jeep, puffed himself up to his full five-foot-seven-inch height, and loomed over Benjamin and Halliday sitting in the shade.

"So, badass Specialist Benjamin, the terror of Anaheim, is afraid of a little old monkey?"

Ben got up. He stood a head taller than the heavy sergeant.

"Afraid? No, Sergeant Clancy," Ben said easily. "But I am uninformed as to the proper military procedure of 'monkey capturing.' So, yes, I was sitting here waiting for someone of superior rank and expertise to come along to instruct me."

Clancy's eyes bulged, and his jaw gaped. The Kid stifled a grin as Clancy turned and marched through the ankle-deep dust toward the whirling dogs.

The monkey spotted Clancy, leapt off Doc's dog, scampered up the stucco wall, caught a roof beam with a long arm, and swung back and forth, high under the eaves, chattering, with the dogs snapping and snarling below.

Clancy kicked his way through the dog pack and shoved Doc's dog aside with a polished boot. The monkey shrieked, leaned his long arm down, and snatched off Clancy's bush hat. He swung himself up onto the tin roof and sat there, chewing on the bush hat.

As Clancy flailed, his wraparound sunglasses tumbled into the dust. Blinded by the harsh light, he tripped over a dog, and fighting for balance, Clancy's combat boot crushed his expensive sunglasses, which made him bellow, whip out his 45-caliber pistol, and shoot wildly.

The monkey ducked and dragged the bush hat over the crown of the tin roof. Clancy chased the monkey around the building, taking pot shots, but couldn't hit the creature, who kept slipping away.

All the bare-chested engineer soldiers tending the big fires stopped and laughed and pointed. Finally, Clancy cursed, yanked Doc's yellow dog out of the pack, and dragged him over to Ben's ambulance.

"Here's the captain's damned dog," Clancy snarled. "Now get your ass back to Daktoum."

The engineers tending the fires kept jeering and laughing. Clancy glared at them and then got in his Jeep.

"Yes, sergeant!" Ben said. "Thank you, Sergeant!"

The Kid revved up the Jeep as Clancy's shining black bald head bounced across the burning camp, rolled out of the gate, and disappeared into the convoy's tunnel of dust.

Halliday and Ben laughed until they fell over.

Ben got out peroxide, and Halliday held the dusty yellow dog while the medic disinfected the monkey bites.

Gunshots rang out from the roaring convoy.

"N-V-A been screwing with that Montagnard hospital near Bridge 39," Ben said.

A big ambulance with red crosses swayed out of the convoy, swept under the signpost into the ruined camp, and stopped near Ben and

Halliday. The slender young captain with dark curly hair in the passenger seat spotted his dog, beamed, and swung open the door.

"Bacsi, Bacsi, come 'ere, boy," the captain called.

The yellow dog leaped up on the captain, marking his olive fatigues with dusty, red paw prints.

"Bacsi, I thought I lost you, boy. Come 'ere."

The ambulance driver—short, skinny, black-haired Mick Donnolly —got out. Donnolly rolled his eyes over blue granny glasses perched on a snub nose and lit a cigarette.

"Bacsi, boy, what happened?" the Captain asked, examining the dog's wound.

"Monkey been eating on him, Doc," Ben said, pointing at the dogs howling at the stucco building. "Same monkey that stole Clancy's hat."

Up on the tin roof, the monkey shrieked and darted around with Clancy's bush hat.

"Clancy's *new* hat?" Doc asked, grinning.

"Broke his twenty-dollar sunglasses, too," Ben said. "Rescuing Bacsi."

"Couldn't happen to a nicer cocksucka," Donnelly said.

Everyone laughed.

Columns of smoke darkened the sky.

"Old Daktoum is burning down, burning down, burning down," Donnelly sang with a South Boston accent.

Doc frowned.

"Sit down here in the shade and drink you a Coke, Doc," Ben said. "Newbie here got ice on his Jeep."

"Can't," Doc said, tugging the dog's ears. "Major Goodby's *special mission*. Find the colonel's driver, Halliday."

"That's *me*."

"Oh. Ron Levin," Doc said, holding out his hand. "Major Goodby wants you at Daktoum at two o'clock. Didn't you hear your radio?"

Halliday looked puzzled, so Ben checked the radio on the colonel's Jeep.

"Wrong frequency," Ben told Halliday. "Tell the major your battery was low."

Halliday grabbed two icy Cokes from his ammo box.

The four men squatted under the shade beneath the big canvas tent flap.

Doc took off his sunglasses and baseball cap and wiped his sweating face. His curly brown hair and large brown eyes reminded Halliday of a dead deer.

"That numb nuts chaplain wants all the guys on the road to wear shirts," Donnelly said, compulsively tapping his leg. "Says our troops are *ruining the 'morality'* of the gook women, inciting them to sin with our '*big bare American chests.*'"

"I bet there's a million gook women incited by your chest, Donnelly," Ben said.

"Very fucking funny, Benjamin, you California whore."

Doc smiled.

A giant burning timber crashed down with a shower of sparks. Beyond the smoke, the steep jungle ridges had almost faded away.

"Hear anything else about us getting hit, Doc?" Ben asked.

"We'd need another doctor," Doc said.

Donnelly rapped out a drumbeat on his leg and stood up. Beneath an engineer bush hat decorated with a peace sign, his pale face ran with sweat.

"We are going to get hit, Doc, I can feel it," Donnelly said. "I only got eighty-one days. Too short for the deep shit, Doc. Send me down to Pleiku, what do you say?"

"Why?" Doc said. "You're no different than anyone else."

Donnelly spit in the dust.

"Jesus Christ, Doc, why? Why's the infantry leaving us here? We don't run patrols, all we got is dozers and dump trucks and graders. Shit, Charlie ain't got no parkways, what's he want us for? Jesus, they should just drop the big one on those fucking gooks."

Doc rolled his eyes. The radio in the large ambulance squawked, so he took the call, and replaced the mike.

"We're going to Bridge 39 with the Colonel and the S-2 truck," Doc said.

The four soldiers jumped into their vehicles, cranked them up, drove out of the burning engineer camp into the infantry's dust tunnel, and headed to Daktoum.

*   *   *

Inside a vast supply depot at Long Binh near Saigon, Colonel John Lehr got out of a Jeep and told his driver to wait. He waved over a heavy, perspiring man in khakis and a white shirt, and they walked down a long row of shipping containers.

Colonel Lehr stopped at three empty containers with their doors open.

"So, you don't actually *have* our five hundred air-conditioning units, Jenkins?"

"I didn't say that, Colonel," the sweating man said.

"But you don't have them."

"We delivered them to Oakland. As contracted."

"And now they've mysteriously disappeared," Lehr said.

"I don't know about mysteriously."

Lehr stopped the large man.

"Do you think I'm an idiot?"

"No, Colonel."

"I've been in Vietnam before, Jenkins. And World War II and Korea. This bullshit stinks of black market. We pay for air conditioners, they never arrive."

"The manifest states that we delivered them," the man said, "With confirmation that they were loaded in Oakland."

"So, I'm guessing, somewhere on the Saigon River," Lehr said. "The air conditioners vanish, and our bonded containers turn up empty? Funny how that works."

"Unfortunate, colonel."

"Right, and I'd say in reply, if I get even a single fucking whiff of how those container numbers ever got out, your ass is grass, Jenkins. I guarantee I will prosecute."

"Colonel, I'm sorry you feel that way."

Lehr was already walking back to his Jeep.

The heavy, sweating man watched Lehr's Jeep disappear down the endless rows of dull black steel shipping containers.

*   *   *

Halliday sat outside the 99th Commander's office, eavesdropping on Lieutenant Colonel Richard Newcomb, inside his plank-lined office in Daktoum's Tactical Operations Center bunker, abandoned by the departing infantry general. The bunker was known as "the Tock."

LTC Newcomb fingered a Band-Aid on his forehead. Lean and crew cut with a set mouth and a long jaw, Newcomb poured over blueprints.

"Pardon me, sir," a deep voice said, entering the room.

The colonel did not look up at the lined, ruddy face of Sergeant Major Bricker, whose sleepy eyes hid a quiet ferocity.

"Yes, Sergeant major?"

"Captain Fairbanks is a real fine West Point engineering officer, sir, and we've got security problems. If Charlie …"

"Sergeant major," the colonel broke in. "Let Goodby handle it. I'll place the bridge approach at 39. I have more experience than any other officer in Vietnam."

"Sir, Major Goodby is a *chaplain*. S-2 says Charlie …"

"The battalion surgeon will visit the native hospital," Newcomb declared. "Show them where we stand."

Newcomb studied the bridge blueprints.

The sergeant major opened his mouth. Then he shook his head and left.

*   *   *

Following the S-2 gun truck, Halliday drove Colonel Newcomb and the sergeant major across the camp, while Doc and Ben trailed in the big, ¾-ton ambulance.

Built for three thousand soldiers, the mile-square Daktoum firebase sprawled across a low bluff above the Dak Poko River to an airstrip lined with helicopter pads and revetment walls. A dusty sea of olive tents clustered around a dirt company street running from the airstrip to the big, sandbagged TOC command bunker, bristling with antennas.

Three artillery batteries—105s, 155s, and 175mm guns—fired from atop the river bluff, directly beneath the steep tangle of Rocket Ridge, towering over the firebase. Daktoum Firebase had been defoliated with Agent Orange down to bare red soil, so that no plants grew between the tents and the sandbagged bunkers and the rusted coils of barbed wire that connected twenty-six squat perimeter bunkers.

The three Army vehicles went out the Daktoum front gate and turned south on half-paved Highway 14, paralleling the airstrip towards a green triangular mountain. They passed their smoldering engineer camp and a tree-shaded Vietnamese ARVN post, went down a long hill, and crossed a gray panel bridge over the Dak Poko River and past a dirt track that ran north to Dak Sut, Dak Pek, Dak Sieang—Montagnard villages and Special Forces camps—lately only accessible by helicopter.

The three vehicles picked up speed as they passed the town of Nhu Can Du and its whorehouse, where slender Vietnamese girls in tight skirts and silky red tops waved honey-colored arms and called out: *G.I., G.I., G.I.,* with taunting laughs. Then they sped south through the jungle, hands on their triggers, eyes on the road, fear of an ambush, fear of a mine, fear producing an almost sexual rush in Halliday.

For an hour, there was only jungle and a Montagnard man in a loincloth, trailed by a young, bare-breasted woman with firewood piled high on her back.

"Pardon, sir," Bricker yelled to the Colonel through the hot air. "I wonder if I might play some music, sir."

The colonel looked over his shoulder at the back seat.

"Johnny Cash, sir."

"Go right ahead, Sergeant Major," the colonel said with his Idaho drawl.

Sergeant Major Bricker pressed his cassette player.

I fell into a burning ring of fire,
I went down down down, and the flames got higher...

The colonel smiled, slapping time with his hand.

Burn burn burn, the ring of fire...

A thatched roof, like a giant axe blade, rose above the green jungle. A dozen longhouses circled the spectacular structure.

"What's that?" the colonel asked.

"Happy House, sir," the sleepy-looking sergeant major said. "Montagnard communal hut—they drink rice wine, dance, do their mumbo jumbo."

The village appeared deserted.

Behind them, a horn honked, and Doc waved.

The ambulance angled off the road onto a dusty track towards an old stucco building covered in red bougainvillea, where a beat-up Land Rover with a red cross sat beneath the shade of a big tree.

The S-2 gun truck led the colonel's Jeep on through a hot dazzle of pale, electric-green jungle. which opened into a bulldozed clearing.

The broad Dak Poko River lay before them, and heat waves rippled off the red-brown water and up into the colorless sky.

A huge black rubber floating bridge crossed the river.

Beyond the bridge on the near side, bare-chested soldiers wrestled concrete buckets pouring bridge supports, while on the riverbank, a dozen Montagnards in loincloths shoveled sand into cement mixers.

The recon truck and the colonel's Jeep bumped along the dusty riverbank to the new bridge site.

An immense banyan tree dominated the forest at the river's bend, where a dozen bare-chested soldiers lounged in the shade of their trucks.

Near the massive banyan, a young lieutenant with a red scarf stood beside a Montagnard soldier in tailored fatigues with an old man in a loincloth. As the young native spoke to the older Montagnard, who wore a scarlet headpiece and silver bracelets, the old man continually shook his head—gesturing at the Montagnard soldier, the new bridge, and the banyan tree.

The banyan's twenty-foot-wide trunk held up a vast overhead canopy, with a dozen smaller trunks rooted like thick columns down into the red earth. Colored blooms dappled the many spreading branches and fell in rainbow heaps all around the thick radial roots of the main banyan trunk.

"Kieu yang ala! Kieu yang ala!" the old man shouted.

Halliday shut off his engine. A sharp, dry smell wrinkled his nose, so he looked closer.

The banyan tree was filled with snakes.

Thousands of snakes lay draped on the branches: glowing-red, striped-green, and brilliant yellow with wicked black diamonds. Snakes: wriggling, sliding, clumped in deadly tangles, forked tongues flickering, kraits and vipers and pythons and sinuous green tree snakes.

Hundreds of cobras lay entwined in clumps—black cobras, red cobras, pale green cobras—even an immense, black King Cobra, slowly swaying high on a banyan shoulder above the undulating carpet of snakes.

"Kieu yang ala! Kieu yang ala!" shrilled the old man.

Colonel Newcomb marched to the lieutenant and the fiercely gesturing Montagnards. The sergeant major followed.

"What's the problem?" Colonel Newcomb said.

The elder Montagnard stiffened.

"Lieutenant Fairbanks," said the officer, holding out his hand. "Welcome to the 99th, sir."

Newcomb nodded.

"Colonel Newcomb. The problem, lieutenant?"

"The tree, sir. It's sacred."

"Sacred?"

"Yes sir. Their religion, a snake god," the lieutenant said, tugging his mustache. "If we take it down, Montagnards say they can't work on the road."

The colonel set his long jaw.

"It's the most expedient approach."

"Well, sir, we could run our cut around it and save the tree," the lieutenant said. "Wouldn't take much more time."

"We didn't even place this bridge approach, sir," the sergeant major explained. "Group S-3 did it. From a map."

"The tree's a security hazard," the colonel said.

"Sir," the sergeant major said. "We do need the Montagnards to mix our concrete."

"Use Vietnamese," the colonel said.

"This is Montagnard country, sir."

"If they won't work," the colonel said. "Hire Vietnamese."

The colonel turned his back and faced the lieutenant.

"Lieutenant," Colonel Newcomb said. "How will you remove this tree?"

"Rome plow blades on 'dozers," the lieutenant said, exhaling and twisting his red neck scarf. "With snake cages."

"Kieu yang ala!" the elder called. "Kieu yang ala!"

Bok, the teenaged Montagnard interpreter nodded. He tapped the colonel's shoulder.

"Colonel sir," Bok said. "Head man say beau coups spirits in tree, snake spirit big magic, best way go long way around, sacred place here, good place, better leave alone, no sweat, spirits help Army, beau coups big magic."

Colonel Newcomb smiled. He nodded, turned, and quickly marched through the red dust.

The soldiers. lounging in the shade of their trucks, got up.

Behind Newcomb, the huge tree rustled, as an eerie quiver swayed the branches.

"Move those vehicles and get your five-gallon cans," Colonel Newcomb ordered the drivers. "Sergeant major, get those men from the bridge."

With a roar of engines and whining gears, the drivers parked their trucks near the riverbank. They unstrapped their gas cans and lugged them to the Colonel, waiting under the outer branches of the banyan.

"Recon," the colonel barked. "Ready your '60."

As the recon truck driver backed into firing position, the concrete-spattered bridge soldiers trotted over with rifles in hand. The sergeant major took off his helmet, wiped his sweating face, and shook his head.

"Spread gasoline over the big roots," the colonel ordered. "Save some for the main trunk. You men be prepared to fire."

Halliday and the drivers hefted their gas cans and slowly walked under the green canopy. The concrete-smeared bridge soldiers followed, pointing their rifles at the big tree as the drivers spread gasoline on each root and trunk, careful of falling snakes.

As they approached the massive main trunk, rainbow waves of snakes slithered onto the large shoulder limbs and wound up the smaller trunks and into the banyan canopy.

Behind them, the Montagnard elder slumped.

When the drivers had spread gasoline on the smaller trunks, they moved towards the main trunk. Agitated snakes fled away from the gasoline and up into the huge tree.

Twenty feet from the main trunk, the men stopped.

At the wide base of the banyan, hundreds of snakes slithered and writhed over the chest-high roots. Except for the snakes rustling up into the tree, the hot, humid jungle was quiet.

"Go on!" the colonel yelled. "Douse that main trunk!"

The drivers balked.

"You candy asses, just *do* it!" Newcomb yelled. "Those men are covering you!"

Splashing gasoline, the drivers slowly closed the circle around the main trunk as waves of snakes skittered up into the big banyan tree.

"Soak that trunk!" the colonel yelled. "As high as you can!"

The drivers flung gasoline all around the colossal trunk.

Overhead, on the large first shoulder of the banyan, the black King Cobra swayed, with its hood spread wide.

The huge snake shot out of the tree, scattering the soldiers. The big cobra hit the ground and swiftly undulated into the jungle.

The colonel ran over, grabbed Halliday's can, and connected the wet gasoline lines from all the trunks.

"Now get the hell away from here!"

Halliday and the drivers ran past the concrete-spattered riflemen as Colonel Newcomb poured a last line of gasoline line almost to the river.

"OK, Lieutenant," the colonel said, handing the empty gas can to the dumbfounded sergeant major. "Light the damn thing. Lieutenant."

The Montagnard elder began to weep.

As Fairbanks approached, the elder ran off, crying a low moaning chant, which pierced the hot silent forest.

"Kieu yang ala, Kieu yang ala!"

Acrid fumes spread across the muggy air.

Overhead, the rustle of snakes grew frantic.

Colonel Newcomb stood, hands on his hips, as Fairbanks bent over, struck the lighter flint, and touched his Zippo to the gasoline staining the red dirt.

"Fire in the hole!" Fairbanks yelled, twisting away into a crouch, and covering his face.

Flames shot over to the main banyan trunk, and exploded with a roaring concussion that knocked over Fairbanks and Newcomb.

The engineer soldiers sprinted to the river as a huge tongue of fire billowed over Colonel Newcomb, lying on the ground, eyes wide open.

As the immense banyan tree erupted into a pillar of flame, whispery shrieks from the snakes filled the air with the terrible stench of a million rotted eggs burning.

The piercing hiss of burning snakes was the most horrible sound Halliday had ever heard, but he couldn't take his eyes off the burnt snakes, shot into the air like living shrapnel, hundreds of serpents writhing, half-alive, and falling from the burning tree in a fiery rain thudding all around the flaming trunk of the great banyan in growing piles of charred, sizzling snakes.

The Montagnards at the cement mixers threw down their shovels, ran wildly down the road after the chanting elder, and echoing his cries: *Kieu yang ala, Kieu yang ala.*

Colonel Newcomb got up from the red earth and stood ramrod stiff in the terrible heat, never flinching from the hot, roaring fire, with his eyes continually blinking.

Bok, the interpreter—the only Montagnard who hadn't run away—stood behind the colonel. His young sweating brown face had turned the color of ash.

A giant burst of flame whipped through the big tree.

"The snake yang has left the tree," Bok said quietly.

"*That's* big magic," Newcomb said. "Solve your problem, Lieutenant?"

"Yes, sir," Fairbanks replied.

The colonel waved Halliday to the command Jeep.

Halliday drove the colonel and the sergeant major, following the bouncing S-2 truck through the track of powdery red earth beside the river, and then jolting their way up and onto the main road near the pontoon bridge.

As they drove to the Montagnard hospital, smoke from the burning banyan tree clouded Halliday's rearview mirror.

*   *   *

At the Montagnard hospital, Captain Ronald Levin walked through the dim old French building and stopped at a high-ceilinged room suffused by a red glow from the bougainvillea vine shrouding the windows.

Doc's eyes were pinpricks from the long drive, and at first, he only saw shining black hair, the perfect rise of a Gallic nose, and high cheekbones. Then, deep haunting eyes, a small mouth, and ghostly white teeth appeared in the dim red light.

Smoke and the smell of pungent French cigarettes rose from an ashtray.

Gabrielle Marchand spread out her arms, balancing a tiny girl with a horribly bent leg.

"Oui, oui..." Gabrielle said, urging the laughing child.

Doc leaned against the doorframe.

Gabrielle looks happy, he thought.

Children curled on the cool polished concrete floor in the heat. Others played quietly; one stared wide-eyed at the ceiling. All the children touched each other or Gabrielle, sitting cross-legged, her worn khaki skirt hiked to mid-thigh. A sleeveless blouse revealed her slender arms and neck.

When the child fell, Doc sharply inhaled.

Many children had missing limbs; one was badly burned. Gabrielle set the girl down and smoked her cigarette.

She exhaled and saw Doc standing in the doorway.

"Oh, Bacsi," she nearly whispered the Vietnamese word for 'doctor' in her husky voice. "Come, sit."

Doc Levin glided across the room and sat amidst the slumbering children.

"How are you, Gabrielle?"

"Well, thank you. Very well."

"We brought malaria pills."

"Merci, merci."

Gabrielle dragged her cigarette, and a warm glow shone on her cheekbones. The burnt-tobacco scent mixed with her earthy body and fleur d'orange.

"The V-C have come here?"

Her eyes narrowed.

"N-V-A," she said. "They say if the village won't pay taxes, they will burn it down."

"You sure they were N-V-A?"

"The elders told me they wore new uniforms," she replied, flicking ash off her blouse.

A burned child reached out, and Gabrielle laid him on her lap.

"Is there anything that you need?" Doc asked.

Her dry laugh made Doc clench his olive bush hat, and he lowered his eyes.

"So many things," she said. "But I am not so sure you possess of any of them."

Doc met Gabrielle's unrelenting gaze.

"I know," he said. "Maybe this time, it will be…"

"Over? Soon?"

Her harsh, quiet inflection was meant only for his ears—the children did not flinch.

"No. Only Americans finish with Vietnam after one year."

From outside came a clattering, and then heavy boots scuffed closer.

Gabrielle frowned, quickly rose, and Doc followed her down the hall.

"I'm looking for the American doctor, Captain Levin," Colonel Newcomb's voice boomed down the dim hallway. "He bought medicine for you people."

Gabrielle led Doc into a spare entry room with an old mahogany desk, where a Montagnard girl shied away from a large American officer, whose hand rested on his pistol.

"Sel," Gabrielle said. "Les enfants, sil vous plait."

The girl disappeared down the dark hallway. Gabrielle turned to Newcomb.

"This is a hospital, Colonel. Children are trying to sleep."

The colonel stood tall in his bulky battle gear.

"Colonel Newcomb," he announced. "99th Engineers."

"Doctor Marchand," Gabrielle replied.

Gabrielle stared at the colonel's watery eyes. She did not take the colonel's outstretched hand.

"If you would like to visit us, please be quiet," Gabrielle said. "Children are sleeping."

Before Newcomb could answer, Gabrielle ushered him down the long, dim corridor and opened a door. A hot room was crowded with children on low wooden beds, where three bare-breasted Montagnard mothers tended small children.

"Amputees," Gabrielle said.

She waited until the colonel had seen the children with no hand, no foot, no leg, no arms, no legs. She closed the door and hurried down the corridor to another door.

"Fragmentation and gunshot wounds."

Another crowded, stifling room, prickly with the smell of alcohol and decaying flesh. The children listlessly stared up at the two tall Americans with pistols flapping at their sides.

As Gabrielle walked on, Doc noticed the silky black hair gracing her tanned arm.

"Malaria," Gabrielle said at a shady room filled with olive-colored Army mosquito nets.

A tropical fan slowly cut the fetid air.

Again, all children—hot and sweating, one wrapped shivering in army blankets. A very young mother in a shiny black skirt gave an ice-bath to a delirious child.

The colonel blinked and knitted his brow. Gabrielle studied his eyes.

On the far side, Ben stood up from examining a patient and walked over to Doc.

"He's got a week," Ben said. "Maybe."

"No," Gabrielle said. "Days."

Ben led the slender doctor over to the small boy, and they whispered to him.

The colonel stood rigid, with a forced half-smile.

Again, Gabrielle searched his eyes.

When Doc Levin and Ben returned, the room's cloying heat made all their faces shine.

"Come," Gabrielle said, leading the three American soldiers down the dim hall to the entry.

As they reached the front room, a strange cry arose.

"Thank you, Dr. Marchand," Colonel Newcomb said, blinking his watery eyes. "I'm authorizing Captain Levin to give you medical supplies."

"Merci, Colonel," Gabrielle said, searching the colonel's expressionless face.

Burns, Gabrielle decided—he's burned his eyes.

Colonel Newcomb nodded curtly, turned on his heel, and marched out. Ben and Doc smiled at Gabrielle and followed.

Stepping out into hot sunlight, Colonel Newcomb's throat caught on a hanging bougainvillea tendril. When he ripped the thorny vine away, it bloodied his hands. Newcomb threw the red-flowered vine away and climbed into his Jeep.

Halliday started the engine, and they drove off.

Standing on her veranda, Gabrielle watched the dust billowing behind the Americans.

An eerie cry echoed from the village and was joined by others until the air filled with wailing.

Sel ran out the front door and took Gabrielle's shoulder.

"G.I.," she cried, tears streaming down her face. "Burn the tree of the Snake Yang."

Gabrielle clenched her teeth.

Wild moans rippled across the darkening forest.

Gabrielle wrapped her arms around Sel.

"Soldiers," she murmured. "Never understand anything until it's too late."

Gabrielle hugged Sel until her breath calmed, and she looked up at the French doctor.

"What happen now?"

Gabrielle plucked a red bougainvillea blossom off the girl's shiny black blouse.

"Who knows?" Gabrielle said, letting the delicate red bloom tumble to the ground.

4.

At dusk, waiting for a tennis court in Saigon, Colonel John Lehr bit his tongue and cursed. His daughter Christina's letter lay crushed in his tennis bag, his own sweaty fingerprints on the blue envelope a reminder of the distasteful message. Lehr had eagerly read the thin airmail letter with a hope that their rift in San Francisco might be healed. But it wasn't. If anything, their differences were even sharper.

As the Cercle Sportif court lights came on, Colonel Eagleton approached.

"Are you OK?"

"My daughter," Lehr said. "*Nineteen*. Goddamned knows everything."

Eagleton slipped on his sweatbands.

"Lecturing *me* on foreign policy," Lehr said. "Jesus, that pisses me off."

Colonel Lehr bent over his racket and touched his toes.

"I was reasonable," Lehr said. "Explained to her how this country—hell, every country—is built on trust. If you can't trust your leaders, what do you have? I asked. '*Peace!*' she said."

Eagleton twirled his racket.

"You have to admit our mission in Vietnam has evolved."

"Hell, Alex, we kicked Charlie's ass in Tet."

Eagleton turned to Lehr.

"John," Eagleton said. "You don't really believe that Ho's done for, do you?"

"Let's just play tennis," Lehr said.

*   *   *

The day after Newcomb burned down the banyan tree, Jack Halliday sat in the sweltering Daktoum TOC, eavesdropping on Sergeant Major Bricker and the colonel.

"Colonel Trinh personally assured me," Newcomb said, rubbing his watery eyes. "He's sending out infantry patrols."

"*Three* a week," Bricker said. "Third Brigade ran thirty, thirty-five every week."

"If Colonel Trinh says Daktoum Valley is secure," the colonel said, blinking, "I see no reason to doubt him. He's a professional military man."

Newcomb waved a stack of documents.

"Hard intelligence," Newcomb said. "Long-range recon, heat-seeking, captured documents, prisoner's confessions. There's been 'no significant diversion of materiel or troops' near us—only one LURP's guess."

"Charlie likes everybody thinking he ain't there until he shows up kicking ass," the sergeant-major said.

A canvas-covered field telephone buzzed.

Red-haired Merton, now the new colonel's clerk, leaned inside Newcomb's door with a smart-ass grin.

"Colonel Trinh on the horn, sir."

"Bonjour," Colonel Newcomb said into the phone.

He waved the sergeant major back.

"Thirteen hundred? Fine, fine. We'll have some lunch and proceed. Au revoir, Colonel Trinh."

The sergeant major grimaced.

"Colonel Trinh and I are flying up to Firebase Paradise," Newcomb said. "With you on board."

"Sir," Sergeant Major Bricker said. "I've got a reaction force meeting ..."

"I want you along," Newcomb said. "And have Merton get me some aspirin."

Clenching his teeth, Bricker went out and got Merton's APC's. When he planted the bottle on Newcomb's desk, the colonel didn't even look up from reading a thick training manual: *Combat Engineer Field Operations.*

*   *   *

Halliday and Merton watched the shiny helicopter land on the Daktoum VIP pad as Colonel Newcomb and the sergeant major greeted two Vietnamese officers: Colonel Trinh, the new Daktoum area commander, and his personal pilot, Major Ban.

As the small helicopter's high-pitched whine wound down, the officers shook hands. Above them, faded American and South Vietnamese flags hung limply on tall poles.

As the four walked past the dusty tents along the Daktoum Company Street, the Vietnamese resembled the Americans' flashy younger brothers—slender and a head shorter, gliding along in tailored tiger fatigues and spit-polished boots. Colonel Trinh grinned and touched his nickel-plated pistol.

Halliday and Merton watched them disappear behind the sagging tents.

"Who's that?" Halliday asked.

"Colonel *Trinh,*" said Merton, spitting into the dirt. "Little shit thinks he's a bad ass. Saigon gave him a new chopper so he's up here showing off."

"You really dig the guy."

"Mail truck got ambushed near his compound in Kontum. Not one of Trinh's dinks even fired a shot. Dunger and Whipley'd grease that guy on sight."

"They'd grease anybody."

"Fucking Dung-*ER,*" Merton shouted, punching Halliday's arm. "Let's go eat, 'cruit."

*   *   *

Colonel Newcomb ushered Colonel Trinh and Major Ban into the big TOC bunker.

Inside, were plank-lined walls with private offices for executive officers and the Colonel. S-3 Operations spread out in a big, open main room, while Commo and S-2 intelligence shared a large sandbagged secure area in one corner.

Colonel Newcomb showed off his spacious office, recently occupied by an infantry general related to Ulysses S. Grant. Colonel Trinh and Major Ban nodded politely with the frozen smiles that Vietnamese often displayed to Americans. Then Newcomb led the Vietnamese and Bricker out into harsh sunlight across a dusty board walkway to a screened briefing room with a long bar at one end.

After a lunch of canned ham, sweet potatoes, red Jell-O salad with celery, iced tea, coffee, and pineapple upside-down cake, Bricker drove the colonel and the Vietnamese around Daktoum's perimeter.

As they returned to the TOC, Bricker said, "If Charlie ever figured we only got twenty-four guards during the day, he'd waltz right in here."

Colonel Trinh stared at the heavy-lidded sergeant major.

"You must not have read our situation reports, Sergeant Major," Trinh said. "No enemy anywhere near Daktoum."

"My ass," Bricker muttered, pulling into the TOC.

"I was just telling the sergeant major," Newcomb said to Trinh. "The Vietnam war's nearly over. Our major concern is completing Highway 14."

Bricker snorted, bit his lip, and then spat into the dust. Colonel Trinh smiled, clapped his small hands, and pointed at the airstrip.

*   *   *

Five minutes later, Newcomb and Bricker—wearing new camouflaged helmet covers and shiny olive flak vests—walked down the company street toward the idling Vietnamese helicopter. The Americans climbed into the two rear seats and the turbine whined to lift speed.

Colonel Trinh's helicopter swept into the sky.

Daktoum soon became a ruddy scar in the green earth between the slash of Highway 14 and the Dak Poko River.

The chopper ascended the lush green face of Rocket Ridge, scarred by bomb craters and burned jungle. As the helicopter cleared the steep ridge, Sergeant Major Bricker raised a bony finger out the open door past Colonel Newcomb.

In the distance, the green ridge tops had been slashed flat.

"Seven Sisters," Bricker said as the helicopter leveled out. "First of the 92nd Artillery."

Perched atop a steep ridge, one small, stark firebase was a warren of gray sandbag bunkers and ammo crate shacks, crisscrossed by trenches zigzagging around a helicopter pad. Bare-chested gunners froze beside a smoking artillery barrel, as they stared at the little helicopter.

This dusty island in the sky was circled by barbed wire, with flashes of wired-on beer cans. The bare red hill fell away on all sides, exposing a litter of tin cans, greasy cardboard, big brass shells, and trash that had been thrown over the wire.

Dense jungle surrounded the small firebase, where ragged artillerymen, tucked away in corners of the funky maze, lounged and smoked. A skinny, bare-chested soldier waved half-heartedly at the helicopter as it banked away to discourage snipers.

"Ladyland," the sergeant major told the colonel, whose eyes continually blinked.

Major Ban flew west to where three scarred jungle hilltops rose out of a twisted landscape of downed tree hulks, blackened earth, and pockmarked craters.

"Hill 8-7-5," Bricker shouted. "November '67, Battle of Daktoum. 73rd and the 4th damn near lost their asses."

Major Ban banked down to treetop and followed the ridge line of virgin jungle past a broad slash of red soil, like the jungle was bleeding. Major Ban swung the chopper into a tight diving turn that pressed them into their seats.

Tall jungle rose around them in three distinct layers of green, so dark and dense that it seemed impenetrable.

"Triple canopy, sir," Bricker explained to Newcomb over the rotor clatter. "Charlie loves to hide in there."

Another flash of red soil, a big circle.

"Arc light—B-52 craters."

Colonel Trinh nodded to Major Ban. The helicopter banked away toward a distant red speck.

Firebase Paradise appeared at the end of a long razorback ridge between two jungle valleys steaming with mist.

"Cambodia," Bricker said, pointing west. "And Laos. Ho Chi Minh Trail down there somewhere. Got big bases, roads, hospitals, everything."

Firebase Paradise grew larger with blasts of white smoke hanging above firing cannons, whose big barrels slammed backwards in recoil. The helicopter climbed and circled.

On the Paradise helicopter pad, tiny soldiers lifted crates from a large heap on a big net.

"Roger that, Viet Loach," the radio said. "Re-supply Chinook came in early. Suggest you return at 1300 hours."

Colonel Trinh threw up his arms. He unleashed a torrent of Vietnamese on Major Ban, who persuaded Paradise Control to let them land on the uneven ground beside the main pad.

The Paradise guns ceased firing and the smoke dissipated.

Colonel Newcomb and Colonel Trinh were to meet with the Paradise commander, while the sergeant major and Ban flew off to Firebase Ladyland to deliver fire control documents to a Vietnamese artillery officer.

Major Ban angled into a tight, curving dive and Paradise rushed toward them until the little helicopter leveled out into a tail-down hover.

As the small helicopter landed on the uneven slope, Colonel Trinh tapped his Rolex to confirm the pickup time, then he hopped out the open door and scampered up toward the main helipad.

As Colonel Newcomb swung his heavy legs out of the rear seat, his eyes watered from the harsh rotor wash. Sergeant Major Bricker slid behind the colonel to go up front and sit next to the pilot.

Colonel Newcomb stiffly lurched after the boy-sized Vietnamese Colonel Trinh, striding up the slope.

As Sergeant Major Bricker got out of the back seat, the helicopter shifted on the uneven ground.

The rotor blade dipped down, and severed Colonel Newcomb's head, slamming his headless body into Sergeant Major Bricker and pinning him against the helicopter.

Blood spurted from the decapitated torso, splattering Bricker and the helicopter bright red.

Colonel Newcomb's head hit the ground and rolled to a stop near Colonel Trinh, whose hands flew to his face, which contorted into a scream drowned out by the rotors.

Trapped by Newcomb's bleeding body against the shiny chopper, Bricker tried to push away the bloody corpse until his legs entwined with the body, tumbling the sergeant major to the ground.

The colonel's severed head lay sideways, eyes wide open.

After an endless moment, a huge black medic scuttled under the whirling chopper blades and muscled the corpse off the sergeant major. The medic dragged off Newcomb's body, leaving a wet smear of blood in the red dust.

Bricker crawled out from under the helicopter blades and collapsed against a low sandbag wall.

Colonel Trinh—with sharp, shifting eyes and short, choppy steps—ducked back underneath the rotors, got into his helicopter, and jerked his hands upwards. Major Ban stiffened and shook his head.

The two Vietnamese faces bobbed erratically, until Colonel Trinh flashed his pistol with its silver barrel pointing up.

The helicopter whined and immediately lifted.

Gritty rotor wash stung the faces of incredulous artillerymen as Trinh's helicopter swiftly banked away.

Colonel Newcomb's severed head stared from the red dust with dead, watery eyes.

The small helicopter whined off into the hazy distance.

"You chickenshit little gook motherfucker!" screamed a bare-chested artilleryman wearing a beaded necklace and silver Montagnard bracelets.

All the artillerymen unloading supplies on the main pad stood motionless as the beating helicopter became a whisper.

"All right, you young troopers," a gruff, hillbilly sergeant yelled. "Show's over, get that god-damn resupply put away!"

The unkempt soldiers scuffled and cursed.

They lugged away the heavy artillery shell boxes and hauled off cardboard C-rations to underground bunkers while the big black medic stretched olive-green ponchos over Newcomb's body. The artillery lieutenant radioed for a Dust-off helicopter, while the medic retrieved Newcomb's head and meticulously wrapped it in another poncho.

Sergeant Major Bricker slumped on the rotting sandbags. Clutching his knees, the sergeant-major waved away the big medic and spurned his offer of a beer and clean fatigues.

Bricker's breath ran hard and shallow.

From time to time, the sergeant-major's bloody fatigue jacket shuddered. Turning his back to Colonel Newcomb's poncho-wrapped body and head, Bricker took out a color snapshot of his wife.

*   *   *

An hour passed.

Shadows grew deep and long. Voices drifted to Bricker.

"…of course, bad fricking luck, asshole. Beau coups bad luck. A fucking *head*, cut off on *our* turf? Fuck me, man. That's some beau coups *bad* karma."

"…Number fucking ten, even if he was a lifer…"

"…Spooky shit, man. I *told* you. Any fucking thing can happen in this shithole…"

Bricker's hands shook as he buried himself in his wife's photograph.

After the artillery shells and C-rations were stowed away into bunkers, the little firebase returned to its squalid life: firing guns, sullen teenagers, sandbags, trash, dust, terrible smells, and rats, trapped on a steep jungle ridge inside coils of barbed wire.

Three young soldiers, in colorless boots, torn greasy fatigues, and faded helmet covers, scuffed past the sergeant major, their sun-dark torsos dulled by dust.

The artillerymen sprawled across a shallow cove of sandbags, smoking and tapping their weapons, jogging their legs, spitting, and pawing the dirt like chained dogs. They muttered harsh curses of black humor while staring at the sinking sun and the indifferent jungle haunting them everywhere past the dull black snouts of their big guns, now silently waiting for Dust-off.

As the light turned yellow, the radio squawked.

From off in the distance came a dull slap of rotors, as all the soldiers turned toward the helicopter—to make goddamn sure that the colonel's head and body were taken the hell off of their firebase.

"There she is," somebody yelled, pointing at a dot in the darkening eastern sky.

The Dust-off helicopter with a Red Cross set down on Paradise, blasting up dust and trash, rattling the beer cans tied on the wire, and flapping the crusty, green ponchos wrapped around Newcomb's bloody corpse.

Under crimson light, the on-board medic stepped onto the metal landing pad, while two artillerymen lifted Newcomb's poncho-wrapped body into the open bay, dragged it across the deck, and strapped it down.

Sergeant Major Bricker stood up on rubbery legs and lurched towards the Huey.

The medic climbed back on board, banged on the co-pilot's Plexiglas window, and flipped a thumb's up before he saw the sergeant major in the bloody fatigues.

"Hold hover," the medic barked into his headset.

The Dust-off helicopter slid a little sideways, barely airborne in the ruddy light.

"Where ya going, Top?" the medic shouted over the clatter of rotor and turbine.

The medic helped Bricker into the bucking chopper.

"Daktoum."

"OK, but we're gonna have to drop you didimau," the medic shouted, guiding Bricker into a green nylon jump seat. "We just got us an Urgent."

"Daktoum," the medic said into the intercom mike.

The helicopter rose and then fell impossibly down the sharp ridge line, quickly dropping off the mountaintop firebase in a beautiful arcing silhouette against the bloody sunset.

As soon as Dust-off was gone, the cannons of Paradise commenced firing.

Big shells cut the heavy air, booming out into the sunset, out into Cambodia and Laos miles across the red sky, pounding the unseen North Vietnamese troops marching and resting somewhere under the vast, triple-canopy forest.

5.

Doc Levin walked from the Daktoum mess hall to the long officer's hootch near the TOC bunker. Doc lay down on his Air Force mattress but couldn't sleep, so he got up and wiped his sweating face with surgical gauze soaked in alcohol.

Doc walked through the ankle-deep dust and immense heat to his new medical bunker. Under the hard afternoon light, it resembled a giant, sandbagged grave, with a squat tower at each end.

All across this wide, chest-high bunker, the 73rd infantry had stretched a broad, Red Cross canvas, used to warn enemy aircraft not to bomb medical facilities. Since the North Vietnamese had no aircraft, the giant Red Cross served only to hold the rotting sandbags in place and was said to make a great target from up on Rocket Ridge.

A smaller, torn, Red Cross flag hung off the entrance tower. Doc paused under the front entrance beneath rain ponchos strung overhead on two-by-fours. Nearby was a sandbagged chamber for storing bodies, which gave off a faint odor of the dead.

Doc knocked his dusty boots on a mud grate and went down a staircase wide enough for two stretchers to pass. Halfway down the dim passageway, medics' voices rose, and boots scuffed on concrete. Waylon Jennings sang on AFVN radio, accompanied by a low moaning.

Doc stepped under the massive roof beams and onto a wooden landing, where rough benches faced a gray steel desk.

The main dispensary room was thirty by forty feet and felt like a large, dank cellar lit by sickly fluorescents. A dozen stretchers on sawhorses lay beneath bare electric bulbs. Every cranny in the sides of this underground room was stuffed with medical supplies.

Two tall medics—Leroy Cullen and Mickey Nimmer—faced off between two stretchers.

"Cullen, don't you get it? Our own fucking Army's leaving us here," black-haired Nimmer said with a wild grin, throwing up his hands. "Didimauing back home."

"Home, don't you go feeding me no know-nothing New York liberal spec-u-la-tion," Cullen drawled. "Doc! Tell this shit-for-brains Nimmer here what's really going on."

"Donnelly!" Doc yelled at the thin soldier in blue Ben Franklin glasses bent over a flame on the floor. "What's with that malaria patient?"

"Just gave him an ice bath, Doc," Donnelly said.

"Give him another."

"If you say so, Doc."

"I say so. Go."

Donnelly hopped back and forth over the tiny flame.

"Donnelly be nimble, Donnelly be quick," he sang. "Donnelly jump over the candlestick."

"Donnelly, I know what you're doing," Doc said. "And I'm not buying it. *Go.*"

Donnelly leaped over the flame and skipped toward a tiny room with four bunks, where the malarial soldier moaned.

"Shit, Doc, I'm just as crazy as Donnelly," Nimmer said.

"We all are," Doc replied. "We're in Vietnam."

A tall, thin, black soldier, Limerick, sprawled face down on a stretcher, reading. His fierce posture said: "don't-even-think-about-talking-to-me."

The concrete floor gave off an oily stench from diesel fuel used to keep down the dust.

Doc crossed the long room, raised a canvas flap, and went into his office in an alcove.

The crowded little room was crammed with medical books, a desk, and two steel bunks. The tactical radio squawked:

"Dust-off Control to Daktoum Three."

"Daktoum Three," Doc answered.

"Roger Three, got you aaah … Field Grade Critical in Zero-Five Mikes. Over."

"OK," Doc said.

"Roger that, Three, Control out."

Doc went into the ward, waved Limerick and Nimmer over, and led them upstairs.

Outside, the sky was on fire as the three hustled out to the airstrip.

A helicopter came in low and fast and then quickly set down onto a metal pad with a faded red cross. Nimmer and Limerick turned away as rotor wash whipped at their jungle fatigues. Doc held his baseball cap tight and craned to see into the helicopter bay, where the on-board medic unstrapped a body wrapped in a green poncho.

Limerick and Nimmer slid the body across the bloodstained aluminum floor.

The helicopter medic stepped out and acknowledged Doc with a touch to his helmet. Sergeant Major Bricker rose from a jump seat and climbed out.

The medic stretched his arms and legs, tapped on the co-pilot's Plexiglas window, nodded, and got aboard.

Dust-off lifted into the red sky and banked east, into darkness.

Nimmer grabbed a stretcher leaning on a revetment wall.

The four surrounded the body.

"The colonel?" Doc asked softly.

The sergeant major nodded.

Nimmer popped the stretcher open, and with Limerick, lifted the body on top and hefted it up. Doc and Bricker followed.

As the four reached the medical bunker, a husky soldier appeared out of the twilight.

Nimmer and Limerick set the stretcher down beside the sandbagged graves room.

"Where the hell's the colonel? Who's that?" Merton said, chopping the air with his hands. "How come you came in with Dust-off, Top?"

"Merton, calm down," Doc said.

"Right, sir, fucking Group's on my ass. Some LURP outfit bags intelligence that an N-V-A *regiment's* in Daktoum valley and no one can fucking find the Colonel. Where is he?"

"Merton," Doc said calmly. "The colonel is dead."

"Dead? *Dead?* You're shitting me, sir? *Dead?*"

"Have Major Goodby call Group. And keep it to yourself."

"How'd it happen, sir?"

"I don't know yet, Merton. Do what I said."

Merton whirled his chunky body around and sprinted toward the boxy silhouette of the TOC outlined in red.

Limerick and Nimmer stood over the body.

"Put it in Graves, Doc?" Nimmer asked.

"No. My office," Doc said. "Keep everyone out."

The sergeant major exhaled. He followed the body down into the bunker, scuffing his boots on the rough steps.

Doc looked out at the darkening camp tents and bunkers. The western sky flamed red, and the steep hills looked like black paper cutouts. Ben walked up and lit a cigarette.

"Notice how Merton watches every chopper, Doc?"

"No," Doc said. "I hadn't."

Venus rose, shimmering in the night sky over Laos. On the thousand-meter hill above Daktoum, the mist caught wisps of red light.

A shadow moved across the dirt lot and became Lieutenant Mac Elroy's sunken face and dark-rimmed eyes. Mac and Doc whispered, and the Lieutenant hurried toward the TOC.

"Spooky shit," Ben said, following Doc down the long staircase into the bunker.

Inside the big dispensary, the incandescent light bulbs above the stretchers had faded to a sickly yellow—the generator was phasing.

"I love your honky ass, *boy*," Nimmer said grinning into Cullen's face from three inches away. "Despite you being a paranoid cracker."

"And proud of it, too, Home. Leastways I ain't no dipshit New York cream cheese fruitcake," Cullen replied with a mad grin. "Ya-cha-cha-cha-chaaa."

"Ya-cha-cha-cha-chaaa," Nimmer mirrored, his nose nearly touching Cullen's.

The two tall young soldiers cackled like madmen.

Doc and Ben passed Limerick reading, and Donnelly lying on a stretcher staring at the huge dark ceiling beams, muttering *Jack fell down and broke his crown…*

Sergeant Clancy bustled down the stairs trailed by his driver, the Kid.

"What's going on, Captain?"

When Doc told him, Clancy nodded and turned to the lounging medics.

"Nimmer, Donnelly, Cullen and the Kid—come with me," the barrel-chested Clancy said. "We got supplies to bring in from those storage CONEXES. Limerick, keep everyone out of Doc's way."

The medics groaned and straggled up the stairs behind Clancy.

Ben followed Doc into his office.

The wrinkled poncho-covered body shone dull and green on the bed under the weak light.

"Unwrap it," Doc said.

Doc went out and crossed the large dispensary room to the small ward alcove, where the sergeant major lay in a bunk bed across from the malaria patient, whose shallow breathing was audible.

Doc found the bottle of scotch in his secret cabinet, poured some in a coffee cup, and gave it to the ruddy sergeant major.

Doc Levin sat on the bottom of the bunk.

"Doc?" Ben called from the main room.

Doc patted the sergeant major's shoulder and joined Ben.

"Colonel's head is gone," Ben whispered as they walked.

"He walked into a helicopter blade," Doc said.

"It's not in the bag."

As they passed by, Limerick flickered his eyes and slowly turned a page of *The Autobiography of Malcolm X*.

In his office, Doc snapped on surgical gloves.

The stiff, blood-encrusted poncho had been pulled back to reveal the naked, headless body of Colonel Newcomb. Ben had cut open the Colonel's bloody fatigues, exposing a pale, hairy torso. Doc examined the body, lingering over the neck, using large gauze sponges to wipe away clumps of clotted blood.

Doc dictated, and Ben wrote on a cardboard death tag with a long copper wire.

"Massive laceration beginning ... anterior thoracic region severing the cranium along with the ... axial skeleton, external carotid artery, surrounding muscles and tissue with a large laceration ending ... posterior, with severed muscles, tissue and the right clavicle, ending in the ... trapezium area."

"Time of death?"

Doc dropped the limp arm.

"Approximately 3 PM."

"You mean 1500 hours."

"3 PM."

"Doc, I love that you don't give a shit about military procedure."

"Like they give a shit about me?"

"Cause of death?" Ben asked with a smile.

"Traumatic amputation of cranium caused by helicopter. It's a … an accidental."

Halliday pulled open the canvas flap and froze in the doorway.

"Holy fuck!" Halliday said.

"What are you doing here, Halliday?" Doc asked.

"Goodby sent me."

"Who let you in?" Ben asked.

Ben stuck his head out the flap.

"Goddamnit, Limerick! Get your dumbass radical nose out of that book and do your fucking job!"

"Forget it," Doc said, pulling Ben back. "Make sure there are no other wounds, bag the body, and put it upstairs. I'll deal with Goodby."

Doc stripped off his gloves, tossed them in the trashcan with Colonel Newcomb's bloody fatigues, and walked out.

Halliday stared at the colonel's naked body.

"Your Colonel caught him a chopper blade," Ben said, removing Newcomb's boots.

Halliday couldn't remember seeing any dead outside of the movies. Until he remembered his friend Chris, who he had watched suffocate in a gravel pit when they were ten. Chris had looked like a wax statue in his coffin.

Halliday studied the colonel's bloody neck. He shivered but didn't feel anything. The body looked like a corpse from a Driver's Ed movie and didn't scare him.

"Don't look at that shit unless you have to," Ben said.

Ben cut away the rest of the colonel's pants and his green Army underwear. As he stuffed the colonel's wallet, watch, and gold wedding band into a clear plastic bag, Halliday looked down, embarrassed at seeing the dead Colonel naked.

"Come here," Ben said, wiring a cardboard tag around the colonel's big toe. "Make yourself useful."

Ben took the upper body, and Halliday, the feet, and they turned over the colonel's headless body. Ben slipped a rubber bag beneath, pulled the long flap open, and rolled the body inside. With a metallic growl, Ben zipped it up and sealed Colonel Newcomb inside the green body bag.

"Get the back," Ben said, gripping the stretcher.

They maneuvered Newcomb out of Doc's room and around the stretchers under dim pools of light.

From the ward bunk, the sergeant major's eyes flickered. Ben glared at Limerick, who didn't look up as they carried the stretcher past the front desk, then up the dank staircase and out into the hot night.

"Set him down," Ben said.

Ben disappeared into the graves room and came back. As they carried the body in, Ben's lighter cast their long wavering shadows onto the sandbagged walls. The heavy air felt almost alive. As they set the stretcher down, something brushed Halliday's leg.

"Jesus!" he yelled, jumping.

Doc's dog thrust his golden head toward the body bag.

"Bacsi, get the hell out of here," Ben said, shoving the dog.

Outside, Ben lit up cigarettes, and their faces flared.

An artillery battery fired.

"Damn dogs," Ben said, petting Bacsi. "They *love* the smell of the dead."

Bacsi lunged toward the sandbagged bunker.

"Strange, your colonel getting his head cut off."

The glowing cigarette light contrasted their sweating black and white faces.

"That bother you?" Ben asked.

Halliday shrugged and looked up toward the black hills.

"I don't know," he said. "No, not really."

"Not much there," Ben said.

"Yeah," Halliday said, his voice cracking.

He remembered his friend Chris's feet kicking and finally going limp in that gravel hopper before he died.

"You OK?"

"Yeah. I watched this kid die once. We were playing..."

Rocket Ridge loomed under a flare light, briefly visible in the dark night.

"Where the hell do they go?" Halliday said.

Under the burning glow of cigarettes, they traded glances. The dog lunged at the dead bunker.

"Goddamnit, Bacsi!" Ben said. "Nobody in there to pet you or give you bacon. And you can't go eating on the dead."

6.

Colonel Lehr played tennis poorly, losing first to Eagleton, who left to take a phone call. After Lehr lost the second set to General Rack Armbruster, Eagleton sat waiting on the white wooden bench while the sweating Lehr sprawled beside him.

Beyond the Cercle de Sportif walls, a heavy Saigon sky yellowed.

"This'll be your last match for a while," Eagleton said.

Lehr glared over.

"Why, Alex? Am I that goddamned bad?"

"No," Eagleton said. "Your command."

Lehr inhaled and got up with a smile.

"I thought so," Eagleton said. "MAC-V's cutting orders. Two Corps."

Lehr tossed his racket into the air and caught it.

"Best god-damned news since I came in country. Where?"

"Combat engineer battalion. A 'challenging' tactical situation— which is why you got it. Vietnamization."

"Of course," Lehr said, slapping Eagleton's back. "How the hell did you ever manage it?"

"Don't thank me yet," Eagleton said.

Eagleton stood, and they walked past the Cercle swimming pool and headed to the clubhouse for a Scotch.

*   *   *

Two days later, Lehr caught an early flight to Pleiku for a morning briefing.

Afterwards, Lehr sat on a jump seat in an open helicopter hatch beside a 966th Group Operations captain.

"Can we cut the bullshit, Captain?" Lehr said into the roar. "What's the real story at Daktoum?"

The younger officer squinted at Colonel Lehr's silver flattop and steely eyes.

"Like they said, sir: it's temporary. Keep the road open, finish the bridge projects, keep the airstrip operational."

"With Vietnamese security?"

"What do you mean, sir?"

Lehr scoffed.

"Tell me there's an American reaction force."

"Most likely."

"Most *likely*?"

"A battalion of the Cav."

"Nobody said that."

"It's ... ah, unofficial, sir."

"Unofficial?"

The captain nodded.

"Yes sir, the ARVNs and MAC-V ..."

"I *know* the ARVNs," Lehr said. "I *worked* for MAC-V."

"Sir, Group didn't pull out that infantry brigade."

"Understood, Captain. Nixon's baby, Vietnamization."

"Sir, Group's 100% behind you."

The helicopter banked as steep green hills drifted through the mist. Lehr had always loved their French name—the Annamese Cordillera.

"Captain," Colonel Lehr said slowly. "Smells like bait."

"Troops can't be used for bait, sir. MAC-V policy."

Lehr laughed.

"Khe Sanh? Dien Bien Phu?"

"Yes, sir."

"Put yourself in my shoes, Captain. An Engineer *battalion* minus, with a couple artillery batteries securing an oversized firebase with no helicopters, no armor, no American infantry. And the South Vietnamese trying to hold a valley that *brigades* 101st, the 4th, the 73rd had trouble keeping. And now this … Colonel Trinh?"

"Sir, you're underestimating the …"

"I hope so, Captain."

"Sir, the 1st Cav …"

"I pray to God that's not bullshit, Captain."

"We have to trust MAC-V."

The Colonel stared hard into the Captain's face.

"Really?" Lehr said. "And you? Can I trust *you*, Captain? Remember, my men are putting their trust in *you*."

Lehr stared out the open hatch.

Dense mist blanketed the landscape and the sky as the dull clattering helicopter absorbed the two men. Three scarred hilltops appeared off in the distance.

"Hill 8-7-5, sir," the captain said.

Lehr nodded.

He remembered the famous photograph. Dead soldiers' boots lined up on Daktoum airstrip, November 1967.

Lehr leaned out and the restless side gunner shifted his gun. The Colonel fitted the cratered green hilltops to the tactical maps he'd been studying.

"Paradise, sir. Over that ridge."

Lehr nodded.

The N-V-A will probe—maybe even overrun those firebases. Overrun, a god-awful hell, his second tour, half-naked V-C sappers coming in the wire throwing explosives. The South Vietnamese panicked despite good training. Killed more of their own than the enemy did.

The chopper changed pitch and descended through the dissipating mist until landforms appeared.

Above the twisting blue Dak Poko River, steep ridges crested in soft emerald waves. The huge scar of Daktoum firebase appeared beside the dusty red streak of Highway 14.

At treetop, the chopper boomed toward Daktoum. Lehr stared at the jungle and recalled the monkeys and birds, trumpeting elephants, and occasionally, the roar of a tiger.

Sometimes at night, all the sounds would stop so you could hear the worst sound of all, your own beating heart.

"Smart little bastards," Lehr shouted to the Captain. "Laying low until the brigade left."

And I'm riding second seat to a cocky Vietnamese colonel who won't get near the fighting.

"We hold Daktoum," Lehr said, pointing at the green hills. "And Colonel Trinh gets a medal."

The captain frowned.

"But if he gets his ass kicked, it will all fall on *us*."

Colonel Lehr clutched the barrel of his M-16 until it shook in his hand. Below the helicopter, on Highway 14, a long line of Montagnard natives led water buffaloes pulling wooden carts, fleeing from some doomed village up in the hills.

The chopper clattered down onto the Daktoum command pad beside two flagpoles.

A dark-haired major with a pale, cheesy face, leaned in and grabbed Lehr's duffle bag. The major sweated under a ridiculous Australian bush hat with one side flipped up. He meekly touched the brim.

"Major Mordecai Goodby, sir," he said. "Acting X-O."

"A *chaplain?*" Lehr said.

"New X-O's on leave. Battalion's shorthanded."

"I can see."

As the helicopter rose, the Captain from Group gave Lehr a half-hearted salute.

7.

Jack Halliday scraped open the door to the briefing room and backed in with a wooden box, clanking with liquor bottles.

"What the hell?" someone yelled.

Startled, Halliday dropped the box with a crash, and the humid air flooded with the peaty smell of Scotch.

A stocky colonel with close-cropped gray hair glared.

"What are you doing here, private?"

"PFC Halliday, sir."

"I didn't ask your name. Why are you here?"

"Moving in, sir."

"Moving in *what*?"

"Club supplies."

"*Club* supplies? In my *briefing* room?"

"Sir, I'm the colonel's driver. I was ..."

"Go on."

"Sir, Captain Ranklin said to set up the bar in the briefing room. It's the only officer's club north of Kontum."

"Jesus Christ."

Major Goodby pulled open the screen door.

"Colonel sir," Goodby said. "I'm having great difficulty locating a helicopter."

"Major," the colonel said. "I don't give two shits if you have to sprout wings out of your ass and fly up there. You get it back here. *Now.*"

"Ah, yes sir," Goodby said, letting the screen door slam and scurrying away.

Halliday swept up the shards of glass.

"Would you like a drink, sir?" Halliday blurted.

"What?"

"The infantry left the mess hall an ice maker, sir."

"Oh, Christ."

Lehr's face reddened.

A faint pain crossed his chest and tightened his left side. The Colonel walked to the screened wall facing the steep ridge.

"All right," he said, exhaling. "I'll have a Scotch. With ice."

"I dropped the Scotch, sir, but I can get another…"

The wooden screen door banged behind Halliday, and Lehr shook his head.

An enlisted man offers me a drink in the middle of a workday. Christ, it's hot.

*   *   *

Lehr sat at a table sipping Scotch while Halliday carried in club supplies.

Outside, Jeeps and trucks churned up fine red dust on the Daktoum camp road. Artillery thumped, going out, and concussions clinked the bar glasses and bottles. The colonel studied his icy Scotch.

Political suicide for everyone in the chain of command clear up to Kissinger and Nixon to redeploy Americans to Daktoum, Lehr thought. So, here I am, in the hot seat. No commander in his right mind would touch this piece of shit—much less in a demotion slot. At least it's not Saigon. *You relish desperate situations, it's the way you show despair, John.* Monique, oh Monique. *You trust the wrong people, John, and you enjoy the chaos that your enemies bring.* Monique. So strange, to think of her as an *ex*-wife. Just one simple signature, and all the flesh and blood, the fire of a marriage vanishes—hah. Not much movement on the Trail. This tactical situation could just look like bait. Maybe the N-V-A won't engage. And there is a reaction force, whoever the hell it is…

"Go see if it's back, Halliday," the colonel said.

Halliday walked through the hot light to the nearby TOC and quickly returned.

"Not yet, sir."

Halliday unpacked glasses and liquor bottles, cases of beer and sodas, Slim Jims, beef jerky snacks, salted peanuts, fried pork rinds, a cassette tape player, and big glass jars of pickled eggs and pickled pig's feet.

The colonel sat at a table, his head and stocky torso silhouetted against the green blur of jungle.

Tough guy, Halliday thought, like John Wayne. He didn't look like he could move that well, but when he started toward me, shit— definitely, nobody to fuck with, an ex- boxer. Lehr? German? He looks like my Lithuanian grandfather, Jadek, white sidewalls, strong nose, and jaw.

Lehr caught his stare.

"Go, see if it's back."

Halliday cursed under his breath.

Lehr watched the tall awkward soldier.

Seems constantly poised to run. Keep him on as my driver? Hair's long, disorganized? Good-looking kid, high cheekbones, strong mouth. If Monique and I had a son… Wonder what he would look like? *You trust the Army too much, John.* Jesus, that woman would let anything come out of her mouth.

"Sorry, sir," Halliday said, entering the room.

Intelligent eyes, Lehr thought—the reverse of Goodby, who explained Colonel Newcomb's death like a Bible story with a profound moral for our times. What moral? Never get in a chopper piloted by a Vietnamese?

Halliday brought Lehr another drink.

The colonel stared into the melting ice as afternoon light angled shadows across the dusty concrete floor.

Newcomb. Poor bastard. Jesus, Lehr thought, shit, *the letter.* Goddamn, never thought I'd have to write one yet. Maybe he doesn't have a family. Of course he does, everyone does. Except me. Oh hell, John, lose the self-pity.

Somebody had gouged F-T-A in the rough wooden table—*Fuck The Army*—and Lehr slid his glass over the carving.

"Go see if it's back."

Lehr drank.

How the hell could anyone forget *that*? Maybe the entire country is coming unglued over this war, like Christina says. Jesus—how can you love and hate your own flesh at the same time? I raised her from when she peed in her pants. And now I have to listen to her lectures on why *I shouldn't kill Vietnamese children*. As if *I* killed children. Jesus. *How can you go to Vietnam, Dad?* I'm a soldier, I have orders, it's my job, I took an oath, I obey my superiors. It's how I make my living and put you through college. Duty, Christina, duty.

"Duty, sir?" Halliday asked, looking up from behind the long plywood bar.

Colonel Lehr glared. He hadn't realized he was muttering. Halliday dusted bottles.

Lehr walked to the screened windows and thrust out his chest. The hot ridge seemed so far beyond this room.

Halliday cut the wrapping off a case of Slim Jims.

"So, you're my driver," Lehr said, approaching the bar.

"Yes, sir," Halliday answered.

Lehr placed his empty scotch glass on the bar and their eyes met. Halliday wiped down the plywood bar.

"Where are you from?"

"Southern Arizona, sir, Tucson."

"Beautiful desert," Lehr said. "I was at Huachuca."

Halliday polished a glass until it squeaked.

"Yeah? Where are you from, sir?"

"Middlebury, Vermont."

"My father went to college there. Before World War II."

"That why you enlisted?" Lehr asked, almost smiling.

"Partly," Halliday said. "I screwed up in school."

"Go see if it's back," Lehr said, his eyes narrowing.

*　　　　*　　　　*

Halliday followed a dusty path lined with half-buried artillery shell casings into the maze-entrance of the sandbagged TOC and crossed the big main room to the Executive Officer's office across from Captain Ranklin's, where Major Goodby sat in darkness, his heavy face placid.

"It's on its way," the Major said. "1800."

When Halliday told the colonel, he wasn't happy.

*   *   *

Thirty minutes later, Lehr and Goodby ducked beneath the whirling helicopter blades. The colonel walked around the nose to the pilot. The vibrating Plexiglas window slid open.

"Why the hell did this take all day?" Lehr asked.

The pilot's eyes blazed.

"Wasn't Priority, sir."

"Who the hell do you answer to, son?"

"Vietnamese Joint Command. Sorry about that, sir."

"It's sorry, all right," Lehr said, turning. "Thank you."

Lehr hustled around the helicopter to Goodby leaning into the open bay. The side gunner pointed out a round object wrapped in a rubber poncho strapped to a jump seat.

Goodby heaved his bulk up onto the aluminum deck and unstrapped the object.

"Bring it," Lehr commanded.

The colonel turned and marched toward the medical bunker. Goodby hustled along, carrying the poncho-covered ball like a servant with a present.

As the helicopter rose, the side gunner grinned at Goodby and instinctively shifted his machine gun toward Rocket Ridge.

Goodby hurried behind Lehr across a small gray bridge and a dusty rutted yard where a stretcher Jeep and a large ambulance parked beside the medical bunker.

The helicopter became a dot in the distance as Lehr and Goodby disappeared into the bunker.

"Atten-SHUN!" yelled a medic, lounging on a stretcher.

All the medics jumped up.

"At ease," Lehr said. "Where's the Battalion Surgeon?"

Clancy pointed at Doc's office.

Lehr walked over, opened the canvas flap, held it for Goodby, and the two stepped inside.

At his desk, Doc Levin looked up, surprised.

"There," Lehr commanded.

Goodby set the poncho-covered ball on the bed.

"Colonel Lehr. Your new C-O."

"Captain Levin," Doc said.

Lehr nodded and departed, trailed by Goodby. As they passed, the medics scowled.

Doc came out of his office as their boots echoed overhead.

"Colonel?"

Lehr was gone. When Doc returned to his office, Clancy followed him in.

"What's this all about, Captain?"

Doc unfolded the green vinyl poncho with dried blood crackling in the folds. Inside, Colonel Newcomb's close-cropped head stared, eyes wide open, mouth agape.

"God-damn," Clancy muttered.

Doc quickly thumbed the eyelids closed.

"Some numb nuts left Colonel Newcomb's head on Paradise?" Clancy said.

Doc re-wrapped the poncho.

"Donnelly!"

Donnelly appeared, scowling, and clenching his fists.

"How can I do ya, Doc?"

Clancy picked up the wrapped head and thrust it into Donnelly's gut like a football.

"Colonel Newcomb's head," Doc said. "Put it in his bag in the dead bunker."

"Jesus, Doc, why me?"

"Why *not* you, Donnelly?" Doc asked.

8.

The next day, driving the colonel's Jeep, Halliday slowed for three Montagnard women crossing Highway 14 with soldiers' laundry piled on their backs. Ben sat in the Jeep ambulance parked above the river.

Halliday turned onto a dirt track leading down to the river, where barelegged Montagnard and Vietnamese women pounded soldiers' laundry. Dozens of olive fatigue pants and shirts were spread out to dry on flat rocks and low bushes.

Halliday pulled up beside Ben's ambulance.

"What's happening 'cruit?"

"Moving club supplies. What are you doing?"

Ben lifted his bush hat and wiped a sweaty brow.

"Clancy's revenge for the 'dog incident.' Making sure laundry girls don't poison our clothes."

Laughter and wet cloth slapping rock echoed from the river.

"Not bad duty," Halliday said.

"Watching laundry girls gonna save us from the N-V-A?"

"So, we will get hit?"

"You tell me—you're the colonel's driver. All I know is Charlie's killing us with the waiting."

They sat in hot Jeeps on worn canvas seats, watching the wet shining legs of the laundry girls' pounding clothes near the river. Rocket Ridge looked small against the colorless sky.

A loud explosion echoed. Halliday jumped out of his Jeep and hit the dirt as a geyser of water shot up above the river.

"Relax," Ben said. "ARVN lunchtime. Killing fish with hand grenades."

"Fucking Vietnam," Halliday said, dusting himself off. "Nothing like I thought."

"Yeah?" Ben said. "What did you think?"

"I don't know, more like the movies," Halliday said as he got back in his Jeep. "Good guys, bad guys, battles."

Ben laughed.

Out on Highway 14, a Lambretta scooter bus rattled by crammed with farmers, chickens, ducks, and pigs. An army earthmover careened past, showering dust on a Vietnamese girl in a conical hat carrying a big red plastic bag.

"Hey!" Ben yelled. "Lam!"

The slender girl waved and ran down the hill. She slipped between Halliday's Jeep and Ben's ambulance.

"Got any beers, Lam?"

The girl, in a purple blouse, bent over between the two Jeeps and unwrapped two cold beers rolled in *Stars and Stripes* newspapers. Lam was a shapely teenager, with long hair and flashing eyes.

Ben and Halliday got out, and the three sat in the shade of the ambulance, while Ben slit the steel cans and pried open the slots. The beer was cold and good.

"Lam, this is Halliday."

"Please to meet you, Howaday," the girl said, elegantly holding out a hand.

Halliday grinned and gripped her strong soft hand, which made her smile.

"Lam's the prettiest coke girl in the Highlands."

"No question," Halliday said.

"How you doing?" Ben asked.

"OK," the girl said. "How you be, Ben G.I.?"

"No money, no girlfriend, no love, number ten," Ben said.

She laughed.

"How's mamasan?"

"Same same," Lam said, looking away. "Sometimes good, sometimes no good. Need beau coups money for B-12 shot."

"Yeah," Ben said.

"Always need more money, G.I."

"A-men. How many beers you got left?"

"Three."

"I'll take 'em, Lam."

Ben pulled out a five-dollar M-P-C note and closed Lam's hand around it.

"Hang onto your beers," he said. "We drink them some other time."

"Too much money, G.I."

"Lam, we rich. Go buy mamasan a shot."

Lam tried to put the beers into Ben's Jeep.

"No way, G.I.," she said. "Too much money."

"I can't drive around with beers in the ambulance."

When Ben stuffed the beers back in her red bag, Lam flashed an impish grin and then snatched off his bush hat. When Ben grabbed her cone hat, she twisted away, and her long hair tumbled over the purple silk blouse down to her waist.

Ben put on her cone hat and Lam wore Ben's bush hat.

"OK," Ben said. "Good trade."

Lam giggled.

Ben's bush hat accentuated Lam's high angular cheekbones and honey-colored skin. Ben snatched his hat back, but when Lam went to grab hers, he held it out of reach, and Lam got mad until Ben let go. Ben dug around under his ambulance seat.

"Surprise, Lam?" he asked, grinning.

Her dark eyes gleamed.

"You got appo?"

Ben gave Lam two dusty apples. She put one in her bag and held up the other.

"Shine it," Ben said.

"Shine,' G.I.?"

Ben polished the red apple on his fatigue jacket.

"Oh, *shine*, G.I., *shine*." Lam repeated, putting the word and the action together.

The radio squawked. Ben tossed Lam the polished apple and put on the headset.

Lam tried to polish the other apple, but her silk shirt was too slick, so Halliday used his T-shirt and then handed it back. When Lam's arm brushed his, Halliday shivered, and she smiled.

"Merci, Howaday," Lam said, taking a delicate bite out of the apple. "Where you live, GI? Back in world?"

"Arizona."

Nearby, an old Vietnamese man poked through the ruins of the old engineer camp.

"Is it beautiful?" Lam said.

"Yeah. But not like Vietnam," Halliday said. "Different. Desert, beau coups dry, cactus, big mountains, no jungle. You want to go America?"

"Maybe," Lam said. "You take me?"

"Sure," Halliday said. "We can ride scooter bus."

Lam put her hand over her mouth and laughed.

Ben replaced the radio headset and got in his ambulance.

"Doc needs me," Ben said, pressing the foot starter.

Halliday and Lam got off the running board and stood in the hot sun as Ben tore off, spinning dust and squealing the tires when the ambulance hit pavement.

Lam held the red apple in her perfect mouth while she coiled her black hair on her head and fitted on the coolie hat.

"Maybe I see you later, Howaday G.I."

"OK, remember, we take scooter bus back to the World."

Lam picked up her red plastic bag, looked back over her shoulder, and smiled. As she glided towards the main road, Halliday caught up with her and shoved four dollars in her bag.

"Buy mamasan a shot."

Lam tried to refuse, but when Halliday wouldn't take back the money, she just looked down. Then her smile shone right at him, as she gently pushed Halliday's shoulder and left.

Halliday watched Lam's lithe, swaying walk until she disappeared over the rise heading down to Nhu Canh Du.

*　　　　　*　　　　　*

As Colonel Lehr unpacked his duffle bag, a crumpled blue airmail letter fell onto the floor of his sleeping bunker.

This large, stark room twenty feet below ground had been built for a general. A comfortable Air Force bed was draped with a mosquito net that hung down to the rough concrete floor, which Lehr knew would seep during monsoon.

He sat at a gray desk topped with a field radio and two field land lines. A fluorescent desk lamp barely lit an old French map of Vietnam pinned to the wall beside a big green tactical relief map of Daktoum.

Lehr opened the letter. Christina's letter was a Vietnam rant which haunted him like the faint scent of orange in the dim bunker.

Lehr stood up. He filled the desk drawer with letters, a shaving kit, a box of cigars, matches, and three books: a Vietnamese-English dictionary, the CIA's *Area Handbook for South Vietnam*, and T. E. Lawrence's *Seven Pillars of Wisdom*.

A black-and-white photograph of his ex-wife tumbled from Lehr's leather briefcase—he thought he had burned all her pictures. But there it was, Monique and Christina, at the Ruby Street cottage in Laguna Beach. Soft light rimmed Christina's blonde, and Monique's brunette hair as the sea softly reflected off their knowing, confident faces. Same eyes—daring, accusing, provocative.

When Lehr heard a knocking, his posture stiffened.

"Come on down," Lehr yelled up the steep stairs.

"Captain Ranklin, sir," a lean soldier said, stepping into the dim room with a crisp salute. "Acting Executive Officer."

Colonel Lehr returned Ranklin's salute and studied the gaunt, prematurely gray officer.

"Colonel Lehr. Your major's orders have been cut."

"That's what Group said, sir."

The two men stood silent in the stifling room.

"R&R?" Lehr asked.

"Hawaii, sir."

"Hard to come back."

"Yes, sir."

When Ranklin's eyes flashed away, Lehr wondered why.

"Things are ... different," Lehr said.

"Yes sir, a big firebase ..."

"Our tactical situation intensified. Vietnamization," Lehr said, contemplating the words. "We're staying. Vietnamese are now securing the valley."

Ranklin frowned.

"You heard about Colonel Newcomb?" Lehr asked.

"Yes, sir," Ranklin said. "Never met him."

"Nor did I."

Lehr took a cigar from his desk drawer and offered one, but Ranklin shook his head.

"Does this room smell like oranges to you?"

As Lehr struck a match, Ranklin sniffed the air.

"Goodby said that French woman doctor stayed here."

"Goodby."

The two traded glances and Lehr exhaled cigar smoke.

"Anything I should know before the briefing?" Lehr said.

"Four regular Army, sir, the rest ROTC and college."

"Anything else?"

"Don't think so, sir."

The colonel took a measured draw off his cigar, tossed the match in an ashtray, and turned to the tactical map.

"South Viet command is forty clicks away in Kontum."

"Colonel Trinh?"

Lehr nodded and puffed.

"I admire the Vietnamese people," Lehr said. "But Christ, the ARVNs? Less so. Too many generals, lack of field-grade combat experience, way too many draftees, corruption."

Colonel Lehr set his jaw and held Ranklin's eyes.

"Think the North Vietnamese want Daktoum?"

"Depends, sir," Ranklin said.

"On what?"

"Opportunity. Scout team heard tanks."

"Not the N-V-A's style," Lehr countered, spitting tobacco.

Lehr watched the gaunt Captain study the map.

"If they really do want it," Lehr said, "Daktoum will be no goddamn picnic."

"Yes, sir."

"Our civilians are sick of this war. So are the military. Yet here we are, 500 engineers and 250 vehicles sitting in Daktoum, looking like bait."

"N-V-A are too smart to take bait, sir."

"But smart enough to hold out seven years against the greatest army in the world," Lehr said. "With no armor or airpower to speak of."

Lehr's face lay in half-light.

Cigar smoke curled off his fist in wisps, enveloping his head, so that the light briefly turned Lehr's face demonic.

The Colonel's shadow loomed against the bunker wall.

Ranklin shivered.

Lehr picked up a field phone, barked into it, slammed the receiver down, and nodded to Ranklin. Lehr palmed his family photograph and slipped it into his fatigue pocket.

The colonel marched up the stairs and out into the stifling tropical afternoon, and Ranklin followed.

*   *   *

Lehr scraped open the briefing room door and nodded at Halliday behind the bar.

"ATTEN-SHUN!" somebody yelled.

A dozen officers and senior enlisted men stood up.

"Carry on," Lehr replied.

The officers shot sidelong glances at Lehr, paid Halliday colored MPC notes for their soft drinks, and then hurried to folding chairs facing two large tactical maps.

A Frenchwoman in a sleeveless khaki dress was silhouetted along the screened windows facing green Rocket Ridge.

Lehr stiffened. Her profile, posture, and long raven hair recalled his ex-wife. She met Lehr's eyes and didn't look away.

"Who's that?" Lehr asked Ranklin.

"Dr. Marchand. Runs the children's hospital at Kon Horing," Ranklin said. "Captain Levin asked her. She's the only other Western doctor north of Kontum."

Lehr walked over to her table and held out his hand.

"Dr. Marchand, Colonel Lehr," he said. "Could do me an immense favor? Come back at the end of the briefing? Thank you."

Gabrielle's eyes flashed. She nodded, rose, and briskly walked outside.

"I will wait in my Land Rover," she told Halliday.

"Gentlemen," Ranklin announced. "Let's get started."

Everyone stood up and came to attention.

Colonel Lehr formally faced the officers and the senior enlisted men, who all saluted, and Lehr returned the gesture.

"Gentlemen," Ranklin said. "The 99th's new commanding officer of Daktoum, Colonel John Lehr."

"At ease," Lehr said. "Gentlemen, please introduce yourselves."

As Ranklin stepped forward, Lehr recalled the personnel files he had skimmed at Group.

A short stocky blond man with a smooth hard face spoke:

"Captain Hardin sir, Fifth Special Forces, working with C-I-D-G Montagnards."

Adventurer. Lehr looked closer—a touch of self-disgust.

"Lieutenant McElroy, sir," a languid voice droned. "Battalion Adjutant."

Lanky college boy. Short-timer, drinks too much. Bags under his eyes.

"Sergeant Major Bricker," a strong voice said.

Big man, third war, at least three tours, like me—tired, drinking, he's seen too much. Was with the dead colonel.

"Major Goodby, sir, Battalion Chaplain."

Most goddamn removed chaplain I've ever met. Touch of righteousness. Or maybe fear?

"Major Sneller, sir, S-3 Operations."

Little man, teeth like a bat, forced smile. Backstabber? Political animal, keeps to himself. Dependable.

"Lieutenant Fairbanks, sir. D Company commander. We're building Bridge 39 and we secure the rock crusher."

A red neck scarf? Sharp, a competent officer. West Point.

"A Company commander is on R&R," Ranklin said. "And the 15th Equipment commander is out on the coast in Qui Nhon, wrangling us a new 'dozer."

"I've been briefed about B and D," Lehr said. "And Charlie company in Kontum."

"Captain Dunkley," a slow voice spoke. "S-4 Supply."

Big, thick glasses, moves like a goofy sailor on shore leave. Silver cross around his neck.

"Captain Levin, Battalion Surgeon."

Smart, Jewish, looks like a disappointed child. Good doctor. Doesn't like the war or the Army.

"Master Sergeant Loudermilk, Intelligence N-C-O."

Mean, efficient. He'll do what you tell him, but if you don't stay all over his ass, he'll go around you. Drinks.

"Thank you, gentlemen," Lehr said. "Captain, the map."

Ranklin uncovered the large green tactical map.

"Our primary mission has been roads and bridges."

The men nodded.

"As you know, the 3rd Brigade has been replaced by an ARVN infantry battalion in Nhu Canh Du. Only other infantry nearby is the 2nd ARVN in Kontum. Besides a few advisers at Ban Sai, the artillery firebases, and the Special Forces camps, we're the only Americans left in the valley. When the ARVNs take command of Daktoum, we'll redeploy, probably to the coast. Current intelligence enemy estimates for the tri-border area are two to three N-V-A *regiments* with enough materiel for three months. So, gentlemen, the question is: does Ho Chi Minh and General Giap want to eat dinner in Daktoum? Not if I can help it."

Goodby choked a nervous giggle.

"Our mission is to secure Daktoum firebase and keep the roads open to Ban Sai and Kontum. And continue to improve Highways 14 and 512. Artillery is coming, two 1-7-5 cannons and an 8-inch gun, plus two dusters and a quad-fifty truck."

Somebody whistled.

"But this is a Vietnamese show."

Colonel Lehr uncovered the Daktoum camp map.

"Our new troop strength is roughly 600, with the artillery. The 1-7-5 battery will dig in along the river and the eight-inch gun will set in east of the medical bunker."

Doc frowned.

"We'll close the A Company compound and move the water point here. As of tonight, we're on 33% alert."

The briefing droned on.

When it ended, Halliday went for Gabrielle. Lieutenant Fairbanks and Major Sneller put on their bush hats and left.

When Gabrielle came in, the briefing room hushed in that uneasy silence that always accompanied Western women in Vietnam. The

Frenchwoman clasped her wrists behind her back and faced the colonel, who motioned her over.

"Captain Levin," the colonel called.

Doc joined them by the dusty screens facing the high green ridge.

"Your village is scheduled for relocation," Lehr told Gabrielle. "Arrangements have been made for your criticals at Pat Smith's hospital in Kontum."

Gabrielle's mouth dropped.

"I'm very sorry," Lehr said. "I'll let you know when."

The colonel shook Gabrielle's warm hand. He walked to the bar and took a dripping can of Coke from Halliday.

Lehr looked back. There was something about the way she moved …

"Dr. Marchand," Doc toasted her with his Coke.

Gabrielle nodded.

She walked to a table and sat in a metal chair. When Doc sat down, her mouth tensed, and her dark eyes narrowed.

Beyond the dusty screens, Rocket Ridge rippled with heat.

"Have you had more malaria?" she asked Doc, gripping the wooden table.

"Unfortunately," Doc said. "Very high temperatures."

"I have had five cases. In two weeks."

"Would you like to examine my Falciparum?"

"Oui," Gabrielle sighed.

"Any day after eleven."

"Oui," she said, nodding and standing up. "I must go."

Gabrielle smiled and headed to the door.

The officers stared covertly at her bare legs, which made them dream of their wives and girlfriends and what it might be like to sleep with her in the heat of an Asian afternoon, which at least two officers were already doing with their Vietnamese laundry women.

"Well, gentlemen," Lehr said after she left. "That's it."

Conversations trailed off, empty Coke cans echoed on the bar, papers shuffled, and rubber bands slapped clipboards as the staff went out into the heat with a shuffle of combat boots.

Lehr and Ranklin stood alone in the large tin-roofed room as Halliday cleaned the ashtrays, wiped down the tables, and collected empty cans. Despite all the screens and a large rotating floor fan, the room was sweltering.

Lehr and Ranklin worked at the maps, the colonel pacing as he questioned and sipping his Coke thoughtfully.

Outside, the steep ridge turned pale under the harsh sun.

"So, we share intelligence with the ARVNs?" Lehr said.

"The Viets *are* taking over the war, sir," Ranklin answered.

"My first tour," Lehr said. "We had an intelligence colonel who said, 'If you really want the enemy to know something, just tell the ARVNs.'"

Ranklin grimaced.

"Think Group will give us helicopter support?" Lehr asked.

Ranklin shook his head "no."

"And this rumor of N-V-A tanks?"

"Speculation, sir."

"Well, work out a plan to blow the bridges from here to Ban Sai. I'll be damned if N-V-A tanks will use my bridges to come up this valley. Put Sneller on it."

"Yes, sir," Ranklin said.

"We're like a goddamn sitting duck," Lehr said. "N-V-A won't engage unless the ARVN commit a sizable force—they'll want a propaganda victory. And the ARVN know that."

When Ranklin looked at his watch, Lehr glared.

"I have a meeting with S-2."

"Go," Lehr said, watching Ranklin leave.

Lehr re-lit his cigar, covered the tactical maps with blue Mylar, and walked to the plywood bar. The colonel reached into his fatigue pocket, took out the photograph of Monique and Christina, and set it on the bar.

When Halliday restocked the small refrigerator with warm soda cans, he saw the photograph of a young blonde and an older brunette. Halliday closed the refrigerator and wiped down the bar.

"What does your father do, Halliday?" the colonel asked, staring at the photograph.

An explosion echoed in the hills.

"Builds missiles, sir."

"You don't approve?"

Halliday scrubbed the bar. When he looked up, the colonel was staring at him.

"I don't know, sir. Sometimes I wonder if he knows what's happening."

"Like burned babies and all that crap? My daughter doesn't approve, either."

Halliday walked to the far end of the bar to wipe it down. The colonel turned the photograph toward Halliday.

"Look, Halliday."

Halliday walked back and looked at the smiling blonde woman and older brunette. Their attitudes were so strong and true that it made him uneasy.

"These two would agree," Lehr said, "that *I* don't know '*what's happening.*' Maybe I don't—who the hell does?"

"Your daughters?" Halliday asked.

"The blonde, Christina. Monique is her mother."

"Bet they miss you, sir."

"Hah," Lehr scoffed. "*Maybe* my daughter—Monique's my *ex*-wife. French."

Lehr made a fist on the bar.

"Monique once told me, 'You trust the Army too much.' Do you think a man can trust his country too much?"

Halliday's eyes shot from side to side.

"Hard to say, sir," Halliday said, looking down. "Maybe, sometimes."

The briefing room door scraped open.

Gabrielle stood motionless outlined in the harsh light, her flushed face sweating under a faded straw hat.

"Dr. Marchand," Lehr said. "Come in."

"I wondered if I might get something cold to drink."

"Certainly," Lehr said.

Halliday took out a cold Coke. Lehr waved off payment.

"Merci," Gabrielle said. "I hope I am not interrupting."

"We were talking about trusting one's country," Lehr said. "You think that's foolish, Dr. Marchand?"

Gabrielle's face tightened.

"Not when one's country proves worthy of trust," she said, moving towards the door. "Merci."

"Dr. Marchand?" Lehr called.

"Yes?"

"I would be happy to help co-ordinate your relocation."

"Yes," she said. "Perhaps. Thank you, colonel."

Gabrielle scraped the door closed behind her.

Heat overwhelmed the room. Lehr walked past the screens, flipped up the blue mylar, and studied the ridges and valleys on the map. Halliday picked up the photograph.

"Looks like your ex-wife, sir."

"Who?" the colonel said.

"That French doctor."

Colonel Lehr grimaced. He walked over, snatched the photograph, and stuffed it in his shirt pocket.

"I don't see it," Lehr said. "Very little resemblance."

Lehr strode into the heat and dust, heading for the TOC.

9.

A month later, stocking the club refrigerator, Halliday felt a wad in his fatigue pants side pocket, $5800 in cash that Captain Ranklin gave him to pay Vietnamese workers.

Someone knocked on the screen door.

Ben stood there in the hot afternoon sun, his exhausted eyes hardened under a battered bush hat.

"Do me a favor?"

"Sure," Halliday replied, opening the screen door.

"Pour me some Scotch," Ben said, coming in.

Halliday stiffened until he remembered that all the senior officers were in Pleiku for a briefing. He scooped ice into a scratched tumbler and poured scotch. Ben drank, exhaled, and tossed his bush hat on the bar.

"Everybody knows we're not going to win," Ben said. "Hell, even Tricky Dick and Kissinger know. No ticker-tape parades for Viet-nam, no sir."

Ben lit a cigarette and set his chrome Zippo on the bar.

"Peace with Honor, *my ass*. Ask Billy Smedley."

"The 'dozer operator?"

Ben nodded, finished his scotch, and glanced outside.

A hazy finger of mist crept over Rocket Ridge.

"More?"

"No, man, enough," Ben said. "You got a brother?"

"Yeah."

Ben stared at his empty glass.

A fly lay as still as death on the sagging screen door, like everything else, slowed by the great heat.

"Powerful thing, a brother—old Billy Smedley proved that right," Ben said. "Got himself greased this morning."

"Mine sweep? Ambush?"

"Hah." Ben's dry laugh was harsh. "There would have been some honor in that. Naw, Billy died like he was on the street—dumb-ass motherfucking pills."

Ben held up his empty glass like a lens.

"Smedley got a letter from his mamma yesterday," Ben said. "His brother was killed in the Delta—Viet Cong sappers blew up a troop ship in Ben Tre. Can I have some more?"

Halliday poured Scotch and dropped ice, clinking in.

"Last night, Smedley and that fool Ellis start washing those shitty village yellow jackets down with whiskey. Early this morning, they're still so fucked up, Ellis thinks Billy's passed out, and when he can't wake him up, he calls us."

Ben sipped his scotch.

"Billy, he's so passed out, he's dead three hours when Doc and I get there. Ellis laughs until he figures out Billy really is dead and starts screaming and hollering so bad, I had to shoot him full of Thorazine and strap him down to his bunk so he don't hurt himself."

Ben tapped the bar in a sharp cadence.

"We found the empty pill bottle—Billy ate 30 damn yellow jackets. And when we carried Billy's body out to the airstrip for the chopper, even that hard-ass revolutionary Limerick starts crying. Know why?"

Ben waited until Halliday shook his head.

"Limerick says two of Billy's brothers already died—one in '66 in the D-M-Z with the Marines, another when the First Cav swept Route 9 into Khe Sanh. How Billy's mother gonna handle that? Four brothers, *four*, while Kissinger be bullshittin' about the *shape* of the goddamn peace table. Four poor black brothers, dying for what? Almost make me believe that Negro genocide shit Limerick always spouting off with his secret Black Power Brothers. Vietnam ain't no war—we're just killing people because we don't know what to do with them."

Ben threw his scotch glass like a baseball that ricocheted off the map of Vietnam and shattered on the concrete.

"Forget it," Halliday said, coming out from the bar.

Halliday stood awkwardly beside his friend.

"Sometimes I can't hardly take it," Ben said.

"Watch yourself, man," Halliday said. "Really."

Ben snatched up his big medical pack, scraped open the door, and went into the hot light, shielding his eyes.

Ben turned and stared through the screen door.

"You working tonight?"

"Naw," Halliday said. "Club's closed. Colonel and everybody are in Pleiku."

"Meet me at the water point," Ben said. "Five forty-five. Bring your weapon."

"Why?"

"I'm sick of this heavy shit," Ben said.

"OK," Halliday said reluctantly.

Ben trudged out into the hot camp.

Halliday swept the broken glass onto cardboard and dumped it in the fifty-five-gallon drum outside.

Ben's chrome Zippo flashed on the bar, so Halliday picked it up, and locked the door.

Halliday crossed the road to his hootch and scooped up his rifle, flak jacket, and helmet.

Nothing moved outside in the heat except the Montagnard interpreter Bok, speeding by on a new red Honda motorcycle and trailing dust. Halliday waved at Bok, tossed his battle gear into the Jeep, and went into the TOC.

Inside, Teletype chattered, and the fans blew hot air, rattling papers on empty desks. The room smelled of diesel, cigarettes, sweat, and dust.

In the open Operations section, Major Sneller flipped through a stack of blueprints. A nervous grimace bared his prominent incisor tooth, the inspiration for his nickname, "Snaggletooth." Halliday knew it was cruel, but because Sneller was so odd, everyone used it. The TOC was nearly empty—Ranklin in the village with his girl, Dunkley target practicing at the dump, Commo playing cards, Mac in his hootch— probably getting stoned, Loudermilk showering before screwing some poor laundry girl.

Merton's desk was empty, but heavy breathing came from the colonel's office, so Halliday peeked in. Merton was leaned back in Lehr's chair with his ruddy face buried in a *Playboy Magazine* and his boots planted on the colonel's desk.

"MERTON!" Halliday shouted, mimicking Lehr's voice.

Merton jerked upright, and the office chair toppled over with a clatter, sprawling the beefy clerk onto the ground. The naked centerfold brunette splayed across the colonel's desk, with a smile so innocent that Halliday wondered if she even realized that she wasn't wearing pants.

"You fucking fuck fucker Halliday," Merton hissed, scrambling up.

Halliday laughed as he studied the girl's curvy backside and shiny legs.

"You scared the shit out of me, 'cruit!"

Halliday kept laughing so hard that Merton had to join in.

"Merton," Halliday said. "I need a favor."

"Fat fucking chance you fucking desert fuck freak. What?"

"Drop me at the water point."

"No fucking way."

Merton righted the chair and brushed dust off the colonel's desk.

"What do I get?" Merton said.

"Get? What do you want?"

"This bimbo," Merton said, flapping the centerfold.

"OK, I'll fly her right over—if you can figure out how to stuff her into your jungle fatigues."

"I'll stuff her all right."

Merton's red face screwed up.

"Scotch," Merton said.

"I can't sell you hard liquor."

"You want a favor?"

Merton's weak jaw thrust out in defiance.

"Merton."

"*Scotch*, you cheapskate cowboy cretin! For your old pal."

"Shit," Halliday said. "OK, but you got it off the convoy."

"Deal."

They went outside.

Merton drove Halliday's Jeep through long afternoon shadows of canvas tents and bunkers, following the river past the artillery beneath Rocket Ridge and then to the tower bunker at the main camp entrance.

Beneath a sandbag-covered roof of the main entrance bunker, an impossibly thin black soldier with bloodshot eyes in oversized jungle fatigues leaned back in a folding chair. His name tag read: Ellis.

"Where you dudes going so god-damn late?"

"Why do you even give a flying fuck, Ellis?" Merton said. "A Company, OK?"

"Cause my gate closes down tight, come 1800 hours," Ellis drawled. "You late, you ain't getting back in. You bic?"

"Yeah, yeah yeah, we fucking bic," Merton said. "Anyway, fuck you, and the dead fucking trick horse you rode in on, Ellis, we're driving back to the World."

"Fine by me wherever the fuck you wanna drive your big fatty white ass, boy," Ellis said. "But come 1800 hours, this gate ain't opening for no living redheaded motherfucker. Bic?"

Merton flipped Ellis the bird and sped the Jeep down deserted Highway 14 toward Nhu Canh Du.

As warm air rushed through the open Jeep, the late afternoon light bathed Rocket Ridge so softly, that it almost looked friendly. Exotic trees teetered on the skyline, while overhead, the sky burned an impossible blue. Even the long red dirt road to Nhu Canh Du gave off a feeling of hope beside the green jungle, and the river glittering with light diamonds. This country is beautiful, Halliday thought. It's taken two months for me to see it.

They passed their burned-out engineer camp, where a tattered Vietnamese family combed through the ruins and drove past the French stucco walls and the old concrete defensive towers around the ARVN camp and then A Company's tiny compound on a dusty bluff above the river.

In a few more days, these twenty tent hootches would be destroyed, and A Company moved up to Daktoum. Merton passed the gate and picked up speed down the long hill to a gray panel bridge and stopped before a dusty bunker. Sunlight flashed on Nu Canh Du's dull tin roofs, peeking through the jungle.

"You fucking owe me, 'cruit," Merton sneered.

Halliday got out and then mock saluted Merton.

The sleepy bridge guard opened his eyes, nodded, and closed them again. As Merton drove away, Halliday hustled across the bridge, thinking Lieutenant Fairbanks would soon be returning from Bridge 39.

A steep dirt track ran around the far side of the bridge down to an engineer water point below, where Ben stood beside stocky blond Sergeant Smith, looking at the Dak Poko River. Halliday ran up, with his rifle and heavy flak vest flapping.

Above them, the whine of a Jeep bounced across the bridge, headed for Daktoum, tires singing across the metal. Lieutenant Fairbanks.

Smitty popped cold beers for Halliday and Ben, and then showed them his water purification trucks—where and how river water was pumped through holding tanks and purified. Then the moon-faced Smitty led them over to a sand beach on the Dak Poko River.

Smitty dragged three stained canvas chairs out from under a truck and set them around a cut-off fifty-five-gallon drum fitted with a cooking grill. Halliday broke up artillery boxes, as Smitty doused the wood with gasoline and lit the fire. As it burned down, Smitty made hamburger patties while Ben cut up and fried an onion, adding cans of beanies and weenies and Louisiana hot sauce.

They sat facing the water and drank beer.

A half-mile away, at a bend in the river, Nhu Canh Du nestled in dense jungle. Cooking smoke wavered the fading light as steaming rice and simmering pork flooded the warm air, and mellifluous Vietnamese voices drifted across the river like a dream.

Barbed wire radiated out from the long gray metal bridge, twisting into the water like a sharp rusty web. Downstream, a water buffalo grazed, silhouetted by the setting sun.

"'cruit?" Smitty asked, holding up a filter cigarette with a twisted end. "You smoked any Vietnamese weed yet?"

Halliday shook his head.

"Guaran-fucking-teed to blow your mind."

They smoked.

The river turned gold.

Glowing strands of mist rose off the shining water and up into the humid air. Like water spirits, Halliday recalled from some movie—the dead haunted water. Halliday took another hit and studied the warm sunbeams falling into the river.

The river turned pink and then deep red, the sky glowing above darkening jungle hills. The red ebbed to a deep purple, mauve, and slowly faded into a dark pearly silver.

The joint went around again. Halliday took another hit. When the silver river mirrored the immense sky, he imagined that the mist rising off the water were spirits of dead soldiers: Vietnamese, Montagnard, French, Chinese, Japanese, Americans, slipping back into the heavens.

Distant gunfire shattered the quiet.

Halliday lunged for his rifle, but Ben and Smitty didn't move. Embarrassed, Halliday reached for the joint.

"Enough," Smitty said, knocking out the flame.

The three sat on the sand beneath the silhouette of the bridge, watching the darkening river.

Downstream, yellow hamlet lights reflected on the black water, while flute music echoed from a scratchy radio somewhere. Up on the bridge, boots shuffled, and flak vests creaked over murmuring and muttering and the faint rustle of clothing. Weapons rattled softly, orange cigarette tips moved like fireflies, intermittently flashing young faces. Conversations rose and fell as young voices quickly pealed up into muffled laughter that rang out across the water and faded.

Smitty dropped three burgers sizzling onto the grill.

"Everybody want cheese?"

"Yeah."

After they ate the juicy burgers and delicious beans, they stared at the black rush of water, and Smitty re-lit the joint.

"One last hit," he said, inhaling.

Smitty handed the marijuana to Halliday, who toked and passed it to Ben.

A tingling fearful excitement raced down Halliday's spine, flooding his arms and legs and groin and shooting out the top of his skull into the balmy night.

Atop the bridge, soldiers whispered, and out on the river, dim yellow lights danced across shining black water. The smell of rice became stronger, and the melodic Vietnamese voices were almost comprehensible.

Somewhere, a helicopter lifted, and the *blap blap blap thump thump thump* slowly faded into the dark thick night and became the quiet brooking of the river at their feet.

"Different fucking world," Halliday said.

"Umm," Smitty agreed. "Sometimes, I don't know where I am."

"What do you mean?"

"I know I'm not back in the World, but where the hell is all this, really?" Smitty pondered, sweeping his hand across the sky, the land, and the river. "Where?"

"Wow," Halliday said. "I just realized that I'm in Asia, in fucking Vietnam. At war."

"Roger that," Smitty said. "So, you were in college, huh? How'd you fuck that up?"

"I don't know," Halliday said. "I lost it, failed out. Didn't have the balls to go to Canada. I guess 'cause my old man was a B-25 navigator in the Pacific, and my mother was an Army nurse in New Guinea, the Philippines, Japan. Everybody's father went, but my *mother* went. How could I not go? In Arizona, they were drafting Marines, fuck that shit, so I enlisted for two years. Why does anybody go? Guilt, ignorance, honor, a weird sense of duty, too many John Wayne movies? So here I am, chickenshit me, in Daktoum. Two months in country, and I just now figure out I'm not back in the world."

"Some guys never figure that out," Ben said.

"Why not?" Halliday asked.

Smitty and Ben traded looks.

"They get blown away first," Smitty said.

Lights from the hamlet flickered through the palm groves, silhouetting the sandbagged gun tower and the fifty-caliber machine gun on the bridge.

Above Nhu Canh Du, a light flared on a small steeple and a cross, which faded into darkness.

Halliday sucked in his breath.

"Smitty?" he whispered. "What's it like?"

"What the hell is *what* like?"

"When the shit comes down."

"Oh, man. Don't ask me that."

Smitty turned. A long moment passed in the dark.

"You just step into it," Smitty said. "Everything's fucking exploding, shit's flying everywhere, and all you're doing is trying not to get killed. Nobody knows what's going on—everybody shooting, guys screaming, people dying, getting shot, calling for their mothers, not like in no bullshit movie, you're completely scared shitless, but jacked up, too."

"Jacked up?" Halliday asked. "How?"

"Like running away from the cops, getting a great piece of butt, and driving a fast car all at once. And fuuuck-ing tiiiiiiime—man, it hauls ass, or else goes so fucking slow…"

Wavering yellow lights shimmered off the black river, shining the back of Smitty's skull.

"Shit, 'cruit, you can't *tell* anyone," Smitty said. "You have to *be there*."

The air grew leaden, still, like death.

Smitty exhaled and stood up. He crushed his beer can and threw it clattering onto a pile beside the water purification vans.

A Vietnamese flute wavered across the water and became quiet laughter.

"I can tell you one thing," Smitty said.

"Yeah?"

"Don't. Ever. Forget," Smitty said, staring at Halliday. "That you ain't coming back out of this motherfucking Vietnam. Never forget, for one goddamn instant or POOF! You're dust, man, pushing up daisies, history, blown clean away, going back to the World in a silver box instead of riding on the Silver Bird. Always keep that in mind, you bic?"

Terror cut through Halliday until his body shook.

"Heeeey Smitty," a playful voice sang down from the bridge. "Heeeey waaaterman. You down there?"

"Of course, I'm fucking here," Smitty called. "Who the hell wants to know?"

"You lazy-ass engineers up for a little night re-con? We could use us a couple more riflemen, Smitty, go check out this village, consort with the Cong, you know, stir it up a little, get some. Heard there's some fine nasty stuff down in that village that we might just want to go get ourselves a little piece of, you bic, G.I?"

"I bic *you*, you tired-ass, Jasper," Ben called. "You just about the tiredest-assed nigger I ever heard of my en-tire fucking life. Who in hell letting you run *night patrols*? You so lame you can't even find no village in the goddamn *daytime*, much less the night. No way, I ain't going *no-where* with your sorry-ass, especially no goddamn patrol."

"Who down there? Who?" the throaty voice from above called. "She-it. Better *not* be that sorry-assed *Cal-i-fornia* medic *Ben*-jamin. Ain't no *god*-damn medic going out on this patrol, uh uh, no sir, not on my goddamn life, sorry about that shit, Jim, we ain't in no immediate need of no medical assistance, 'specially coming from *Cal-i-fornia* land of the fruits and the nuts and the Tricky Dicky Nixons. How come you can't find yourself no decent company, Smitty? Whatchyou hanging 'round with nut cakes for?"

"Decent company, my ass," Ben said, laughing. "You better *listen* to what this medic tells you. I know your nasty-ass habits, Jasper, I do. I may just ship your sorry non-commissioned ass off to the island of the Black Syph."

"Black Syph, my black ass," the voice came back. "You honkies and fruitcake medics get yo' sorry butts up here, didimau baby, 'cause this here night patrol is saddlin' it up ASAP and movin' out, in zero-two mikes, you bic, G.I.? And bring you lock and loads, we be having us a arms inspection."

"We *bic*, you sorry ass," Ben yelled. "And we be having us a *short* arm inspection."

"In your dreams, Ji-im, this is your weapon, this is your gun, this is for fighting, this is for fuuuun."

The night hooted with laughter.

Down on the river, Ben and Smitty stood up.

"Ready?" Ben asked Halliday.

"I guess," Halliday said, shifting from foot to foot.

Under the dim glow of charcoal, Smitty and Ben traded glances as the three young soldiers rustled around the dark water point, collecting flak jackets, helmets, weapons, and ammo bandoliers. They climbed up the dirt track to the guard tower, angled through the barbed wire barricade, and walked onto the steel panel bridge.

Lit by dim glowing cigarettes, soldiers milled around the empty bridge. The throaty voice walked out of the blackness.

"Ben-jamin-coming-into-Los-An-gel-es, my main mother fucking man, wha's happenin', brother?"

A tall black man greeted Ben with a series of fist taps, thigh raps, and arm slaps.

"Under what fucking rock you been hiding, Jasperman?"

"I been doing me some international travel."

"International *what*? Only in your sorry-ass heavily-grunt-ified and fully blown mind."

"That be *international* grunt humping to you, home. Laos, Cambodia, you know, study you geography, French Indo-fucking-china. Join the Army, see the world, go to beautiful tropical places, and blow all those pretty people the fuck a-way, the 'meri-can way."

"*Cam-bodia*, what the fuck you want to go to Cam-bodia for?" Ben said. "What the hell's over there, anyway? Good place for you Jasper, all those snakes and monkeys with all your best gook buddies, the N-V-fucking-A."

"Leastways I ain't looking at no drippy peckers and telling people 'bend over' all day long. How you been, man?"

"Number two or three. How about you?"

"All right. Who this di-min-utive honky dude?"

"Jasperman," Smitty laughed, gripping his arm hard.

"Smitty brother. What's happening, water-fella, watermelon?"

"Just making water, baby. Long time. You been out humping the good fight?"

"Yeah, ain't that some shit. 'Leastways nobody but Charles and the snakes fuck witchyou out there. No scared-shitless green-ass L-T's or fat damn drunk lifers. Who else wit' you?"

"Halliday."

"Holi-day," Jasper said. "Gimme five,"

Halliday slapped a clumsy hand gesture.

"When you get here, 'cruit, yesterday? Day before?"

"Two months ago. How could you tell I was a 'cruit?"

Jasper threw back his head and laughed until Smitty and Ben joined in.

"*Tell*? Maan, you got 'cruit written all over you in glow-in-the-dark-letters—you tense, you make noise, you scared, you ain't been laid for way too long, its like you waiting for the movie to begin—all that nasty-ass stink of 'cruit. But no sweat, everybody's a 'cruit—even a couple of these tired-ass foo's," Jasper said, motioning to the men behind him.

"Gentle-men," Jasper said. "Pre-pare to stand by."

Jasper stiffened his posture, executed a precise hand signal. and the murmuring soldiers in the dark went silent.

"Pa-*trol*, pre-*pare* to move out," Jasper said. "We wasting time up on this sorry-assed bridge. *Move* out."

The patrol straggled away.

Jasper and Ben and Smitty and Halliday walked down the bridge, followed by a huge black soldier, a wiry white soldier with a machine gun humped across his shoulders, and a black soldier in a do-rag with a grenade launcher slung barrel-down. A skinny black soldier and a hulking white soldier both in new fatigues brought up the rear.

When Jasper stopped at the squat tower bunker at the far side of the bridge, the soldiers halted like a single organism.

"Cook?" Jasper called up into the low tower. "You up there? You awake?"

"Yeah," said the unseen soldier.

"You listen up hard, now. That L-T come by? You tell him we out setting ambush."

"OK, Sarge."

"You got the password?"

"Yeah," the voice in the bunker droned.

"Stay *awake*, Cook, I do not want to have to kick your skinny ass, which you know I will."

The loose column of young soldiers slowly weaved through the barbed-wire barricade, walked down the bridge approach, and onto the road through air so hot and thick that Halliday imagined he was swimming. The night was so dark, that in his stoned state, all Halliday could do was try and keep his feet moving and not fall or run into anything.

"What's happening in Cambodia?" Ben whispered to Jasper.

"Why? Ain't no medical business out there."

"Jasper, don't give me that lifer need-to-know bullshit."

They walked silently.

"N-V-A getting ready," Jasper said. "Not much shit going south. Maybe the 66th resting up to push into Parrot's Beak, maybe the 28th hit Dak Sieang, or cruise on down to the Ia Drang or Ban Sai, maybe the 40th even come up and kick the shit out of Daktoum like everybody keeps saying."

"I ain't holding my breath," Ben said.

"Hey that's some heavy shit—your newbie Colonel losing his fucking *head*."

"Literally," Ben said. "I seen it."

"No shit?"

"No shit."

"What's the new one like?"

"Well," Ben said, "this Colonel's got himself a head. So far."

Jasper laughed.

"He's OK," Halliday chimed.

Jasper turned around.

"What the fuck you know about colonels, 'cruit?"

"Halliday drive for the man," Ben said. "He run his officer's club."

"*Officer's* club? In *Daktoum*? What kind of sorry-ass shit is that?"

"Colonel who lost his head started it."

"No wonder we losing this god-damn war," Jasper said. "Officers don't need no fucking *club*—their whole *life* is a *club*. But this new old man ain't so bad, Holiday?"

"He's OK," Halliday said. "3rd tour. Been in the bush."

"No, man. Not *in* the bush. *Over* the bush. In a helicopter, maybe. Colonels don't go *in* the bush, they barely even touch the fucking ground unless they in a trailer or some shit—or else they shot down," Jasper said. "Your Colonel must have done sorryass nightmare bullshit, like banging him Westmoreland's wife or Nixon's daughter, to get his ass shipped to Daktoum and head up this circus—taking orders from the *gooks*. *She-it*, no fucking way would I answer to no Colonel Binh or Trinh or Minh Binh Phu motherfucker—no way in hell. Not even if Nixon, his-sorry-assed-bullshitting-self, come over here and fly me back to the World in Air Force One with ten horny wimmens. I'd go to Cam-bodia first, join me up with old Ho himself."

"*Shi-it*, you ain't joined up with old Ho *yet?*" Ben said. "Jasper, you even *look* a little like old Ho—you grow you a pointy little beard, get all skinny, and shit, paint your face yellow, maybe even find you some extra-large black P-Js."

Jasper laughed.

"Them lifers keep giving me shit, I may just do that," Jasper said. "I do love them Vietnamese wimmens."

"*Wimmens?* Where'd you learn to speak, Jasper? You so sorry-assed. You from *De*-troit? Mo-Fo town?"

"Don't you start that Mo-Fo town shit with me, you Cal-i-fornia fruit pie. You cain't beat Jasper."

"How's Linh?" Smitty asked the tall sergeant.

"Aww, man, bitch driving me crazy. *'Jasper G.I., you like Linh? Linh good to you, Linh do what you want, Linh make you beau coups happy, Linh give you beau coups love. You buy Linh liddle gold necklace?'* Bitches everywhere all the damn same: All of 'em got that 'buy me' shit on their radar. Hey Smitty…"

Jasper turned back.

"Hey Smitty, I give you some money—get the mail courier pick me up something gold in Pleiku P-X, twenty-five, thirty dollars?"

"No sweat, Jasper."

Jasper held up his hand. Everyone stopped.

When they started again, the patrol moved like cats through the night.

Under the darkness and the silence, Halliday's mind went wild. What little of the landscape he could see took on the shapes of rifles and cone hats, lost legs and coffins, bloody limbs and machine guns ready to blast—and the only way he put them out of his mind was to concentrate on slow-dancing with Gayle McDonough and sliding his hands down over her fine round hips.

Hot jungle closed over the road.

As Halliday walked, leaves brushed his arms, fear gripped his throat as his tight chest filled with dense night air, pungent with tropical decay.

Suddenly the patrol stopped.

Halliday's heart beat up in his throat, his legs felt like lead, and he gripped his rifle so hard that it shook.

Jasper's strong hand fell hard on his shoulder. When Halliday's eyes adjusted, they stood in the middle of a village—he could barely see thatched roofs. What was he supposed to do? He reached to flip his weapon off safety, but Jasper squeezed his shoulder.

Momentarily calmed, Halliday stood still.

A breeze whipped across his jungle fatigues, and he stiffened. When the breeze rippled his thigh again, he whirled his rifle until Jasper's touch eased him. Again, the breeze brushed his leg.

Instinctively Halliday reached for it.

A beautiful little hand gripped his palm.

The hand gently tugged until Halliday relaxed and let himself be pulled into the night.

Halliday heard soft laughter but all he saw was Jasper, lifting a tiny, giggling woman into the air.

The patrol spread out around a low building. When the hand departed, Halliday stood alone in the dark.

Jasper whispered sharply.

The skinny new man and the black man with the M-79 posted around the dark banana grove as shadowy young women circled the large G.I.'s like gentle night winds.

Halliday heard an older woman's voice—prodding curt commands to slender young females gliding all around the big battle-dressed G.I.'s. The night was so dark that all Halliday could see were flashes of long hair, smiling white teeth, and the whites of eyes briefly sparkling the night. He felt silky hair rustle his arms as girls spun by, brushing their bodies against the teenage soldiers, and whispering, '*You liike, G.I. you liike? You wan' me? You wan' me now? You liike me?*'

Jasper kissed his girl, Smitty had his arm around one, and Ben whispered to another with long hair down to her waist. Halliday clutched his weapon. His legs tingled and his groin stirred. Impulsively, he brushed the thigh pocket of his jungle fatigues and felt the wad of piasters that Ranklin had given him to pay the Vietnamese workers.

Halliday panicked—shit, why in hell did I bring that? I'm outside a whorehouse with a ton of money, scared shitless, can't see anything, trying to figure out if I even *want* to sleep with a whore I don't even know what a whore is and I'm horny but it's an unsecured village where do I put my money and what do I do with my weapon and what if they go through my pants and steal it while I'm sleeping, what if Charlie comes in and slits my throat and what if I get the clap do they really send you away to an island and never let you go home for the rest of your life because of the Black Syphilis and then they tell your parents you died in the war and you live the rest of your life like a leper. I'm scared shitless, I can't speak Vietnamese, what if everyone leaves me, what if all the women are V-C and have razor blades in their ...

"Hello G.I.," a quiet voice called.

A small hand slipped into Halliday's.

"Hi," Halliday said, his voice cracking.

Jasper disappeared into the thatched building. Ben and Smitty were nowhere in sight.

Under the moonless night, only the two new G.I.'s in the black banana grove stood near an older woman sharply speaking Vietnamese. Halliday looked from the jungle to the building to the girl's dark outline.

She slipped her arm around his waist and curled her head in the crook of his arm. Halliday squeezed her. She was small and delicate, with firm limbs and warm hips.

Whispered Vietnamese came from the shadows.

The girl's head resting on his chest and her thin arms draped on his hips stirred him. Out of the inky night, Halliday caught a sparkle in her eyes as long hair brushed his arms and stoked the warmth below his belly. She loosened her grip.

Another short, whispered stab of Vietnamese came from the old woman. The young woman held him tighter.

"You wan' me, G.I.?"

Her small chin rested on his chest, so her words murmured deep inside him.

"Yeah," Halliday said, not knowing.

She turned sideways, and her breath came faster. Another short command, and the girl slid out of Halliday's embrace and tugged him toward the dark building.

"Come, G.I."

They moved through the hot night to the small building that had swallowed all the soldiers. Halliday was pulled through a fabric doorway and down a long hallway towards a faint scarlet glow.

The rug door rustled shut behind them, and they passed raised cubicles draped in heavy red cloth. Muffled movements and caresses and heavy breathing echoed as if from far away and somewhere, faint laughter trilled. The girl paused and parted a carpeted door to giggling and a muffled groan from Sergeant Jasper, so they fled.

The girl led him to the end of the passage.

Halliday couldn't see anything, so he stood out in the dark hall trying to decide whether to take his weapon in until her hand reached through the curtain and tugged him inside. He sat down, put his rifle in and moved to swing his feet in, until her hand stopped him.

"No boot, G.I."

Reluctantly, Halliday took off his jungle boots and swung his body and feet into darkness, blindly pushing his weapon alongside the wall—

a bullet still in the chamber. He groped through the darkness and found the girl, huddling knee to chin in a corner. Halliday touched her legs, but she pulled away and leaned against a rolled up thatched mat.

The airless chamber was stifling, so Halliday unbuttoned his shirt and moved to the girl. When he touched her, she curled back into herself. Confused and apprehensive, Halliday waited in the dark, sweating.

"What?" he finally asked.

Again, he reached out, and this time, she pressed his hand to her knee. An endless moment passed in the heat and the dark with the powerful marijuana throbbing and stirring his passion, his confusion, his fear. The disembodied sounds of all the other soldiers floated around him so the air sighed with a thin wild wind and the only true sound, her gusting breath.

His hand covered hers and moved to her neck. He stroked her nape and gently lingered behind her ears like Jennifer had shown him, until her breath became more than fear and her small ripe body trembled.

Kissing her first on the cheek, he moved to her tiny rosebud of a mouth, which lay softly against his young mustache, barely responding to his kisses. He moved his hand to her slender waist. Not knowing what to do, he kept up childlike little kisses until slowly, she relaxed.

Passion rising, he strained his body over her, momentarily breaking off and falling against the wall to catch his breath. She stretched her legs and Halliday felt hot silk rustling the heavy air.

Suddenly he reached out and kissed her hard, flattening her small lips and pressing her breast so roughly that she drew back. For a moment, Halliday battled her, trying to pry her limbs apart. Then he laid back, panting, as sweat trickled down his neck.

A quick faint voice pierced the darkness—the mamasan again—and the girl's hand moved through the black night to stroke his heated chest, exploring downward with an innocent touch. Heat charged out of his belly and down his loins; bursts of energy jerked his legs.

Halliday reached for her breast. This time she allowed his hand to stay. It was a small breast that barely filled his hand through the high-necked silk blouse and as he squeezed it, her nipple stiffened beneath his palm.

When Halliday kissed her again, her mouth parted and his hand moved beneath her silk shirt with ease, to her smooth flesh and tiny heart pounding beneath a beautiful little mango breast, and when she moaned, his hand moved under the silk to the other breast and he held that tight, too.

He moved down her waist to the smoothness of her belly, around the silk trousers and her curvy hip and cupped her bottom and rubbed the backs of her legs until she moaned. Hearing her own strange new voice, the young woman wrenched away with a sigh and curled back into a ball.

"What the fuck?" he hissed.

Mamasan's voice drifted into the room from somewhere, and again, the girl reached out. He hugged her, sensing her feeling and her fear because he feared his own fire of emotion and the barely controlled heat stirring his belly. She stretched out again, kissed him deeply, and with a strong tender motion, he lifted the bottom of her silk shirt. There was no resistance as he pulled the top easily over her head, and she offered her breasts to the darkness and his touch.

Halliday grew hard and his hips twisted under the baggy jungle fatigues. He struggled to strip off his t-shirt soaked with the damp tropical night. She touched his chest, and he lengthened his caresses from her silky shoulders to the silk covering her hips, finally catching the elastic waistband of her shiny trousers, and slipping them down off her smooth hips and thighs, gently stretching them over her strong thighs, calves and ankles before flinging them into the night.

Halliday's hands roamed across her small body. Together, his fatigues and underwear slipped down and off until he was naked. Instantly, he feared for the $5800 in his pants. Bolting up, he wrapped his pants around his rifle and faced the girl.

She laid there, breath pounding.

Halliday pulled her toward him. His hardness was large against her small limbs and as it brushed her smooth belly, he took her small hand and wrapped it around him, and she held it so delicately that her fingers were like a hot wet breeze. Gasping, Halliday drew her towards him, her hand slipping from his sex as he swallowed her tiny hard body with his arms, enveloping her limbs. The girl felt so tiny and delicate and tender and round upon his skin that he relaxed his grip.

Streams of electricity ran off his warm fingers into the hot-liquid sheen on the backs of her legs, the flesh so achingly alive that he thought his fingers might just melt into her skin. She came alive under the electric charge of his hands with a soft, sharp cry of abandonment. Her legs slowly parted and wildly brushed his legs with her velvet thighs until he cupped the roundness of her buttocks with his hands and squeezed them so hard that a moan escaped her and flooded out into the night.

He kissed her as tenderly as he ever had any woman, his body aching with what was to come. He easily lifted her beautiful bottom up and poised her center near his until the two bodies met. For long lovely seconds, he slowly moved into her heat. When he could not take the inching slowness any longer, he plunged into her with a groan and a violence that caused her to cry out a birdlike moan of pain and desire.

For what seemed like forever, Halliday felt the fury of her tiny body beneath him and through him and with him and in him and as suddenly as she came, he came in great gulps of breath and blood and semen flooding out of his young body and into hers with equal fury and mystery.

He held and stroked her, comforting. After a long while, he felt powerful emotions shuddering through him and through her as she lay in the afterglow darkness nestled beneath him. She was so soft and tender and giving—I've never been this way with any woman, Halliday thought.

*   *   *

Slowly, the hot, dark Vietnamese night filled with fear until the war had returned.

The dense night air muffled all sounds as apprehension crept into Halliday. I'm naked. With a young naked woman. In an unsecured Vietnamese village. At night with $5800. Dumb shit, she might have the clap. Why didn't I ask her for a rubber? Where are Ben and the others? I don't even know the password. What if I get left behind? Could I even find my way back? Oh fuck, Halliday what a stupid shit you are.

He fumbled for his fatigues and rifle and felt for the wad of money —it was still there. Halliday grabbed his Marlboros, shook out a cigarette, and stuck it in his mouth.

He clicked open Ben's Zippo and struck the darkness into flickering light. The girl's round hips and legs curved across the rumpled bed. He followed the shiny black hair up to her face, modestly turned away from the flame. Halliday drank in the young woman's body until he recognized the high, angled cheekbones, pursed lips, and shining eyes.

"Lam?"

The Coke girl, Ben's friend from the road.

"Yes Howaday G.I.," she said in a soft voice. "Lam."

Halliday dragged on his cigarette, snapped the lighter shut, and exhaled an uneven breath. The cigarette glow outlined their shadowy faces.

"How long have … Lam? I mean, in this …"

"Firt day, G.I.," she said.

"Firt day."

He dragged off his cigarette.

"So, you no go …?" Halliday asked, faltering.

"No. You firt, Howaday. Choose you."

Me first, he thought. Oh Jesus.

He dragged the cigarette, exhaled, and leaned back under the stifling darkness, the silence pounding his watery brain, forcing a whirr of images and thoughts. He reached out to touch Lam's shoulder. *Me firt, me firt.* Oh shit, how the hell can I deal with this, I never slept with a virgin before. He thought of Marti his first and Steph crying and Jennifer's laugh and Sarah making him wait so long, his mother, his grandmother, his friends Linda and Laura and sweet Mary Jeanne. *You first, you first.*

Beside him, Lam rustled as heat from her small body spread out across the vast night.

"I see you Howaday. Wan' you firt. You no number ten G.I., you know, Lam know."

"Why not Ben?" he asked.

"Don't know," she said. "I see him, hide. Just want you."

She curled against him. Halliday kissed her and stared at the blackness.

Suddenly, the crimson curtain opened.

A match was struck, lighting their shining naked bodies as Jasper's gleaming face peered into the cubicle.

"Hol-i-day man, *get the fuck up*, holiday's over," Jasper said. "We moving it out, this patrol done finished, time to di di mau. Pull up your pants, mutter your sweet nothings, and pay the lady, or we be leaving without you."

The cloth curtain dropped.

They lay in each other's arms. Halliday wondered, pay the lady, pay the lady, is that what it was all about?

Lam kissed his cheek and found his fatigues, and then she lit a candle on a narrow shelf before a small shrine that Halliday hadn't noticed. Lam's long hair covered her slim body, sitting cross-legged as he pulled on the jungle fatigues over his pale skin. Lam handed Halliday one boot, and then she laced his other under the dim light. When Halliday grabbed his rifle, he saw a statue of Buddha beside a creased photograph of an old Vietnamese man with a wispy beard.

"I'll come back and see you, Lam."

"Maybe yes, maybe no, G.I., beau coups N-V-A, beau coups V-C, maybe G.I. go Kontum, maybe anything happen, Howaday," her voice hummed with musical pidgin.

"Holiday! *God-damnit!* We moving out!"

He took ten dollars from his wallet and put it on the shelf next to the Buddha and then kissed Lam hard and sweet.

"No ten, only tree dollah, Howaday."

The curtain parted behind him as her words echoed down the dark hallway, but he didn't look back.

As Halliday stepped out of the house, a full moon burst over the banana palms.

The patrol waited a hundred feet away, their cupped cigarettes glowing from the shadows of the silvery palm leaves. A murmur followed Halliday's appearance.

"About god-damn time," Jasper whispered loudly from the moonlit grove.

The tall sergeant grabbed him hard.

"You was in there a goddamn *hour*. Now I ain't no believer in no short-timers, but that silly-assed Lieutenant be by soon, and if we ain't back, he'd love to bust me for leading this half-assed *ambush*—shit, we been out here twenty minutes—I should have just left your 'cruit ass," Jasper said angrily, only releasing Halliday's shoulders to give a hand signal.

The patrol crushed their cigarettes and moved out, walking a dozen feet apart down the moon-dappled road, the straggling line of soldiers keeping to the shadows of the tree line. Halliday, second to last, walked a little dazed through the moonlight, filled with Lam.

After twenty minutes, Jasper appeared. They were close to the bridge now.

"Your first Vietnamese woman, 'cruit?" Jasper asked.

"Yeah," Halliday said.

"Fine lady, huh?"

Halliday mumbled.

Under the moonlight, a stand of giant bamboo looked like the black-and-white bars of a vast jailhouse.

"Don't that beat shit," Jasper muttered. "Fighting some drag-assed war nobody—not even their gooks—can figure out. Hell of a way to meet people."

Jasper shook his head.

"I love that little yellow woman, she treat me right. Every time I see her, I say Jasper, this could be the last time, do not hold back 'cause if you get your ass shot off out on old Ho's Trail, you do not want to re-gret holding back with no woman in your last dying breath. Dig? Cain't hold back *nothing* in god-damn Viet-nam."

"Yeah," Halliday said, thinking maybe it was the first time he hadn't held back.

The patrol walked down the road towards the bridge.

Beyond Nhu Canh Do, a flare burst.

Everyone fell flat to the ground.

The flare slowly spun down through the night like a ghostly firework, shining on the metal bridge, the road, the wide black river, the shaggy green jungle.

After the flare went out, a soldier went in to give the password. On his arm signal, Jasper led the patrol angling through the barbed wire past the Claymore mines.

Most of the soldiers disappeared into the bunkers at each end of the bridge.

Jasper, Smitty, Ben, and Halliday stood in the moon shadow of the tower bunker above the water point. Jasper spoke on the radio and then turned to Halliday.

"What's your girl's name?" Jasper asked. "I'll keep an eye on her."

Halliday hesitated.

"Lam," he croaked, looking down.

"Lam," Jasper replied. "OK. Will do."

The big recon sergeant touched his helmet and climbed up into the bunker.

"Good luck," Jasper called over his shoulder, "'cruits!"

"Take care, you tired ass," Ben said.

"Good luck," Halliday whispered.

Ben and Halliday walked across the bridge to the Daktoum side.

"Lam?" Ben asked. "Our Lam?"

"Yeah," Halliday said, looking at his feet.

"Man," Ben said, exhaling loudly.

A rumbling clanked through the night.

"Viet-nam," Ben said. "Some fucking war."

Ben looked away as the rumbling grew closer.

Watched by the tower guard, Ben and Halliday carefully slipped through the barbed-wire barrier and the Claymores until they stood outside of the wire on the bridge apron.

The rumbling grew louder.

"You got a sister?" Ben asked.

"I told you, no," Halliday said, catching Ben's eyes in the moonlight. "Just a brother."

"OK, then," Ben said. "Lam is like my little sister."

A tank roared out of the darkness.

At the last moment, the tank locked a churning tread, spun around, and stopped before them with a great groaning and clanking of hot steel. The big tank sat there, engine throbbing in the darkness, a hulk of clicking metal, stinking of hot grease and diesel fuel.

A billow of dust caught up with the tank, showering the bridge and Ben and Halliday with a thin wavering cloud that cast wispy shadows across the yellow moon.

The tank hatch popped open in the moonlight.

A skinny teenager scowled under square, rose-colored glasses. His bare, moonlit torso shone with sweat, and a greasy helmet proclaimed: "Roadkill," in childish ballpoint letters. Montagnard bracelets jingled his wrists, while a big peace sign glittered on his pale chest.

"Climb aboard, sinners," Roadkill said. "Whorehouse Express is moving out."

10.

Two large twin-towered Chinook helicopters landed and dumped a dozen supply pallets on the medics' pad. After the Chinooks rose into the air, Doc Levin and Clancy and the medics ripped into the pallets.

Cases of bandages, intravenous fluids, alcohol, whole blood, splints, stretchers, and morphine flowed off the airstrip and into the six black metal shipping containers scattered around the medical bunker. Just as the sweating medics thought they were done, another Chinook landed.

The big helicopter's cargo bay was so packed with large boxes that the side machine gunner was nearly obscured.

"Five minutes," the crew chief yelled to Clancy, over the high-pitched whine of the turbines.

Moving easily for a heavy man, Clancy ran over and called back the departing medics.

The cargo stank of new rubber. The medics unloaded so many boxes that when they finished, their faces were uniformly grim. They unloaded enough body bags for a thousand dead.

*　　　　　*　　　　　*

Dr. Gabrielle Marchand sat smoking on sandbags with her legs crossed at the medical bunker entrance with her black hair gathered up under a bush hat.

The idling Chinook helicopter growled a dull scream as the sweat-streaked medics hauled stacks of body bags into containers. Finally, the Chinook's turbine rose into a hover, the rear hatch closed, and the big helicopter slowly lifted away. The medics filed past and gave Gabrielle a look. A white woman in Daktoum was a fantasy as remote to the soldiers as peace.

Gabrielle stood up and stepped on her cigarette as Doc approached, wearing an olive-green T-shirt. Short damp curls ringed his slender face.

"Boots," Gabrielle said, indicating the airstrip.

"Boots?" Doc asked.

"Last year. The boots of all the dead soldiers, filling up with rain," Gabrielle said. "Their general lined them up so the press could take photographs."

When Gabrielle followed Doc down into the medical bunker, Nimmer, Limerick, Ben, Cullen, the Kid, and Donnelly all traded glances.

"All right, you big-eyed nosy troopers," Clancy said, hefting Ringer's up into the rafters. "Keep on working."

The medics stacked boxes atop the low massive beams and on shelves in the wooden bunker walls.

Gabrielle trailed Doc through the olive stretchers on sawhorses and into his small office.

The fluorescent tube flickered on Doc's clean uniforms atop a file cabinet. Stacks of reports and medical journals were strewn across his desk. Gabrielle set her medical bag on the floor and held up a cigarette.

"OK," Doc said, rummaging for an ashtray.

Gabrielle lit up.

"So, Doctor," she said, sitting on the bed. "You have luck with your anti-malarials?"

"The Vivax strain," he said, sitting at his desk.

Doc passed her a journal summary, which she quickly scanned as tobacco smoke filled the room. Gabrielle finished the article and pointed at a photograph of a blonde woman.

"Your wife?"

"Un huh," Doc said. "She's pregnant with our first child."

Gabrielle's mouth turned up.

"So far from home, you and me."

"I thought you grew up here?"

"What is left of my family are in France," she said with a thin smile. "With most of my friends. A few in Saigon."

"Must be hard," Doc said.

"I try to see the good bits in life."

Doc waited until she met his eyes.

"Even so," Gabrielle said. "Sometimes, I get the cafard."

"Cafard?"

"Cockroach," she said. "Like to be down, you know? On the ground. Depressed. I think Algerian soldiers named it in our war before Dien Bien Phu. A loss of purpose, that's it."

Gabrielle studied her cigarette. As a jet roared overhead, emotion creased her face. When Doc touched her hand, her mouth almost turned up.

"Merci," she said quietly.

She shook her head, and her face tightened.

"Since the Montagnards refused to work on your road," Gabrielle said. "They have no money. Now the V-C want taxes. And your Colonel speaks of relocation."

"To protect them from the V-C," Doc said.

"*Protect*? They have lived here for 700 generations," she said. "Would you move because a general wants to 'protect' you? I wouldn't."

"What would you do?" Doc asked. "Leave them to the V-C?"

She stood up.

"Your Colonel wishes to see me," she said.

Gabrielle stubbed out her cigarette.

Doc leaned over to embrace her, but instead, he fumbled for her medical bag, which she took from him.

"Merci beau coups, ami Bacsi," she said, speaking the Vietnamese word for "doctor" like an endearment.

Gabrielle opened the canvas flap and left.

Doc slumped in his chair. He tried not to give into the first strong feelings he had felt in six months. Doc studied his wife's photograph, trying to banish Gabrielle, even though the strong scent of her cigarettes and orange still lingered.

When Gabrielle stuck her head back in his doorway, Doc jumped.

"I thought you were going to show me your malaria patient and explain the treatment," Gabrielle said.

"Of course," Doc said. "Give me a minute."

*   *   *

Waiting outside the colonel's office in the TOC, Halliday rubbed his eyes. Lehr entered, nodded curtly at Merton, went in, and shut his door. The phone rang.

"C-O, 99th Engineers," Merton said. "Yeah, you silly son of a bitch, what the fuck do you want?"

Sweating, red-faced Merton paced and grimaced. He sat in his chair and stretched his feet up on his desk.

"He's *here*," Merton snarled. "Where the hell else would he be—on R&R? Why? Your old man's in a bad mood?"

Merton huffed, threw down the phone, and swung his feet to the floor. He opened the colonel's door and walked into the adjoining plank-walled office, where Lehr was studying a green operations map spread across his desk.

"Excuse me, sir."

"What?" the colonel said, glaring at Merton.

"Colonel Eagleton's on the horn, sir."

Lehr flipped over the map.

"Sir ..." Merton began. "Word is sir ... Saigon gave him a case of the ass."

"What?"

"USAR-V, MAC-V—the big boys, sir."

"Merton, speak English."

"Colonel Eagleton's Saigon highers are bugging him."

Lehr spun his chair around, frowned, stood up, and lifted a canvas-covered field phone.

"Sir—remember," Merton said. "You're meeting that French doctor at noon."

Lehr's frown drove Merton out of the office.

"Colonel—no, I have not relocated them yet..." Lehr spoke into the field phone. "*What?*"

When the door banged shut, Merton glared at Halliday.

*   *   *

When Lehr burst out of his office, Merton handed him Ranklin's new security plan. Lehr shook his head.

"I need a chopper to Kon Horing," Lehr said.

"No choppers, sir," Merton said.

"What about those three across the strip?"

"F-O-B's sir—spook shit—nobody can use 'em."

"I'll see about that. Halliday, get my M-16, Merton…"

"Sir …"

"Set up a bunk in my office," Lehr said.

"A bunk? In *here?*" Merton repeated, scratching his head as Lehr marched away. "O-K, sir. Whatever you want."

Halliday ran out as Merton cranked the phone.

"Supply, S-4, whatever. This is Merton. Yeah, yeah, yeah. Listen, I need a fucking Air Force bed, yeah, *now*. For the old man, that's who, here in the TOC, *yeah*, got it? ASAP!"

*   *   *

Across Daktoum airstrip, three Huey helicopters waited beside a sandbag revetment. The crews lounged in their open bays on stained olive jump seats and on the ground in the shade. M-60 machine guns hung down on their mounts under canvas covers and brass ammo belts glinted in the sun.

Underneath the middle chopper, a slender soldier lay on the rough pavement with his ear to a transistor radio. His fingers tapped the chopper's hot aluminum skin to the beat of the music: *there's something happening here, what it is ain't exactly clear, there's a man with a gun over there, telling me, I got to beware.*

The other side gunner lay on his back throwing his camouflaged bush hat up and down.

Across the strip, a colonel marched towards them.

"Stubbsy-man," the gunner called up into the bay. "Field-grade brass on approach with what looks like a case of the ass."

Lehr halted before the middle chopper.

"Afternoon, Colonel," Stubbs, the pilot said, sitting up and swinging his legs out the bay door.

"Afternoon, Captain. I need your chopper."

"Colonel," Stubbs said. "I'd sure like to, but we're standby for the spooks and the beanies. Fly Over Border."

Stubbs pointed towards Cambodia and Laos.

"Emergency. I need to go to Kon Horing," Lehr said.

"Tell you what, Colonel," Stubbsy said. "Captain Hardin over in the indigenous area might be able to cut us loose for an hour. Long as you're willing to stand down and get dropped if we get a call, then I'm happy to take you."

Colonel Lehr was gone before Stubbs had finished speaking, powerfully striding across the airstrip.

On the river bluff, a 1-5-5 cannon roared out, drowning out the gunner's music.

*   *   *

Lehr sat in the open bay of WO2 Stubbs's helicopter, skimming treetop at a hundred miles an hour, heading for Kon Horing village. Captain Mike Hardin sat in an olive jump seat with his M-16 pointed out. Bok, the 99th's Montagnard interpreter, sat in the open bay door with his feet hanging out. His impassive face reflected the rushing green jungle.

"What happened?" Hardin shouted over the turbine roar.

"Not exactly sure," Lehr yelled.

"Intel, we got," Hardin said. "Says Colonel Trinh put the local V-C up to it—some beef with the District Chief."

Lehr glared at the captain.

"Spooks," Hardin explained. "Just passing it on, sir."

A black column of smoke rose from a clearing in the jungle, and the helicopter banked around it.

The concrete walls and caved-in roof beams of Gabrielle's hospital smoldered with blackened clumps of furniture. Red bougainvillea blossoms from the massive vine along the front drifted across the ruins like drops of blood.

Beyond the hospital, Kon Horing village lay in chaos.

Half the stilt houses had been burned. Tribesmen and women carried cooking pots, baskets, clothing, rice, wine jars, tools, and furniture out of thatch houses.

A dozen Vietnamese soldiers prodded the Montagnards to a long row of shiny South Vietnamese Army trucks.

As the helicopter descended, a bare-breasted old woman smoking a pipe combed through the ruins, ignoring the helicopter circling the destroyed hospital.

Lehr studied eighteen-year-old Bok's chiseled face, his prominent lips, and the deep pools of his eyes under heavy brows. Bok wore tailored tiger fatigues over a rock-hard body. Lehr knew that Montagnards rarely showed feelings to outsiders except when they drank rice wine.

The moment they touched down, Lehr jumped out with Captain Hardin, who hand-signaled "five minutes" to Stubbs. Bok trotted off to find the village elders, while Hardin went to the Vietnamese soldiers poking through the empty huts.

Gabrielle's hospital was destroyed, and the village was being abandoned. What had been her life for five years had vanished in an hour.

Bok returned with a wiry older man in an embroidered indigo vest and a loincloth. Silver bracelets clinked on his arms, and his hard eyes were watery.

"Chief man now," Bok told Lehr. "Two elder die."

"What happened?"

The two Montagnards—the elder in loincloth, the younger in fatigues—conversed rapidly in the whispering language.

"He say beau coups V-C come morning, kill two elder, tell everyone leave, say N-V-A say come back two day kill everybody. V-C burn and leave, 'cept for few. ARVN airplane come shooting, so all V-C, maybe some N-V-A, run into hospital. ARVN airplane bomb hospital, kill many people."

"How many beau coups N-V-A?" Lehr asked.

The two Montagnards spoke again.

"Two hundred."

"Two hundred?"

Captain Hardin ran up with his M-16 slung barrel down.

"Yah, two hundred," Bok said finally. "Head man say snake yang gone now, all luck gone, no care who have village, same same N-V-A, V-C, ARVN, G.I.—he no care."

Lehr nodded at the old man. He walked beside Hardin back to the helicopter.

"A lot of N-V-A for broad daylight, sir," Hardin said.

"What else did you find out?" Lehr asked.

"ARVN drivers had orders to come here *before* the attack."

Lehr's face screwed up.

"Yes sir," Hardin said. "Somebody knew this was going to happen."

Hardin pulled out a wad of Vietnamese piasters, peeled off a stack of bills for the elder, and told Bok to thank him.

The three soldiers got into the waiting helicopter and Hardin gave a "thumbs up."

"Another thing, sir," Hardin yelled over the hover roar. "ARVNs don't want Dr. Marchand in their relocation camp—or at Pat Smith's. Some bullshit about 'security.' "

As the helicopter lifted, the old woman combing through the hospital ruins carefully gathered up a small gray bundle out of the wreckage. She pressed the bundle to her withered breast, but it was little more than ashes, so the bundle crumbled and was swept up into the rotor wash.

The thumping chopper banked into the colorless sky.

Colonel Lehr leaned out of the open door, watching the old woman in the smoldering wreckage of Gabrielle's hospital. As she still clutched the smear of ashes to her breast, Lehr realized that the bundle was all that remained of a baby.

*   *   *

Lehr walked back across Daktoum under a bleached sky.

A 175mm artillery gun lumbered by him on clanking tracks and angled into a broad cut of red soil lined with new blue-green sandbags.

Out on the river bluff, a 1-5-5 gun roared out a round with pale-yellow flames and the concussion shook the ground.

Three bare-chested soldiers with rivulets of sweat streaking dusty skin bent away from the firing gun, with their hands cupped over their ears. The artillerymen opened the smoking gun, flipped out a long brass shell, and clanked it onto a pile on the red ground. Then they hefted a new, white-tipped round into the hot gun breech.

Lehr walked to the dusty, sandbagged mess tent.

Twenty enlisted men were lined up under the shade of the tent flap. Sergeant Clancy glared at Donnelly's sparse mustache and rectangular blue sunglasses.

"Why the hell I gotta do it, Sergeant Clancy?" Donnelly said. "You know I'm short."

"You're the ambulance operator, Donnelly. I don't give a damn how short you are."

"What about the Kid? How come he don't he do it?"

"Don't give me no lip, Specialist. Unless you want to spend the rest of your tour in LBJ jail?"

Clancy glowered as the colonel approached.

"Afternoon sir," Clancy said to the colonel.

Lehr nodded to the sweaty line of unkempt young soldiers wearing stained, baggy fatigues, and scuffed jungle boots. Lehr pushed through the dusty screen door into the hot mess hall.

Vietnamese women in starched white uniforms doled out spaghetti with thick red sauce, watery creamed spinach, fruit cocktail, and Wonder Bread. The colonel took his metal tray and nodded.

At the command picnic table with a red-checked oilcloth, Ranklin sat beside the French doctor. The colonel walked up, pursed his lips at the lean, prematurely gray Ranklin, and sat down. Gabrielle wore a sleeveless dress, and her long hair flowed over her bare arms, again reminding Lehr of his ex-wife.

"Too many Montagnard refugees, too many forced relocations," Ranklin said.

"Have you coordinated fields of fire with the new artillery battery?" Lehr asked Ranklin.

The Colonel unwrapped a paper napkin and took out his fork and knife.

"Yes sir," Ranklin said.

"Get me a full report. 16:30 hours in the TOC?"

"Right, sir."

Ranklin nodded to Gabrielle, looked back at the colonel, and then excused himself. The lean officer angled across the crowded mess tent with a quick step that made Lehr think that Ranklin was avoiding something.

All the soldiers in the mess hall covertly glanced at the tanned Frenchwoman with the dark circles around her eyes.

"Dr. Marchand," Lehr said. "May I use your first name?"

"Gabrielle," she said, reaching out.

Her hand was tough and strong, slightly moist with a delicate touch.

"Gabrielle," Lehr said.

"Colonel, if you could possibly wait until after monsoon for the relocation …"

"Later," Lehr said. "Right now, I'd like to eat my lunch."

As Doc entered the mess hall, the colonel caught his eyes and frowned, so the medical captain took his tray and sat with Halliday and Ben.

By the time Lehr got up and escorted the laughing Gabrielle outside, the rare sound of a woman's joy had charged the mess hall with boyish excitement.

*   *   *

Gabrielle stood smoking at the edge of darkness.

Lehr's eyes opened to her naked body standing in the harsh beam of light falling down the airshaft of his sleeping bunker, twenty feet below ground.

At lunch, Gabrielle had genuinely laughed, and so had he—though she had sensed Lehr's cold, leaden nature, his joy had pierced her and then sucked them both down these dusty steps beneath the ugly crossed entrance beams that Gabrielle despised, down into the darkness of that awful general's bunker where she had broken a bottle of fleur d'orange.

The colonel took her standing up.

He had kissed Gabrielle once and only held her briefly, so she felt his 45-caliber revolver against her hip and his stiff webbed belt against her belly. When she felt her skirt pulled roughly up over her hips, and his hands on her buttocks driving her into him, Gabrielle gripped him even harder. When Lehr ripped off her delicate silk panties, tearing them apart, her long-untouched flesh suddenly bared in the heated air, released such a dormant animal craving, that she quickly opened his starched fatigues and stroked him hard.

After they finished, the two staggered away, gasping for air. Hot sweat ran down their faces and heaving bodies as they tumbled across Lehr's bed.

It became so unbearably hot in the big sleeping bunker that Gabrielle shoved Lehr away, stripped off her damp khaki dress and brassiere and threw them on his footlocker. Naked but for the silky torn panties around her waist, Gabrielle bent over, searching for another cigarette.

Lehr pulled up his pants and leaned, fully clothed against a broad post beside the mosquito net gathered above the bed.

The low room pressed at Gabrielle as she recalled that thin hard general who had lined up all the hundreds of empty boots in the rain— for that bizarre ceremony on the airstrip. She imagined that general living down here, breathing this stale air.

"Ohhh," she exhaled, lighting her cigarette, and leaning on a post near the bright shaft of light.

She remembered at that hideous time the general had proclaimed a victory. Five hundred men, dead. For a hill that they abandoned the next day.

"They will come," she said.

"The N-V-A?" Lehr said, his breath deepening,

Outside, artillery skittered away in booming echoes, which became deep rumblings in the hills. She remembered her father the colonel, and she guessed that the tactical situation would never stray far from Lehr's mind.

Gabrielle turned to face him. She let her cigarette burn low and took a final puff. She walked into darkness, tore off her ripped underwear, and threw them on Lehr's footlocker. She hooked her brassiere and then smoothed her khaki skirt.

"You want to save Daktoum, Colonel?" Gabrielle said. stepping into the skirt, "But how?"

Lehr came over, gripped her shoulders, and inhaled.

"The V-C burned down Kon Horing. They took hostages and hid in your hospital," the colonel said. "So our *allies*, the South Vietnamese, bombed it. I'm sorry."

Gabrielle crumpled on his footlocker.

"Goddamn both sides," Lehr said. "Makes no sense at all."

Gabrielle did not cry, no, just like her father, she did not cry. Ever.

"Stay at Daktoum as long as you want," Lehr said.

11.

Lehr marched past the tents on the company street and over to the medical bunker, where Doc sat outside the entrance on a bench, examining his yellow dog for ticks.

"Doctor Marchand's hospital was bombed this morning," Lehr said, squinting, "N-V-A, ARVNs. Some relocation Juliet Foxtrot."

"Is it destroyed?" Doc said, pushing the dog away.

The colonel nodded.

"Any problem with Dr. Marchand helping us here?" Lehr said. "For a limited time?"

Doc searched the colonel's face.

"No, sir."

"That hospital was her life."

The doctor nodded.

"Captain," Lehr said over his shoulder, walking away. "I'll provide her with quarters."

*   *   *

At the bottom of Lehr's bunker stairs, Gabrielle's pale angular face peered from darkness.

Lehr stood up at ground level.

"The ARVN commander barred you from the relocation camp. And all the civilian hospitals in Kontum province."

Gabrielle looked up.

"I'm very sorry," he said. "I've arranged to have you help us here—if you want to."

"Oh," she said.

"Good," Lehr said.

"Why not?" she said listlessly.

*   *   *

When Lehr opened the club screen door, Halliday stopped wiping down the plywood bar. Lehr's boots scraped the gritty concrete passing the screens facing Rocket Ridge.

Outside, artillery roared and rattled the bar glasses.

"Drink, sir?"

Lehr shrugged. Halliday polished the scratched glasses.

"Stupid bastards," Lehr muttered.

"Sir?"

Goodby pushed at the screen door and entered with a blue airmail letter clutched in his sweaty hand. His puffy face was flushed like he had been slapped.

"Colonel ..." the Chaplain said in a falling cadence that begged for a congregational response.

Lehr turned and glared.

"I have a letter," Goodby said, letting his mouth hang open. "It came care of the Chaplain's office."

Goodby handed Lehr the sweat-stained envelope and hovered nearby.

"What, Goodby?"

"Well, sir, since the letter came care of the Chaplain..."

"Yes?"

"Just that ... you might want to ... consult with me."

"No," Lehr said.

The overweight Chaplain exhaled. He glanced at the concrete floor and pressed his hands together. With a nod, Goodby lumbered out of the briefing room.

Outside, Goodby's step lightened considerably.

Ten minutes later, Halliday carried a plastic bucket across the camp road past a 3/4-ton truck. A machine gun hung limply from the bed center post, and the exhausted gunner slumped against the cab. The passenger door opened.

Sweating profusely under a flak vest and helmet, Ben dragged out a large medical pack and his M-16 rifle. His chest was crossed with ammunition bandoliers.

"Where you been?" Halliday asked.

Ben mock-saluted the driver, and the truck lurched off.

"Fucking mine sweep. Ambush."

"Jesus."

"Don't know if he was in on it, but if he was, I'd like a word. I'm too short for this shit. I didn't sign no contract for no goddamn N-V-A."

Ben pawed at the dirt.

"You seen Lam?" he asked, looking up at Halliday.

"No," Halliday said, looking away.

"She picked you that night," Ben said. "Lam could use a friend."

Ben waited until Halliday met his eyes. Ben shook his head, and trudged around the tall sandbagged TOC walls.

Halliday crossed the road and entered the overheated mess hall, where a pimply soldier with a shock of white-blond hair stood above three Vietnamese women scrubbing immense greasy pots on the ground. Soap and water ran down their legs as they chattered.

"Come *on*, mamasans, get the fucking lead out."

Halliday eased around the women and went into the mess hall office. The wide-mouthed mess sergeant led him into a freezer and dropped a dripping block of ice into his plastic bucket. Halliday's fatigues spattered dark from the icy drips.

When Halliday yanked open the club screen door, a blue airmail letter lay open on the bar, and the colonel was pacing back and forth. Halliday lifted the ice into the sink with the unusual sensation of his fingers going numb with cold.

"What?" Lehr sputtered, holding up the letter. "In hell does she think *I* can do?"

"Sir?"

"My daughter, Christina. How old are you, Halliday?"

"Twenty, sir."

"She writes the goddamn *Chaplain* when I don't return her letters."

Halliday chipped at the ice in the sink.

"How come you didn't answer her, sir?"

"What can I say?"

"She's your *daughter*, sir," Halliday said.

"She only writes about Vietnam," Lehr said, glaring. "And thinks that I'm Richard Nixon."

Halliday stopped chipping.

"I tried to explain," Lehr said. "About duty, sacrifice, my responsibility to my country, my family, my career ..."

"What did she say, sir?"

"Oh, 'bombing, defoliation, the CIA, napalm, the murder of innocent civilians'," Lehr said. "There are no goddamn answers, Halliday. It's war, people get hurt and die. It's shitty. Does she think that I *enjoy* writing the parents of that dead black soldier? How the hell does she think I'm paying for drama school?"

Halliday chipped away at the block of ice.

"I guess it really bothers her, sir."

"Of course, war has too goddamn many casualties. On all sides. Does she actually believe that I don't understand that? I'm a goddamn combat commander. My *job* is dying kids."

Lehr moved to the bar. The ground rumbled under a distant B-52 strike.

"Pour me a Scotch."

Halliday poured the golden liquor over ice as the colonel tapped the bar. Lehr sipped and the glass frosted in the heat.

"Christ, I understand her idealism. But '*There's absolutely no justification for killing someone because of political or religious beliefs.*' Has she forgotten Hitler, Stalin, Mao? The Civil War? I'm a soldier. I train, I get a mission, I perform my duty. I don't get paid to make moral decisions."

The colonel sipped his Scotch.

"But what if, sir?" Halliday said. "Your duty was not ... *right*? Like if you got orders to kill ... when you didn't believe that you should."

"What do you mean?"

"What if the people giving the orders are wrong?"

"It's not our job to question orders. You know that—the chain of command."

Lehr's hard eyes softened.

"But what if the order was dead wrong, sir," Halliday said. "Like Geneva Convention wrong?"

The colonel glared at Halliday.

"I don't know, Halliday," the colonel's voice wavered and then turned gruff. "I've never had that happen."

Lehr recalled the old woman with the bundle of ashes, the dead baby, Gabrielle's face.

"Is it really that clear, sir?" Halliday said. "Even like what we're doing here in Vietnam?"

"She says crazy things," Lehr said.

Artillery rounds rocketed away.

"I love my daughter beyond words," Lehr said. "I want her to be proud of me."

Halliday hit a chunk of ice, but it wouldn't crack.

"Play some music," Lehr said expansively, stuffing the letter into his pocket.

Halliday reached back to the grimy back bar shelf, grabbed a plastic cassette, and popped it in the cheap tape player. A tinny carnival blare of rock and roll filled the briefing room...

... *down yonder in Viet-nam,*

"You thought I wouldn't like that?" the colonel said, forcing a grin. "But Halliday, I do possess a sense of humor. And you think exactly like my daughter."

A helicopter landing drowned out the music.

Lehr stood up.

"That F-O-B bird is back. Go find the recon sergeant. I need to talk to him."

.... *open up the pearly gates,*
I ain't got time to won-der why,
Whoopee we're all going to die!

Halliday ran out.

Lehr walked behind the bar and ejected the thin plastic cassette. He read: *Country Joe and the Fish.*

Colonel Lehr dropped the cassette on the floor, smashed it with his boot, and threw the tape in the trash.

        *   *   *

Five exhausted infantrymen lumbered across the sticky airstrip, lugging weapons and battered rucksacks.

The helicopter dipped its olive-colored nose and thumped away, banking over the rough airstrip and the washed-out green hills. The chopper quickly became a tiny dot heading for Pleiku, sixty miles south.

Halliday ran toward the team. So much grime lined their faces that they looked like old dirty men and Halliday bristled at their body funk.

"Who's the recon sergeant?" Halliday said.

Four soldiers swept past him without even looking.

"I don't talk to no-goddamn-body before I sleep," a familiar voice growled.

"Jasper?" Halliday asked.

"Yeah," Jasper said, not stopping. "Who that?"

"Halliday."

"Hol-i-dayman, god-damn. Who want me?"

"Colonel."

"Aw, shiiiiit."

        *   *   *

Lehr stood at the green relief map with his hands behind his back as Halliday entered.

When Jasper set his rucksack down, Lehr turned and came over to the bar.

"Sorry to bother you before stand down, Sergeant...?"

"Jasper," the tall black N-C-O exhaled.

"Like a beer, Sergeant Jasper?" Lehr said.

"Wouldn't turn one down, sir."

Halliday popped a cold Bud, which Jasper immediately drank down. When Halliday handed him another, Jasper took a long, slow, first sip.

Lehr waved the sergeant over to the big map.

Jasper sat down.

"My orders are to report to the ARVNs," Jasper said.

"What?"

"My highers say this is an ARVN show."

Lehr leaned toward Jasper.

"You can't brief the Daktoum firebase commander with a need to know?"

"I'm telling you what they *said*, sir."

"When's your briefing?"

"Tomorrow. In Kontum with my highers, the ARVNs."

Jasper looked to Halliday and his eyes said: "Be cool."

"Between you and me, sir," Jasper said. "I don't trust them goddamn ARVNs as far as I can throw 'em."

Jasper got up, went to the big map, and tapped his beer near the Laotian border.

"66th N-V-A regiment. Disappeared. 28th, building up here, along with the 18th and the 24th."

Jasper ran his elegant fingers along Rocket Ridge.

"40th Artillery, 615th Heavy Mortar Battalion, beau coups 122s, 152's, 82's, plenny of rice. Digging in deep. Supply lines leading to Rocket Ridge. Shit on the fan, sir."

Lehr stared at the green map. Jasper sipped his beer and lost focus out in the pale green mass of Rocket Ridge beyond the dusty screens.

"Need a hop to Kontum tomorrow, sergeant?'

"Fine by me."

"VIP pad, 0800 hours."

"I'll be there," Jasper said. "I never spoke to you, sir."

"Never seen you before, sergeant."

Jasper picked up his rucksack and downed his beer.

"Can I take some beer for my men, sir?" Jasper said, holding up the empty can.

"Certainly," Lehr said.

Halliday put a case of cold ones in a box, which Jasper hefted and left. Lehr walked to the bar and sipped his Scotch as if Halliday wasn't there.

"Close the club tomorrow," Lehr said. "I'll be in Kontum. Don't let anything that sergeant said leave this room."

"What does it mean, sir?"

"Maybe nothing. Maybe everything."

After the colonel walked out, Halliday swept the floor until red dust streamed up the yellowing wall of screens facing Rocket Ridge. Halliday wondered what Jasper had meant, and then he remembered the hard glint in Lehr's eyes when Halliday played *Fixing to Die Rag*.

When Halliday dumped the dust in the trash, there were chunks of black plastic, the smashed Country Joe cassette.

"Goddamn him!" Halliday said.

"Goddamn who?" a languid voice called through the screen door. "Charlie? Merton? The colonel?"

Lieutenant Mac Elroy walked in, tossed a worn army baseball cap onto the bar, sat down, and polished his aviator sunglasses with a handkerchief.

"PFC John Halliday, R-A, Sigma Chi," Mac declared.

"What, Lieutenant?"

"Brother Halliday," Mac said. "Recall how propitiously that I saved your ass from going on mine sweep? Now, you have a golden opportunity to pay back your old adjutant..."

"What, Lieutenant?"

"Scotch, Halliday," Mac said, holding up four fingers.

"I can't sell bottles, Lieutenant. You know the policy."

Mac smiled for so long that Halliday counted the black rings around his eyes.

"Merton says you owe him," Mac countered.

"Fuck," Halliday muttered.

"Nobody will know."

Halliday looked at the smashed Country Joe and the Fish cassette.

"What the hell, Lieutenant," Halliday said.

"My man," Mac said, pointing. "Johnnie Walker Black."

"When the colonel leaves, I'll bring them to your hootch."

"You're invited, Halliday. Tomorrow, in the old mess hall near Bunker 11. Best fucking short-timer's party ever."

12.

After Lehr left the next day, Halliday drove Major Ranklin down the long red dirt hill on Highway 14 past the burnt-out Engineer camp, and rattling over the double Bailey steel bridge, where ARVN soldiers lounged around sandbagged positions at both ends, grilling shining fish.

Where three roads converged, they entered tree covered Nhu Canh Du beneath the big triangular mountain.

"Left," Ranklin said.

They passed the Tan Canh whorehouse in the banana grove with its girly dazzle sprawled in hammocks on the porch, laughing, wearing red and purple silk blouses, and waving at G.I.s. Halliday looked for Lam but didn't see her.

When Halliday slowed the Jeep in front of faded stucco shops, eyes peered from shady porches and open storefronts where old women with betel-stained teeth sold black-market tiger fatigues, Coca-Cola, marijuana, cigarettes, beer, tape players, unit patches, pills, and black silk dragon jackets proclaiming: *When I die, I'll go to Heaven, because I've already been in Hell, Daktoum, Vietnam, 1969.*

Two ARVN soldiers walked by holding hands; an old man balanced a fat bag of rice on an ancient black bicycle. Red and yellow patriotic banners hung above the street while a loudspeaker blared discordant music and fervent Vietnamese.

"Here," Ranklin said.

Halliday drove up an alley lush with purple bougainvillea and pulled into a dilapidated plywood car shack. Ranklin dragged out a sheet of plywood and concealed the Jeep.

"Come on," Ranklin told Halliday.

Halliday followed the major up a steep path to a small house.

Grinning, Ranklin waved Halliday across a sloping dirt yard, where two naked children chased clucking chickens and a rooting piglet. A duck roasted on a wood fire. Ranklin caught up the children, who giggled as he gave them chocolate bars.

A pregnant young woman ambled out of the house and kissed the Major.

"Tu, this is Halliday."

"Hello Halliday."

Tu guided Ranklin's hand to her bulging belly, as she led them inside the hot dark house to teak armchairs beside the sagging screen window. There were woven mats on the concrete floor, a large, polished table, and an altar with family photographs, candles, incense, and fruit around a gold Buddha.

The window looked over the dusty pastel storefronts, the whorehouse, and the dull yellow walls of the distant, tree-shaded ARVN camp and Rocket Ridge, looking small.

"Baby come tee-tee time," Tu said.

Halliday nodded. An older woman brought Halliday a cold Coke.

"Trinh," Tu told Halliday.

"Thanks, Trinh," Halliday said, smiling.

The woman returned to her pot, simmering with pork.

"Why don't you eat with us?" Ranklin said, getting up.

Halliday smiled. While the thin graying major whispered to Tu in the corner, Halliday looked out the window, and tried to dismiss his fears about what Jasper had said.

Out on dusty Highway 14, a Jeep and a Lambretta bus puttered past, followed by the tinny whine of Honda scooters. The Duster tank and the 99th ambulance were parked in front of the whorehouse, which made Halliday nervous until he remembered that the military police had left with the infantry.

Tu and Ranklin's murmurings made Halliday wonder if the major might take her back to the states.

The old woman served them pork and rice and vegetables at the low table and afterwards, Ranklin disappeared into the back bedroom, while Halliday napped in the armchair.

*   *   *

Two hours later, when light had softened the Duster and the big ambulance still parked beside the banana grove. Girls were lined up on the porch for Roadkill's inspection as he stood beneath the 40mm pompom guns, dickering with mamasan.

The unkempt buck sergeant looked like a refugee from a time-travel Western with his long, twirled mustache, silver Montagnard bracelets, and neck beads. A peace symbol hung around his filthy flak jacket, and a small Swedish K automatic rifle slung from his shoulder. Roadkill was from East Texas and on his second Vietnam tour. His nickname came from Bong Son after his tank ran over three enemy soldiers.

"OK mamasan, forty bucks each, OK? Now you're sure they bic *beau coups* boom-boom?"

"Ya, ya, bic, bic. No sweat, no sweat."

"Mamasan, you *sure* these chicks understand? We're talking beau coups subcontractor-style boom-boom here."

"Yah, understand. You gimme money now, G.I., you go now," Mamasan said. "ARVN soldier come titi time, no good you be here, gimme money, go away now."

"Fuck them ARVNs—we'll goddamn light up their skinny yellow asses, right, Dingalinger?"

Roadkill glared at his replacement driver, James Slinger, a plump, recent high school graduate, in Vietnam one month.

"Sarge, just get 'em so we can get the fuck outa here."

"Hang on Dingalinger, me'n mamasan're doin' bidness."

"We don't get in before dark, gate'll search the Duster."

"'cruuuuuit—have some faith in the Roadkill. My bidness is the road, and you know how I love my bidness. Anyway, that fucking Lieutenant owes me. Big time."

Roadkill pulled out his plastic-wrapped wallet, and an ace of spades fell out. He scooped up the card and then counted out eighty dollars MPC into mamasan's hand. She herded the two chosen girls over to the tank—one, flat-faced and sullen; the other, young, pretty, and terrified.

Roadkill lifted the flat-faced girl onto the Duster. But the pretty one fought as Slinger pulled her down inside the hot cramped tank interior, which stank of hot metal, grease, diesel fuel, and body funk.

*   *   *

Gabrielle still sat at the bottom of the staircase in Lehr's bunker. Her eyes were watery, and her throat burned from hours of smoking cigarettes. She had cried once and even made vengeful plans before abandoning them with a sigh, realizing it was better for the villagers if she stayed away. Finally, Gabrielle decided she would help in Daktoum, before going off to Genevieve's in Saigon to raise money for a new clinic. Gabrielle went upstairs and walked across the camp.

Walking on the airstrip, two soldiers cast long shadows as they approached a parked helicopter.

Gabrielle inhaled and flipped her cigarette away. Then she went back to Lehr's bunker and fell asleep.

*   *   *

Lying in his helicopter bay on the far side of Daktoum airstrip, Pilot Jimmy Stubbs listened to the two medics, laughed, and then refused. But Cullen and Donnelly kept hammering away at Stubbs's desire, the deal all set up and ready to go, the rare situation of only clueless Goodby above the rank of captain remaining at Daktoum, with all the other officers and N-C-Os at Mac's short-timer's party. Stubbs's chopper was only standing by tomorrow for a mid-morning cross border ARVN extraction—with a 25% likelihood.

"How about Clancy?" Stubbs protested. "He sticks his nose in everything."

"Taken care of," Donnelly said, nodding.

"No way," Stubbs said, folding his arms. "How?"

"Black Jack Daniels," Cullen drawled with a lizard's smile as he rubbed his close-cropped scalp. "Clancy's got a big old soft spot for Black Jack. Anyway, Home, you owe us."

"Cullen, I can't do this shit—they'll take away my wings."

"Ain't gonna get caught, Home, no way."

"No fuckin' way, Stubbsy," Donnelly piped up. "We're clean as flounder."

"Tell you what, now, Home," Cullen said. "We give you the Air Force bed, private room, and first pick of the women."

When Stubbs turned to red-haired Long, lying in the helicopter bay on the nylon seats, the co-pilot grinned.

"What the fuck? Over," Long declared, tossing down an R. Crumb comic book. "What can they do? Send us to Vietnam?"

*   *   *

Tall curly-haired Ray Nimmer had already preselected the four best girls and had given cash to mamasan. Nimmer spent an hour with Hoa, a tiny girl he liked, and then he held sick call and gave all the girls penicillin shots.

When Cullen's radio call came in, Nimmer loaded the four girls into the big ambulance, drove south from Nhu Canh Du, and turned onto a short dirt road through dense jungle, which led out to a defoliated red dirt field strewn with mounds of garbage.

Smoke drifted into the sky above the dozen Vietnamese in black peasant clothes combing through greasy garbage, which could contain live ammunition. Nimmer parked the ambulance in a scrap of shade.

Five minutes later, when a helicopter boomed in, shaking the treetops, Nimmer hustled the four girls out in their shiny red and purple blouses. Leaves fluttered and tree limbs swayed as the helicopter clattered down, the door gunners scanning the tree line, where the V-C could launch B-40 rockets.

Dust and garbage billowed up, and coolie hats sailed off under the hard rotor blast that flapped the scavengers' trousers.

Nimmer snapped open stretchers on the helicopter deck, laid the wide-eyed girls down, and covered them with army blankets, saluted Stubbsy, and jumped out.

Under the waning light, the helicopter lifted out of the huge red dust cloud and cleared the treetops.

A dusty red haze of garbage slowly drifted to earth.

Nimmer's ambulance was already bouncing down the rutted road. He squealed tires turning onto Highway 14 and sped off toward Daktoum, racing to beat the sunset curfew.

Yellowing jungle streamed below the girls on the stretchers. Riding in a helicopter for the first time, their faces showed fear and wonder as big, gold-tinted tropical trees rushed beneath their feet. Hypnotized by the streaming wind and the booming scream clatter of the helicopter, they watched the huge red sun sink into the dark hills of Cambodia.

*   *   *

Standing beside the airstrip, Leroy Cullen and Mick Donnelly heard the approaching Huey. The sun flashed into low black clouds on the western hills and streaked the sky red.

"Shit," Donnelly said, "Vietnam's fucking beautiful."

"What the fuck do you know?" Cullen said, grinning. "You're from Boston."

"Like I don't fucking know?"

"Vietnam sucks."

"Sure, but it's still goddamn pretty."

*   *   *

Stubbs's helicopter quickly clattered onto the Dust-off pad.

Donnelly and Cullen and the two door gunners grabbed the stretchers and made two trips across the gray wooden bridge, carrying the girls right past the main medical bunker and down into an abandoned ward bunker.

No one on Daktoum firebase noticed.

*   *   *

Sergeant Clancy lay resting in his sleeping hootch, passing a bottle of Jack Daniels from hand to hand, contemplating why Donnelly and Cullen had given the liquor to him.

A knock echoed on his wooden doorframe.

"Sergeant Clancy?" a young voice asked.

"Yes?"

"You said to call you at six o'clock."

"Eighteen hundred hours."

"Yes sergeant."

Footsteps walked away.

"Hey, Kid? Why don't you come in? We can walk over to the mess hall together."

The footsteps returned and the tent flap opened.

The Kid—Jamison, a tender, pale-skinned 18-year-old, stood uneasily in the entrance. Clancy lay on his bed wearing only undershorts in the great heat.

"Sit down."

The round tent ceiling radiated down from a single center pole. Clancy's neat hootch exuded the order of a lifetime soldier. The Kid sat at a desk that Clancy had crafted from plywood and artillery shell crates. As Clancy dressed, the Kid picked up a book and thumbed the glossy pages.

"You interested in military uniforms?" Clancy asked, pulling on his fatigue pants.

"Some," the Kid replied. "One night when I pulled C-Q at Ft. Leonard Wood, I read a real good book about them."

Clancy, in fatigue pants and bare feet, cracked open the Jack Daniels.

"Ever taste sour mash whiskey, Kid?"

"No sergeant, I don't think so."

Clancy took two glasses and a bottle of water from his footlocker. Then he poured three fingers of rich brown liquor in each glass and splashed them with water.

"Real branch water, Kid, not Army water. And this is Kentucky sipping whiskey. The trick is you sip it, real slow. Let the whiskey warm your mouth."

The Kid held the glass, sipped, and smiled shyly. Clancy pointed at the book.

"What's your favorite uniform?"

"Oh," the Kid said. "Revolutionary War."

Clancy beamed and slipped on his fatigue shirt.

"You know, that's always been one of my favorites, too."

*   *   *

Riding in the turret, Roadkill didn't slow the Duster tank rumbling past the Daktoum gate. He gave a stiff-armed Nazi salute to PFC Lester Ellis, the thin black soldier with bloodshot eyes sitting in the squat tower. Ellis flipped Roadkill off.

"I told you," Roadkill yelled at Slinger as they rumbled across the firebase past the TOC. "Nobody fucks with my tank, nobody."

The Duster idled along the powdery firebase roads to their riverside position on the Nhu Canh Du end of the camp. Slinger maneuvered the Duster into a bulldozed slot near the perimeter wire, surrounded by sandbags, so that the 40mm guns faced Rocket Ridge, looming overhead in deep shadow.

Slinger shut off the engine, and Roadkill slid off the tank.

"Sure as hell ain't no Chevy," Slinger said in the driver's port. "My damn hands tingle for an hour."

"Pussy," Roadkill said.

Slinger shook his head.

"Here's the deal," Roadkill said, tossing his stained flak vest onto a greasy cot. "We get 'em out, lock 'em in the CONEX, chow down, and then open for biz say 2130 hours, when all of them lifers are good and juiced."

"Rog'," Slinger said from inside the hatch. "OK. Let's boogaloo, babysans!"

Roadkill leapt onto the Duster, yanked out the two girls and swung them off the tank. Slinger jumped down and unlocked a metal shipping container, where the last light glimmered on a tall pointed stack of 40mm shells.

Roadkill held the girls close and pressed a greasy index finger to his lips.

"No talk-talk, babysans, OK? G.I. come back soon. Bic?"

The flat-faced girl muttered; the pretty girl looked away. Roadkill led them into the container and gave them sodas. Slinger grabbed two C-ration meal boxes.

"They ain't gonna eat those," Roadkill said. "They only eat gook food."

"They might," Slinger said, tossing the rations into the container with a thud. "G.I. chop-chop, number one."

Roadkill slammed the container door and locked it.

Inside the hot, dark, metal box, the pretty girl began to cry.

* * *

Inside the abandoned underground ward bunker, Nimmer and Donnelly settled the four girls in with cokes and beer and candy. This was a medics-and-chopper-crew-only operation with tight security. Since Nimmer knew the girls, he stayed behind, while Donnelly and Cullen and Stubbsy and the helicopter crew went to eat.

"Babysans," eighteen-year-old Nimmer began, pushing two steel army bunks together. "Let's play some cards."

Nimmer took out a worn black deck with a fierce eagle on the back and shuffled as the four teenaged girls sat cross-legged around him. They chattered in Vietnamese with a flurry of black hair, dark laughing eyes, and bright blouses smelling of jasmine. Nimmer dealt everyone a card.

"Don't look," he said. "Put it on your forehead. Like this."

Nimmer held a three of spades on his forehead and the giggling girls mimicked him.

"Now," he said. "Whoever gets the *low* card - 2, 3, 4 - takes off one clothes."

"What clothes G.I.?"

"You know, shirt, pants, skivvies, whatever you got."

Nimmer pulled at his sleeve and grabbed one girl's silk trouser waistband.

"Number one *high* card—King Queen Ace—you put one clothes back on, you bic?"

"Bic, bic," the girls laughed.

They had a great time.

When Stubbs and the chopper crew came back, Nimmer was in his undershorts—the girls had figured out the game, and besides, they had too many ribbons, silver rings, and necklaces. Stubbs and the chopper crew laughed at Nimmer as they cracked open cold beers, and somebody lit a joint.

* * *

Sitting in the deserted mess tent, Donnelly and Cullen watched Clancy and the Kid.

"That Clancy," Cullen said. "Beau coups sneaky."

Donnelly tapped his cigarette ashes on the metal tray.

"Uh oh," Donnelly said. "Here comes King Shit."

Sergeant Clancy smiled and leaned over their table, gripping the red oilcloth, while Donnelly tapped out a beat.

"Evening, troopers. So, Limerick's duty medic?"

"Sure is, sarge."

"You men do me a favor?" Clancy said easily. "Tell Limerick if he gets anything he can't handle, he should call Spec Five Benjamin—*not* Sergeant Clancy. Understand?"

"Sure, sarge."

"No sweat, sarge," Donnelly said, fingers drumming.

"And if Limerick need a doctor, which he probably won't—that French woman's over at the Hilton—but remember to knock first and ask real nice."

"No sweat, Sergeant Clancy."

"Don't forget to remind Benjamin."

"That's a no sweat, Sarge, we won't."

As Clancy's broad back moved across the mess hall towards the Kid, Cullen and Donnelly grinned.

"Bing-a-fucking-go-go," Donnelly said.

"We home, Home," Cullen said.

Cullen punched Donnelly's shoulder and grinned.

"You cracker son of a bitch."

*   *   *

At Daktoum, the night was balmy and silent. Occasionally, an artillery round rocketed overhead toward Cambodia.

After dinner, Ben and Halliday sat smoking up on the medical bunker roof. To the east, flares lit a distant ridge where tracer bullets streamed out of the sky with glowing red trails and guttural electronic bursts.

Ben flipped his cigarette at the machine gun tower near the bunker entrance.

Halliday kicked at a rotting sandbag and flashed on sleeping with Jennifer during the Big Snow. She hadn't written once in three months.

Artillery rocketed out. Flare light flashed on the black hills.

"What are you thinking?" Ben asked.

"How I blew it with this girl back in the World."

He thought of that incredible day with Jennifer skiing the high bowls on Agassiz. And making out in the trees.

Ben stared at the wavering flare light and the red tracers.

"Man, glad I ain't in the infantry," he said. "Or artillery."

"Me, too."

"My old man was Infantry," Ben said. "An L-T, in Italy."

"Mine was in the Pacific, B-25. Met my mom in the Philippines. Army nurse."

"You told me," Ben said. "No wonder you're in Vietnam. Romantic shit like that."

The tiny red glow of a cigarette moved toward them.

"Benjamin," a voice said, walking across the roof.

Donnelly sat with a lit cigarette dangling from his mouth.

"Clancy says he ain't to be bothered. You're supposed to help Limerick."

"He told me," Ben said. "So, you guys are slick as shit."

"Tight as young pussy," Donnelly said, grinning. "You two gonna participate?"

"Probably not," Ben said. "Halliday?"

"What?"

"Nimmer, Cullen, and Donnelly masterminded some boom-boom over in the ward bunker."

"No," Halliday said.

"Don't say I didn't ask ya's," Donnelly said, walking away, and flipping his cigarette butt into the hot night. "Good luck."

Halliday stood up.

"I'm going to Mac's short-timer's party," Halliday said. "Want to come?"

"Drink with sorry-assed lifers?" Ben said. "Hell, no."

*   *   *

Halliday walked for ten minutes across the immense dark firebase towards a large tent near the wire. The tent vibrated with muffled voices, and when the flap opened, a wedge of light spilled cigarette smoke and raucous voices across the night.

Halliday went through the big canvas flap into the harsh light. Folding tables filled with bottles and glasses were packed with disheveled junior officers and beefy sergeants, who stared with flushed faces at Halliday. Mac sat a table with a smashed chocolate cake topped by a fat burned-out candle. The cake proclaimed in big red sugar letters: MAC DEROS DAKTOUM '69.

Captain Hardin stood up, clapped Mac on the back, nodded to Halliday, and left. Sergeant Loudermilk glowered from a dim corner table with two jowly sergeants.

"Halliday, my man," Mac slurred. "Have a drink with your really really really goddamn shooo-rt ex-Adjutant."

Mac gave him a coffee cup filled with scotch and ice.

"Cake!" Mac said.

When Mac grabbed a chunk of cake with his fingers and slapped it before Halliday, Lieutenant Fairbanks threw back his head and roared. Major Goodby and Captain Dunkley—drinking orange sodas—frowned.

"Fuddie-fucking-duddies," Mac stage-whispered. "Halliday, let's drink to my extreme foresight in keeping you off mine sweep. Here's to your higher calling as club bartender and colonel's driver, HEAR HEAR!"

"Hear hear!" Fairbanks echoed.

Halliday toasted, but Mac forgot, and turned to Fairbanks, whose curly black hair looked crazy. Dunkley, Goodby and Loudermilk glowered.

Halliday grinned. Fuck them. Only reason I'm here is because I'm Lehr's driver. Halliday remembered Denny from recon, killed on mine sweep, and took a long pull off his drink.

Sergeant Major Bricker sat alone in a corner, staring at the tent ceiling. Halliday recalled Colonel Newcomb's headless body and how it didn't seem to be a person at all.

When Mac arm-wrestled Fairbanks out of his chair onto the floor, Halliday got up. All the drunken sergeants gave him the stink eye as he pushed out through the tent flap.

*   *   *

Business was good for Slinger and Roadkill. They had commandeered an empty bunker close to the river bunker line. An olive-green Army blanket split a sandbagged chamber into two "rooms" where the tankers had dragged in cots.

Roadkill spent the first hour after dinner with the flat-faced girl, while Slinger lay behind the blanket wall with the pretty girl, who was shaking. Slinger had to threaten to slap her before she slept with him; it was not a pleasant experience.

Roadkill got up and lit a cigarette.

Carefully cupping the flame in his hand, Roadkill walked along the river bunker line, passing the word to all the guards—short-timers were ten bucks.

After an hour and a half, the flat-faced girl was into profit, but the pretty one was a problem. Only one G.I. had managed to be with her, and even that guy—a hulking mechanic from Mississippi—complained that she bit him.

Roadkill ushered in a chatterbox bunker guard to the flat-faced girl, and then he parted the blanket and went to the pretty woman huddled in the sandbagged corner.

"Babysan," Roadkill said. "This shit has to cease. Bic?"

Roadkill squeezed her arm. She squirmed and her breath fluttered.

"Goddamnit now, I pay mamasan beau coups bucks for you to go boom-boom. Bic?"

"Bic," the small voice said.

"So, get with the fucking program! Boom-boom!"

"Too much boom-boom, G.I."

"Hey! Boom-boom is your job—you're a fucking whore."

Roadkill yanked the girl up.

As he dragged her across the dirt out into the night, the girl made cries like a trapped animal.

When they reached the tangle of barbed wire on the bluff above the black shining river, Roadkill pushed her against the wire so the barbs bit through her blouse and silky pants.

"Look, babysan," Roadkill hissed. "Out there, *everything* is V-C. You no go boom-boom? OK, then I throw you over this fence into the fucking river, where G.I. shoot you dead like a fucking V-C, you bic?"

Weeping silently, the young woman went limp.

"Bic," she whispered, trembling.

"You better fucking bic."

When Roadkill yanked her back from the wire, a barb ripped her skin. Roadkill dragged the girl back to the bunker and threw her onto the empty cot.

He went outside, lit a cigarette, and waited for the next customer.

*   *   *

After dinner, the Kid returned to Clancy's round tent and sat beside the burly sergeant on his neatly made bunk. The Kid thumbed through the shiny uniform book that Clancy had found on R&R in Hong Kong's China Fleet Club.

"Want to see a picture of my dress greens?" Clancy asked.

"Sure," the Kid said.

Clancy rummaged through his desk drawer and handed the Kid a color photograph. The husky sergeant's uniform was cut sharp, and Clancy's expression and physique embodied all the strength and courage of the military. The Kid sipped the strong bourbon.

"Ever think about a military career?"

"Not really," the Kid said.

"Travel, benefits, friends all over the world," Clancy said. "But it can get lonely."

Clancy's warm thigh pressed against the Kid, who did not move away.

"Wartime's not so bad, is it, Kid?"

"No, not yet."

The liquor made the Kid feel like he was glowing.

"Sergeant Clancy?" he asked. "What's it like? In battle? Is it hard to be brave?"

Clancy thought for a moment.

"You find strength, you find out that you can cut it—just keep your head down and do your job."

The Kid sipped his bourbon.

"Did you ever see the movie *Seven Sinners*?"

"Of course, I did."

"John Wayne looked good in that uniform," the Kid said.

"Yeah," Clancy said. "Certainly did. Real good."

The Kid smiled and felt a warmth growing in his belly.

"Here, let me show you my favorite," Clancy said, leaning in and turning the page.

*　　　　　*　　　　　*

After leaving the party, Halliday walked across the big dark camp and passed the flickering camp movie projected on a plywood screen mounted on the back of the TOC. Never one to pass up a movie, Halliday slumped on a wooden bench. A black-and-white World War Two film was set in Hawaii with Kirk Douglas, John Wayne, Brandon DeWilde, Patricia Neal, and Paula Prentiss. A few soldiers sprawled on the wooden benches were drinking, but no one even hooted or threw beer cans at the screen. The wartime Honolulu scenes were beautiful and romantic, but when John Wayne lost his leg in a sea battle, it was depressing, and Halliday stumbled away.

*　　　　　*　　　　　*

The medics and the helicopter crew slept with the four Vietnamese girls in the old ward bunker. Everyone got half a night each with a girl except Stubbs, who had his own girl. Nimmer, Donnelly, and Cullen each got first shift since they had set up the deal.

For a while, the four young soldiers and their girls quietly lay in steel bunks in separate corners of the big abandoned bunker. It was so dark in the underground room that they couldn't see a thing. At first, they laughed and jeered against the night like children—hooting and falsely groaning and breathing hard, jiving each other until their fear went away. One by one, they grew silent and sank into themselves, and into the girls beside them until no one cared what was true and what wasn't, and their bodies became their entire world.

*　　　　　*　　　　　*

Ben climbed off the medical bunker roof and walked over to the CIDG indigenous compound beside the dark airstrip.

Inside a big sagging tent, candles flickered over Captain Hardin, lounging amidst reclining Montagnard soldiers in tiger fatigues, whose chiseled faces lay in shadow.

The hot damp tent was pungent with ripe fruit, cooked rice, and unwashed bodies. Ben squatted beside Hardin under a pall of tobacco smoke trapped by the canvas ceiling.

"Hey, Cap'n. You seen Jasper?"

"Gone," Hardin answered.

"Recon?"

Hardin's eyes were somewhere far away.

"When?"

Hardin shrugged.

"Back tomorrow. Maybe."

Ben got up to leave and paused at the entrance flap.

"Cap'n?"

"Yeah."

"This offensive?"

Candlelight struck Hardin's cheekbones and glittered his eyes. Lying amidst the Montagnard troops with such a fixed stare, Ben wondered if Hardin was smoking opium.

"Make you a believer," Hardin said. "Vietnamization. Or bust."

"And we're the bust?"

"That's a rog."

All the reclining Montagnards watched Hardin out of the corner of their eyes, like they were stalking a large animal.

"People say this firebase is bait," Ben said.

"I've heard that."

"And?"

Hardin looked at Ben and shrugged.

Artillery buffeted overhead with a sucking sound that echoed away and became a distant rumble.

"Well," Ben said. "Good luck, Cap'n Hardin."

"Yeah, Ben. Good luck to you."

Hardin stared at the shadows of his soldiers flickering up on the tent ceiling. The Montagnard soldiers watched Ben flip open the tent flap and then slowly pass out into the black night along with a billow of tobacco smoke.

*   *   *

Out on the camp road between the TOC and the river bunkers, Halliday ran into Smitty, the water point guy, and Jonesy, the club driver.

"We're celebrating," Smitty said, handing Halliday a bottle. "Jonesy here ran the goddamn road without a convoy!"

"You're fucking nuts," Halliday said, sipping Scotch.

"Tits on a bull," Jonesy said. "We're here to tell."

They went over to Halliday's hootch and drank to blasting Motown music on a tape player. Smitty and Jonesy—both from Detroit—laughed and danced and bumped and whirled and clomped their boots on the rough plank floor.

Halliday sank into his bunk, smoking and muttering.

You were so goddamn sweet, Jennifer, Halliday mooned, what the fuck was I thinking, I really blew it. He recalled the way Jen moved in that green corduroy skirt, her impish smile, the yellow leaves falling, drinking, and laughing at football games, skiing with her and the twelve-foot snow.

Didn't I treat you right, now baby, didn't I?

The music worked on Halliday. Lam was great, but I was stoned. And horny. She can't even speak English.

When Smitty and Jonesy yanked Halliday off the bed to dance, his feet didn't work, and the room whirled and blurred. Halliday staggered back to his bunk.

And Lehr and his daughter. How come he spills his guts to me? Everyone thinks he's a hard ass; but he's just hardheaded, like my old man. All that ancient shit those World War Two guys yack about, discipline, duty and then you die, what the hell kind of life is that?

Halliday's thoughts drifted—Lam is so pretty. But she's a whore, fuck! How could I like a whore? No, she's just a girl, at war. But I can't even talk to her. So, fucking what, Jennifer could talk, and I didn't really try with her. Maybe Lam can...

Halliday passed out.

Jonesy and Smitty drank and danced to Motown music until dust rose off the floorboards and they were drunk and sweaty and breathless and happy.

*   *   *

Roadkill collected ten bucks from a fat, wheezing hulk of an artilleryman who went into the happy-time bunker. The skinny tank sergeant figured his "little talk" had done the trick so he dozed on a filthy cot under the stars beside the warm Duster, while bunker guards came and went.

A low cry awoke Roadkill.

A flash of black hair and pale legs rushed past the groggy Roadkill.

"Son of a BITCH!" he yelled, lurching up and grabbing the big artilleryman by the shirt. "What the fuck did you do?"

"Nothing, man, I didn't even screw her!"

"Bull-shit, fuckface!" Roadkill said, shoving the big man away. "*Slinger!*"

Slinger, asleep on a cot, bolted up in the night.

"Get the fuck up—we got us a problem! That little bitch cheeked it and now I got to go find her."

Roadkill grabbed an M-16 from the stack and threw it at Slinger. He grabbed another rifle and snapped in a fresh clip.

"Be cool, Sarge," Slinger said.

"Get your ass up and watch the other one, Newbie," Roadkill said, jerking his thumb towards the bunker. "I gotta go hunt down that pretty little bitch."

Roadkill ran off into the night and clicked a round into his M-16 chamber.

*   *   *

The short timer's party was over. Drunken junior officers and N-C-Os swayed out through the tent flap into darkness as sergeants and lieutenants stumbled off to tents and hootches in twos and threes, hollering obscenities and long nasty farewells to the swaying Lieutenant Mac Elroy. Mac shambled out with Fairbanks, whose red neck scarf was tied around his forehead like a hippie.

The two young officers paused at a metal piss tube and peed into the big artillery shells filled with gravel and lime. To the south, toward Kontum, tiny flares popped and swayed.

"I am so fuck-ing shoooooooort!" Mac yelled. "Only one more fucking day in this shithole."

"You are really really short, buddy," Fairbanks mumbled. "Shit. I'm short, too, five fucking eight. That's fucking short."

"Fucking right."

As they wandered away, Fairbanks tripped over a tent stake and fell flat on his face.

"Son of a bitch!"

Mac roared.

On the ground, Fairbanks laughed harder.

The round bouncing white glint of a woman's bare posterior streaked past Mac and disappeared into the darkness.

Mac lurched after the jiggling white bottom but stumbled over Fairbanks and landed right beside him.

"Fucking weed," Mac said, looking at the dark sky. "That shit really bends your mind."

"That's a roger-dodger," Fairbanks agreed.

They got up and weaved arm-in-arm through the dark camp.

*   *   *

Down in the medical bunker, a drunk from Headquarters Company split his arm on a metal tent stake.

Limerick set down his dog-eared copy of Eldridge Cleaver's *Soul On Ice*. He laid the drunk on a stretcher under a surgical light, cleaned the wound with hydrogen peroxide, and listened to the soldier yap about some "gorgeous redhead." Then Limerick woke up the sleeping Benjamin to suture.

Half an hour later, Ben closed and bandaged the wound, peeled off his latex gloves, threw them in a trashcan, and went outside.

Ben climbed up on the medical bunker roof, sat down on the sandbags, and lit a cigarette.

"Shit," Ben muttered out loud. "Getting hit, again. I am way too short for this shit. Hardin knows what he's talking about—after three years with those 'yards."

Ben blew smoke toward the dark lump of the abandoned ward bunker.

Maybe I should just go climb in with a Vietnamese girl. I don't need anything that bad, 'cept maybe Lam. Shit. God-damn, why did she pick Halliday?

Pale beautiful legs and twinkling white buttocks swayed through the dark night.

What the hell?

Ben looked hard—a Vietnamese woman running without any pants. God damn it, Nimmer, I knew this fucking thing would turn to shit. Clancy'll have my ass, bust me down to private E-1 for letting those dumbshits bring in whores.

Ben took off. He caught up with the girl, grabbed her waist, and lifted her off the ground. Her pale, shapely legs kicked fiercely, while her breath rasped borderline hysterical as her white bottom jiggled up against him.

"Calm the hell down, Babysan," he laughed. "Where do you think you're going? You ain't even got any pants on."

"G.I. say me V-C, say he kill me," a tiny frantic voice cried. "Make me beau coups boom-boom."

Ben turned her around and pulled back her long hair.

"Lam?"

"Who you, G.I.?"

"Ben."

She stopped kicking and Ben set her down.

Lam spread her hands over her naked lower body, and Ben looked away.

"What are you doing here, Lam?"

"Mamasan make me. Lam no can do."

Lam bolted away, and Ben grabbed her.

"Hold on, damn it, Lam," he said, turning her toward him. "Which Bacsi said he would kill you?"

"No Bacsi, G.I., no Bacsi."

"Then who the hell ..."

When Ben heard running footsteps and the clatter of a weapon, he swept Lam into the dead bunker and eased her onto an empty stretcher.

"Stay here, Lam," he whispered.

"Numbah ten G.I.," she whispered. "Say me V-C, say he kill me."

"Nobody's going to do nothing to you, Lam."

She gripped his arm tight.

"Lam," Ben soothed. "Stay here. I come back tee-tee time."

Ben touched her shoulder.

Ben went outside and hid in the entrance shadows. Boots thumped and a silhouette loped across the dark airstrip toward Cambodia.

Ben ran down the wide medical stairway.

Limerick dozed on the desk with his head beside the radio. As Ben dug into the big cardboard box of discarded fatigues, Limerick jerked awake.

"Wha's up, Benjamin?" Limerick asked.

"Anyone besides Nimmer and Donnelly bring in girls?"

"Not that I heard."

Ben stuffed fatigue pants and a sleeping bag under his arm. He ran upstairs and went back into the dead bunker.

"Here," Ben said, handing Lam the pants. "Go to sleep."

Lam's hands shook.

"G.I. say he kill me."

"Nobody's going to kill you."

"Numbah ten G.I. kill me."

"Bullshit, Lam," Ben said softly.

"No bullshit, G.I."

Ben spread the sleeping bag over the stretcher while Lam slipped on the pants.

"I'll stay with you," Ben said, his lips pursing. "Goddamn Halliday."

"Howaday?"

"Go to sleep."

Ben unfolded another stretcher and lay beside the small woman in the baggy fatigue pants, resting his hand on her shoulder. After a few minutes, her erratic breathing deepened into the sudden sleep of a child.

Ben dozed with his head near the entrance maze so that the dawn light would wake him.

*   *   *

Gabrielle awoke in Lehr's comfortable Air Force bed.

She sat straight up and lit a cigarette. Even though she slapped her face hard, the faces remained—glittering eyes, Montagnard faces—the thin old woman with wispy hair and tough watery eyes, shrapnel in her foot, the boy, Diep, leg blown off by a mine, Sel, the little girl with the rare strain of malaria and the beautiful smile on that little burned boy.

Gabrielle inhaled.

Her glowing red cigarette dissipated all the images.

All the faces and bodies had seemed as real as the rough redwood beams looming overhead in the colonel's bunker.

After she finished the cigarette, Gabrielle stared up at the darkness until she fell asleep.

*   *   *

Roadkill searched for half an hour, combing the airstrip, hootches and bunkers for the girl. But Daktoum firebase was very dark and filled with dozens of unused tents, abandoned buildings and crumbling bunkers. The young soldiers mostly avoided the empty spaces—snakes had been seen slipping into old bunkers and curled in loops in tent rafters. A deadly bamboo viper had been killed inside one empty hootch and Merton swore that he saw a King Cobra crawling into a foul old ammunition bunker. The thought of snakes so chilled Roadkill, that finally he just cursed the pretty girl and trudged back across the camp to his Duster.

*   *   *

Roadkill threw his flak vest into the dirt alongside the Duster, grabbed a beer, cut a thin slit in the top with a P-38 can opener, and drank.

"So?" Slinger said, coming out of the bunker.

"*So?*" Roadkill mimicked. "So, fucking *what?*"

"What happened?"

"What the fuck do you think happened?" Roadkill said, his mouth full of beer. "Does it fucking look like I fucking found her?"

Roadkill rapped the beer can on the tank.

"This fucking caper better not fucking backfire."

"No sweat," Slinger soothed.

"Don't 'no sweat' me, mother fuck."

"Hey man," Slinger said. "Look. All we gotta do is get the other girl out of here when the gate opens. That runaway bitch ain't tied to us. Nobody can prove nothing."

Roadkill cocked his head.

"Maybe."

"Well, maybe's all we got, man."

Roadkill chugged his beer and tossed the can away with a clatter. He lay on the cot beside his Duster and stared up at the dark starry night until he slept.

*   *   *

Clancy awoke in his circular tent and glanced at his glowing wristwatch. He flipped up his mosquito net, slipped out of bed, and went out to pee. When Clancy returned, he set his flashlight lamp-down on the artillery box beside the bed so that only a faint light glowed. Clancy shook the sleeping Kid.

"Hey Kid," he whispered. "Time to go."

The Kid murmured and turned over.

"Hey," Clancy said. "Kid. You gotta get up."

The Kid awoke to Sergeant Clancy looming over him in the dim light.

"You gotta go," Clancy said. "Can't be seen coming out of my hootch."

"Oh, yeah," the Kid agreed, clutching his blanket.

The Kid sat up, swung his feet out of Clancy's bed and shivered. At night, the jungle mists in Daktoum made the highland air almost cold. Clancy watched the young man bend over to retrieve his jungle fatigues.

"I... liked last night, Kid."

Fear crossed the Kid's face.

"Don't worry about me, Sergeant Clancy."

The Kid slipped on his socks, thrust his feet into worn jungle boots, and quickly wound the long laces around his ankles. He took his fatigue jacket hanging on the chair, and then hugged Clancy.

"Good night, Sergeant Clancy."

"Good night, Kid."

*   *   *

Outside, deep blue darkness slipped towards dawn as a weak pulse of light on the horizon tugged at the black night.

As the Kid groggily walked back to the medical sleeping bunker, shadowy figures rushed past carrying a stretcher. When three more stretchers hustled by, the Kid broke into a run and caught up with them.

"What happened?" the Kid asked breathlessly.

"Shitfire, what are you doing up, Kid?" Donnelly asked.

"I heard you guys."

"We got patients to get out," Donnelly said, grinning, with a cigarette in his mouth.

"Yeah," Nimmer said. "Should have seen the treatment."

The Kid wondered why the patients were Vietnamese girls.

*   *   *

Inside the dead bunker, the whine of a starting helicopter woke Ben. Dim blue-gray light bathed the maze entrance. Ben's hand still lay on Lam's shoulder.

"Wake up, Lam," he said, shaking her. "We got to go."

Lam stiffly stood up and followed Ben outside.

In the baggy American combat fatigue pants, Lam looked like a Vietnamese Charlie Chaplain, which made Ben smile. He grabbed her hand.

"Come on, dee-dee."

As they raced toward the low whine of the helicopter on the airstrip, a faint thump echoed near Nhu Canh Du.

"Shit," Ben yelled, running faster.

A mortar shell exploded a half-mile away, smashing into the end of the airstrip.

The helicopter blades whipped faster.

The barely visible pilots and gunners tensed under the growing light as the turbine approached lift speed.

Inside the helicopter bay, four girls already lay on stretchers that Nimmer and Donnelly had strapped to the floor. When Ben ran up with Lam, the Italian door gunner instinctively shifted his machine gun.

"You dog, Benjamin," Nimmer yelled over the turbines.

"Shit, shit, shit," Donnelly said, flinching at the mortars.

The hollow-faced gunner leaned out of his perch and watched the red-yellow mortar bursts come closer. The helicopter blades spun faster.

"Walking 'em up," the door gunner said on the intercom.

"No shit, Sherlock," Stubbsy said. "No sweat."

The blades made a thick biting sound approaching hover speed as rotor wash kicked up dust and pebbles.

Mortars exploded closer, flashing brilliantly red-yellow in the dawn light. Sulfurous black smoke drifted by.

"Charlie's got our fucking number," the Italian gunner said into the intercom mike.

"Where's the trust?" Stubbsy asked coolly.

The turbines screamed and the blades thumped deeper.

Donnelly panicked and jumped out of the helicopter, followed by Nimmer. Bolting away, they grabbed their bush hats as grit from rotor wash bit their faces and arms.

They dove into a sandbagged pit near the helicopter revetments.

Inside the chopper, Ben held the fearful Lam tight, and the other girls twisted on their stretchers.

Beyond the straining chopper, Daktoum camp siren moaned as the big TOC mound slowly appeared in the blue light. Groggy soldiers rushed from hootches in shadowy waves, their weapons clattering. Mortars exploded, soldiers threw themselves on the ground, crawled away, and scurried into foxholes and bunkers.

Mortars kept parading up the airstrip, closer, sets of orange flash-balls exploding, and cracking louder and louder as they approached the straining helicopter.

The turbine reached hover speed.

Stubbs skittered the bird sideways, hovering out of the walled revetment. The second they were clear of the walls, the helicopter shot banking up with a thumping scream, straining every weld and bolt and chain in a steep, arching climb that moved away from the hot-yellow mortar bursts.

A mortar cracked in right beside the revetment.

"Charlie's got his shit to-gether, J-im," the Italian gunner said over the net.

"So do we," Stubbs said.

"Stubbsy, roll her my way," said the youthful gunner with the concave face, hanging off his perch as he searched for the mortar flash. "Get some."

"Roger that, Jockey, see the flash?"

"Yep."

The helicopter banked around in the growing light until the side gunner faced the jungle between Daktoum airstrip and Nhu Canh Du.

Under the clatter of the thumping helicopter, the machine gun chattered, brass shot out into the air, and cordite smoked off the hot gun and drifted through the open bay.

The girls cried and held onto each other. Lam squeezed Ben's arm, her eyes shining with terror while the four girls on the stretchers moaned and squirmed.

A tracer bullet flared past the open hatch making a beautiful glowing green line.

"Shit!" Ben yelled.

"Taking A-K fire, Stubbsy," the intercom crackled.

"No shit, Sherlock."

The left side gunner relentlessly pounded the ground around the flash, but there were no more mortars. And no more tracers.

"Charlie dee-dee'd, Stubbsy."

"You're Silver Star material, baby."

"I'd rather be Silver Bird material."

"Taking it treetop," Stubbsy said.

They rolled the helicopter over, quickly descended and then skimmed fast toward Nhu Canh Du with soft green forest rushing beneath them in the dawn light.

Outside, on the gunner's perch, thin pucker-faced Jockey grabbed a new belt for his smoking machine gun, spit on the barrel, smiled when it sizzled, inserted the first round, and snapped the cover down. But they took no more fire.

Nothing flashed, nothing moved in the vast, gray-green tree shadows streaking below.

"Papasan's already back in the sack, bopping ol' mamasan," Italian said on the net.

Co-pilot Long glanced at the cargo bay and motioned Ben to pick up the headset.

"Ben," Stubbsy said. "We'll hover over the street and drop them."

"OK."

Ben kept the headset on as Stubbs switched to Daktoum Net. The camp was awake, on 100% alert. Mortars had hit a hootch and there were wounded.

"Shit," Ben muttered.

*   *   *

When Ranklin heard mortar rounds from inside his house in Nhu Canh Du, he switched on his radio and threw on his fatigues. Tu lay in bed with the sheets over her body.

As the sound of a helicopter approached, Ranklin grabbed his weapon and radio and ran out the back door toward the tree-skimming bird. He sprinted down the yard, out the gate and into the dirt street.

The chopper descended, nose-up, in the wide triangular lot at the edge of Nhu Canh Du where dirt Route 512 met half-paved Highway 14.

Ranklin pumped through the narrow alleyway toward the cloud of red dust billowing over the sleeping town. The door gunner whirled his machine gun, but Ranklin didn't notice. He jumped up into the bay just as the last of the girls on the stretchers bailed out the other side.

Ben eased Lam out of the helicopter, dipping and swaying in a foot-high hover.

"Come Daktoum tomorrow!" Ben yelled. "Get Bacsi job."

Lam nodded and sprinted away. The baggy jungle fatigues flapped around her legs under the biting wind.

The other girls ran to the whorehouse where Mamasan waited on the porch, but Lam took off the other way, toward the dirty pastel buildings.

Stubbs spun the bird around, nosed it down, picked up speed and swiftly rose until the cloud of dust over Nhu Canh Du was only a thin red smudge on the green earth.

High above Daktoum, the helicopter leveled off into a wide slow circle.

"F-O-B One to Daktoum Tower," Stubbs radioed.

"Go ahead, One. This is Tower. Over."

"Still taking fire? Over."

"That's a negatory, we're all-clear. Over."

"Request permission to land. Over."

"Roger that, F-O-B One, come on back in. You got a ... zero-to-three ground wind out of Sierra-Echo. Tower Out."

"Thank you much, Tower. F-O-B One, approach. Out."

Stubbs banked the helicopter over in a fast tight circle, screaming turbines and swiftly spiraling down as much for show as for evasive action.

Ranklin and Ben faced the spinning green landscape below, their heads light with vertigo.

After the helicopter touched down on the Daktoum airstrip, Ben and Ranklin scrambled out into the warm yellow light.

Laughing over the intercom, Stubbs maneuvered the helicopter across Daktoum airfield to the F-O-B staging area.

"Where the fuck did that Major come from?"

"He damn near shit when he saw those girls."

"Must have been some great nookie, Major."

"Better hope that hard-ass Colonel don't get wind of it."

"Girls? What girls?"

The intercom net crackled with obscenities and wisecracks.

Stubbs settled the helicopter on the far side of the airstrip and shut off the turbine. The long helicopter blades slowly wound down under the rising sun.

Overhead, a thick bank of mist covered Rocket Ridge.

*   *   *

When Ranklin rushed into the TOC, Daktoum firebase was still on alert. Fifteen minutes had passed since the first mortar, yet the command bunker was curiously empty—except for Captain Sneller, Chaplain Goodby, and Sergeant Loudermilk, the radio operators and the S-2 section.

Ranklin remembered Mac's short-timer's party, cursed, and ran out of the TOC.

The camp monkey, in a new cage atop the TOC, screamed and leaped from side to side, bouncing off the chicken wire.

*　　　　　*　　　　　*

A harsh, burning face slapped Halliday immediately awake and coughing hard. Groggy, he tugged at ropes binding him; painful tears streaked his cheeks. Claustrophobic and half-dreaming under a terrible hangover, Halliday struggled as black-headed monsters appeared. Jerking in horror, bound tight, and coughing uncontrollably, Halliday screamed as the monsters came closer.

But the huge glass eyed monsters only untied his ropes, and then pulled something over his hot face. A rubber mask soothed his burning nose, and mouth as the monsters muscled him off a truck bed. They dragged him across a dirt lot and down uneven wooden steps into a small dim room, where they threw him on a bed and laughed.

"What do you want?" Halliday asked through his mask. "Am I dead?"

The monsters roared and doubled over.

Finally, through a hangover stupor and burning tears, Halliday focused on the black-headed creatures with shiny glass eyes. It was Smitty and Jonesy, wearing gas masks.

"You fucking assholes!" Halliday screamed.

"You slept through a mortar attack," Jonesy said, his voice muffled under the mask.

"Some dimfuck thought we got overrun," Smitty said. "And set off CS gas that blew back into the camp."

Halliday felt like he was at the bottom of a toilet as the two men in gas masks laughed. God, he thought, I've never been this hung over.

Like a zombie, Halliday struggled up and fumbled for his flak vest and rifle. Under the mask, Smitty's eyes sparkled.

"You really didn't hear the mortars?"

"No."

The two masks laughed again.

"You're lucky you didn't get blown away," Jonesy said.

"*I'm* lucky?" Halliday said. "I would have haunted your sorry asses for all eternity."

*　　　　　*　　　　　*

When Ranklin's neck finally stopped tingling from CS gas, the Major carefully blew his mask clear and lifted it. When his eyes didn't burn, Ranklin removed the rubber mask. The gas had dissipated.

Ranklin entered the long, screened BOQ hootch divided into spacious officer and N-C-O rooms. The partygoers were asleep, so Ranklin ran room to room, kicking the metal beds.

"Alert! Get up, damn it, alert!" Ranklin yelled, banging wood doorframes. "Up, Up!"

Ranklin yanked sleeping bags and pulled blankets off beds, stirring the shocked, mumbling men. He kicked Mac's bunk repeatedly before the bleary Lieutenant even moved. Most of the N-C-O's ran off in battle gear before the junior officers even got up.

The officers slunk away, dragging rifles and flak vests and helmets, lurching toward their duty stations with hangdog looks at having slept through Daktoum's first mortar attack.

*   *   *

At first light in Pleiku, Colonel Lehr and Doc Levin caught a small LOH helicopter to Daktoum. Fifty feet below, waves of green jungle washed by.

"Daktoum's under fire," the pilot told Lehr beside him in the front seat. "I'll go make my Oasis pickup, and we'll wait for another sitrep."

Lehr nodded and glanced back at Doc in the rear seat. Except for perfunctory courtesies, the two had not spoken.

Ridgetop firebases appeared in the distance.

General Armbruster had been affable, joking about Lehr's backhand, enthusiastic about the ARVN army in this new N-V-A offensive, confident that "our Vietnamese brothers could protect Daktoum." Colonel Trinh spoke of "a great victory."

Only Eagleton had been blunt—over an afternoon drink in MAC-V's lush courtyard villa beside a fountain.

"Don't count on any American infantry, Lehr."

"And the Cav'?"

"Forget the Cav'," Eagleton said with hard eyes. "If you're overrun, *maybe*. Politics. At the highest level."

The chopper skirted a broken ridge, where, on a shattered hilltop, blackened trees lay smashed like kindling.

At least Eagleton was honest. Vietnamization. How about bait, pure and simple.

The small chopper briefly circled the debris-strewn red scar of Fire Support Base Oasis before corkscrewing down onto a metal-grid pad. A grinning Artillery Captain wedged a packed duffle bag into the back seat and climbed in beside Doc.

"Going home," he said, grinning.

The small chopper lifted off Oasis.

As the helicopter followed the long, blasted line of Rocket Ridge toward Daktoum, the intercom net crackled.

"Daktoum's an all-clear, colonel," the pilot said. "No incoming for fifteen minutes."

The red-brown cut of Daktoum firebase appeared on the green valley floor, and as they descended, everything grew bigger: the airstrip, the long road, the artillery positions on the river, the bunkers and tents, the dusty trucks, the lumpy walls, and rotting sandbags.

As they left the small helicopter, bags in hand, the colonel's steely gaze caught Doc's eyes. He nodded and marched down the dusty company street toward the TOC. Doc headed for the medical bunker.

*   *   *

As Lehr carried his green canvas bag into the TOC, the monkey chattered overhead.

"Where the hell is everyone?" Lehr yelled across the TOC to a red-eyed Merton.

Sergeant Major Bricker ambled out of his office.

"On the line, sir," Merton said.

"No more incoming?"

"No, sir."

"Sound the all-clear," Lehr said.

Merton hit a switch and a police siren moaned outside.

"I smelled C-S gas," Lehr said.

"Bunker one-five thought they had a probe."

"And tripped *gas?*"

"Yes, sir," the red-faced Sergeant Major said.

"That's a Juliet-Foxtrot," Lehr said.

Lehr tossed his bag in his office and headed for the back entrance.

"Going out to the line," Lehr said over his shoulder, his boots echoing out the rear maze entrance.

Merton widened his eyes at the sergeant major.

"Shit's gonna fly, Top."

*   *   *

Crossing the ankle-deep dust on the firebase camp road, Lehr pulled out a cigar stub and stuck it between his teeth. As he looked up from lighting it, Halliday walked toward him.

"Ahhh … morning sir," Halliday said. "Need your Jeep?"

"No."

Clenching his smoking cigar in his teeth, Lehr walked toward the crooked tangle of barbed wire overlooking the river.

Firefight trash—shredded plastic, metal, wood, and paper wadding —was strewn all around the wooden pallet paths, and rusty beer cans glittered, hanging on the barbed wire.

Soldiers trudging back in flak vests and weapons looked away when they saw Lehr.

When the monkey screamed atop the TOC, Lehr looked back. Soldiers were shuffling out of the officer's hootch, their hair and uniforms disheveled, and some of them were still struggling into battle gear and blinking at the bright light.

They slept through the attack, Lehr thought.

"Get the hell going!" Ranklin yelled at the officers.

Lehr loped over to the officer's hootch.

When the stragglers saw Lehr, they hustled away before the colonel bulled into the hootch.

"What the hell is going on with my firebase?" Lehr said.

Ranklin's mouth opened, but nothing came out.

"What the hell happened, Ranklin?" Lehr said. "Staff meeting—ten minutes!"

Lieutenant Mac Elroy staggered out in a wrinkled green T-shirt and shorts. Bent over in his doorway, his ass stuck up in the air as he searched for his boots.

Lehr stormed over, caught a foul whiff of alcohol breath, and yanked the lieutenant up by his T-shirt, ripping it.

"*You*," Lehr said in a low deadly voice. "Get the hell off my firebase. *Now.*"

As the colonel marched out, a helmet lay in his path, and he kicked it with a loud thwack. The helmet shot down the long hootch hallway, out the back door and into the dust.

*   *   *

Halliday sat on the bench outside the colonel's office.

"Go prepare the briefing room," Lehr snapped.

Halliday stumbled out of the TOC and careened across the hot red dirt to the screened room. He swept the floor, lined up chairs, and set out ashtrays. Halliday was erasing the blackboard when the door scraped open, and Lehr scowled at him.

"Halliday," Lehr roared.

"Sir."

"Did you sell liquor to Lieutenant Mac Elroy?"

"Yes sir," Halliday said in a small voice.

"God damn it, son! Do you think this is a *game*? Jesus," Lehr said, hitting the bar with his fist. "Officers, N-C-Os so blind drunk they couldn't even hear a mortar attack? Christ, a man was wounded badly."

"Sorry, sir."

"That's not enough, Halliday—you're finished as my driver."

Halliday's face fell.

"What will I do, sir?" Halliday said, thinking like a smartass, does that mean I can go home?

"You have two days to find something, or else go out to a line company."

Harsh morning light flooded the briefing room.

"You couldn't see how good you had it," said the colonel. "Just like my daughter. You think you *know* the world, when you can't even see what's going on in front of your nose!"

Lehr jabbed his arm at the green wall of jungle.

The colonel walked over and grabbed Ben's chrome Zippo off the bar. He lit his cigar and looked at Halliday.

"My advice? Keep your goddamn eyes open, Halliday," Lehr said, absently slipping the chrome Zippo into his pocket.

*   *   *

Under the flickering fluorescents, Sergeant Clancy and the medics worked on the mortar attack casualties.

Gabrielle labored over the only serious wound—a skinny, dark-haired young soldier with a chunk of bicep torn off by shrapnel. Blood slickened the loose, black fatigue shirt that had been her father's.

"Kid!" Clancy yelled. "Get that F-O-B chopper for Medevac."

The Kid ran out.

Gabrielle held pressure on the wound until the morphine took hold, and the wounded soldier stopped thrashing. She irrigated the wound, quickly bandaged it, then re-checked his pulse, breathing, and blood pressure.

"Got a chopper," the Kid yelled down the stairs.

Gabrielle waved Donnelly and Nimmer over, taped down the thick white bandage, and held the glass IV bottle. They lifted the stretcher and rushed the patient up the wide staircase and out into the hot morning light just as Stubbs skittered his helicopter across the airstrip.

As the helicopter settled, Gabrielle and the medics lifted the stretcher into the bay. She held the wounded man's good hand and studied the young soldier's thin smile and morphine-glazed eyes.

The three stepped away, the chopper lifted, and whopped off into the hot blue sky.

As Gabrielle, Nimmer, and Donnelly crossed the gray bridge, Doc ran over from the VIP pad. Doc walked beside Gabrielle.

"Only one critical?" Doc asked.

"Yes," Gabrielle replied. "But he will lose the arm."

They stopped at the entrance to the medical bunker.

"All the other wounds are minor," Gabrielle said, gripping Doc's shoulder as the medics clomped downstairs.

Gabrielle lit a cigarette as the helicopter flew down the valley. She turned and the deep black circles around her eyes were veiled in cigarette smoke.

"There's blood on you," Doc said.

He offered his handkerchief, and Gabrielle wiped her fatigue blouse clean.

"It's started," she said, handing it back.

"What makes you think that?" Doc said.

"This is when they always come," Gabrielle said.

She pointed beyond Rocket Ridge, where a deep valley lay smoking with mist.

"Summer monsoon," she said. "The crachin mist will cover Daktoum and the hills, so the helicopters cannot see to fly."

Gabrielle's eyes were bloodshot, and her long black hair was tucked into her fatigues.

"Two years ago, they came inside this camp."

Gabrielle dragged on her cigarette and ground it out with a shrug. She nodded and walked across the open dirt lot, her footsteps raising silky puffs of dust.

Doc stood up.

"Welcome back, Cap'n," Ben said, stepping into the light.

"Yeah," Doc replied, leaning against the sandbags.

"You missed all the shit."

"Not quite."

"Hey Doc, I'm going to Nhu Canh Du. That Vietnamese girl we talked about to clean the dispensary? That still cool?"

"Oh," Doc said. "Yeah."

Ben walked over to the small Jeep ambulance parked near the black metal shipping containers.

"Hey Doc?" Ben called.

"What?"

"Donnelly's trying to jive a purple heart out of Clancy. He and Nimmer got scraped up diving into a bunker. Don't believe him—I saw them. They didn't do shit."

"OK," Doc answered, watching Gabrielle cross the dusty lot and turn onto the company street to Colonel Lehr's bunker.

Clancy's voice boomed from below, so Doc walked down the dim stairway into the weak fluorescent light.

*   *   *

Ten minutes later in the briefing room, staff officers and sergeants sat rigid and sweating, with their eyes locked straight ahead. Outside, the firebase was quiet—no artillery, no aircraft.

Lehr could barely contain his rage as he took the lectern. He stared at each man with a look of contempt.

"Cut the crap, gentlemen," he said, in a low, flat voice. "There is no goddamn excuse for this morning."

With his hands behind his back, Lehr paced among the rows of seated men. The colonel's jungle boots scraped across the gritty concrete.

"The buck stops here. We have five hundred men. Against two or more N-V-A *regiments* dug into Rocket Ridge and all over the Badlands between here and the Trail. The South Vietnamese are tasked with our security. It's their duty to engage the enemy. We are here as support. The 99th Engineers are not leaving, nor can we count on any American infantry."

Colonel Lehr looked over each officer again, turned sharply, marched out of the briefing room, and slammed the screen door.

The officers and sergeants sat in the heat.

Then Ranklin stood, uncovered the green map with the acetate overlays and grease pencil circles and arrows, and began the nuts and bolts briefing. Operations. Work parties. Air defense coordination. Mine sweep. Perimeter defense. Reaction forces. Re-supply and convoy security. Water-point security. Casualties. Weather. Weapons. Intelligence. Fields of fire.

"Major Ranklin," Chaplain Goodby asked. "What's our ... evacuation plan? In case…"

"You heard the colonel," Ranklin said. "There is no evacuation plan. We stay at Daktoum until we're ordered to pull out."

13.

As Colonel John Lehr walked to his sleeping bunker, mist drifted over the company street and wavered the hard light. Out on the airstrip, Captain Mike Hardin and Bok loaded Montagnard soldiers into six thundering Sikorsky helicopters that rattled like huge metal locusts.

Lehr felt like lying down. He had never experienced this before. His step slowed, and his body seemed unresponsive—he even had to rest against a sandbag wall. His left arm ached, and his breath grew shallow and labored.

Three medics with chrome stethoscopes flashing on faded-green fatigue pockets ambled by with clipboards.

Nimmer, Donnelly, and Cullen stopped talking as soon as they saw the colonel.

Lehr quickly heaved himself off the sandbag wall and slowly moved toward his sleeping bunker.

It seemed an eternity before he reached the entrance, where Lehr rested again, then eased himself down, step by step. Entering his stuffy bunker, he sensed something, but did not switch on the light.

Gabrielle sat in the center of the room on a chair, her face shadowed by a shaft of stairwell light. Lehr cursed under his breath—he had forgotten her. He dragged himself to his bunk and sat down.

As his eyes grew used to the light, he saw she was naked.

A silence followed before her bare feet padded across the dusty concrete.

Lehr smelled orange mixed with the musk of her body.

His lips were like stone as Gabrielle ran her fingers over his hair, his neck, and his shoulders. Finally, she knelt and removed his boots and cotton socks. As she touched her head to his feet, her hair brushed his legs. She reached her hands under his fatigues and ran her fingers along his muscular calves.

An artillery cannon fired with a dull concussion.

The colonel did not move—it was almost as if his breath had stopped. Gabrielle loosened his fatigue jacket, stripped it away, and then peeled his olive drab T-shirt over his head. Lehr lifted his hips and let her pull down his fatigue pants and shorts, until he sat shaggy and naked in the dark. Though it was very hot in the bunker, Lehr did not sweat.

She found his penis and gently rubbed and stroked it. Nothing. She caressed him intently, but his remoteness grew.

Finally, Gabrielle stood up, walked across the room, and lit a cigarette.

Under the flame, Lehr's muscular bulk loomed out of the darkness and vanished. Gabrielle coughed and then exhaled.

"What will happen now? she said.

She dragged on the cigarette and stepped into her dress. Then she slipped on her black military shirt.

"The luck is all gone from this place," she said.

Lehr stared straight ahead.

"My father was a colonel," she said, sitting on his footlocker to put on her shoes. "In our Indochine War."

Lehr turned.

"His troops were ambushed in a famous battle. Mang Yang Pass."

Gabrielle stood up, smoothed her skirt, walked across the concrete floor, and stepped up into the harsh shaft of light.

Her footsteps grew faint and disappeared.

*   *   *

Doctor Ronald Levin sat at his desk writing on thin blue airmail paper. He reread the letter to his wife Holly and closed his eyes. Doc stood up, walked to the wastebasket, and ripped the letter into blue shreds.

Beyond the canvas door, a medic's cassette player droned:

Find yourself at war
While waterfalls of pity roar
You feel to moan but unlike before
You'd discover that you'd be
One more person cry-ing.

Someone knocked on the wooden doorframe, so Doc lifted the canvas flap. Gabrielle brushed by him and sat down on the bed beneath the photograph of Doc's wife.

Gabrielle scanned Doc's boyish face.

"So, Bacsi," she began. "I will help you."

"We could use another doctor."

"The mist comes now, Bacsi," she said, brushing aside a tendril of black hair. "The crachin, we French call it, one more reason for the cafard, all that gray sky."

Doc locked eyes on her.

"I need something," she said.

"Of course," he said. "What?"

"May I take a bed here? I will need to be close ..."

Doc nodded. He spotted a scrap of blue paper on the floor and scooped it up.

"Thank you, Bacsi."

Gabrielle rose suddenly and moved past him out the canvas door with a light step. Doc followed as Gabrielle bounded through the stretchers on sawhorses past the main desk, where Benjamin stood beside a pretty Vietnamese girl.

"Captain Bacsi Levin, this is Lam," Ben said. "She's going to clean our dispensary."

Doc came over and shook the girl's hand.

"*Who* gonna be cleaning *my* dispensary?" Clancy boomed, bolting over.

"Lam is," Ben said.

"Oh no she ain't," Clancy argued. "I got plenty of medics sitting on their dead asses."

"Who says?" Ben protested.

Ben and Clancy faced off, hot-faced. Lam cringed.

"Sergeant Clancy," Doc said. "I told Ben to hire her."

"You think about discipline? Security, Captain?"

"She's being cleared by S-2," Doc said. "The medics will need help."
Ben smiled.

"Come on, Lam," Ben said. "I'll show you around."

The burly sergeant glared, quickly wheeled around, and tripped over Doc's golden dog, sleeping on the floor. The dog yelped.

"God-damn it," Clancy muttered. "Dispensary ain't no place for a damn dog."

The playful retriever nuzzled his head into Doc's palm.

"It's OK, Bacsi," Doc said. "OK, boy."

Clancy stopped at the reception landing and walked back.

"OK, Captain, I can live with the girl cleaning," Clancy said. "Could I have a word?"

"Go ahead," Doc replied.

The hefty sergeant took off his hat and rubbed his bald head.

"I think it might be a good idea that the Kid ..." Clancy blurted in a quiet voice. "Change jobs."

"Why?"

"I don't think he can a ... take it—you know, the casualties—when we get hit."

Doc frowned.

"He's a good ambulance driver. Are you sure?"

"Yes, sir, "Clancy said, exhaling.

"Well," Doc said, studying the sergeant's impassive face. "I'll see what I can do."

Clancy turned away.

Doc went into his office, followed by his golden dog.

As Doc sat on his bunk and pulled his dog's ears, the field phone buzzed.

"Battalion Surgeon," Doc answered. "OK, ten minutes."

*   *   *

When Lehr entered the TOC, yet another blue envelope with the familiar rose-colored ink sat on his desk. A spear of feeling cut through the dull pain lingering in his chest.

The colonel sat heavily down, stared at the feminine handwriting, and fingered the airmail letter. Then he buzzed Merton to send for Captain Levin.

*　　　*　　　*

Halliday shuffled across the camp road to the TOC and stopped beneath the camp monkey's rusted cage high on the sandbagged walls. The monkey mimicked his slumping shoulders and hangdog head, but Halliday hardly noticed.

Halliday thought of his father in the hospital with polio and John Wayne losing his leg in the movie. The thought of losing his own legs scared him so much that he shook.

When Halliday lurched into the TOC, the monkey screamed, grabbed his cage, and beat his feet on the rusty wire.

Inside, the TOC was quiet and the heat, stifling. Halliday floated through the command bunker, so disconnected from body and mind beneath his shame and hangover that he didn't notice Major Ranklin glaring from his office beside Sergeant Major Bricker.

In Operations, Major Sneller, sitting beside a grimacing Dunkley, arched a crooked grin at Halliday. Loudermilk scowled, and Fairbanks' red neck scarf flashed by, hurrying into Commo, where radios squawked, and teletypes churned out rolls of orders and intelligence from Saigon and Group.

Halliday entered Merton's office and slumped into a chair.

"Jesus, 'cruit, the old man didn't order you shot or nothing," Merton said. "One shitty job's the same as any other. Big fucking deal —you're still in the fuckin' Army."

Merton quit typing and waved mimeographed orders.

"In-country R and R—Vung fucking Tau, where pussy runs like water. You want 'em? Two authorized—nobody wants to go."

Halliday stared at him.

"Consolation prize," Merton said. "I put your name in—with your pal Benjamin's. Colonel will sign 'em, no sweat."

Doc Levin walked into Merton's office with his black medical bag.

"Halliday, Merton," Doc said, nodding.

"Colonel's waiting, sir."

*   *   *

As Doc approached Lehr's desk, he noticed the colonel's faint pallor and flushed temples.

"Can you examine me?"

The colonel stripped to the waist. Doc listened to his heart and lungs as Lehr described his symptoms. Doc put away his stethoscope and blood pressure gauge.

"So?" Lehr asked.

"You should go to Saigon."

"Why, Captain?"

"I can't be sure unless I see test results."

"What is it?" Lehr said. "In your wildest opinion."

"Your heart."

Color returned to the colonel's face. He buttoned his shirt.

"You should go to Saigon," Doc repeated.

"And lose my command? You'd like that."

Doc's gentle brown eyes stared steadily into Lehr's gray.

"I won't order you," Doc replied. "But I could."

Lehr ushered Doc to the door.

"If it happens again," Doc said. "I want to know."

"Thank you, Captain Levin," Lehr said.

"Immediately," Doc said. "Unless you want to die like a salesman in your chair."

*   *   *

The colonel's battered office door scraped shut.

When Doc walked into Merton's stark office, Halliday was slumped over, head in hands.

"What's wrong?" Doc asked.

"Colonel fired him," Merton said, grimacing and grinning. "*And he don't wanna do mine sweep.* Who the fuck would?"

Doc left the outer office, and then he came back in.

"Has the colonel found another driver?" Doc asked.

"Not yet," Merton said.

"Halliday," Doc said.

Halliday looked up.

"How would you like to drive the ambulance?"

His face brightened.

"Really?"

Captain Levin nodded.

"Sure, Doc."

"Let me clear it with the colonel."

*   *   *

That evening at last light, Halliday stood with seventy-seven other young engineer soldiers in a loose formation near the mess hall.

Smitty, the sergeant of the guard, read the orders: tactical responses, policies, passwords, and a threat about falling asleep. Many of the dusty, battle-dressed teenagers were bone-tired from working on the road. All they wanted was a few hours sleep before their watch.

Lieutenant Fairbanks, the Officer of the Guard, performed a cursory weapons inspection and then dismissed the restless, bored soldiers.

As the sunlight faded, the teenaged soldiers straggled through the red dust to twenty-six fighting bunkers circling the big camp.

Halliday walked to the river with his rifle, sleeping bag, flak vest, helmet, ammunition, gas mask, and two cans of Coke.

Two hundred feet beyond the last sleeping hootch, a dusty wooden walkway led to Bunker 15 on a low bluff overlooking the Dak Poko River beneath the darkening jungle ridge.

Bunker 15 was a squat, two-story tower of uneven, gray sandbag walls covered in rain ponchos to keep soil from leaking. Beneath the tower, a dank, sandbagged chamber held wooden cots where off-duty guards slept.

Halliday climbed up a crude ladder to a parapet under a sandbagged roof. The other two guards had thrown their flak vests and helmets in the stinking room below and sat up top. The young soldiers checked the radio and the night vision starlight scope, while one clipped a belt into the M-60 machine gun and chambered a round.

For two hours, the three teenagers in faded jungle fatigues sat atop the low sandbagged tower and listened to the rush of the Dak Poko River.

They smoked cigarettes and drank Cokes and told the truth and told lies about their families and their cars and their buddies and their girlfriends and sex and high school and stereos and motorcycles and favorite foods and movie stars and wild adventures, while beneath them, the silver river flowed by, slowly turning black.

For once, the air was sweet and balmy and free of mosquitoes, and as stars appeared in the sweep of black sky, the soldiers even forgot their fear.

After everything had been said, the talk slowly petered out, and the teenagers grew silent as the immense jungle night enfolded them, each in their own loneliness and insignificance.

Leaving one guard on top, Halliday and the other soldier grabbed their M-14 rifles and climbed down to the ripe sandbagged chamber where they fell asleep on stinking cots.

A few hours later, Halliday awoke, furiously scratching his crotch. He eased up into a sitting position and cradled his M-14. Goddamn it, crabs. Again! Fucking crabs—makes me feel so guilty, like beating off. Goddamn filthy fucking bunkers.

A hand reached through the darkness and smacked Halliday. A sleepy soldier passed him a glow-in-the-dark watch reading 4 AM. The third guard lay snoring on his back, still wearing his flak vest. Halliday stood up.

"Bunker one-four," the soldier whispered, laying on his cot and curling his sleeping bag around him. "Ellis."

The soldier immediately went limp.

Halliday hauled out his gear and climbed the ladder.

Inside the parapet, he slipped on his flak vest and steel pot, checked his rifle, and cranked the command post landline.

"Sergeant of the Guard," the line echoed.

"Smitty," Halliday said. "Why the hell did you let Ellis take last watch? You know he's gonna wake up the whole camp—the colonel'll be pissed."

"Halliday, just stay the fuck awake. The old man ain't your concern no more."

The landline went dead.

Halliday sat in the dark behind the low sandbagged wall. He fingered the machine-gun bolt, the trigger, the safety, checking and rechecking the belt. He peered out at the dim curve of the river and the vague outline of the steep ridge.

Ellis. Lester Ellis. Permanent day gate guard, crazy bastard, and king of the stoners. Ellis's eyes blazed bright red, and his speech and movements were so slow, it was as if he lived in his own private time scheme.

"The Law, man," Ellis always told anyone who would listen, slapping the three-foot-long plastic rocket he always carried on his shoulder, "*This* is my goddamn LAW."

The Light Anti-tank Weapon was a quintessential American plastic throwaway killer. Lester Ellis shot off as many LAW's as he could. He was a firepower freak, laughing like a banshee every time he lit up a LAW rocket and blew away whatever was in sight—mostly jungle.

Ellis's assignment to permanent guard duty derived from what was called "an unusual personality profile," which meant one step shy of criminally incorrigible and barely able to deal with authority. Since the Army often found it impossible to admit mistakes, especially with regular army enlisted soldiers at war, Ellis lived his entire Vietnam life in bunkers—at the front gate, all day—and at night on the bunker line —constantly getting high and shooting off just enough military fireworks to keep him giggling.

Where the fuck is Ellis coming from? Halliday thought, always waking the camp up. Funny—artillery fires all night long, but *that* never wakes anyone. Guess you get used to some sounds when you're asleep, but why? How does your dream mind know which sounds are good and which ones are bad?

Halliday stared out at the night.

The jungle inhaled.

Below, the swift river was strangely hushed. Halliday shivered in the pre-dawn chill and wrapped his sleeping bag around him. The constantly rushing river was lulling and would also muffle any movement—especially half-naked Vietnamese scrambling up the bank with their bodies so black with grease that you'd think that they were the night.

Smitty said that the V-C used B-40 rockets to blow up a bunker, and then they'd whip into camp with explosives taped on their bodies, ripping charges off and throwing them into tents, blowing G.I.s away to Kingdom Come.

Ellis wasn't afraid of anybody or anything. Or maybe he was just beyond caring. "Whatever I do in this hell-hole Vietnam jus' fine," Ellis once told Halliday and Ben, as he offered them a hit of his special 'day weed,' "cause the Lord, he do what he want with me. Always has, always will. There it is, man, there it right fuckin' righteous is, you dig, man, you dig?"

Halliday sat quietly behind the parapet wall.

Four to six AM was the longest two hours of guard duty. The darkest part of the night, the sleepiest, when all the energetic teenagers atop the bunker towers were at last overcome by exhaustion, their alertness dimmed, their relentless spirits, ebbed.

The night split open.

A stream of fire flew down from the next river bunker, flashed across the shining black river like the hand of God unleashing a cracking fire bolt.

Halliday flattened behind the parapet wall.

A huge concussion rocked the river line bunkers and shook the defoliated forest across the Dak Poko River.

The silence that followed was split by Ellis' long, high-pitched giggle, right after his brand of retaliating Jehovah had lit up the stump-covered hillside and woken up the entire bunker line along with half of Daktoum camp.

Voices cursed the night in a cacophony of American dialects:

"You motherfucker Ellis you ... "

"Jerkass, I get my hands on your skinny-assed neck, I ... "

"Silly son of a bitch ... "

In Daktoum, the response was standard.

Lehr immediately awoke and grabbed the PRC-25 radio on the floor beneath his bed.

"Sergeant Smith?" Lehr asked over the radio. "Problem out there, riverside?"

"Ahh, checking on it, sir. Bunker ... ahh, one-four reports movement," Smitty said.

"Put up a mortar flare and let Fairbanks know," Lehr replied. "Keep me posted."

"Yes, sir."

"Who's out on one-four?"

"Ellis."

"Brandywine clear."

"Lifeline clear."

Smitty cranked one of five telephone lines in the TOC.

"Tubes Inc.," the mortar pit answered.

"Ordering a flare over sector one-four."

"Roger that, lighting up one-four."

"Drop one," Smitty said. "Standby for another."

"Over easy. Drop-kicking you one, hold one."

Smitty shouldered the radio and ran outside.

A hollow sound punctuated the night as a parachute flare rocketed over the camp.

The flare popped like a dying incandescent bulb, and a tiny parachute rocked a brilliant light down through the darkness.

On the bunker line, guards ducked below sandbags to hide their silhouettes from snipers.

Under the harsh illumination, the defoliated jungle hillside became a moonscape of stumps and branches, big broken trees, and eerie shadows shapeshifting under the flare, slowly rocking toward the shining black river.

A loud clear voice called out.

"SH-IT! Ain't nobody out there. Charlie ain't no god-damn fool, Ellis. You think he gonna let you see his skinny yellow ass? Hell, no. Charlie be underground a hundred feet by now. You done scared him away, fool. Damn you anyway, Ellis! You smoke so goddamn much weed you can't even tell shit from Shinola. Damn your skinny ass anyhow."

Murmurs and curses rose from the bunkers and echoed out into the night. After the second flare fizzled out, Sergeant Smith arrived at Ellis' bunker.

"Who goes there?" Ellis stage-whispered down from the low tower, rattling his rifle.

"Knock that shit off, Ellis," Smitty said. "Coming up."

Smitty climbed the rickety bunker ladder and stepped inside the low sandbagged parapet. The stink of cordite hung in the bunker.

Lanky, red-eyed Ellis stood in the dark, his M-16 pointing out. A used LAW cartridge lay at his feet; another round hung on his shoulder. Three LAWs were stacked on the wall.

Two shadowy soldiers wrapped in sleeping bags, muttered.

"Ellis," Smitty said. "Those LAW's cost Uncle Sam ninety-one dollars each."

"Sergeant, you know, that I know and that I could give a fat clusterfuck if they cost Sam a thousand dollars. If I gots to use the LAW to save *your* ass—sin loi, motherfucker, then you go tell Sam he can sue old Ellis for his ninety-one dollars."

"You saw movement, Ellis?"

"Through the scope, check it out, sergeant."

Smitty bent down and gazed through the Starlight scope, but all he could make out was a pale-green maze of twisted stumps across the river.

"Nothing out there, Ellis."

"I seen movement, Sergeant."

"I believe you, Ellis," Smitty said, sighing. "Just call me before you fire a LAW."

Ellis grunted as Smitty stepped over the parapet and went down the ladder.

"Sergeant?"

"Yeah, Ellis," Smitty said, his head just above the sandbags.

"Sometimes I ain't got no time to call you," Ellis said. "You know, tactical necessity."

"Try."

Smitty climbed down to the ground.

*   *   *

Inside the Sergeant of the Guard bunker, Smitty leaned his M-16 against the sandbags and cranked the landline telephone.

"Bunker one-one, watch the river," Smitty said. "We've got possible movement."

"Fucking Ellis."

"Bunker two, stay awake. Just watch the river."

"Roger that shit."

"Bunker one-three—keep your eyes open."

"Gotcha."

"Bunker one-five?"

"I know, I saw it," Halliday said.

"Saw what? The movement?"

"No, Ellis' light show."

"Everybody saw it. Halliday, just stay awake."

"Right on."

Smitty hung up the phone. His supernumerary stared out the gun port.

"Going over to the TOC," Smitty said.

*   *   *

As Smitty entered the big command bunker, Lieutenant Fairbanks lay on a cot writing on a yellow legal pad, his gaunt tanned face looking serious.

"Ellis?" Fairbanks asked, not looking up.

"Yeah."

"Anything out there?"

"Don't think so."

While Fairbanks scratched at the yellow paper, Smitty sipped coffee in silence.

*   *   *

Down in his sleeping bunker, the colonel hung up the mike on the radio beside his bed. Lehr remembered Christina's unopened letter, so he got up, padded barefoot across the concrete, grabbed the blue envelope, and ripped off the end.

A photograph of a droopy-eared basset hound gazed mournfully out. Lehr opened the greeting card. Inside, it read: "I wish you weren't so dog–gone far away." Below, in the familiar artful handwriting: "I miss you, Dad. Love, Christina. P.S. Soon we'll be together again, forever."

The colonel's eyes misted, and he inhaled sharply. He shook his head at how long he had waited to read his daughter's letter, afraid of another anti-war rant. Lehr got in bed, turned off the lamp and immediately fell asleep.

*   *   *

Halliday was having trouble staying awake. He slapped his face, pinched his arm, even tried to get himself scared, but nothing worked. He was fading.

You know, Halliday you dumbshit, he argued, fall asleep, and you could just wake up in Kingdom Come.

Something on the defoliated slope across the river made Halliday start. Staring into the darkness produced the barely perceptible image of Bonnie Wilder, a beautiful, high-kicking cheerleader who lifted her long slender leg and curled it around Halliday's sleepy mind.

Bonnie Wilder. Her young pouty face with a cocky hint of trouble, spun through Halliday's brain, kicking *stand up and cheer* out in the haunted tree stumps. Bonnie, perfectly shaped in all the right places, kicking her heart out for Verde High. The rocking peaches of her perfect ass took his breath away.

Halliday squinted across the dark river, where he could almost see Bonnie on the sidelines, kicking her shiny white legs high for the team *just for you, Jack* her sly, smart-ass grin always inferred *I know you want me and maybe, I even want you.*

Halliday shifted the rifle in his lap.

Faint movement rustled through the dim, slanting silhouettes of smashed trees angling up Rocket Ridge.

Halliday murmured, the senior trip—those white shorts, impossible to look away from Bonnie. Camped on a sandbar on the Colorado River near Needles—barbecuing burgers and getting drunk. They sat, not talking for the longest time, just looking at each other and trying not to feel the heat rising.

Halliday wiped sweat off his brow.

Again, the trees across the Dak Poko seemed to be shaking as Bonnie led Halliday away, her laughter echoing off the sandstone walls as they ran up a narrow side canyon.

Beyond the barbed wire and across the Dak Poko River, a finger of mist drifted past Halliday's bunker.

Bonnie stopped on a moonlit sandbank and started dancing. Halliday caught her up around the waist. After he stole a kiss, she whispered, *I won't tell if you won't.* Bonnie spun away and ran up the narrow canyon on a long sandbar through moon shadows and then around a bend in the river to a crescent-shaped beach. Halliday chased those long, shiny legs and perfect bouncing bottom until Bonnie stopped in a shaft of moonlight, turned back, and grinned as she wiggled off her shorts and panties and stood there, in only a bra and gold sandals. She kicked off her sandals, smiled sweetly, and sidled into the desert pool. Halliday tore off his Levi's and T-shirt and waded into the warm water after her.

Across the Dak Poko River, the defoliated tree stumps wavered as Bonnie whirled away from Halliday, dipping her pale body down into the black water. When she stood up and looked over her shoulder, her wet, moonstruck hips swayed and sparkled, shining her back, her legs, her pale white bottom, stunning his eyes with a sweet, lovely, jiggling movement, movement, MOVEMENT?

Halliday jerked straight up, grabbed the landline, and furiously cranked it while kicking awake the sleeping guards.

"I got movement, I got movement, Smitty, I got so much fucking movement!"

"Who is this?" the phone demanded.

"Halliday. Smitty, I got movement, the whole fucking hillside, thousands of gooks. What do I do?"

"Unless they come across, hold fire until I get there."

"I'll try."

All the riverside phones in front of Smitty buzzed. He quickly answered.

"That hillside ..."

"Got it one-one. Hold fire. Do not fire unless fired upon. Repeat, do not fire."

"Smitty, battalion-sized movement."

"Got it one-three, hold fire."

"We're cool."

"Holy shit, Sarge ..."

"I know, one-two, hold fire."

"Roadkill," Smitty told the radio mike. "Hang loose. Wait until they start it. Do not shoot first."

"Gotcha, sarge."

Smitty cranked the landline to Lehr.

"Brandywine," the tired voice said.

"Battalion-sized movement on five river bunkers, sir," Smitty said.

"*Battalion?* Overrun Ops," Lehr ordered, already snapping on his gear.

"Yes sir."

"I'm moving, Sergeant, meet you at one-five, ASAP."

Jesus, Lehr thought as he ran up his stairs in the dark, *Jesus, here we go.*

*   *   *

Smitty cranked the line to the TOC. Fairbanks answered.

"Battalion-sized movement, sir. Brandywine's got us on overrun."

"Roger that, Smitty. Get control moving—air, arty, Spooky. I'll wake up the camp."

Smitty grabbed the radio and changed frequency.

"Lifeline to Kontum control," Smitty said.

"May I take your order, Lifeline?" the radio crackled.

"Control, battalion-sized movement out here at Fort Apache, river perimeter."

"Spooky's ahhh already moving over your A-O, bring him up on your net, Lifeline. And ... got your tac-air standing by ... at first light."

"Roger. Request Death Cong stand by."

"You got your Death Cong, alerting Dust-off, too."

"No friendly ops, Control?"

"Ahhh. No sir, so Charlie's still got himself a pair. Ahh, and you've got yourself a free fire from Nhu Canh Du to Cambodia. Over."

"Thank you much, Control. Lifeline Out."

"Good luck, Lifeline. Control Out."

Smitty grabbed his steel pot, threw on his flak vest, bolted a round into the chamber, slung bandoliers of ammo around his chest, grabbed the radio, and rushed through the door.

He ran smack into Lehr, who had a glitter in his eye.

The colonel chuckled at their collision and grabbed Smitty's shoulder as they hustled along toward the river.

"Everything rolling, sergeant?"

"Like clockwork, sir."

"Got your radio? I'll run the net from the bunker line."

"Got it, sir," Smitty said.

Near the TOC, Fairbanks fell in beside the moving Lehr and Smitty. The three battle-dressed men moved swiftly through the dusty camp toward the river bunker line, hugging the sandbagged tents and bunkers.

As they approached the dark bunker line, a faint glimmer of false dawn appeared on the eastern horizon.

The bunker guards were quiet, and alert as silent soldiers poured out of the hootches on all sides and moved towards the river line.

By the time Lehr, Fairbanks and Smitty reached Bunker 15, most of the camp was in bunkers and foxholes. The three leaders lightly stepped across the pallet boardwalk and started up the ladder.

Atop the dark bunker, Lehr tapped a soldier bent over a machine gun. He didn't realize that it was Halliday.

"You saw them?" the colonel whispered.

"Yes, sir, eleven o'clock."

"Give me the starlight."

"Yes, sir."

Lehr put the scope to his eye.

"Christ, that's a lot of movement," Lehr said. "What in hell is Charlie doing? It's almost first light."

"No idea, sir."

Lehr put down the Starlight scope and faced the darkness, thinking. Smitty took the scope and intently studied the hill. The colonel turned back.

"As soon as they clear the ridge, call in the Death Cong and throw a mad minute on them," Lehr whispered to Fairbanks. "Get everybody under cover. Spooky can work them from the ridge line to the river and directly above us. As soon as it gets light, we'll bring in Tac-air and shotgun rounds from the artillery."

"Roger, sir."

"Got your co-ordinates?"

"Double-checked them myself," Fairbanks said.

Smitty was still glued to the Starlight scope.

"No firing until we're fired upon," Lehr said to Fairbanks. "Yellow flare means we've tripped gas. Got that?"

"Yes, sir," Fairbanks said, heading down the ladder, whispering into the radio.

"Everything set, sergeant?" Lehr asked Smitty.

Smitty stared through the Starlight scope at the dark hill.

"Sergeant?"

"Just one thing sir."

"What's that, Sergeant?"

"It's not the N-V-A, sir."

"What?" Lehr whispered. "Then who the hell is it?"

"Take another look, sir."

Lehr grabbed the device, put a practiced eye to the scope, and stared.

Behind Lehr, the enlisted men tensed.

Finally, the colonel exhaled, took his eye away from the scope and turned to Smitty.

The eastern horizon glimmered with a pale thin line.

"You're right, Sergeant," Lehr said. "Not the N-V-A. Or the V-C."

"No sir."

"Who is it then?" Halliday asked.

"Monkeys," Lehr and Smitty said.

"*Monkeys?*"

"Battalion of monkeys."

"Driven down the hills," Smitty said. "Probably fires up there from incendiary rounds."

And under the first dim glimmers of light, Halliday and Lehr and Smitty and the guards laughed so hard that their hilarity passed down the bunker line.

But when the laugher reached the guards on Bunker 16, they couldn't hear it clearly because of the rushing river and mistook the sound for something else, and in fear, shot off all their magazines and M-60 machine gun in a mad minute of fire that caused all the river bunkers to join in. The soldiers hit a dozen animals and wounded more before the shadowy pack of monkeys bounded over the ridge back into the jungle.

Lehr barked: "Cease fire, cease fire, cease fire!" into the radio.

After they finally stopped shooting, Colonel Lehr signaled the all-clear, sighed, and slowly climbed down the ladder onto the ground.

Under first light, Rocket Ridge emerged from the night like a great ship. The colonel shook his head at the steep ridge and headed across the red dust to the TOC.

14.

All morning, Halliday and Ben ran up and down Daktoum airstrip, trying to hitch a ride south for their unexpected R&R.

A dozen helicopters worked the still air above Daktoum, ferrying re-supply and re-enforcements to a fierce battle that Captain Hardin and his Montagnards were fighting against a dug-in N-V-A battalion near Hill 875 and Cambodia.

When Warrant Officer Stubbs flew in to refuel, Ben and Halliday ran across the strip.

"Where ya' going, Stubbsy?" Halliday asked.

"Nha Trang. Taking an N-V-A prisoner to MAC-V."

Within five minutes, the helicopter lifted Halliday and Ben with their small weekend bags. They grinned as Daktoum fell away behind them.

Mist rose out of all the green valleys endlessly folding into the hazy distance into Cambodia as the helicopter leveled at three thousand feet, where the air was pleasantly cool. Ahead, puffy white thunderclouds stacked up over the blue South China Sea.

Lulled by the helicopter, Halliday and Ben fell asleep.

They awoke, descending towards the spectacular bay of Nha Trang, where dazzling white beaches curved along the turquoise sea.

"My kind of Vietnam," Ben said.

The chopper set down beside a neat tropical terminal.

Ben and Halliday waved to Stubbsy, ran off, and quickly boarded a camouflaged C-124 cargo plane loading pallets for Tan Son Nhut airbase in Saigon.

Ten minutes later, they rose above the sea, banking over pale-yellow rock formations and verdant jungle and into the puffy white clouds.

The C-124 soared to ten thousand feet and followed the coastline south to Saigon.

*   *   *

Under a cloud of marijuana smoke, Lester J. Ellis walked back from guard duty on the river. He ducked under a long steel runway panel supporting three layers of sandbags and slipped inside his sleeping bunker.

Ellis had papered every wall with what he called, "the finest Playmate collection in all goddamn Viet-nam." Nearly fifty sets of shiny American breasts, buttocks, thighs, calves, bouffant hairdos, bright eyes, and girl-next-door smiles floated off the walls in a fantastical adolescent dream.

Ellis stripped off his battle gear, tossed it in a corner, and went outside.

Blinking at the hard morning light, Ellis slipped on his Stevie Wonder wraparound sunglasses and ambled over to the mess hall, his mouth already watering for strawberry jam.

Ellis glided under the dusty tent flap and nodded to the cooks, whom he supplied with weed. He piled his tray high with eggs, bacon, potatoes, orange juice, toast, jam, and coffee.

Ellis sat alone in a corner, studying the long canvas room as hot sunlight streamed through the torn screen window.

Ellis liked to watch people, so he ate lazily, having no other duty besides a one to six guard shift at the main gate. Savoring his bacon, Ellis watched the colonel get soft-boiled eggs and toast and eat alone at the command table.

Lehr was ambushed by the chunky chaplain, whom the colonel dismissed.

Ellis listened to the Frenchwoman talking to Doc and frowned, thinking, no way could I listen to that shit for a lifetime, no damn way, Jim. Wimmen. Talk too fast, always getting up in your business about something you don't really give a shit about or don't want to say the answer to 'cause no matter what you say, it'll be wrong. Anyway, why the hell is she even up here at Daktoum? Ain't no wimmen in Vietnam, 'cept Donut Dollies and nurses. Just like some lifer officer to get himself a white woman clear the fuck up here. Well, no, thank you, especially, with her stinky-ass French cigarettes.

Sergeant Clancy set his tray down at a nearby table.

Uncle Tom motherfucker, Ellis thought.

Clancy carefully wiped down the red-checkered oilcloth with a paper napkin, walked to a trash bucket, tossed away the napkin, brushed off his hands, and sat down.

A moment later, the pale young medic who looked like a girl joined Clancy.

Under wraparound sunglasses, Ellis watched the sergeant and the skinny white kid talking with their heads close. Ellis zeroed in on their hushed talk, through a dozen mess hall conversations and the buzz of flies.

"Had to, Kid."

"Why, Sergeant Clancy?"

"It's better for everyone."

Young-assed medic, Ellis mused, big soft lips, curly hair, sissy white skin, walk all funny. Shee-it.

"So, I don't have anything to say about it?" the Kid said.

"No."

When the young medic stood up, Clancy caught his arm, quickly glanced around, and then let it go.

"You can still come visit."

Ellis sipped his coffee and spread a layer of strawberry jam across his toast. After the young medic left, Clancy scowled.

The hot room grew loud with a clatter of silverware, metal trays, and coffee-quickened voices. Lester J. Ellis ate his last piece of strawberry toast, burped, and got up. He scraped his steel tray into a garbage can and left.

*   *   *

Late that same afternoon on the sprawling American base at Long Binh near Saigon, Halliday and Ben drew bunks in a long transient barracks with slatted windows.

They walked a mile across Long Binh's paved streets, past rows of air-conditioned trailers and dusty tropical buildings encircled by a concrete perimeter wall.

"Weird," Ben said, walking along. "Can't even *see* the bush. I don't dig it."

The heavy Saigon air stank of dust, exhaust, rotting vegetation, and cooking rice as they passed by a line of shabby temporary buildings. Hand-painted red and yellow signs proclaimed: Laundry, Souvenirs, Barber, Tailor, Massage Parlor—and New York Bar, where "hostesses" in miniskirts slouched in dusty chairs, eyeing the soldiers.

"Man, we ain't even off post yet," Ben said. "What the hell kind of war they fighting down here?"

Halliday and Ben entered a wire cage beside a massive concrete guardhouse, where a military policeman with polished boots, shiny helmet, and dead eyes checked their passes and waved them off-post.

The streets and sidewalks of Long Binh were a rush of soldiers and Vietnamese—dubious friends and potential enemies. Sullen Vietnamese flew by in cyclos, and Pedi cabs as old French taxis jostled around the waves of pedestrians, speeding military trucks, and Army sedans.

"Man in the shower said three thousand V-C sappers live in Saigon," Ben said. "Hang onto your wallet. If you hear incoming, get flat."

Halliday and Ben walked on a crowded street reeking of sour sweat, tropical rot, and fermented fish sauce. The swampy Saigon air muffled the constant roar of aircraft and helicopters as the dirty yellow sky turned luminous and slowly faded.

Slashes of red, yellow, green, blue neon flashed *American Bar, Girls, Girls, Girls, New York Club, G.I. Welcome* and *Short Timer Bar,* the bright primary colors tinting the passing faces and traffic and dust beneath a dull sky laced with tangles of barbed wire on every building.

At intersections, soldiers manned machine guns in high parapets behind grenade-screens.

As dusk became night, the Long Binh camp perimeter shot out a dirty, unsettling light that hung over the teeming streets.

"You wan' girlfriend, G.I.?" a woman purred, her soft arm slipping under Ben's. "Number one Saigon bar, no booshit Saigon tea, no number ten nothing, pretty girl, nice girl, good place, come on I show you now, you come now, OK?"

She led Halliday and Ben into a dark, immense, pink room with high stucco ceilings. In the back, under a dim pool of light, a Vietnamese family sat at a massive teak table eating an elaborate evening meal, attended by black-clad servants.

The small, shapely woman led the tall American soldiers through the long room past the family, who ignored Ben and Halliday as if they were as insubstantial as ghosts.

She ushered Ben and Halliday down a long corridor into a formal parlor room filled with low leather couches, where a dozen graceful Vietnamese women in miniskirts and silk gave off scents of jasmine, rose, and frangipani.

*　　　　　　*　　　　　　*

On the Daktoum bunker line, Ellis stretched his arms and legs before settling in atop Bunker 14. Ellis felt good and figured that he might just stay up all night. Maybe I'll even get me a Charlie. Now that would be something.

*　　　　　　*　　　　　　*

The Daktoum medical bunker was nearly empty.

Weak fluorescent light fell on the dull, olive-green stretchers. In his small office with the door open, Doc played Hearts with Gabrielle, who chain-smoked and listened to Eric Satie on the cassette player.

Gabrielle's silly laughter at Doc's jokes drove the medics out of the bunker, where they usually spent evenings playing music and cards, telling stories, arguing, drinking, and writing home. Gabrielle's nakedly feminine voice had provoked the medics' vulnerability and their deepest fears, which they worked very hard masking each day in so many ways —smoking, lying, joking, drinking, cursing, bragging, dreaming, scheming—to keep their terror at a manageable level.

Clancy, freshly showered and barefoot in blue shower shoes, an olive towel around his neck, flapped down the bunker stairs into the light.

He stood on the rough wooden landing, surveying the medical bunker.

Through Doc's open door, Gabrielle's pale hands flashed as she shuffled the black cards. Cigarette smoke whirled around her pale face and long dark hair.

Clancy sat on the waiting bench opposite the front desk.

Donnelly, the night-duty medic, read a well-thumbed magazine under buzzing fluorescent light, his dusty boots up on the desk. Clancy started to order Donnelly to take his feet down but instead, pursed his lips and inhaled. When a mosquito droned by, Clancy instinctively swatted at it.

"Pretty slow tonight," Clancy said.

Above the magazine's *HOT ROD* in blood-red letters, Donnelly peered over blue-tinted glasses.

"Yep," Donnelly said. "Doc and that French broad playing hey diddle diddle's the only fucking action around here."

Donnelly frowned and went back to his car magazine.

"Kid been here?"

"Nope," Donnelly said.

Clancy sighed and stood up.

"If you see the Kid—ask him to come by my tent."

"OK, Sarge."

Donnelly rolled his eyes and watched Clancy slapping up the gritty stairs in shower shoes.

"Hey Sarge!"

Clancy's expectant face peered back out of the darkness.

"I think the Kid's moving his shit into his new tent."

Clancy exhaled, nodded, and walked upstairs.

*   *   *

Puffing and red-faced after fifty pushups, Lehr decided there was nothing wrong with his heart. He got up, folded an Army blanket in half, placed it on the bunker floor, and did fifty sit-ups, thinking he should get a carpenter to put up a wall rack. Stay in shape. Nothing wrong with my ticker. The latest situation-reports from the battle to the west were encouraging. Maybe the South Vietnamese can contain the N-V-A. Shit, with all our artillery and air they should be able to. Weather's holding, could be a mild monsoon. If the N-V-A don't move soon, it'll be too late for an offensive, and Eagleton'll be wrong.

* * *

At dawn in Saigon, Halliday and Ben awoke in a big mahogany bed beneath a white mosquito net in a hexagonal room filled with windows.

A tall, beautiful Vietnamese girl lay between them, so when they awoke, their first sight of each other was over her spectacular breasts, which made them laugh as hard and as ridiculously free as only teenagers can.

* * *

"*Two* gun trucks?" Lehr said to Chaplain Goodby from his desk. "You do realize that we're short of men and vehicles?"

"Yes, sir," Chaplain Goodby said, invoking his deepest preacher's voice. "Group Chaplain gave orders for immediate distribution to the Montagnards."

"So, a tactical necessity?"

"Oh," Goodby said, his eyes darting like flies. "Yes, sir."

"All right then, I'll find you some security."

Colonel Lehr stood up.

"Merton," the colonel yelled through his open door. "Have Ranklin find a couple gun trucks to escort the Chaplain so ... what are these supplies? Bibles?"

Goodby stared down at his new olive bush hat with the silver Chaplain's cross.

"Clothing, sir."

"We're *clothing* these people now. In old uniforms?"

"You could say that sir," Goodby said, his knuckles clenched.

Lehr sat down, nodded dismissal, and grabbed a stack of yellow Teletype dispatches as Goodby hustled out.

"Goodby!" Lehr said. "Why the hell are *you* distributing uniforms? Why not S-4?"

"It's a special situation, sir."

Goodby turned and almost made it out the door.

"*Special* situation?"

"Thank you so very much sir, for getting the security."

Goodby slipped out of Lehr's office.

"Goodby!" Lehr yelled.

Major Goodby came back in.

"Spit it out, man, what are these uniforms? Military?"

"Not exactly, sir."

"What are you taking to the Montagnards, Major?"

"Clothing."

"What *kind* of clothing, Goodby?"

As Goodby looked from side to side, Lehr glowered.

"I want to know."

"Brassieres, sir," Goodby said.

"Brassieres?"

"From the Greater Atlanta Council of Churches."

"Out of the blue, the Atlanta Council sends the 99th *brassieres*? Why in hell would they do that? Is there something I don't know?"

Goodby exhaled and then looked down.

"I sent them a letter."

"That said...?"

"It ... wasn't ... right."

"*What* wasn't right?"

"That American soldiers see half-naked women ..."

Lehr stood up.

"You get the hell out of my office, Goodby!" Lehr said, jabbing his finger at the pasty chaplain. "We are in a serious tactical situation here, major! Not some goddamn dubious morality play! You take those brassieres up to the Montagnards yourself. The V-C are not idiots. Why the hell would they ambush a chaplain with a truckload of D-cups?"

*   *   *

Whenever Doc touched Gabrielle's hand playing cards, his body trembled. Every day, Doc looked forward to the simple joy of Hearts, the ease of the rules, the predictable gambits, the luck of the draw, and the intimate small talk.

Outside Doc's office, the medics were hot, sullen, and resentful. Clancy had made them clean the bunker twice, even after Lam had meticulously dusted and swept. Doc made a mental note to have Clancy knock off the busywork, then he smiled and waited for Gabrielle to play a card.

Gabrielle threw down an eight of hearts and laughed like a girl at her mistake as the eight slid across the metal chair seat they were using between the bunks as a table.

The card landed near Doc sitting cross-legged on his bunk in his socks.

"Pardon," Gabrielle said, brushing Doc's leg as she retrieved her card.

Captain Levin felt a warm rush tingle his groin. But Bacsi licked Doc's face, which made Gabrielle laugh, breaking the spell. The photograph of Doc's wife hung between them on the rough redwood beam.

*   *   *

Surrounded by the large cardboard boxes of brassieres, Goodby sat in the Chaplain's Tent and wrote thank-you letters to the Atlanta Council. Goodby loved writing because it allowed him to make his readers feel needed. He knew that they wanted to hear how they were "good Christians helping the war effort." He knew he was writing white lies but justified his petty falsehoods as little parables to show each pastor "how eagerly the primitive tribeswomen took the brassieres" and "immediately donned the prized garments"—"which quickly became a badge of honor and virtue and among these pious women," "who no longer had to endure the terrible embarrassment of uncovered breasts." Goodby always ended each letter with the hopeful flourish—*"perhaps we may even look forward to some native baptisms."*

In the late afternoon, Goodby gathered up all the letters and walked them over to the S-1 mailroom tent.

Goodby stepped out in the hot sun, shook himself, set his jaw, and resolved to get the brassieres to the Montagnards—even if he had to take one box at a time. The thought of giving brasseries to village women filled Goodby with such inspiration that his step lightened as he passed two soldiers in worn fatigues huddled under a tent flap smoking a hand-rolled cigarette.

"Good afternoon, troopers!" Chaplain Goodby said.

"And a good good afternoon it is too, good Chaplain, sir," a soldier said, inhaling. "Good luck."

"Thank you, troopers," Goodby declared. "You do realize that the work of the good Lord doesn't need luck."

"Oh yeah."

"Of course, Chaplain. We know the Big Guy is way way beyond luck. We just wanted to offer him a little more."

They laughed, and the Chaplain joined in.

*   *   *

That evening before guard duty, Lester J. Ellis sat in the doorway of his bunker relaxing in a beach chair that he built out of artillery-crates. He drank beer and counted a rainbow wad of Military Payment Certificates. A fatty reefer burned on the rim of a cut-off Budweiser can wedged in the sandbags.

A generator started up.

Behind Ellis in the dimness, blue bulbs glowed on his shriveled Christmas tree with brass shells on all the dead prickly branches between dusty aluminum-foil stars and balls. Ellis decorated it the previous Christmas after trading pot to a helicopter pilot who brought in the little pine trees from Dalat.

Ellis carefully stacked his pot money, slipped on a rubber band, and went into his bunker. He reached under the fine, upward-pointing titties of Miss September 1967, and removed an empty sandbag from a crevice. Ellis squeezed his wad of money back into the bag and dreamed of the Cadillac he would buy back in his World, South Side of Chicago. Ellis imagined climbing into his white Cadillac convertible with the white leather interior like the salesman at the Pleiku convoy point had shown him in his big shiny book. Ellis slipped the sandbag back under Miss September.

"Get back Cadillac!" Ellis yelled, putting on his combat gear and heading out.

Outside of the bunker, Ellis grinned at the setting sun and nearly tripped over a gray dog.

"Man, you a number ten worthless old hound," Ellis told the dog, whom he sometimes fed. "You ain't done nothing about my rats. That's your job, dog, your canine M-O-S, rat catcher. You better get with the motherfucking program, hound, or else you miss out on your promotion. You got to get you some rat body count. This is war, dog, Viet-nam, hound! Get them rats 'fore they get you, or me!"

*   *   *

The bloody sun descended into the west and the Daktoum night was cool and dark and uneventful.

Ellis got loaded and pulled guard. Colonel Lehr did sit-ups and wrote his daughter. Gabrielle smoked her thirtieth cigarette and then slept fitfully in Doc's office, while Doc—still elated from the game of Hearts—lay awake in his narrow bunk in the officer's hootch. Ranklin dreamt of his wife, who had Tu's face. The Chaplain sipped cold Pepsi from his small refrigerator and wrote long letters to his wife and parents and grandparents. Roadkill got up in the middle of the night with Ho Chi Minh's Revenge from the pork noodles he had eaten in Nhu Canh Du. Nimmer dreamed of naked girls, Clancy of the Kid, Loudermilk of making Sergeant-Major of the Army, Donnelly of getting on the Silver Bird and telling war stories to his partners in Southie, and Sergeant-Major Bricker of his strong handsome wife and her fondness for hiking and making love in the outdoors.

Out on the bunker line, sleepy guards tried to stay awake, conjuring up family and siblings and wild times and old 1932 hot rods and new Firebirds and GTOs and movies and books and Japanese cameras and stereos and baseball and football and milkshakes and hamburgers and steaks. They spoke of anything but Vietnam and tenderly of the soft flesh and silky hair and beautiful touch and sweet whispering voices of the women who they thought could save them.

Overhead, the stars were hidden, and the sound of the unseen river was almost soothing. Artillery rocketed out so softly that even the distant bombing in Cambodia and Laos rolled in like gentle thunder.

Mist rose out of the deep valleys around Rocket Ridge and covered the camp at Daktoum.

*   *   *

At dawn, Colonel Lehr sat sipping coffee on the wooden steps of his sleeping bunker in view of his nearby latrine, which had been built for an infantry general.

Gabrielle pushed open the creaking latrine door, stepped outside, and washed her hands at a water can on a little wooden stand, before she turned and saw Lehr.

"Good morning, Colonel," she said.

"Good morning, Dr. Marchand," Lehr said, standing up and running a hand through his short silver hair.

"Beautiful, no?"

Under the dim sunlight, the colonel's skin looked pale.

"Monsoon's late," he said. "Maybe we'll luck out."

"Maybe," Gabrielle said flatly, running her fingers through her tangled hair.

"How are your quarters?" Lehr said.

"Out-standing," she said.

Lehr looked into her eyes.

"I feel good, living underground like a mole," she said pleasantly. "The doctor and I play the cards at night and speak of the little things."

She separated her dark hair into three thick masses.

"I despise games," Lehr said. "Except poker and chess."

"And war," Gabrielle said, braiding her hair.

They stood face to face under the soft gray light. The colonel reached for Gabrielle but changed his mind mid-gesture and crossed his arms.

"How long will you be with us?" he asked.

"Until the end of monsoon, or ..."

"Or what?"

"You tell me, Colonel," she said.

Gabrielle finished the braiding and tossed her hair over her shoulder. She flashed a smile and impulsively walked towards the medical bunker.

Lehr shook his head and threw his cold coffee onto the red earth. Then he stepped beneath the ugly entrance beams and went down the stairs.

As soon as Lehr was underground, his chest tightened and fluttered. Gasping, he struggled to his bed and collapsed. Pain cramped him into a ball.

Lehr inhaled with long, slow, deep breaths, and after five minutes, his body relaxed, and the pain ceased.

Lehr got up, straightened his uniform, and headed upstairs to the mess hall.

*   *   *

That night on the Daktoum bunker line, a dense mist muffled conversations and made the soldiers' fingers itch at their now-cool metal triggers.

"New moon," Roadkill said to Slinger as they sat atop the Duster. "Bad motherfucking luck. Like eating apricots before an op or someone bumming out a good buzz."

Down the bunker line, a soldier coughed and hacked until someone yelled.

"Play some music," Roadkill told Slinger. "Take the edge off. Just keep it down so the O-G don't bust us."

Slinger snapped a cartridge into a tape player, and the wild electric organ of The Doors floated across the dark night,

… lost in a ro-mance, a wil-der-ness of pain, and all the child-ren are in-sane…

"Dig it," Roadkill said. "If we only we had some weed."

"What about that spade cat, Ellis?"

"You ain't back here yet?"

Slinger jumped down and ran his fingers along the Duster tank, tracing the warmth and streaking three dusty lines across the warm metal. He grabbed his rifle and walked along the perimeter to find Ellis.

Behind him, The Doors' organ trilled to a crescendo. As Slinger walked, the long riff faded into the rushing river.

*   *   *

When Slinger found Ellis' guard bunker, it was midnight.

"He's gone, man," a small soldier with a large mustache called down from the tower. "Making his rounds, be back tee-tee time. Pull yourself up a sandbag."

"Well, then," Slinger said easily. "Fuck me, man."

Slinger climbed up the wooden ladder.

On top, inside the low wall of sandbags, Slinger took off his helmet, lay back in his open flak vest, and stared at the black night where a few stars peeked through the drifting mist.

"When I was little, every summer I stared at the stars for hours," the guard said. "Down the Jersey shore, at my Jadek's place, me and my cousins laid on the hot grass, our glass jars glowing with fireflies, looking for shooting stars, and listening to the ocean roar until we fell asleep."

Stars drifted by, and the river whispered like the sea as Slinger dozed off, dreaming of his life.

*   *   *

With a high-pitched cry, the camp monkey finally broke out of his cage on the TOC, scampered down the sandbags, and raced along the Daktoum camp street.

The monkey ran to the mess hall and tilted the wooden lid off a stinking 55-gallon drum, which thumped on the ground.

The sleeping Vietnamese KP's moaned but did not wake. The monkey reached his long arm into the drum and fished out two blackened bananas and an apple. Then he climbed up the mess tent and sat on the broad sagging canvas top, eating the soft fruit.

Doc and Lehr both masturbated that night—each with a pang of embarrassment and guilt because Gabrielle, who they fantasized—might have been there—had either of them asked. Or so they thought. Doc dreamed of his wife bearing his child as he walked naked through the jungle with Gabrielle. Lehr's Gabrielle was mixed with the faces of his ex-wife and his daughter combined, three visions, three bodies drifting into one that melted together in Lehr's sweaty, troubled sleep.

*   *   *

In Saigon, on Tu Do Street, Ben and Halliday sat on stools beside Vietnamese bar girls. Halliday's was perfect—tall and friendly with a flashing smile, fine breasts, long legs, honey-colored skin, and long, shiny, black hair. Halliday sipped his weak drink and smiled at Ben's sardonic grin.

"Man, I don't know," Ben said. "What if she's really some demon V-C Saigon ride? Ain't no way to tell."

Halliday frowned. The girl clutched his leg under the table and leaned close, her long hair falling across his arms as her scent overcame him. When she whispered in his ear, Halliday's spine tingled.

"I go work now," she said, slipping a napkin into his hand. "You come this place go upstairs drugstore, we be there, titi time, you go now, bring friend, too, OK, G.I.?"

Halliday and Ben freshened their drinks under the table from a pint of Chivas. Drinks were expensive—two dollars—for terrible Japanese whiskey.

Later, they walked through jostling Tu Do Street, high, but not drunk. Beneath a red neon sign flashing *Texas Playboy Bar*, a Military policeman and a Saigon cop had blocked a Jeep. Scooters and bicycles and army trucks sped by in the hot blaring night.

"What the hell?" Ben said, looking closer. "That's Jonesy!"

The M-P held a nightstick over Jonesy.

"I'm a courier—yeah, V-I-P flight," Jonesy yelled. "On Priority for my C-O. You know, the real war!"

By the time Ben and Halliday ran over, the M-P was unbuttoning his pistol.

"Move on," the M-P said.

"Excuse me, Sergeant," Ben said. "He's in our unit."

"Well, I'm hauling him in for drunk."

Jonesy dug into a leather dispatch case and produced sweat-stained papers. When the M-P grabbed them, Jonesy scowled and lunged, but Ben held him.

"He's our battalion courier," Ben said to the M-P. "Daktoum, Two Corps."

"I can read," the M-P retorted. "He's also pisspot drunk."

"Maybe give him a break," Ben said. "We ain't from Saigon. We'll drive his Jeep. We don't get down here much."

Anger tightened the M-P's tanned face. He grimaced and then stepped back formally.

"Orders say VIP escort to Tan Son Nhut 0300 hours."

"We'll have him there," Ben said. "My word."

Jonesy glared at the M-P.

"Just get his fucking Jeep off my street," the MP told Ben, scribbling on a card. "Here's the freqs for his escort."

"Thank you, Sergeant," Ben said. "You won't regret it."

"Better fucking not. I never want to see this asshole again."

The M-P Jeep screeched into the red neon night reflecting off chrome Honda motorcycles and dull-olive military trucks cruising the narrow streets below five-story buildings under the foul air that haunted Saigon day and night.

Ben jerked the Jeep into gear, and Jonesy and Halliday bobbed like punching dummies. They cruised Tu Do until Ben found a walled compound with a blue tin "Hotel" sign. They drove through the gate past an old man sitting in a guard booth with a M-1 carbine.

In the room, Halliday's fear of losing his legs became so strong that he and Jonesy kept drinking until they passed out. Ben roused them at two AM.

By four AM, they were strapped in the back of a C-124, the only passengers, bound for Daktoum.

*   *   *

Ellis woke up sweating in a strange bunk in some brother's tent. Passed out, again. Shit, almost dawn, better get back. Never like to lay my head nowhere but home.

Ellis stood up, and a plastic LAW cartridge clattered against his M-16. Mosquito nets shadowed the young soldiers, sleeping under nets like cocoons in a science fiction movie. In one corner of the six-man tent, a weak incandescent bulb burned, and Ellis moved toward it.

Outside, he tripped on a tent rope.

"Motherfucker!" he hissed.

Ellis stared into darkness, remembering where he was.

A billow of fire lit up the river as a bunker exploded in a roil of smoke, debris, and dirt.

"Motherfucking dinks," Ellis muttered, already running past the rows of tents.

Sleepy young soldiers dragged rifles and flak jackets out into the darkness, bumping each other in dim light from the burning bunker and popping flares. A torrent of red tracer bullets ricocheted across the camp.

Another explosion.

Now even naked soldiers careened out of dusty tents with rifles and a few shots rang out past the fiery bunker.

Then the whole perimeter line lit up, and flames silhouetted the looming TOC bunker.

A hundred weapons shot into the hills beyond the burning bunkers. M-16s zinged, M-60s chattered, fifty-caliber machine guns pumped out rounds, mortars thumped and crashed, and 40-millimeter pom-pom guns pounded.

"HOT DAMN!" Ellis shouted on the run.

*   *   *

"Far fucking out," Halliday said ten thousand feet above Vietnam looking through the transport window at a billowing fireball exploding in the black jungle below.

"Napalm," Ben said.

*   *   *

Slinger never knew what hit him.

His body blew into the merged myriad fragments of flesh and uniforms and weapons and flak vests that used to be four American soldiers.

*   *   *

Ellis saw the silhouetted pieces of soldiers spew up from the fireball, followed by a clatter of metal and wood debris.

Bullets and shells and mortars and flares and grenades careened all around the firebase in a hard smoky rain.

Another explosive roar, another slow-motion fireball.

Ellis ducked behind a sandbag wall just as a thick shower of timber and tin and canvas tumbled out.

Then a naked, black-streaked sapper flew by so fast that Ellis thought it was a ghost, and then he ran after it.

        *   *   *

Soldiers screamed and crashed into each other as tracers crisscrossed the camp.

Across from the TOC, Halliday's old sleeping hootch roared into flame and broke apart like a cherry-bombed dollhouse, just as groggy Lehr, radio in hand, stepped from the shadows of his sleeping bunker to find Daktoum burning.

        *   *   *

"I'll get you, motherfucker," Ellis hissed, firing a burst at the fleeing sapper.

The small N-V-A soldier stumbled and screamed in pain when a bullet hit his calf. Ellis fired again, but the man limped away and disappeared between the row of tents.

        *   *   *

Daktoum lay smoking under a half-dozen rocking flares. Artillery and machine gun fire pounded the hills, soldiers huddled underground in foxholes and sandbagged doorways and in shallow bunkers, suspicious of anything that moved.

The monkey screamed.

Hugging sandbagged hootches, Lehr ran toward the last explosion. The colonel's adrenalin and sense memory pounded him back to Korea, when his company had prowled for days, rooting out snipers.

A grease-smeared sapper flashed toward the mess hall.

The colonel took a shot and missed.

A soldier smacked into Lehr.

"Watch out, motherfucker," Ellis cursed.

"He's in the mess hall."

"I'll get that asshole dink," Ellis hissed.

M-16 fire zinged overhead.

Lehr craned to see. Smoke billowed, and they coughed.

Ellis dropped to his knee and armed a LAW rocket.

"Teach that little bastard," someone said.

Lehr turned just as Ellis' LAW rocket roared a long rope of fire lashing into a brilliant yellow stream, which exploded with a red-orange burst.

The mess tent deflated like a shredded balloon. Flaming canvas fell everywhere in foul, black puffs.

"Why the hell'd you do that?" Lehr yelled at Ellis.

"Who the hell are you, telling me shit?" Ellis yelled.

"Colonel Lehr," the commander barked.

"Shit," Ellis muttered.

The fallen mess-hall canvas rustled. Lehr's radio crackled as a thin gray line lit the eastern horizon.

"Hold fire," Lehr told the soldiers running up. "Hold fire!"

Lehr's order passed from soldier to soldier until the shooting died away until the only sounds were the roar of burning hootches and the chattering monkey.

"Mountain Range to Hill Station, any incoming?" Lehr asked on the radio. "Over."

"Negative," Ranklin answered in the TOC. "Two K-I-A Victor-Charlies, over."

"Another trapped in the mess hall, request an interpreter, over," Lehr answered.

"Will do, Mountain Range, over."

"I want that prisoner, over."

"Shee-it, *prisoner*." Ellis muttered. "Not likely after I fry his ass again."

Lehr scowled at Ellis.

"You want I should light up that mess hall, Colonel?"

"No, goddamnit," Lehr said. "I want that prisoner."

Fires burned and the rustling continued under the collapsed mess hall.

As they waited, small-arms fire chattered from the bunker line along Highway 14.

*   *   *

Three breathless soldiers smelling of hot metal dragged Lam through the darkness. They ducked behind a sandbagged wall and thrust the young woman at Colonel Lehr.

"Medics dispensary girl, sir."

"You speak English?" Lehr asked.

"Yes, G.I.," Lam said.

"V-C in there," Lehr said. "Tell him to surrender, Chieu Hoi—or else we'll shoot him."

Lam nodded. When her clear sweet voice rang out with Lehr's message, the soldiers shifted uneasily.

"Fuck you, G.I.!" came back, followed by a bitter torrent of Vietnamese.

M-16 fire ripped into the mess hall.

"Goddamnit," Lehr yelled. "CEASE FIRE!"

"He call me 'tool of invaders'," Lam translated. "Curse me, curse you Vietnamese."

"Tell him again," Lehr said. "Say he that doesn't need to die, he can see his family again."

Lam's sweet voice sang out.

Another tortured curse came back, ending in a scream.

Lehr cursed and yelled, "Fire!"

The soldiers blasted the ruins of the mess tent until explosions rocked the tent.

"Hold fire!" Lehr commanded.

"Aww Jesus Christ Almighty," said the mess sergeant. "Look what you done to my poor mess hall."

The mess sergeant with the lined face and crooked grin crawled on his hands and knees behind a sandbagged wall.

"Hope you-all like C-rations."

Lam called to the sapper, but there was no answer.

The smoking black heap of crumpled canvas was quiet, so the soldiers waited.

The sky slowly brightened into soft pink streaks until Rocket Ridge loomed under a smoky mist.

Thirty soldiers surrounded the collapsed mess hall. On Lehr's orders, they slowly advanced with fixed bayonets, tightening the cordon, and cautiously kicking lumps beneath the rumpled canvas.

When the monkey screamed from the TOC, M-16 fire raked into it, puffs of dust spraying from the old sandbags.

The soldiers carefully turned over canvas, poking at heaps and stepping over wood and rusty screen. Pots and pans and chunks of counters and tables and chair legs were kicked away. A shredded green oilcloth shone with the glitter of forks and knives surrounded by pools of chili and yellow peaches and catsup.

Finally, the soldiers found a fierce boy—maybe sixteen, in undershorts, clinging to a pan of peeled potatoes bloodied by his calf wound.

The hulking young Americans in heavy green battle gear stood above the thin grimacing Vietnamese boy writhing in his underwear, his grease-blackened body matted with red dust.

A stretcher was called for and quickly appeared.

Lam walked alongside the two large G.I.s carrying the boy.

"You were in my dream," the boy said in Vietnamese, half-dazed. "Your brother was with us last night."

His words struck deep. Lam's brother could be fighting for either side. But she didn't know the sapper, and he had never seen her. The G.I. stretcher-bearers ignored Lam, who told the boy to be quiet and rest.

Nearing the medical bunker, Lam spotted a thin body twisted on the barbed wire, her breath stuck in her throat—she knew it was her brother.

In the harsh sunlight, his stiff outstretched arms and hands gripped barbed wire, and his head hung down onto his thin chest, his legs and feet crossed at the ankles in a perfect last posture.

Lam abandoned the stretcher and bolted toward the body with her heart pounding.

Waiting for the stretcher, Clancy saw Lam run and immediately went after her. As Lam came close to the perimeter wire, the corpse's gaping wounds, and frozen face made her shake violently. It wasn't her brother.

"Where the hell you going, girl?" Clancy yelled, running up. "These G.I.s are blood crazy. You're Vietnamese—they'd shoot you in a minute."

As Lam walked beside Clancy to the medical bunker, she thought, I must leave Vietnam.

*   *   *

A helicopter circled the smoking Daktoum firebase.

Rosy light bathed the faces of Halliday, Ben, and Jonesy.

"Mess hall," Ben said. "And bunker one-four."

"Sappers," Jonesy said.

"Shit. They got my fucking hootch," Halliday said.

"Halliday, you would have been a dead man."

"Right," Halliday said, his voice wavering as the chopper banked over. "Never happen, G.I."

*   *   *

That night, a black King Cobra snake slid under the Daktoum perimeter wire and slowly wound its way across the red earth and into an abandoned bunker. The big snake immediately cornered a large rat, ate it whole, and then it coiled up in a corner. As the lump of the rat slowly made its way down the snake's long spine, the King Cobra fell asleep.

15.

A week later, Gabrielle sat near the medical bunker entrance smoking, while roaring green helicopters ferried boyish South Vietnamese troops in new uniforms to a raging battle. The hills resounded with artillery.

Clancy poked his head from the entrance tunnel.

"Fever's breaking," Clancy said.

Gabrielle stubbed out her cigarette, ran her hands through her hair, and walked downstairs, wondering how long it had been since she'd bathed. The smell of beans and spaghetti wafted up the stairs, overcoming the pervasive smell of alcohol.

Donnelly, Cullen, Nimmer, and Limerick squatted around burning plastic explosives, heating cans of C-rations. Gabrielle walked between the stretchers and went into the tiny wardroom, across the bunker from Doc's office.

She leaned over the bottom bunk and replaced a cool cloth on Halliday's sweaty forehead, which made him murmur.

*　　　　　*　　　　　*

In a fever dream, Halliday sat with two hundred teenagers in an airliner shaped like a giant silver penis. Three John Wayne movies flickered on large screens and every soldier held giant baby rattles and M-16s that took potshots at the screens. All the cabin rugs and side panels were red-and-white striped, while the dark-blue ceiling sparkled with stars. Between the portal windows were portraits of George Washington, Teddy Roosevelt, George Patton, William Tecumseh Sherman, George Custer, and Audie Murphy. Each stewardess was a past Playmate of the Month dressed in camouflage corsets, black stockings, and high heels, and they carried trays of cheeseburgers, French fries, apple pie, and ice cream, which dripped down their long sleek thighs.

The Playmates sauntered down the aisle, tittering and coyly shielding their pubis while grinning soldiers licked melted ice cream off their flanks.

Halliday unbuckled his chrome rodeo-seat buckle and strolled to the front, where grinning Joe DiMaggio, in his Yankee uniform, held hands with giggling Marilyn Monroe, whose pleated white skirt billowed up, flashing her legs and white panties. The famous couple streamed soft drinks directly into soldier's mouths from golden machine-gun nozzles. Halliday sucked at Marilyn's dispenser, while on the screens, three movie John Waynes simultaneously cinema-assaulted Pork Chop Hill, Iwo Jima, and Normandy.

Gorged on Coke, Halliday followed Miss February 1968's swaying buttocks as she merrily wriggled away from the groping soldiers' hands.

An immense explosion blew off the plane's tail section.

A long, bloody vortex of body parts and entrails poured into the rushing night, where bandaged young soldiers clung hand-to-hand, while their amputated limbs whirled away in the plane's wake.

Shattered plastic Statues of Liberty, shredded toy flags, broken plastic guns, and twisted model-plane fragments rattled in the howling tailwind.

Specters of the recently-dead spiraled through the blowback—led by John Wayne in buckskins and a tricorn campaign hat, blowing smoke off a huge six-gun in his right hand while firing a machine gun with his left.

Half of Duke's face was rotted away like a corpse—flaky moldering skin and white hair clung to his smashed, desiccated skull. The Duke's good side was freshly made up and camera-ready, his eyes done, lips shining, tanned skin flawlessly brushed and dusted with expensive powder. As Duke Wayne sailed along spearheading the howling vortex of specters, phantom limbs, and battle debris, a wailing scream escaped his half-rotted throat: *Whoopi—Tee-Yi-Yo, get along little doggies, it's your misfortune and none of my own!*

*   *   *

After lunch, Gabrielle watched the thick, gray mist creep across the hills in sinuous blankets until it covered Daktoum valley and seeped into every tent and bunker, chilling the young soldiers and their officers.

The air became so laden with moisture that it was hard for Gabrielle to breathe, and it soon turned into a sad rain, with none of the grace of a spring shower in France. She shivered, suddenly nostalgic for the heat that everyone had so recently cursed.

Wind blew in from northern Laos, down from the ten-thousand-foot mountain, Fransipan, near the French hill capital of Sapa on the Chinese border, where Gabrielle had vacationed with her father as a girl, taking refuge from the sweltering Hanoi summers.

Gabrielle poked at the bulging army poncho above her, and water splashed onto the ground.

Now the enemy will come, she thought, remembering her father the colonel, eternally dissecting the French disasters at Mang Yang and Dien Bien Phu. Under the rain and mist, she thought, helicopters won't fly, planes can't see to bomb Rocket Ridge, and even the camp mortars would have to be careful when they fire—afraid of detonating on the mist and showering their own troops with friendly fire.

*   *   *

For days it seemed, Gabrielle sat chain-smoking beneath the plastic rain flap strung from the squat tower above the medical bunker entrance. She had to get away from the clammy, unwashed stink of young males. Her boots were covered in red mud, her ears haunted by the funereal rock and roll and the bittersweet country music that the medics played all day long until Clancy made them shut it off.

At night, the young soldiers twisted in dank, unwashed sheets and in sleeping bags that never dried out. They spent long days in damp fatigues, enveloped in their own swampy teenage odors, soured by cigarettes, twenty-year-old canned food, instant coffee, and stale beer. Gabrielle's orange water barely covered her own dense scent.

The waiting became so powerful that Gabrielle could think of nothing else.

Water dripped everywhere, even into the numerous fighting holes on the huge American base, and many soldiers feared that Daktoum might prove impossible to defend.

Low spots turned into shallow pools rimmed with red clay. Rain drenched the once-dusty paths that ran through the poorly drained camp, and rotting sandbags took on so much weight that they continually broke, so the sound of dirt plopping into the mud in a ghostly randomness haunted the soldiers almost as much as the constant drizzle.

Gabrielle wondered if only the cold made the soldiers shiver. Or was it a deep collective fear that threatened the camp like a ball of cobras coiled in a tree.

Gabrielle dragged her cigarette.

She absently checked the web belt at her waist, sensing how thin she had grown eating the awful C-rations. The belt buckle felt cold, and she remembered how just last month, all the metal—the trucks, the guns, the shells, and her keys—had burned her fingers.

Halliday emerged from underground with an olive-green towel around his neck and crossed an immense puddle on shifting wooden pallets thrown into the mud.

A Jeep splashed by Halliday and stopped at the medical bunker's back entrance.

Major Ranklin jumped out and hustled around to take the arm of a very pregnant Vietnamese girl. They ran down the back stairs.

*   *   *

Inside the TOC, a hopeful Lehr ripped open a blue airmail envelope. But Christina had written another garbled, incoherent rant about the war, this time typed instead of written, which ended "it is an individual's duty to accept responsibility for every heinous act of her government."

All day long, Colonel Lehr monitored Daktoum Net, the Seven Sisters' radio, and the Vietnamese infantry hill battles raging to the west, in teletype reports that Loudermilk brought in on long manila rolls. Major Sneller picked at his teeth and monitored the mine sweep team, which had been ambushed three times today, trying to keep the road open to Ban Sai.

Worst case for Daktoum? Lehr thought.

No re-supply, intense rocket, and artillery fire. No air ops because of low ceilings, the Vietnamese infantry support bogged down at Hill 670—nasty goddamn fiasco. The road falls, no choppers. Food reserves? 25 days, plenty of C's, Ammo? Maybe ten days—get Ranklin on that. Water? Purification unit vulnerable on the river. Solution? No, wait, we've got five hundred cases of beer and soda that Halliday ordered by mistake. Combat mistake. Halliday. Abandoned, by our own command? Well, at least, it's begun. Hope we can hold this goddamn place.

Merton entered the colonel's office carrying a blue "Top Secret" paper cover. The fleshy enlisted man's face was redder than usual as he stole glances at Lehr while he read:

MSG 067 13 May 1969

    TO: COMDAKTOUM

    FROM: COMUSARV

    NO INCOMING NO OUTGOING US MAIL UNTIL FURTHER NOTICE   STOP

What? Lehr thought, no mail? Whose idea is this?

*   *   *

Halliday plodded through the mud to a sandbagged wooden shack beside the officers' hootch and opened the door to a shower, where a bent nozzle shot scalding streams of water from 55-gallon drums on the roof.

Overhead, the flaming gas heater roared, so Halliday stripped, got wet, and soaped up.

A muffled thump echoed, like the single beat of a drum.

Seconds later, an inconceivably loud, horribly contorted sound fell out of the sky like a train hitting the earth.

An earsplitting 122mm rocket slammed into a nearby hootch and whipped Halliday into pure animal fear.

Naked, all soaped up, Halliday flew out of the shower. Another distant drumbeat, another horrible roar dropped him flat—bare-assed, face down in the red mud.

A huge explosion rocked the camp.

Half-crawling, fear choking his throat, Halliday slid across the mud and crawled into a foxhole.

Halliday crouched in the muddy hole with his knees clutched to his chest, cold water up to his ass.

Dull thumps echoed off the hills and with each terrible explosion, fear pounded him.

The horrible rip of rockets kept slamming and screaming at Halliday's ears, tearing at his arms, his mind, his soul, his body that just wanted to run.

"Oh God, oh God, please save me, God, please!"

Another rapid salvo came in so close that it felt like knives stabbing his eardrums.

A violent wrenching of metal careened overhead.

Smashed wood and clods of mud and debris spattered into his hole, shredded canvas snowed the drizzly air, and the harsh stench of cordite bit his face.

Halliday wanted to run. But something—army training, shame, a rational flash—curled him tighter into a naked muddy ball, panting and shaking uncontrollably, his humanity reduced to sheer animal terror.

A ghostly image—gunfighter John Wayne—cracked into Halliday's febrile brain. The phantom image vanished under the next crash of rockets, which seemed to be moving away.

After what seemed to be hours, Daktoum firebase lay deathly still.

This unearthly silence caused Halliday's desperation to subside, leaving only a manageable general fear and a deep embarrassment of crying out for God. He should be at the medical bunker, he was the ambulance driver, he was alive, and he hadn't really panicked, so he wasn't a complete coward.

Halliday uncoiled and slowly stood up in the muddy hole. The weak siren atop the TOC whined the All Clear, so Halliday hoisted himself out and headed for his clothes.

He couldn't find the shower, panicked, and collapsed into a crouch, gripping his naked muddy genitals.

Somewhere, the monkey chattered.

Halliday came back.

The shower and his fatigues were gone, blown into olive-colored smithereens strewn all around in the red mud, bits of torn metal and splintered wood flecked with soap and muddy scraps of leather, his combat boots, he guessed.

Halliday scraped off whatever mud he could, but the red clay was hardening. Humiliated and vulnerable, naked, and muddy, Halliday scuttled around the huge puddle near the medical bunker.

He hugged the sandbagged walls heading toward the Waiting Room bunker, where Halliday had moved after becoming ambulance driver.

Scuttling down the stairs, Halliday ran into Donnelly, wearing a flak vest and steel pot, which made the small soldier resemble an olive-colored mushroom wearing blue sunglasses.

"What the fuck happened? Mud wrestling, cowboy?"

"Fuck you, Donnelly," Halliday said.

Halliday stepped into the clammy bunker, embarrassed at Donnelly seeing him naked and muddy. Halliday took clean fatigues out of his footlocker and pulled them on over the mud. He found socks, quickly laced his spare boots around his ankles, slipped on his battle gear and grabbed his weapon.

Halliday ran up the wooden steps out into the drizzle and quickly stepped down the rear medical bunker staircase.

Inside the big, low-ceilinged room, muffled cries of young soldiers rose from the stretchers, where medics tended the bloody wounded. Ranklin's pregnant girlfriend stood against the back wall.

A meaty black hand grabbed Halliday.

"Where you been?' Clancy demanded. "Hiding with that chickenshit Donnelly?"

"I got pinned down."

"*Pinned down,* my ass—plenty of time to get back after them first rounds. Get your shit together, young trooper, you're the ambulance driver—wounded all over this firebase and you jerking off in some hole …"

"The shit was hitting all around."

"Bull crap, trooper."

"Fuck you, Clancy," Halliday muttered.

"What you say, troop?"

"Nothing."

"Get busy tagging these wounded. Your weapon clear?

"What?"

"Did you clear your goddamn weapon? Let me see it."

Clancy grabbed for his M-14. Halliday jerked it back.

"It's not cleared," Halliday said.

"Get your ass upstairs and clear it," Clancy said, turning back to the busy room. "All I need is another goddamn green-assed trooper discharging a weapon in my bunker, bad enough Nimmer shoots a hole in Doc's wife's picture. What the hell's on your face, trooper?"

"Jesus," Halliday breathed, slipping up the muddy steps.

Halliday nearly collided with Ben and Cullen angling down a stretcher with a big blond soldier, whose childish face had a yellow pallor as he floated down the dark stairs past Halliday.

Outside, Halliday pointed his M-14 at the hills and pulled the trigger. A round zinged up over Rocket Ridge. Shit. Halliday flipped on the safety, ran downstairs, and threw his rifle and gear behind the front desk.

"Halliday, get some wounded tags," Clancy yelled. "Follow Doc."

Halliday grabbed a stack of tags by their copper wires and rushed to Doc, making his rounds through the low room. Doc caught Halliday's elbow and kept him from ripping out a plastic tube dangling from a glass IV bottle.

"Slow down," Doc said.

Doc looks younger, Halliday thought, younger? Doesn't make any sense. War was supposed to make you older, weird fucking war, no nurses, no Hitler, no Mussolini, no Tojo, never see the goddamned enemy...

"Write just what I say," Doc told Halliday, calmly guiding his shoulder.

Halliday readied his pen.

"Traumatic amputation of right toe ..."

"He got his toe shot off?"

"Sshh, Halliday," Doc whispered. "He doesn't know."

"Know what?" Halliday whispered back.

"Be quiet," Doc whispered.

Doc took Halliday aside.

"He still thinks he has a toe," Doc said. "It's called a Phantom Limb —the nerve endings are all there, so the brain registers that it has a toe."

"When will he find out, Doc?"

"In the hospital. Later."

Clancy hustled over.

"That trooper knows god-damn well he ain't got no god-damned toe, Doc," Clancy said to the wounded man, who turned away, "Because he shot it off himself."

"Clancy, you don't know that," Doc said, frowning.

"I seen this before, in Korea—man's a chickenshit."

The patient grimaced.

Doc opened his mouth, but Clancy set his lips and strode away, moving from stretcher to stretcher, helping the medics. Halliday trailed Doc and wrote down his words on casualty tags, trying not to think about the phantom limb.

"Gunshot wound right buttock. Condition stable, IV administered 1610 hours, blood pressure 120 over ..."

"Wound, shrapnel, upper anterior right thigh, massive lacerations..."

What if your whole body was blown up? Does your mind think everything's there?

"Halliday, pay attention," Doc whispered. "Superficial shrapnel wound, chest lacerations, possible concussion, pulse 65, blood ..."

"Traumatic amputation of left hand caused by massive shrapnel wound. Ringers lactate I-V and one-quarter grain morphine administered 1600 hours."

What a weird job, Halliday thought. Must be a lot of phantom limbs in Daktoum. Maybe even a whole goddamn phantom village, full of phantom limbs, maybe even John Wayne, like in my hole when I was getting rocketed. How can the Duke be a phantom? He's not even dead.

"OK, Halliday, that's it," Doc said.

Halliday followed Doc onto the broad entrance landing, where he surveyed the room.

A dozen onlookers haunted the darkened corners of the big bunker —Ranklin and his girlfriend, Lam, sergeants, officers, friends of the wounded—pressed up against the rough board walls out of the way, their faces hard and empty and sad.

"Call Dust-off," Doc told Halliday. "Get the wounded to the landing pad."

"Roger, Doc."

Clancy hustled over.

"We need clean stretchers," Clancy said.

"How could we be running out?" Doc asked.

"Get 'em, Halliday," Clancy said. "More I-Vs too, splints, pressure dressings big 'n little, morphine, body bags."

"We can't be out of body bags," Doc said.

"We will be," the sweating black sergeant said. "Once Charlie starts this shit, he don't back off. It ain't like he believes in God or anything, Doc."

Doc stared at Clancy with exhausted eyes, shook his head, and walked to Gabrielle, working on a blond soldier with a sucking chest wound.

The large teenager gave out a short little sigh and expired.

Gabrielle bent over the corpse, checking the pulse.

There was nothing left, she decided, nothing—just a dead, pimpled, teenaged face, with dead eyes glazed in an awful and lifeless innocence, nothing profound. She closed the dull, pale-blue eyes with a practiced thumb and glanced up at Doc's shadowed face. He didn't react.

Turning away, Gabrielle stripped off her bloody gloves and threw them into a metal trashcan overflowing with torn fatigues, bloody human tissue, and soiled bandages.

*   *   *

"How long before Dust-off?" Clancy asked Halliday across the busy room.

"Ten minutes."

Clancy pointed at the dead soldier.

"Get this guy tagged and bagged and take him up with the wounded."

Halliday reached atop a low beam, peeled off a rubber bag, and carried it to the baby-faced dead soldier, whose corn-silk hair matched his wispy mustache.

The soldier's mud-stained fatigues were cut off in tatters all around his pale naked body. Halliday wrote: KIA, Cause of Death: chest wound on the tag. Killed In Action. Dead, Halliday decided, doesn't faze me as much as I thought, like Newcomb. Look at his face, there's nothing fucking in there. Nothing. Where the hell did he go?

Doc's dog, Bacsi, slipped under the stretcher, tail wagging, and Halliday eased him away with his boot. He stared at the dead ruddy face with the open mouth that the respirator had twisted into an odd smile. Like he tried to laugh off death, Halliday thought.

He grabbed the blood-smeared steel dog tags off the soldier's neck: Earl Jimmy Holt, US 68797676. Halliday wrote the service number on the cardboard tag and then twisted the copper wires around the dead man's wrist.

When Bacsi licked at a pool of blood on the floor, Halliday dragged the whining dog away into Doc's office.

Halliday tried to maneuver the dead man into the body bag, but he weighed a ton, and when he tried to pull the bag up from the ankles, the unwieldy body flopped the bag onto the floor. Donnelly laughed.

"Dust-off, five minutes out," Clancy yelled over from the radio. "Wrap it up! Get those wounded out to the strip! Halliday, what the hell are you doing?"

Ben handed off his stretcher to a line company soldier.

He came over and rolled the big dead man on his side, while Halliday slid the bag underneath. Ben opened the long flap, they rolled the body in, and then they folded the other flap over the dead man.

Halliday yanked up the heavy zipper, but it caught.

"Halliday," Ben laughed. "Don't cut off the man's nose."

Halliday tucked the nose in, zipped up the bag, and the big ruddy blond boy disappeared.

Clancy hustled over, grabbed the front stretcher pole, and with Halliday on back, joined the procession.

The tattered, bloody, wounded, decorated with smeared white bandages, swayed up the stairs, moaning and murmuring and mumbling through dazed lips.

Clancy and Halliday tugged the heavy body up the dark staircase.

Outside, under low clouds, a line of stretcher-bearers crossed the puddles on a trail of dirty wooden pallets.

The medics set down the stretchers near the airstrip.

A lone helicopter crossed a bloody patch of light in the gray sky and thumped in.

As soon as the whining Dust-off ship clattered in, the on-board medic jumped out.

Two wounded in muddy bandages lay in the open bay.

"No supplies," the medic yelled.

Under the cutting rotors, the medics loaded the wounded. Grimy lines in the chopper medic's face deepened as he scanned casualty tags and strapped down the new wounded.

The pilots anxiously searched the misty hills for flashes as Clancy and Halliday brought up the dead man.

"Never happen," the helicopter medic yelled over the roar, shaking his head. "We're way too heavy."

Clancy opened his mouth as the medic banged the co-pilot's window and held his thumb up.

The Dust-off medic hopped back onto the deck and scuttled around the wounded, checking for bleeding, and untwisting plastic tubes on fluid bottles as the rotors screamed and the blades blasted down grit. The helicopter clattered into the darkening sky, heading south to Pleiku.

Clancy yanked the dead man around.

A recoilless rifle round sang in overhead and cracked into the airstrip fifty yards away.

The medics scrambled for cover.

Halliday dropped his stretcher and dove beside a sandbagged wall. The dead man slid halfway off the stretcher onto the ground. Clancy's eyes narrowed.

Setting the stretcher down, the burly sergeant marched to Halliday, cowering beneath the revetment wall.

"What in hell you doing troop?"

"Fucking incoming, Clancy."

No more rounds came in.

Clancy stood, chest thrust out above Halliday, clinging to the sandbags.

"You *dropped* that man."

"He's *dead*, Clancy."

"He coulda been wounded."

"Then I wouldn't have dropped him!" Halliday said, still flat on the ground.

The medics slowly got up and watched the hills for recoilless flashes.

Ben came around the far side of the revetment and glared at Clancy. He rearranged the dead man, took the front poles of the stretcher, and told Halliday to grab the back.

"Give the man a goddamned shot," Ben told Clancy. "He ain't ever treated wounded before—or been under fire."

"*Shot…*" Clancy spat.

Nimmer, Limerick, Donnelly, and Cullen stood in a half circle watching Clancy, hands on hips, face to face with Ben.

"What in hell you troopers goggling at?" Clancy said, turning and marching to the bunker. "Like you ain't got nothing to do?"

The medics rolled their eyes, made faces, and flipped off Clancy behind his back as they re-crossed the gray bridge and the big muddy pools.

Ben and Halliday carried the body behind the medics.

Clancy stood in front of the morgue and glared at each medic, and then he followed them underground, blustering commands all down the long stairway. Halliday and Ben set down the dead man.

"Let's get him off," Ben told Halliday.

Lifting the bag by the rubber handles, they dragged the body into the sandbagged chamber.

Outside, Ben collapsed the bloodstained stretcher and tossed it on a stack under the rain flap.

"Ever since the Kid left, Clancy's had a case of the ass," Ben said. "Don't go dropping no wounded."

"I won't."

Halliday put a cigarette in his mouth, and Ben lit it.

"What the hell's on your face?"

Halliday touched his cheek.

"Oh. Mud. I was in the shower when …"

"You got caught bare-assed? Your first rocket attack?"

Halliday nodded, lowering his eyes.

"Shit, no wonder you freaked out."

"Fuck, I didn't freak out."

Ben lifted an eyebrow. They smoked silently as Clancy's voice echoed up the stairs.

Lam came up with a trashcan. Ben nodded to her, flipped his cigarette into the mud, and went underground.

When Halliday got up, Lam caught his arm.

"Hi," he said.

Lam dumped the trash in a fifty-five-gallon drum and set the metal can down.

"What on your face?" she said.

Halliday blushed.

"Mud," he said.

Lam put her hand to her mouth and smiled—for the first time since she had seen the body that looked like her brother.

"No good," she said.

"You've got that."

Halliday squeezed her shoulder and quickly kissed her. She pressed against him and laid her head on his chest.

"OK, G.I.?"

"I guess," he said, running his hands down her body.

"Halliday!" Clancy yelled from underground.

Halliday grinned at Lam and ran down the dark stairs.

*   *   *

Underground, Clancy theatrically blustered, directing the cleaning and restocking of dressings and I-V bottles. The medics were happy to be busy and not have to think about all the dead and the wounded. Ranklin and his pregnant girlfriend and all the buddies of the wounded and dead had departed. Lam swept the floor, and Cullen went to the front desk and snapped in his "special" tape cassette.

Music filled the room: *go to Wover-ton mountain, if you're look-in' for a wife, Clip-ton Clowers, has a pretty young daughter, he's might-y hand-y, with a gu-n-and-a-knife*

*   *   *

Gabrielle scrubbed her hands and arms with alcohol, walked into Doc's office, and sat on the bed. As Doc leafed through a medical book, she took off her baseball cap, ran her fingers through her black hair, and closed the canvas flap door.

*   *   *

Clancy, hefting supplies up into the rafters, shook his head when Doc's office flap closed. Halliday and Ben handed him cases of Ringers' Lactate.

"Halliday," Clancy ordered. "Get that body out."

Halliday nodded.

"That's your new job." Clancy said.

"What?" Halliday asked.

"You in charge of the dead."

*   *   *

"*What?*" Lester J. Ellis said to the red-faced Sergeant Major Bricker. "You making *me,* in charge of the *gooks?*"

"Yep," Bricker nodded, and blew his nose. "Make sure them Vietnamese stay in this bunker when they ain't working. Our troopers are trigger-happy."

"Whatever you say, Top," Ellis said.

After Bricker left, Ellis surveyed his spacious new bunker. He wrinkled his nose at the scent of the eleven women and two old papasans hunkered beside a pile of cloth bags and baskets on the rough concrete floor.

"OK, all you gooks, listen up," Ellis said, rapping the stock of his M-16 on an overhead beam, like he had seen this badass Special Forces dude do.

The Vietnamese women squatting on the floor studied the lanky black soldier with bloodshot eyes peering over big wraparound sunglasses.

"My name is Ellis, me Ellis. Bic?" Ellis said, jerking his thumb at his chest and adjusting the LAW cartridge strapped across his shoulders.

"Aa-lis, Aa-lis, ya, bic" the Vietnamese repeated, nodding.

"Yeah, *right,* me—Ellis," Ellis went on, pointing. "Now, you—gooks. And me, I *ain't.* Bic? Me, same-same *King* of the Gooks. You bic?"

"Bic," they echoed. "Aa-lis, Keeng-ow-guhks."

"Yeah, right, you got it, yeah. I'm King of the Gooks."

"Keeng-ow-guhks, Keeng-ow-guhks."

The women smiled in that fawning way that G.I.s liked, except for the prettiest one, the medics' girl, who just stared up at the bunker ceiling.

"Whatsamatter her?" Ellis asked.

"Dead V-C scare her," an older woman replied, glaring at the others.

"OK, you tell her," Ellis declared, shaking his LAW. "King of the Gooks will personally grease every god damn V-C in this half-assed town! She's got nothing to worry about it, you bic?"

"Bic. Keeng-ow-guhks shoot beau coups V-C," the woman told the girl.

"Don't you forget it, neither. King of the Gooks is the baddest ass in all Daktoum."

*   *   *

As soon as the wounded were flown out and Daktoum was quiet, Lehr grabbed Major Ranklin and the Kid to survey the damage.

The three climbed into the command Jeep and churned through the mud.

The monkey scampered alongside them and disappeared after they crossed the main camp road.

The Kid drove past a jagged heap of wood, ripped canvas, and twisted screens, which was all that remained of the officers' hootch. Under sunset light, red streams of water arched from a shot-up water tank like a fountain of blood. The Kid studied the hills for rocket flashes.

"Put out the word," Lehr told Ranklin in the back seat, "All officers sleep at duty stations, and their men—underground, or on the bunker line."

On the company street the torn canvas of a ruined tent revealed the young soldiers' lives—cheap steel bunks draped with olive mosquito nets, battered wooden footlockers, and gray wall lockers covered with snapshots of girlfriends, wives, mothers, cars, nude pinups—all peppered with shrapnel and shining like an underground art exhibit under the crimson light leaking under the black clouds in the west.

A helicopter thumped overhead.

Night fell quickly.

Artillery flashed under darkening mist where a battalion of ARVN infantry were pinned down south of Bridge Two. Jesus, Lehr thought, those goddamn steep valleys around Hill 670 are no place to be at night.

Flares drifted through the dark and the air vibrated with the propeller roar and electronics growls of a Spooky gunship shooting sheets of red tracer bullets.

After a helicopter landed on the medical bunker pad, Lehr ordered the Kid to where soldiers dragged barricades across the Daktoum airstrip. A quad-fifty truck and a Duster tank took fighting positions behind the temporary wire, and machine guns were set on top of two nearby bunkers facing Nhu Canh Du's dim yellow lights.

At the wire barrier, the Kid stopped beside a truck with four fifty-caliber machine guns on a revolving turret. It had painted flames like a hot rod and a Death's Head on the hood.

As they drove, the light faded, and the lumpy bunkers disappeared.

Lehr knew the bunker line by heart, having checked it every evening since Mac's drunken fiasco. No need to check now, Lehr thought, it's started.

They passed a Duster tank with 40mm guns trained down the airstrip. They won't probe from this side, Lehr thought, too much firepower. A tanker flipped a cigarette in a red streak.

Lehr motioned the Kid west, passing the main gate, crossing the airstrip, and following the dirt track around to the bluff with all the river bunkers.

The Jeep's knobby tires made sucking sounds as they wheeled past a gun battery, thundering shells at the hill battle.

Near the ruined mess hall, Lehr had the Kid stop.

On the river line, the destroyed bunker was barely visible, as guards readied a machine gun inside the ruined walls. Lehr frowned when a cigarette glow revealed a pale face, a rifle barrel, and a helmet.

When low voices hissed awareness of the colonel, the cigarette went out.

Sergeant Smith stepped out of the night.

"Problems, sergeant?"

"That gook on the wire's beginning to stink ..."

"Throw lime on it," Ranklin said.

"I know, sir, but..."

"It's there to remind the enemy," Lehr said. "Vietnamese believe when a body doesn't go home, the spirit wanders, tormented in hell."

"We aim to uphold that belief," Ranklin said.

"Understood, sir," Smitty said. "But it's spooking *our* men."

"Tell them to say a prayer," Ranklin said.

The night went quiet except for distant rumblings.

Sergeant Smith slung his weapon and walked away.

They slowly drove back to the TOC.

Somewhere out there in that jungle, Lehr thought, there's three full regiments of North Vietnamese regulars.

                    *   *   *

Ten minutes later, Halliday stood in battle gear before Lehr's desk.

"Halliday," Lehr said. "You have keys for the containers?"

Halliday's face reddened. The last thing he had done at the Officer's Club was mistakenly order five truckloads of soda and beer. Lehr stood up.

"Let's go."

They walked through the mud past the command Jeeps to the wrecked briefing room with its smashed wood and canvas, twisted screens and metal.

"How are your new duties?" Lehr said.

Halliday shifted his feet. He felt the dried mud on his neck and flashed on the big dead kid with the peach-fuzz mustache.

"OK, I guess, sir."

An artillery round hurtled out, rattling a corrugated roof panel, the blue flame briefly lighting Lehr's face.

Above jungle ridges, the battle flashed onto the clouds.

"Halliday," the colonel said. "I didn't want to let you go. But my own driver selling liquor was inexcusable."

"No sweat, sir," Halliday said, toying with the mud.

"Where are the keys?" the colonel asked.

Halliday opened the eight shipping containers lining the camp road, packed with beer and soda.

"How is your daughter, sir?"

"Fine," Lehr snapped as he checked the containers. "She's 'taking responsibility for her government's action,' whatever the hell that means."

"She feels strongly, sir?"

"Who knows, Halliday, do you feel that way?"

"Probably not, sir."

"OK, I'm done," Lehr said, exiting the last container.

Halliday locked the containers and handed Lehr the keys. The colonel skirted the tangle of wood and screens and stepped onto the concrete slab where the club bar had been.

Overhead, the clouds above Rocket Ridge flashed.

"Halliday," Lehr said, turning. "Your generation strikes me as undisciplined."

Halliday could barely see Lehr under the bursts and flames of artillery. His feet got tangled up in the screens.

"You're easily seduced," Lehr said. "By ideas that I wouldn't give the time of day."

Lehr walked to Halliday.

"But, hell, who really knows," the colonel said, kicking the screen away and ripping Halliday's pant leg. "Maybe what you people are *'into'* is for the better."

The colonel paused.

"Maybe you will," Lehr said thoughtfully. "Really learn to lo…"

The black night went quiet.

"Learn to *what*, sir?" Halliday asked.

The colonel shook his head

"Nothing," Colonel Lehr said. "I have to see Doc."

As they walked back, Lehr gripped his shoulder.

"Here we go," the colonel said with an odd finality.

Halliday started to ask "what," but Lehr's hand just steered him through the dark camp toward the faint glow of the medical bunker entrance.

"Good luck, Halliday," the colonel said.

Warmth spread from Halliday's shoulders to his chest then up to his forehead and throat as he walked beside the colonel across the open lot.

Artillery flashes lit their way, and the concussions skittered little waves across the black pools of monsoon water. A generator sputtered into a comforting hum and provoked catcalls from soldiers' tents which briefly glowed and then went dark as the teenagers closed the flaps for the nightly blackout.

Halliday followed Lehr down.

Underground, the fluorescent lights momentarily blinded them. Chaplain Goodby sat at the reception desk reading a Bible—his hootch had been blown up.

Medics lounged on raised stretchers, while a cassette player droned a nasal song that Lehr recognized ... *upon your magic swirling ship...* as one of Christina's favorites.

"ATTEN-SHUN!" Clancy called out when Lehr entered.

The medics slowly rose off their stretchers.

...my senses have been stripped ...

"At ease, sergeant," Lehr said.

...my hands can't feel to grip ...

"As long as we're taking fire," the colonel said, standing between the stretchers. "No saluting—unless you're trying to get me shot."

Nimmer laughed, provoking Clancy's glare.

... wait only for my boot heels to be wandering...

"Shut off that damn record," Clancy ordered.

"Captain Levin's in his office, sir," the bulky sergeant told Lehr.

"How'd things go today, sergeant?"

"Only problem was Dust-off not taking our dead, sir," Clancy answered. "Halliday will get them out tomorrow."

Lehr nodded and walked toward Doc's office.

"Colonel?" Clancy asked. "How's your new driver?"

"Fine, sergeant."

"He's a good soldier, sir."

"Seems to be."

"The best, sir."

Under the medics' sidelong glances, Lehr knocked on Doc's door.

"Come in," Doc said pleasantly, opening the canvas flap.

Doc and Gabrielle sat cross-legged on the beds facing each other. Black playing cards were strewn across a folding chair.

"Colonel," Gabrielle said, holding the Queen of Spades.

"Any problems today, Captain?" Lehr asked Doc.

"Besides the wounded and the dead? No."

"Did your men perform adequately?"

"As adequately as I did."

Lehr squinted at Gabrielle.

Her creased black fatigues were caked with red mud, and her black hair was disheveled; her nicotine-stained fingers held a cigarette that curled smoke up to a dim light, yet she seemed happy. Lehr turned to leave.

"Captain Levin," Lehr said, glancing back and trying not to look at Gabrielle.

Doc looked up.

"Take nothing for granted," Lehr said. "Dust-off, the convoy, generator, fuel, even food and water. Conserve your supplies. Make fall-back plans."

The colonel's ice-gray eyes glinted.

Then Lehr was gone, and the falling canvas flap wavered Gabrielle's pall of cigarette smoke.

As Lehr's boots echoed upstairs, Gabrielle fingered the Queen of Spades and threw it down. Impulsively, Gabrielle grabbed an orange from the shelf beside the photograph of Doc's wife, which had shattered when Nimmer demonstrated the 45-barrel safety to Doc.

"Your Colonel is an unusual man," Gabrielle said, tossing the orange.

Doc stared at his cards.

"General Giap surrounded Dien Bien Phu for three months before the siege," Gabrielle said, pointing up. "The Vietnamese say Giap is behind this."

"Umm," Doc said.

"Today on the radio your Nixon said 'Peace with honor' like it was 'bacon and eggs'."

"He's not *my* Nixon," Doc said.

Gabrielle dropped the orange, and the cards scattered. She tossed the orange to Doc like they were lovers.

Doc caught it and quickly replaced the orange beside his wife's picture.

"I could," Doc said. "Get you choppered out to Saigon."

"Why?" she asked.

"You don't have to be here," he said.

"I want to," she said.

Doc touched her hand.

Gabrielle didn't respond. Then she gripped his hand so tenderly
that Doc rested his head on her shoulder.

Doc opened his eyes to his wife's smashed picture and left his head
on Gabrielle's shoulder for a few moments. Then he moved away and
began shuffling the cards.

*   *   *

Lam watched thin black G.I. *Ay-lis*, reading a magazine in his
corner under the single bulb in their large, damp bunker. She thought
of her dead mother and of mamasan, who would beat her when she
returned to Nhu Canh Du. I cannot leave Daktoum and all G.I.s think
we are V-C.

"OK all you gooks," Ellis called. "Lights out. Now don't go playing
grab-ass in the dark neither, 'less you want to play grab-ass with me."

When the light went out, Lam lay in her cot and thought for a long
time about what it might be like living in America with Halliday in a
house with a swimming pool and riding in his big car through desert
sand and mountains.

*   *   *

Halliday lay on a stretcher in the Daktoum dispensary with his eyes
closed, feeling lonely. He sank into the dark, fervid place where Bonnie
danced naked on the moonlit Colorado riverbank. But her face kept
melting into his mother's, which was weird, so he drummed Arizona
and his mother away by remembering Lam that night at the Dak Poko
water point. Suddenly he wanted to see her and touch her and speak
quietly with her in pidgin, *you firt, G.I., you firt Howaday.* But no one
was allowed near the Vietnamese bunker and besides, he hadn't even
tried to be alone with her.

Halliday stared at the redwood beams in the bunker that Clancy
said no rocket could penetrate, but no one knew if it was true. He
slapped a mosquito on his neck, which was still smeared with mud. Ben
ambled over and kicked his stretcher.

"Come on man, you can't be breathing this nasty bunker air all
night. Let's go up on the roof and watch the war."

They went upstairs and hoisted themselves up onto the low, sandbagged roof.

In the west, distant ridges flashed with shifting light and smoke as Spooky droned a wall of red tracer bullets, pounding the night with electronic growls, which felt oddly comforting. Artillery flame light danced across the tattered mess hall canvas, and all the outgoing fire made Halliday edgy.

They crossed the roof to the sandbagged machine-gun tower, where Nimmer and Donnelly sprawled, drinking beer.

"Ninety-fucking five at Fenway yesterday," Donnelly said. "Almost as hot as fucking Viet-nam. No wonder the Sox lost."

"The Sox always lose. And the Yankees always win, get used to it," Nimmer said. "They opened the fucking hydrants in Flatbush."

"You ever done that?" Donnelly asked.

"You ain't lived until you been knocked on your ass by a fire hydrant."

Nimmer opened beers for Halliday and Ben, who sat on the low wall. Flare light flashed on their faces as Donnelly lit a joint and passed it around.

After they smoked, Donnelly slapped out drumbeats on his thighs.

"Sound effects," Donnelly declared, as he snapped on an army radio. "The war channel."

Static crackled out of the small speaker.

"Roger that," said a curt, disembodied radio voice. "Roger Death Cong."

"Shi-t," Donnelly whispered, doom creeping into his voice from the radio's panicky tone. "*Death Cong*? Must be gooks in the wire up on Ladyland—them 1-5-5s firing point blank. Gooks fucking everywhere."

Donnelly clicked off the radio and lit a cigarette from the one he was smoking.

"I'm too old for this fucking shit," he said, the cigarette glowing on his stubbly face.

Freaky, Halliday thought, as Donnelly's face faded in and out of the dim battle light. He's way too freaky. Anywhere but Daktoum, Donnelly would be in a padded cell. Halliday sipped his beer and tried to forget the day, the mud, the wounded, the dead, Bonnie, Lam, the fucking world.

"JESUS, MARY, AND JOSEPH!" Donnelly said, jumping straight up.

A shadowy figure appeared right beside Donnelly.

"Re-lax, Dickwipe," a wild and weary voice said. "You ain't gonna die. Least not tonight."

Artillery flashed on a grinning, wraithlike soldier with a gold tooth.

"You dudes want to smoke some shit?"

Flare light revealed a shadowy beard on a long face and greasy hair falling over threadbare tiger fatigues like a loose skin. Thin lips twisted into a cunning smile over a pointed jaw. The red-rimmed eyes were the worst with damage so naked and deep that Halliday didn't want to imagine what he might have seen or done. But he couldn't turn away.

His M-79 strap had painted skulls and crossbones, and bandoliers of grenade shells crossed his chest.

With shaking hands, Donnelly cracked another beer and handed it to the soldier.

"Light," the man said, digging into his ammo bag.

Donnelly struck his Zippo so the man could see inside.

"Whatta ya got? Apricots?" the stoned Donnelly said, spotting a plastic bag. "You got fucking apricots? Dried LURP apricots? Shit, I love dried apricots."

"Here you go, man," the stranger drawled, tossing the bag to Donnelly, who caught it. "Eat all you want."

The grinning stranger produced an empty M-79 shell with a curved brass stem and packed the huge pipe.

"Don't smell like LURP apricots," Donnelly said, holding up the bag in the dim light.

The stranger lit the pipe, sucked in, and exhaled.

"Do they really look like *apricots*, numb nuts?" the stranger asked, holding a burning match near the bag.

"JESUS CHRIST!" Donnelly yelled, jumping up. "JESUS FUCKING CHRIST! THEY'RE FUCKING EARS! EARS! JESUS, MARY, AND JOSEPH!"

The stranger laughed a shrill, almost silent whistle and snatched back the bag.

"Shut the fuck up," he told Donnelly, passing the pipe.

Donnelly stared at the black sky, tapping his feet, and drumming his fingers on the sandbags.

"Fuck this shit," Ben said, walking away.

Halliday stood up, but the stranger thrust the pipe in his hands, so impulsively, he sucked on it. The dope looked black under the glow. The pipe went to Nimmer and back to Donnelly, who shook his head, and re-lit his own joint.

Halliday smoked again and his dull beer high brightened. The night turned razor sharp, until he felt omniscient, hovering above Daktoum in the raised machine-gun pit, sagely observing the war with an extreme clarity. Tracers, explosions, distant bombing, flashes, outgoing artillery, the dark circle of young soldiers formed a perfect world, composed just for him.

"What kind of black pot is this?" Halliday asked.

"*Pot?*" the stranger roared, bringing Nimmer in on the joke with a back slap. "The pot's just there to keep the flame burning, newbie. *Opium*, man, pure fucking poppy. What the fuck you think this war's all about?"

He swept his hands out across Cambodia and Laos.

"Golden Triangle, man, world's largest opium producer. Right over there, a dozen miles. Guess who owns the *only* airline in Laos? Air America, run by the C-I-fucking-A! You think *Nixon* burning the Turkish opium fields was an *accident?* No way, part of the master plan. Hell, even President Thieu's cashing in. Beau coups gold, man."

The stranger grinned, sucked on the pipe, threw back his head, and squealed a maniacal giggle without a shred of joy.

"Ain't this Vietnam a motherfucking self-fulfilling fiasco? Righteous bureaucratic bastards, sucking the taxpayer's tit dry by hauling opium out on the government's dime, then drop-kicking old Joe Six-pack's ass and making him pay for his high and dying for *freedom*. War on drugs, or drugs on war? You tell me. Chicken or the egg, you know? There it *is* man. There it fucking *is*."

The night went quiet and clear.

"Well," Halliday said. "Vietnam's no John Wayne movie."

"No shit, Sherlock," Nimmer said, laughing.

The stranger got serious.

"I seen him."

"Seen *who?*"

"John Wayne, man," the stranger said. "Right here. In Daktoum. Last year."

"John Wayne?" Nimmer asked. "In Daktoum?"

"That's a fucking rog. Wasn't even wearing his rug."

"Wayne wears a *rug*?"

"Fucking John Wayne is bald as a cue ball, man."

"No!"

"Oh yeah, man, I seen it! He choppered in, stayed a couple hours, had some drinks, drove around in a Jeep. We even gave him an M-60, but he just laughed and gave it back."

"No shit."

The freaky unkempt soldier quickly packed his bag.

"Goooooooood luuuuck," the wild voice said, moving into the darkness. "You sorry ass motherfuckers'll need it!"

Donnelly lit a cigarette and snapped on the radio. Strained voices crackled through the tiny speaker.

"Fire, fire…fire illumination!"

"Roger, six-fiver."

"Jesus Christ!"

A thundering explosion rumbled across the valley and the radio hissed static.

"SIXTEEN, SIXTEEN, SIXTEEN."

"TWELVE?"

"B-40's SARGE!"

"DINKS, DINKS IN THE WIRE!"

"Niner, Seven. PUT OUT FIRE!"

"FUCKING SEVEN, MEDEVAC!" said a tinny desperate voice on the radio, while in the background a soldier screamed. "MY LEGS, MY LEGS…"

"HANG ON, TEN."

Donnelly turned off the radio.

"Oh man, this is too too much, this is too goddamn motherfucking much," Donnelly said, madly puffing his cigarette. "Jesus Christ, they're overrunning Ladyland. I gotta get the fuck outta here before I get killed."

Under the wavering flare light, Gabrielle's face briefly flashed near the entrance and disappeared. Doc climbed onto the bunker, walked over, and sat on the sandbags.

"Doc, Doc, Doc, Hickory Dickory Doc," Donnelly said, clutching Doc's arm. "You gotta get me outta here."

"Calm down, Donnelly."

"If those dinks overrun us, I'll fucking shoot myself, Doc. They took Ladyland, tonight, Doc, Nimmer tell him—my nerves are fucked up, Doc, you know they are, you gotta get me outta here, Doc, I'm gonna die, I know it. I'll be on your conscience, Doc, promise me, Doc, PROMISE ME, PLEASE!"

"Calm down, Donnelly," Doc said. "No one leaves Daktoum before their time."

"Doc, its *dinks* we're treating here, just fucking dinks, not even G.I.s," Donnelly pleaded. "Humpty-Dumpty ding-dong dinks. It ain't worth it, Doc, nobody knows we're up here, the war's over, you know the fucking Paris peace talks and all. I don't wanna die, Doc, I don't, I been here eleven fucking months, Doc, I done my duty, you know I have."

"Donnelly, are you smoking pot and drinking beer?"

"Tits on a bull, Doc. Jesus! You gotta help me out, I'm gonna die here, I know it! I know I am, Dooooc."

Donnelly fell at Doc's feet and bawled like a baby, clutching his legs. Doc put his arm on Donnelly's shoulder.

"Take him downstairs," Doc told Nimmer. "Half dose of Thorazine."

Nimmer shuffled over, tucked the sniffling Donnelly under his arm and stumbled with the small man across the sandbags and then thumped down the stairs.

Doc sat calmly on the rotting sandbags, staring out at the dark night lit by rocking flares and artillery flashes.

Halliday shivered.

He kept hearing the man on the radio screaming for his lost legs until fear licked at Halliday's body like icy flames, the fear of ending up like Donnelly, sobbing in the dirt or his greatest fear, to be crippled like his father or worse, losing a leg.

Doc rose, nodded to Halliday, glided across the roof like a ghost, and disappeared underground.

Overpowered by the opium, Halliday heard every one of Doc's quiet footfalls resounding across the night.

John Wayne invaded his mind. John Wayne in Daktoum?

Halliday staggered up.

He tried to shake off the image of John Wayne as he lurched across the bunker roof. Halliday grabbed the back entrance post and swung himself around and down into the staircase, his mind racing before his body as he careened onto the stairs and fell, ass over teakettle down, tumbling, down, down, his heavy body and hauntingly-clear opium mind registering each scuffed wooden wall and dusty ceiling board and mud-worn step as he rolled, slowly, acrobatically and forever, over and over, inevitably down until he landed in a heap at the bottom of the long medical stairwell.

       *   *   *

Halliday awoke, face down on a worn wooden step, tasting mud, his body finally caught up to his reeling mind. He rolled over and stared up the long stairway to the starlit opening.

A flare flashed, and a dog stood framed in the entrance, his jaws tearing at what Halliday thought was a man's hand.

Then the night went dark, and under the opium, he couldn't tell if the image was real or not. Halliday didn't think he could manage to climb up and find out, so he just crawled on his hands and knees into the medical bunker.

A dim light burned in the far corner, where the duty medic dozed at the front desk.

Halliday spotted an open stretcher on the concrete floor and dragged himself onto it. He passed out and fell into bloody fantastical war dreams of the silver airliner—only this time, the passengers were all Daktoum soldiers, and the grinning pilot was John Wayne, wearing a tricorn Revolutionary War hat above the Duke's half-rotted face.

16.

"Wake the fuck up!" Ben said, kicking Halliday's stretcher on the floor. "They're bringing in what's left of Paradise."

Halliday sat up, his eyes, wild and unfocused.

"Get up, man," Ben said, upending the green stretcher and sprawling Halliday onto the muddy, bloodstained floor. "Dust-off coming in, tee-tee time."

Halliday heaved up his dazed body, smacked into a big post, then groped his way up the back stairs, using his hands to climb the steep wooden steps, slowly steadying himself by sliding along the right wall.

Only when daylight hit his eyes and seared through the opium fog, did Halliday realize that he was in Vietnam. He fumbled at his pants and took a long piss at the tube, squinting under the shattering gray light.

Nimmer and Limerick and Donnelly came out, followed by Ben, who jammed a can of Coke and a tropical chocolate bar in his hands. Halliday popped the aluminum tab and washed down the chocolate, the acrid bubbly sweetness sizzling his throat and forcing the day on him.

Halliday crushed the can under his boot, lit a cigarette, and sat on the sandbag wall, shivering under a low mist obscuring the ridges. When a thumping chopper broke the silence, Halliday rubbed his scratchy eyes and shook his head hard, as if it could pound some sense into himself.

When the black speck in the mist became a helicopter, the medics tossed away their cigarettes, grabbed stretchers, and ran across the gray bridge out to the medevac pad.

The chopper landed, and the medics dragged wounded soldiers in bloody fatigues up off the cold vibrating metal deck and carried them in stretchers across the mud back to their bunker.

Clancy and Halliday waited for the last wounded man, a lanky soldier with glazed eyes. Clancy grabbed the man's wrist and put his ear on the chest.

"He's dead," Clancy said.

"Take him," the on-board medic ordered.

"We ain't got no Graves."

"TAKE HIM OFF!" yelled the medic with cold, fierce, exhausted eyes.

"You don't want to be giving me no shit, Specialist," Clancy said. "You better goddamn come back for him then—we ain't getting many slicks, things being what they are."

The co-pilot glanced back at Clancy through the Plexiglas and opened his palms. The rotors spun faster.

"I ain't promising nothing," the medic said.

Clancy shot the medic a hard look and grabbed the dead man's stretcher so swiftly that Halliday barely caught the back stretcher posts sliding off the metal deck.

The chopper lifted and banked toward Cambodia.

"Goddamnit," Clancy cursed as they marched through the mud. "These stiffs gonna get all maggoty—we ain't equipped for no Graves."

They set the stretcher down in the mud near the dead chamber. Clancy went inside, came back with a bag, and quickly zipped the dead man inside.

"Hold your breath, Halliday."

Inside the chamber, the big, dead, blond kid's body funk hit them hard as they rolled off the new dead man. Halliday held his breath so as not to gag and then left quickly.

"Go over to the TOC, Halliday," Clancy said. "Have that young-assed Major get us a chopper for these dead."

Halliday moved away.

"Trooper, where are you going?"

"To...."

"Get your *god-damned rifle and battle gear!* I don't need no Colonel jumping deep in my shit when you show up unarmed in his TOC."

"OK, Sergeant Clancy, OK."

Halliday stuck out his tongue at the retreating Clancy, which felt childish but good. He ran through the mud to the waiting room, groped down the dark stairs, and felt his way through the blackness by the wooden mosquito frames over to his bunk, where he rooted out his flak vest and steel pot, grabbed his rifle, and headed upstairs.

As Halliday hustled toward the TOC, a rocket hit the officer's hootch, exploding what was left of the tent canvas into a thousand puffy wisps that drifted slowly to earth. A tremendous roar rang in Halliday's ears.

Halliday threw himself down and tasted red mud.

Breath heaving, he strained to hear another incoming *pop* from the hills. When it didn't come, he scrambled into a fresh one-man foxhole —one of many Lehr had the 99th's bucket loaders dig. Halliday slumped into the hole, which felt like a fat blanket of dirt.

All he could see was the gray sky overhead.

*   *   *

Lester J. Ellis supervised "his" Vietnamese as they unloaded hundreds of cases of beer and soft drinks into his huge new sleeping bunker.

"OK, Papasans, get a fucking move-on," he prodded two old shitburners lugging soda cases.

Goddamn lifer motherfuckers, Ellis muttered, as he architected all the drink cases into tall, color-coordinated rows. What the hell they gonna do with all these sodas?

"Papa-sans, you tell me something, OK? How come *your* ARVN gooks cain't never do nothing right, while *their* gooks regularly kick our ass?" Ellis asked the old Vietnamese men. "Now if all the bust-ass gooks are V-Cs, how you all ever gonna kick any butt, if your side got all the second-rate gooks?"

When Ellis and the Vietnamese had finished, the entire bunker was lined with tall walls of red Budweiser, Carling's Black Label, and red

Coca-Colas, with a chest-high wall of green Seven-Up cases splitting the big bunker.

Ellis had the Vietnamese stack cases of Pabst Blue Ribbon and wall off his private sleeping area. Ellis fashioned himself a doorway and hung up a big dusty Texas flag that his mother had sent him.

After they finished, Ellis passed out Cokes all around, popped a warm can of Carling's, and hoisted himself up on the low green wall of Seven-Up cans.

"OK, cherries, listen up," Ellis called. "King of the Gooks is putting out the *Word*!"

Ellis towered over the women, the three children, and two old papasan shitburners, squatting on their haunches.

"OK, now all you mamasans, papa-sans, and girlsans too, this here is the *word*. Ain't none of you, none, not one swinging dingle or dangle, my gooks, better *never ever*, motherfucking even *think* of making off with, drinking, sneaking, poaching, or selling—even *one* goddamn can of beer and soda. No takey take! *Bic*? Number fucking ten, you bic? No takey take! Bic? OK?"

Ellis pointed to the cases of beer and sodas, shook his head, and made a cross with his fingers, like warding off the Devil or the Evil Eye.

"Bic, Keeng-ow-guks, bic," said the sharp-eyed woman who understood the game and led the dutiful Vietnamese in an acquiescent group murmur.

Major Ranklin walked into the bunker and right over to Ellis, sitting on the green Seven-Up cases.

"Ellis! What the hell is going on?"

"What you mean, Major?"

"*King of the Gooks*?"

Ellis stared at Ranklin.

"You know, Major, chain of command, all that," Ellis said. "Military principle. Discipline, respect, control, order. These gooks don't understand nothing except authority."

"You don't know that, Ellis."

"They ain't never responded to nothing else, sir."

"Cut the crap, Ellis. Now!"

Ellis glowered at Ranklin.

"Look. No more of this demeaning talk, Ellis, understand? No more King of the Gooks."

Ellis grinned and nodded at the Major. Then Ellis snorted, slid off the green Seven-Up wall, flipped up the big Lone Star flag, and withdrew behind his Pabst Blue Ribbon walls.

Ellis stretched out on his comfy Air Force mattress, opened a well-thumbed *Playboy* magazine, studied Miss June on the glossy back flap of the centerfold, and then reread her personal biography.

When Ellis heard Ranklin whispering, he peeked through a gap in the Texas flag and saw the Major and the pregnant Vietnamese woman getting all cozy.

Then rockets started falling, and all the Vietnamese huddled together on the floor.

*   *   *

When the rockets finally stopped, Halliday thought about climbing out until he remembered getting caught naked in the shower. Goddamn N-V-A—timing their rockets to catch us getting out of our holes.

Halliday shivered. He cautiously stuck out his head, but hollow *pop pop pop* sounds echoed, and he ducked back down. All he could see was gray sky and dark mist and a pole with wires running to the TOC. How in hell do voices transmit over wires, they told us in science? Electrons? Protons? Sound waves?

Three rockets slammed in, three freight trains ripped at his eardrums. Shock waves rippled the muddy water, debris hissed overhead, canvas, shattered wood, and clumps of earth slapped into tents. Halliday curled his body together tight until his fingers and toes clenched like claws.

Another deadly *pop*.

Halliday tensed for the impact. One thousand one, one thousand two, one thousand three, one thousand four, one thousand five …

As the rockets roared in, Halliday twisted himself even tighter to keep from running.

Another *pop* from Rocket Ridge.

Again, a rocket smashed in.

Mud spewed over Halliday with a tremendous ripping sound that threatened to drown him. His fingers tore at his left side, scratching and compulsively clutching himself, squeezing every muscle in his body to kill his intense desire to run. Halliday twisted into the smallest possible space and prayed to God, to Mary, to Jesus, to anyone.

Three more *pops* like giant wine corks echoed off the ridge as the Duster tank on the river line opened-up.

Rockets exploded on the airstrip, with huge orange flames and thick black smoke. Chunks of pavement clattered down. Another rocket screamed in, spraying mud over Halliday.

Slowly, Daktoum firebase fell silent. No outgoing, no incoming. Then the 1-5-5 battery blasted an artillery shell echoing off through the hills.

Another rocket screamed in close.

The explosion flung chunks of red earth on Halliday, smacking his cheeks with flecks of mud.

A 1-7-5 cannon thundered out a round, and another 1-5-5 gun started firing.

Halliday poked his head out of his foxhole and stood up.

"You fucking gook fuckers!" Halliday yelled and immediately felt ridiculous.

Daktoum firebase was quiet.

"So where are *you*, John Wayne?" Halliday yelled to the empty firebase, "*You* and all your phony movie star bullshit! How come you never went to war? Show yourself, chickenshit! You made me come here, you and your goddamn war movies!"

Halliday thought, shit, I'm losing it—screaming at the N-V-A, then John Wayne?

The Daktoum cannons roared out shell after shell into the hills. Between outgoing rounds, Halliday heard a dull *pop*, and sank back into his hole.

The rocket smashed in so close that splinters, smoke, dust, and metal tore through the air.

Halliday groaned and buried himself even deeper.

He covered his face like a child. Shit, they almost got me, he gasped, shaking, and trying not to cry.

When he opened his eyes, John Wayne's steely eyes and square, jutting jaw were right in front of him. Halliday closed his eyes and shook his head to banish the fantasy.

"Fuck you, John Wayne," Halliday cursed, reaching for his rifle. "Chickenshit."

Halliday looked again, and Wayne glinted back, his eyes as mean and narrow as in a hundred movies.

Halliday remembered the Duke smacking a cowardly Marine with a rifle butt in *Sands of Iwo Jima* and clanged a round into his M-14.

"You never went to war. You owe me," Halliday said. "Get me the fuck out of here, Duke."

The Duke stared through Halliday and slowly evaporated.

John Wayne's deep voice echoed through Halliday's head, *keep your eyes open, Pilgrim.*

Halliday blinked his eyes, but there was only the muddy red foxhole.

"Fuck!" he cursed. "Fuck, fuck fuck! Fuck me! I'm fucking losing it. John Wayne? Fucking opium, fuck, fuck, fucking Vietnam!"

Halliday banged his helmet into the dirt where Wayne's face had appeared.

*　　　　　*　　　　　*

After the police siren wailed the all-clear, Halliday climbed out of the hole. Just in case, all the way to the TOC he hugged the sandbagged tents and bunkers, crouching through smoky air stinking of sulfur and cordite.

A soldier hustled by down the company street.

Halliday turned and saw a burning hootch and wondered if he should he put out the fire, until he remembered Clancy.

*　　　　　*　　　　　*

Inside the TOC, Major Ranklin sat at his cluttered desk.

"Sergeant Clancy sent me to get a chopper for the dead."

"Forget it, Halliday. Try the Vietnamese," Ranklin said. "I've got General Armbruster tomorrow. You medics handle the bodies—just grab a slick from the airstrip."

"Sir, nobody likes to take the dead."

Ranklin shrugged and bent over a yellow stack of teletypes.

Halliday scowled, rushed away and nearly ran into Merton.

"Watch where the fuck you're going, 'cruit."

A fierce grin gleamed on Merton's ruddy face.

"Hot enough for you, 'cruit? Huh?"

Halliday nodded.

"Hey," Merton said. "You know, Nimmer? Got stuck in here during the attack. Says he saw a King-goddamn-cobra this big around. Going into a bunker."

"Bull-shit."

"Swear to God, who's flying up here tomorrow."

"What?"

"God himself, General Fuckface Patton Armbruster and half of fuckin' Saigon, plus your normal shitload of two-bit dink generals, Minh, Dinh, Binh, and Phu. Some combat excursion to get medals for the scrambled eggs set, big fucking deal, blah blah blah—FUCK all of them," Merton said. "We're not even supposed to *be* in Daktoum. Fucking MAC-V, no mail, no reporters, fuck every single dink on both sides, sorry-ass fuckers, screwing up my adolescence, the best years of my fucking life rotting away in this shithole. What the fuck are you doing here anyway, Halliday?"

"Getting a chopper for the dead."

"Oh, *right,* cow-fucking-boy! I can't even get choppers for the living. You want one for the dead?"

"Should I ask Lehr?"

"Fuck no, shit for brains, he's already *completely* pissed that *our* dinks refused him one this morning."

"You sure?"

"I'm his goddamned clerk—I know more than he does."

Merton grinned an evil look, stiffened his chubby body, saluted Halliday with an extended middle finger, and then turned away.

"Gooood luck, Halliday, you asshole."

"You too, dickhead."

Halliday nodded at the Kid, sitting on a bunk near Lehr's office, cleaning his weapon.

Outside the TOC, Halliday scuttled away through the ominous dull yellow light, skirting sandbagged walls, bunkers, and foxholes. Artillery roared through the jaundiced mist and billows of gun smoke haunted the camp in dirty little clouds. Halliday didn't see any other soldiers—even near the still-burning hootch on the company street.

Under the lowering sky, Halliday crossed the huge shining pools on pallet walkways. The red cross atop the medical bunker was smeared with muddy boot prints, and the sandbagged machine gun tower slumped towards a collapse.

How come everything looks so clear and detailed? Halliday thought, skimming his hand across a shiny plastic sandbag.

An artillery round roared out so close that Halliday nearly fell over.

"Fuck you!" he yelled, having forgotten the eight-inch gun behind the med bunker.

Halliday scraped his muddy boots on the steel grate and headed down towards a low moaning and the steady drone of medics. He rounded the entrance at the bottom of the stairs.

Wounded soldiers lay everywhere on stretchers. Coils of plastic tubes wound from their bloody arms up through a blue layer of cigarette smoke and into glass intravenous bottles hanging from nails on the redwood beams.

"Roger that, Oscar-Charlie two," the radio crackled.

"Lost in a romance, a wilderness of pain," a tape player sang softly. *"And all the children are insane."*

"Ahhhhhhhh," somebody cried.

"No sweat, you'll be back in the World titi time, gimme that clamp, Pepper."

"Oh Gaaaaawwwdddd, noooooo."

A parade of stretchers flowed through the dim, steep staircases, the filthy, bloody wounded, rushing down, and the green-bagged dead, heading up.

Gabrielle worked on a shaking patient, while beside her, a small soldier with a shaved head sobbed into a muddy handkerchief. Every detail imprinted on Halliday's brain.

Shiny metal scalpels cut and probed flesh, while bloody shrapnel fragments clinked into steel trays. Black blood-pressure bubbles puffed and deflated, sighing the air. Medics rushed from stretcher to stretcher, cutting flesh, clearing airways, stopping blood, soothing, grabbing dressings and needles and gauze and tape.

Bible in hand, Chaplain Goodby moved gravely down the shadowy rows of wounded, his cheerful smile somehow attached to the wrong face.

Bravery? Suffering and blood.

The wounded drilled into Halliday's mind as he passed out supplies and instruments. Each of their sweat-soaked, filthy, jungle fatigues stank with unique scents: a chilly biting dust, an oily sourness, the rank sweetness of a polluted swamp, a heavy pomade of mud, a gagging, unwashed funk poorly drowned in Old Spice and Right Guard. The odors stung the air, suffused under the impossibly warm salt of blood.

"Doc. Over here, vitals."

"Shit, where's that I-V, Nimmer?"

"OK, now man, this is gonna hurt a little."

"Quarter grain morphine."

"I don't give a damn what he says."

"Ah, ah, ah, ah, ah, ah ahhhh!"

"Where are you from?"

"He's stable. Where are those low vitals?"

"Troy, upstate New York."

"Halliday, cut the man's fatigues off," Ben ordered, shoving scissors at him. "Find out where he's hurt. Gotta be more than this scalp wound."

Ben turned away.

A stretcher dropped down onto sawhorses, and Halliday cut off the dazed, groaning soldier's fatigues and underwear until the young soldier lay naked with only muddy boots and shreds of dirty fatigues around him like a filthy green halo. A dried smear of blood lay atop one pale thigh. Gingerly, Halliday rolled him over.

"Fuck," he whispered.

A baseball-sized chunk of flesh was ripped out of his back thigh.

"Here, man, let me at it," Ben said, dousing the wound with alcohol.

Ben applied a pressure dressing streaked with yellow ointment, tied it on, and quickly taped it.

"Give him a tetanus shot."

Halliday gave the injection, found a blanket, wrapped up the wounded man, and elevated his feet. When Halliday looked up for something to do, Clancy grabbed him.

"About time you got here, trooper. Where's that goddamn Donnelly?"

"How would I know?"

The burly sergeant slapped a wet strip of gauze in Halliday's hand.

"Stuff this in your nose and come with me. We got us a chopper, but they won't take no dead."

The alcohol-soaked gauze cooled his nose and killed his sense of smell. Halliday trailed Clancy up the dark stairs.

Outside, a dead man lay in the mud, wrapped in a blood-encrusted poncho with a rangy dog sniffing at the corpse.

"Get the hell out!" Clancy yelled, kicking mud at the dog.

"You got a tag?" Clancy asked.

"Tag?"

"Death tag, Goddamnit! Always have 'em in your pocket."

"I don't have one."

"After we stick him inside, go downstairs, get some tags, look at him, figure out what killed him, write his name and service number on it, and tie it to his toe."

"How do I know who he is?"

"*How do I know who he is?*" Clancy mimicked. "His god-damn *dog tags*, College Boy! What the fuck you thinking?"

They pulled off the crusty poncho, rolled the dead man into a body bag, and dragged him into the dank morgue.

Halliday came back with a cardboard tag and pulled the corpse over to the maze entrance, where he could see. Revulsion and curiosity rose in his throat.

The soldier was young and black with a patchy beard. Halliday found the dog tag laced in the soldier's boot: Lemuel Richard Carden, RA 18917013 Blood Type O POS Baptist. A blue class ring circled the dead man's stubby right finger—Roosevelt High, 1968. Had to be thousands of Roosevelt Highs—one kick-ass soldier and one crippled hell of a commander-in-chief. Crippled, like Dad, who flew in WWII. Both warriors, Teddy because he liked to charge, and Franklin because he won the war.

Halliday couldn't find any wounds until he accidentally nudged the dead man's head, which flopped over to reveal a grapefruit sized hole in his throat. Halliday jumped. Poor fuck, dying up on Paradise for something nobody, not even John Wayne, could figure out.

"Fuck this stupid war and all the civilian idiots who sent us here!" Halliday yelled.

Halliday spotted John Wayne and threw himself behind a sandbag wall.

Halliday whipped out his forty-five and held the shaking pistol on Wayne.

The big black hat bent down and struck a match on his cowboy boot, which lit up buckskin chaps, a denim shirt, black vest, and the Duke's signature red kerchief.

John Wayne inhaled a hand-rolled cigarette, looked up, and blew smoke at Halliday.

Wayne sat down on a wall of sandbags near the bodies, which seemed to emanate a dim blue light.

Through the alcohol gauze, Halliday smelled putrefaction.

Wayne stared at the shaking Halliday, holding a 45 pistol.

"Fuck, Duke, you scared me," Halliday said.

John Wayne scoffed.

"Your whole war's *phony*, Duke, fucking phony," Halliday said. "Look at this Kid—dreaming chicks and cars and the good life he'll never have. Fighting for *freedom*. Freedom for *who*? The press, the brass, the tennis courts in Saigon? The advisors, the CIA drinking scotch and fucking Vietnamese chicks, planning assassinations, while hissing *body count body count* to generals living on yachts, saving their own asses by sacrificing his? We been here *years*, Duke—nothing's better, nobody's learning nothing. This kid is going home in a box, and they'll shove a flag at his mother, and somebody who never had the balls to go will call this kid a hero. It's sick, Duke."

The Duke tilted his head.

Halliday kicked fine red dust up into a plume.

Duke just sat smoking between the bodies.

Standing over the dead black soldier, Halliday's 45 pistol pointed at Wayne.

"OK, Duke, I get it, you don't want to talk about it," Halliday said, and then he asked in a little boy's voice. "Can you tell me something about death."

John Wayne narrowed his eyes, slowly took off his black cowboy hat and wiped his brow. Something rustled—a skinny black dog poked its nose in. Halliday grabbed for a clod to throw, but the dog bolted away. When Halliday turned back, the Duke's eyes locked on him.

"Death?" Wayne said in his matinee voice.

"Yes," Halliday repeated in a small voice that meant 'no'."

"What do you want to know?" Duke said. "Pilgrim."

Outside the eight-inch artillery fired and the shell rocketed away. The unearthly blue glow emanating from the movie star made Halliday shiver.

John Wayne adjusted his black cowboy hat and kept his steely eyes on Halliday. One side of his face had never looked better, but underneath, there was meanness and treachery, like in *The Searchers*. The Duke turned so the rotted side of his face looked right through Halliday and then, Wayne was gone.

Halliday stood in the sandbagged morgue bunker, staring at the dead black kid. Snapping his 45 back in his holster, he searched the body for a cause of death, but all he could find was a tiny piece of shrapnel in the chest. Halliday started to write it down, until he remembered the gaping hole in the throat.

Lemuel Carden's face looked unusually calm.

Never knew what hit him. Better off dead than crippled. Crippled? Shit, *crippled!* Being crippled is worse than dying.

Halliday wrote on the tag: "massive shrapnel wound thorax area" and attached the thin copper wires to Lemuel's muscular wrist. He ran his hand across dead man's smooth cheek, like he would to a girl. It felt cool, prickly, and rubbery.

Halliday quickly zipped the bag shut and dragged it to the darkest part of the chamber with all the others.

He heard something rustle and whirled around to find a black dog. Halliday heaved a dirt clod, that went wide.

"Get the fuck out of here!" Halliday yelled.

Man, I must be losing it. Dreaming ghosts. He pulled out the alcohol sponge, but the sweet, awful stink of death overwhelmed him, so Halliday crammed the gauze back in his nose and wondered if he'd ever forget that smell.

*   *   *

Soft rain pelted Halliday's face as he stepped out of the dead bunker into gray light.

Clancy rose from the muddy staircase.

"Chopper coming in," the big sergeant said, stepping under the rain tarp. "Get those bodies out on the strip."

A helicopter flew out of the black wall of clouds.

Limerick, Cullen, Nimmer, and Ben emerged and helped Halliday drag the bodies out of the sandbagged morgue onto stretchers. They humped the bodies out to the airstrip over the little gray bridge that Ben was calling The Bridge Without Joy.

As they waited on the tarmac, rain misted their faces, shining the dull-green body bags. The unforgettable stink of death rose all around them, a scent that contained every good and terrible smell in life, like velvet shit-fire cut with sweet mother's milk.

The chopper screamed down the airstrip, clattered hard onto the tarmac, and the medics hoisted up the bodies.

The gunner's left arm was nearly shot off above the elbow, and his arm hung by a thin strip of cartilage and was tied off in a crude tourniquet. His face contorted as he cradled the machine gun with his good shoulder.

"Doc," he said in a hoarse voice barely audible over the rotor wash, "Just gimme morphine to make it in."

Clancy and Ben set down their body and ran over to the gunner. The big sergeant checked the gunner's pulse and breathing, and then he jammed a morphine syrette into the gunner's thigh, while Ben rewrapped the stump with a new pressure dressing and quickly secured the useless arm in a makeshift sling.

"Go lay down," Clancy ordered the gunner.

"No fucking way," the gunner said. "I'm OK, I'm all strapped in. We need this gun."

"You'll fall into the jungle."

"So fucking be it."

Clancy shrugged and turned back to the waiting medics holding the bodies. Their fatigues and the body bags flapped under the rotor wash.

"Get them goddamn bags onboard!" Clancy yelled.

The pilots made hurry-up gestures through the Plexiglas, as sobbing erupted inside. A lanky black soldier sprawled across three filthy bodies already piled on the aluminum deck.

Ben jumped up and bent over the sobbing soldier.

"Jasper?"

The tall sergeant lay atop three dead men.

"I ain't leaving them," Jasper told Ben. "Just get me the hell out of here."

"You OK, man? You OK?"

Jasper's face was so pale that it almost looked like he was dead. The pilots banged on the Plexiglas.

"I ain't leaving nobody, no-how," Jasper said.

Jasper didn't even know who Ben was.

"OK man," Ben said, nodding.

The pilot banged the Plexiglas window. Ben squeezed Jasper's shoulder and stepped out into the rotor wash where the medics waited with the fresh bodies.

A rocket screamed in and exploded two hundred feet away.

The medics abandoned the bodies and hit the ground as the pilot lifted the helicopter, banking away in a swift booming arc and up into the darkening sky, where the lift ship slid away toward the heavy clouds in the east.

The medics lay flat for a full minute.

The chopper disappeared into the clouds. No more rockets came in.

"Let's go," Clancy ordered, getting up. "Goddamnit!"

The medics rose, picked up the bodies, and carried them back. They slid the heavy bags off of the stretchers and dragged the dead back into the morgue.

The firebase was quiet, no Duster fire and no artillery. The medics stood uneasily outside the bunker entrance.

"How come those Dusters didn't fire?" Clancy said. "They had to see that flash."

"Maybe we're running out of ammo," Cullen said.

"Cullen, you don't know a goddamn thing about our goddamn ammo! Or *any* goddamn thing," Clancy said, heading downstairs behind Nimmer, and yelling over his shoulder. "Don't go starting no bullshit rumors, trooper!"

"Fucking gooks," Cullen said to Ben, Limerick, and Halliday. "Why the hell would they shoot at our dead?"

"Maybe heard you were throwing N-V-A out of choppers," Ben said tightly.

Cullen made his hard grin.

"Speaking of bullshit rumors," Cullen said. "Wasn't me. But, back home in Oklahoma, Home, we'd a hung them little bastards up on the nearest tree."

Limerick gave Ben a disgusted glance.

"You'd have probably hung *me* up, too, right, Cullen?" Limerick said. "And laughed about it. I've seen those souvenir postcards of your fucking lynchings. Families, smiling like they were at a picnic. You're fucking sick. All of you."

Their faces dripping with rain, Ben and Limerick glared at Cullen.

"No siree," Cullen retorted with a thin-lipped grin. "We like your kind real good."

Limerick narrowed his eyes and went downstairs.

"Grow the fuck up, Cullen," Ben said.

Ben shook his head and followed Limerick downstairs.

Cullen scoffed and removed his helmet.

As the airstrip faded into darkness, Cullen scratched his sweaty, close-cropped head.

When the weak all-clear siren wailed from the TOC, Cullen faced Halliday.

"And you, Home, I do believe you are a chickenshit," Cullen said with his joyless grin.

He grabbed Halliday's shoulder hard.

"I can see it in your eyes—just like Donnelly."

"Fuck you, Cullen," Halliday said, shaking the bigger man's arm off. "I haven't run from any duty. And I haven't begged Doc to leave."

"We'll see, Halliday, we'll see."

Halliday shook his head and went downstairs.

Cullen stood alone in the dusk, staring at the dull dirty light in the west.

                    *   *   *

A few minutes after the last rocket slammed into the airstrip, the Kid drove Lehr and Captain Dunkley around the bunker line.

When they finished, the Kid parked behind the TOC and forgot to switch off the Jeep's blackout lights.

"Goddamnit, Jamison!" Lehr yelled. "Pay attention."

The Kid shut off the lights, but his ears burned as he followed the Colonel inside the command bunker.

The Kid sat down on his cot in the hallway outside Lehr's office just as Merton stomped out.

"What the fuck's the matter with you, Long Puss?"

The Kid looked down.

"Oh, oh, oh," Merton whined. "*What?* Some suck-face lifer chewed your sensitive little ass out? Big fucking deal. Get the fuck over it. Who gives a shit what they think? Who the fuck are *they* anyway? Green fucking machine—just out to kill us any way they fucking can. Jesus Christ, I used to think all we had to worry about was the fucking enemy, but noooo, it's our own fucking idiots trying to fucking grease us, too. Fuck them, fuck the government, fuck those fucking civilians who fucking sent us here. I gotta go write my girlfriend. Go have a fucking beer, Kid. Just remember, not one swinging dick besides your mamma ever gives a flying rat's ass how the fuck your sensitive little ass *feels, bic?* Nitey night, liddle baaaab-y boooy."

Merton blew a loud raspberry through his fist and disappeared into his office.

The Kid scanned the dimly lit TOC.

In the open S-3 area, Sergeant Edison read Norman Mailer's *Armies of the Night* by flashlight with his feet on a desk near the restricted S-2 area behind a sandbagged wall.

The Kid reached under his cot and took out the book that Clancy had given him—Marlowe's *Illustrated History of Military Uniforms*. He thumbed the glossy pages until he found a stocky French commander in a field uniform.

As the 1-7-5 guns on the river line behind the TOC boomed out, the Kid studied a photograph of John Kennedy's funeral—the riderless horse with the tall shiny boots in the stirrups backwards, the shiny black coffin on the black caisson, the six tall riders on six black horses.

The generator phased and the lights faded as the room dimmed.

The Kid exhaled, turned the pages, and read in near darkness: *Eighteenth-century military dress consisted of: tricorn hat, long-skirted coat, waistcoat, and breeches with long canvas gaiters to mid-thigh with multiple buttons.*

The Kid smiled at a black Revolutionary soldier wearing tight knee breeches with high gaiters and a long-skirted coat.

Teletypes chattered from the S-2 section.

Eerie wails of radio squelch—crisp static and moaning band drift signaled that something was happening. When the Kid looked up, Edison was gone, and Major Sneller leaned back in his office chair, chuckling over a thin book with red cartoon letters: *Jokes For the John.*

As radio communication intensified, Sneller shook, but continued to chuckle.

A laugh came from the sergeant major's office with a clink of glasses.

"So, tell me Top," Loudermilk's wheedling voice soothed. "What really happened up there on Paradise?"

A bottle clinked sharply.

"Be good for you to talk, Top," Loudermilk purred. "Just between old soldiers."

Straining to hear, the Kid didn't see Sergeant Clancy sit down on the cot beside him at a respectable distance.

"Kid."

"Good evening, Sergeant Clancy."

Clancy wore fresh jungle fatigues and smelled like Old Spice. His watery eyes were bloodshot, but his wide mouth fell into an easy smile.

"How's it going, Kid?"

"OK, Sergeant," the Kid replied, closing the book.

Major Ranklin walked past, ignoring them.

Ranklin beckoned to the chuckling Sneller, who set down his toilet joke book. Ranklin led Sneller into the S-2 office and closed the security door.

The Kid and Clancy sat alone in the big main room.

"It was real good having you in the medics, Kid."

The Kid smiled.

"I wish I was still there."

Clancy's knee brushed the Kid's.

"I keep thinking about that night," Clancy said.

The Kid smiled and fingered the military history book.

Clancy nodded, made eyes out the front entrance, and left.

A few moments later, the Kid headed out. As he glided by the sergeant major's office, Sergeant Loudermilk splashed liquor onto the sergeant-major's fatigue shirt hanging on the back of a chair. The Kid screwed up his face in disbelief but kept on walking through the entry maze.

Outside under starlight, Sergeant-Major Bricker urinated into the piss tube.

The Kid hurried away toward the abandoned ammo bunker that Clancy had suggested once before.

*   *   *

The next morning inside the bustling TOC, the Kid swept shards of red-brown mud off the floor in preparation for the generals from Saigon. An hour before, a rocket attack had killed two artillerymen and wounded four engineers.

Carrying a long sheet of Teletype paper, Major Ranklin rushed past the Kid. Lieutenant Fairbanks, now battalion intelligence officer, followed, wearing a fresh red scarf.

Sergeant Loudermilk stopped Ranklin with a thick hairy arm.

"Sir," whispered the gum-chewing sergeant. "I think he's ... you know, at it again."

"Goddamnit," Ranklin cursed. "After Colonel Lehr ..."

"Don't know where he got it," Loudermilk said.

Sergeant major Bricker ambled out of his office toward the S-3 section, where Edison and Lundly were preparing the large briefing map of the Daktoum A-O.

"Major," Bricker greeted Ranklin.

Ranklin edged Bricker toward a corner.

"Top, Sergeant Loudermilk will do the briefing."

"*What?*" the soft-spoken Bricker yelled.

Ranklin smelled alcohol.

Across the TOC, Loudermilk rubbed a meaty hand through his short, bristly, red hair.

"Where's Colonel Lehr?" Sergeant-major Bricker asked, staring hard at Ranklin.

The Kid stopped sweeping.

Bricker's droopy eyelids were ringed with dark circles, and his loose ruddy face paled as he preceded Ranklin into Lehr's office. Loudermilk sidled away with a light step.

Someone elbowed the Kid off-balance.

"What the fuck are you staring at, sweeper boy?" Merton said. "Get your ass in gear, or I'll ship you out to the goddamn infantry, lunchmeat."

The Kid scowled at Merton and swept the heap of dried mud toward the exit.

*   *   *

Crisply uniformed, Colonel Lehr regarded Ranklin and Sergeant major Bricker, whose eyes looked glazed as he argued to give the briefing. Lehr's powerful arms thrust together on the battered desktop, fists touching. Lehr glinted his pale gray eyes directly at Bricker, who smelled like alcohol.

"Sergeant Major," Lehr said. "Our tactical opinions aren't worth a damn to Saigon, and I really don't give a shit about this briefing—let Loudermilk present it. Concentrate on the Command Sergeant Major —about our enlisted men—no fresh food, water shortages, the wounded, the dead, the soldiers' morale in the siege—maybe you can get through to him—they don't listen to me. They have their own agenda."

Lehr stood up.

"Shall we, gentlemen?"

Ranklin left. Lehr caught the sergeant major by the elbow.

"Might be a good idea," Lehr said, "to change your fatigue shirt."

Bricker stared at Lehr for a moment and then nodded.

*   *   *

Colonel Lehr waited beneath the twin flagpoles near the rain slick airstrip, wearing a helmet and flak jacket over his last pressed pair of combat fatigues. Major Ranklin, an artillery lieutenant colonel, Captain Dunkley, and Sergeant Major Bricker stood at the end of the company street.

A twin-engine, black-and-white plane dropped out of the gray sky and made a tight, quick landing on the rough airstrip. The plane roared, weaved to avoid rocket craters, and fast-taxied across the tarmac to the VIP pad.

Colonel Eagleton—in new fatigues, polished boots, and battle dress —opened the rear hatch and unfolded the aluminum steps. He nodded to Lehr, standing at attention.

General Armbruster, General Cade, General Nguyen Lin, Colonel Trinh, and Sergeant Major Stack briskly stepped out of the plane. They nodded and swiftly marched down the company street, sweeping up the reception party to the TOC.

General Armbruster beckoned Lehr beside him.

"How's that backhand, Lehr?" Armbruster said, nodding at the pockmarked airstrip. "Damndest clay courts I've seen."

Lehr made a tight grin. The Americans paired up with their escorts, the Vietnamese with each other.

Daktoum firebase seemed deserted. The artillery crews on the river were the only soldiers visible, and the engineers were underground, out on the road, or on the bunker line.

Half the tents on the camp street were ruined. The red-brown mud was littered with soldiers' toothbrushes, torn *Playboy* pinups, a teddy bear leg, a ripped red flag with a snake on it, a torn photograph—just a smooth forehead and shining blonde hair—making it impossible to tell if the woman was a mother, a sister, or a lover.

The South Vietnamese officers nervously scanned Rocket Ridge beneath roiling clouds. Their uniforms seemed too large, with numerous medals and decorations which gave off the impression of small, overly plumed birds.

"How many rounds?" General Armbruster asked Lehr.

Armbruster had a strong jaw and a tough grin. He moved like a boxer.

"Thirty," Lehr said. "So far today. 1-22s."

"Effective weapon."

Colonel Trinh magnanimously waved to Firebase Paradise, while General Lin pawed a chrome 45 pistol at his belt. Trinh's cocky walk and attitude had always pissed Lehr off.

"Your monkey, Colonel?" Armbruster asked as the camp monkey scampered by, trailing a leash.

The monkey scaled the TOC and ducked under a tower.

"Gutsy bugger," Armbruster said.

"Monkey see, monkey do," General Cade drawled. "Just like most folks."

Cade's laconic Georgia accent set Lehr on edge but amused Armbruster.

"So, Lehr," Armbruster said. "Colonel Trinh's operation?"

"The one he's running from 30 miles away?"

"It's their war, now, Colonel," General Cade said.

"Maybe. But they don't seem compelled to hold this valley," Lehr said.

Armbruster shot Lehr a glance as they reached the TOC.

The command party stepped through the maze entrance into a scrubbed TOC, which was empty except for Sergeant Loudermilk, S-2, and Commo.

In the open operations section, a dozen chairs faced a large map of Daktoum firebase and a larger relief of the Cambodian-Laotian border. The pilots followed the party in and carried two shiny olive mess coolers.

"Thought we could save some time," General Cade said. "If we ate while you briefed."

The Vietnamese general smiled and nodded. Sergeant Major Stack passed out steak sandwiches on fresh French bread with coleslaw, hot French-fried potatoes, icy Philippine beer, and generous slices of German chocolate cake.

"Gentlemen," Loudermilk began. "Daktoum is in the second week of frequent N-V-A rocket and mortar fire…"

Toward the end of the briefing, Sergeant Major Stack passed out paper cups of dark-roast coffee.

"Unless there's a timely infantry operation to neutralize enemy rockets and artillery on Rocket Ridge," Loudermilk concluded. "Daktoum will suffer heavy casualties unless the 99th and the artillery are pulled back, the enemy withdraws, or the enemy's rocket and artillery positions are destroyed."

The command party finished their sandwiches and started on the chocolate cake.

"We just don't have the manpower," Lehr said, "to assault their positions."

"Air power," Colonel Trinh interrupted.

"Dug in too deep," Lehr said. "Even B-52 arc lights haven't stopped them, or their resupply—and the ceiling's getting pretty dicey for Tac-air."

"Colonel, I perhaps think you underestimate your own air power," Trinh said. "We already have a fine body count."

"Maybe out in the jungle," Lehr said. "But besides a few sappers, the body count here in Daktoum, Ban Sai, and the firebases is mainly American."

"What are you inferring, Colonel Lehr?" General Cade asked. "American infantry?"

"Unless there's another force that thinks that rooting out N-V-A artillery positions is prudent and possible."

"Vietnamization," Colonel Trinh said, looking at his general, who turned to General Armbruster.

"Our role, Colonel Lehr, is not to suggest tactics," Armbruster said. "This *is* a South Vietnamese show. We're here to offer support capacity."

Lehr flushed and Eagleton glanced over in sympathy.

"General," Lehr said to Armbruster. "If this weather holds, the N-V-A will continue to kick the hell out of Daktoum, the ARVNs and all our firebases. The enemy has what? Six, eight, ten thousand? If our choppers can't get in and the road gets cut, Ben Sai could fall. The N-V-A could even bring Russian tanks down Highway 14."

General Cade's grin said: "that's exactly what we want."

"Colonel Lehr, I do think your statement assumes an awful lot," Cade said. "And, further, it carries a not-so-subtle inference that our brave allies and good friends the South Vietnamese will not meet with success on the field of battle."

"Sir," Lehr addressed Armbruster directly. "Every major Highland siege battle—Dien Bien Phu, Khe Sanh, Bu Prang—shares a similar pattern. The North Vietnamese dig in deep with a lot of personnel when it's quiet, and then they bring out the heavy weapons as soon as the monsoon slows air ops. The only way to counter this is infantry. Beg your pardon, but at this juncture, the most effective infantry in South Vietnam is American. At least a battalion, two. Root out those positions."

General Cade sighed.

"Thank you much, Colonel Lehr," Armbruster said.

General Armbruster stood up and shook Sergeant Loudermilk's hand. When Lehr got up, a hand gripped his shoulder, and he turned to see Colonel Eagleton's tight smile.

"We're scheduled for departure," Eagleton said.

The command party filed out of the TOC.

Outside, the gray skies were misty.

"Colonel, your points are well-stated, and I might add, not dissimilar from my own," Armbruster said, walking beside Lehr. "Unfortunately, the defense of Daktoum is as political as it is military. I couldn't bring an American infantry *company* back in here, much less a battalion. My hands are tied."

"Sir, you are the commanding general of Vietnam."

Armbruster glanced over with a hard, compassionate stare. He looked past the broken tent hootches to the jungle hills.

"You'll hang on, Colonel."

"Hang on?"

"I read your casualty reports—I read *all* the casualty reports in Vietnam, Lehr. I feel for your men and their families, but whether we like it or not, ultimately, the battle for Daktoum valley is a South Vietnamese show. Our orders come from the top. I do mean the *very* top—and I don't mean the Army, the Joint Chiefs, or D.O.D."

Out on the airstrip, General Cade checked his watch, frowned, and signaled the pilot. The small plane fired up and carefully maneuvered out from the parking revetment.

The command party shook hands, swiftly moved up the aluminum steps, and boarded, until only Eagleton and Armbruster stood beside Colonel Lehr.

"John," Armbruster said to Lehr over the propeller noise. "I am genuinely sorry about your mail and Saigon briefing the press that there's no Americans left at Daktoum. The moment the South Viets get control, we'll open things up a bit."

Armbruster nodded, made a tight smile, and held out his hand. Lehr hesitated. Then he shook the general's hand.

"Practice that backhand," Armbruster said with a smile, before turning and entering the small aircraft.

Cold son of a bitch, Lehr thought.

Eagleton gripped Lehr's shoulder.

When Armbruster reached the hatch, he turned back and flashed a grin before ducking inside the small cabin.

Eagleton looked deep into Lehr's eyes, nodded, and then climbed the ladder.

The co-pilot pulled up the ramp from inside and buttoned up the hatch.

The small black-and-white plane quickly taxied onto the main strip, revved its engines, and took off.

Lehr waved the command party back to the TOC.

As the hum of the small plane melted into a rumble of artillery, Lehr felt a stab of pain on his left side. His muscles cramped so tight that he almost cried out.

*   *   *

Gabrielle and Doc sat inside the small medical office, playing Hearts with the worn Death's Head deck that the airborne brigade had left behind. Doc shuffled and dealt. He turned over the Queen of Spades.

"The Queen's coming up a lot, lately," Doc said.

"Superstitious, Bac si?" Gabrielle asked, studying her cards. "Or do you think I'm cheating?"

"Both."

Bacsi licked Doc's arm, but he pushed the dog away and played the eight of Spades. The field phone buzzed, and he picked it up.

"Battalion Surgeon," he said.

"Hiya, Doc," Merton's harsh voice said. "Colonel wants to see the French doctor."

"OK," Doc told Merton, placing the phone back on its canvas case.

Doc's eyes narrowed as Gabrielle toyed with her cards.

"Colonel Lehr wants you," Doc said, trying to sound unconcerned.

When Gabrielle played the King of Spades, she inadvertently flashed Doc her Jack.

"Until I come back?" she teased. "You do promise not look at my cards?"

Gabrielle rose from the metal bed and lit a fresh cigarette from the one smoldering in the ashtray.

"Promise?" she said.

Gabrielle took a long drag.

When her hand trembled, she hid it behind her back, and beamed at Doc. Her unwashed hair drooped in strands from Doc's extra baseball cap. Gabrielle snatched up her black medical bag, quickly drew open the canvas flap, and left.

*   *   *

As Gabrielle walked across the red mud in the dusk, the only sound in the camp was the whine of the generator.

Whenever Gabrielle entered the TOC, she felt the soldiers' eyes on her body. Even right in the colonel's outer office, Merton openly glanced at her hips.

"Ain't here," Merton said. "Doctor Mar-chand. Try the Hilton."

"Hilton?"

"His *sleeping* bunker," Merton said, smirking.

Gabrielle left the office, crossed the TOC with her head held high, and went out the front maze entrance.

Only a thin slice of green jungle hills in the west were visible under the dimming sky as she hurried along the ruined company street with its mud-stained borders of white rocks. The mist muffled the soldiers' voices and footsteps—what little life that was left on the firebase.

Inside one smashed hootch, three emaciated camp dogs fought over a bone. Gabrielle shuddered and rushed along. As Lehr's bunker loomed up out of the mist, the flak vest that Doc forced her to wear felt heavy.

She stepped beneath the crossed timbers and went down.

"You're here," Lehr called from the darkness.

She groped through blackness, blindly drawn through the dank room until she pressed her body against Colonel Lehr, who, after a very long time, yielded—ever so slightly—to her.

*   *   *

Afterwards, they lay naked on his silky poncho liner, their unwashed bodies adding to the thick decay that overwhelmed Daktoum.

"They don't care," he whispered.

Gabrielle lay on Lehr's chest, feeling his words murmur through her chest.

"It's no longer a war of principle, or men's lives or even honor. Only politics."

Gabrielle sat up.

"What did you expect, Lehr?" she asked. "A war by its nature is corrupt."

I'd rather be destroyed, Lehr thought, shaking with anger.

"So," she said. "What will you do now, Lehr?"

Her whisper assaulted him like a knife.

Lehr slapped Gabrielle.

His sharp slap instantly fell dead in the cool humid room. The pain of inflicting and the pain of receiving hung as heavy as the strong odors of their bodies. Lehr immediately regretted it and waited for tears, so he could comfort and embrace her, but Gabrielle only gasped.

"So then," she whispered. "You will just wait."

Lehr nearly cracked at the sound of her voice. His powerful body shuddered, and his strong boxer's arms clutched her as fear and desperation and abandonment pounded his every capillary.

Finally, Lehr exhaled and loosened his grip.

Then Gabrielle rolled over and engulfed him—until Lehr moaned and his hips jerked unexpectedly, like an adolescent. Afterwards, he slept, lost to the horror—until the enemy artillery started up again. The rockets continued sporadically throughout the day and night.

17.

The next morning, Halliday dozed on the medical bunker's long wooden bench in the waiting area with his head propped on a stained flak vest left by the wounded.

"Get your ass up!" Clancy yelled, kicking the bench.

Halliday sat up with buggy eyes.

"Where's that girl? Bunker's a goddamn mess—you medics don't do shit!"

Groggy, Halliday realized that Clancy meant Lam.

"Get your ass moving, Halliday! She's in that shit-burner-laundry-girl bunker out on the river with crazy-ass Ellis."

Halliday shook his head. He lifted his flak vest and helmet off the floor, grabbed his gas mask, and shuffled out the back, dragging his rifle up the wooden steps.

"And figure out how to get a chopper for the dead," Clancy called after him. "Maybe get some of those sodas Ellis sitting on—we only got a couple days of water left."

"Yeah, yeah, yeah," Halliday muttered as he trudged up the muddy stairs.

Outside, the mist had turned to light rain. Halliday put on his battle gear and went out. Thick red mud stuck to his combat boots. Then the rain stopped, but the mist was still so thick that he could barely see the antennas atop the TOC and the jerry-rigged wooden rocket deflector.

He walked toward the river bluff, where the crumbling bunkers and tangles of barbed wire loomed out of the mist.

Outside the oldest bunker in Daktoum, built by the 101st airborne four years before, Halliday scraped off his boots.

The mist shifted, and the body, hanging on the wire with outstretched arms, disappeared. He waited for the body to reappear, but only the tops of the tower bunkers were visible.

Halliday descended twenty steps underground until the smell of rice cooking came from a dim blue light reflecting off hundreds of Pabst Blue Ribbon beer cases. A big, glowing Texas flag hung over a door-sized break in the blue wall.

"Ellis?" Halliday called through the flag.

"Who asking?"

"Halliday from the medics."

"That's the password. Open, sesame."

Halliday pulled aside the Texas flag.

The room was ablaze with naked women. A hundred glossy *Playboy* Playmates pinups covered all the beer case walls clear up to the ceiling.

Tall, thin, red-eyed Ellis sat on his bunk, feeding the camp monkey C-ration peaches off a fork.

"Where'd you get all these centerfolds?" Halliday asked.

"Finest collection in the whole damn Central Highlands, maybe in all goddamn Vietnam. Lucky they weren't in my last bunker when it blowed up. I had me a pree-mun-ition, and saved most the good ones, just lost all my duplicates."

"Where the hell did *he* come from?" Halliday asked, nodding at the monkey.

"Just showed up. Anyway, he don't smell no worse than them gooks, all that fish heads rice nook mom bullshit," Ellis chuckled. "And he certainly smell *way* better than that gook on the wire. Now that dude, he *stink*."

"I thought I saw a body," Halliday said, "How come we don't bury it?"

"Major says scares the shit outa *their* gooks—dead spirits are all unsettled, freaking and deaking, and wandering and lost 'cause it ain't been buried at home with their people."

Halliday looked doubtful.

"Makes as much sense as any other damn thing in this shit-hole Daktoum."

Ellis cocked his head.

"How come your babysan stay in here so much?"

"Busy," Halliday said.

"Yeah, like everybody else *ain't*?"

"Well, I'm here to get her."

"Lucky I ain't charged you no rent."

"No sweat, Ellis," Halliday said. "Next time you get the clap, your shot's free."

"Ellis he don't get no god-damn clap. I *honor* my body. I always wear me a raincoat."

"Where is she?"

Ellis pointed out the flag-covered entrance.

Halliday pushed through the Lone Star flag and walked past the blue stacks of beer cases into a dimly lit room with tall, red walls of drink cases. Vietnamese talked around a rice pot on the floor, steaming on the low blue flames from C-4 plastic explosives.

Three Vietnamese women and two old men squatted around the pot.

"Where's girlsan?" Halliday asked. "Lam?"

A long-faced, sharp-eyed woman grimaced as Ranklin's girlfriend, Tu, with a new short haircut, pointed to a shadowy corner with stacks of red Coca-Cola cases.

"Over there, G.I."

Lam lay on a filthy army cot staring at the low ceiling.

"You OK, Lam?" Halliday said.

She looked over.

"Sure, Howaday G.I."

Halliday adjusted his helmet.

"Sergeant Clancy sent me."

"Where you take me?"

"Go America on scooter bus," Halliday said.

"You crazy, G.I.," she said, smiling and hitting his arm.

The monkey chattered, the rice steamed, and Vietnamese women conversed in melodious lines.

Lam sat up, smoothed her long hair with delicate fingers, and reached beneath the cot.

"Lam?" he said, sitting down. "How are you?"

She turned her brown almond-shaped eyes to Halliday.

"OK, G.I.," she said. "Where you live, America?"

"In the desert, you know, cowboys and Indians. Why? You want to go there?"

"You take me?" she said.

"What about mamasan?"

Lam shrugged and reached under the cot for her cone hat.

"We should go," he said.

Halliday took Lam's arm. As they walked, Lam's hip brushed against his, making her smile. Tu watched them.

Shit, Halliday thought, asking to go home with me? Lam's pregnant. Oh man, it can't be mine, there had to have been a lot of guys.

"Ellis," Halliday called in, pushing aside the Texas flag.

"Yeah?"

Ellis smoked a big bomber as he fed the monkey peaches. Lam shook out her long silky hair, which brushed his arm.

"Clancy asked me to score some soft drinks."

"That's a negatory on that shit, Jim," Ellis said, exhaling marijuana smoke and slowly shaking his head. "Colonel say no beer no soda for no-motherfucking-body—unless he say so."

Ellis offered the smoking joint.

"Want some do?"

Halliday didn't, but he walked over for a social puff. Taking the joint back, Ellis accidentally jerked the fork, and the monkey screeched and bit Ellis's finger.

"God-DAMN! Dirty ass monkey!"

The monkey snatched out a dripping peach, shot past Halliday out under the Texas flag, and scrambled up the bunker staircase. Ellis sucked his bloody finger, and Halliday stifled a grin as Lam's hand circled his waist.

"God-damn monkey! I *never* should have done *shit* for you, *fool,*" Ellis ranted. "Ungrateful wild-ass animal—no god damn respect—same same as *all* you gooks!"

"Come on over and get a tetanus shot," Halliday said, pushing the Lone Star flag aside.

"Fuck that tetanus!"

Halliday became conscious of the melody in his voice. Good dope, he thought. When Lam's warm hand brushed his hip, all the naked girls on Ellis's walls seemed to stare right at him with such intense longing that Halliday felt the glossy women dancing down his spine and warming his belly.

"We go now, G.I.?" Lam said, tugging his hip.

"Yeah."

Lam coiled her black hair atop her head, put on the straw cone hat and followed him upstairs.

Outside, raindrops glistened on the entrance beams.

The wall of mist shifted so the stiff arms and torso of the dead N-V-A soldier stretched over the barbed wire.

When Halliday steered Lam away from the lime-whitened corpse, her warm body brushed his, and he pulled her close.

"G.I.?" she whispered.

"Yeah," Halliday said breathlessly.

"We go now?" she said, her dark eyes staring.

"Yeah," he said.

Lam slipped out of his arms and sauntered away.

Halliday caught up and turned her honey-colored face toward him. She smiled, and her black almond eyes danced under the coolie hat. His mind raced—America? Is she pregnant? My child? *You first, G.I., you first.* First.

Her hips rocked the silky black pants as her tiny bare feet in green flip-flops delicately stepped over the red mud.

The fog shimmered and pulsed. Good shit Ellis smokes.

Suddenly, Halliday grabbed Lam's shoulder and kissed her tenderly, leaning so far over that his helmet tumbled into the mud with a loud plop.

He broke away with an embarrassed grin. Lam stared and her lips parted.

"Number one?" he asked.

"Number one," she nodded, looking down.

Halliday drew Lam so tight that he felt her heat through the silky pants.

Three quick rounds popped, muffled under the fog, and Halliday yanked Lam down into a crouch. He looked for a bunker until he realized that the rounds were outgoing flares.

Halliday grinned like a schoolboy as he shivered at Lam's kiss rippling through his body. As he picked his helmet up off the mud, Lam smiled.

"Come on," Halliday said, grinning and squeezing her.

She looked down at her bare feet in the green flip-flops, rimmed with red mud.

"Go where, G.I.?" she asked in a soft voice.

"Just come on," he said, grabbing her hand and gently tugging her away.

They moved quickly under the fog, his heavy boots and her green flip-flops sliding across the viscous red clay. Sandbagged walls loomed and dissolved in the mist as they passed smashed wood and collapsed wet heaps of canvas.

Bunkers and olive drab tents swirled in and out of view until they reached a broad gray mound of sandbags, the Waiting Room, Halliday's underground hootch.

They scraped red mud off their shoes and headed down.

Halliday led Lam into a very dark corridor between metal bunks with wood frames and mosquito nets. He stopped at his bed, peeled off his combat gear, and tossed it on top.

He yanked up the damp mosquito net and eased Lam onto a thin mattress where he had not slept in weeks, wiping the red mud off her bare feet with a dirty T-shirt. Then he removed his boots, slipped into bed beside her, and yanked the mosquito net around them. Lam's hat tumbled off when Halliday moved in to kiss her, but she held his face and ran her smooth fingers across Halliday's cheeks and pressed her fingers on his eyes.

"Ahhhh," he sighed. "Oh God."

When she moved her hands, he could barely see her face in a dim glow from the stairwell thirty feet away.

"Miss you Howaday," she whispered.

He rolled over, kissing her hard, his hands tugging off her silky clothing, and she, his fatigues, until a pile of olive drab and black silk lay crumpled at the foot of his bed. His hands covered her body as they fell together, wildly kissing and touching under an overwhelming desire from weeks of fear until his limbs shuddered. All the blood and gore and horror of weeks tainted the darkness with dim glowing red images that seemed to overwhelm him and burst off his cock.

She pushed him onto his back and knelt above him, resting her hands on his shoulders as she lifted her hips. All the sensations were dizzying, her rocking satin flesh and soft breath, their warm centers slipping against each other like they were roped to their souls.

The fear of rockets, dying, getting crippled, John Wayne, C-rations, the heat, the cold, the dead, the wounded all faded away as her smooth tight body slipped up and engulfed him, and her cooing breath trilled like the floating harmonica creeping down the stairs, accompanied by boot steps.

Halliday gasped and touched Lam's sighing mouth.

"Fuck me," he whispered.

The harmonica walked into the bunker on heavy boots.

Your mer-cury mouth in the mission-ary times. ...

"Motherfucking AFVN radio always playing that scratchy-assed folksinger bullshit," a voice said. "How come they ain't never play no soul music."

"Turn it off, Jim."

The music faded and quit. Black voices, three? Four? Halliday guessed.

"Over this way."

"Can't see *shit*."

A leg cracked against a steel bunk.

"Goddamn!"

"Light a match."

"Negative on that shit, no lights."

"Who says?"

"Me, Limerick *says*. Clancy catch us here, he court-martial us all."

"Court-martial? What the fuck for?"

"I don't know, ... treason."

"*Treason*? What the hell you gonna talk about? Overthrowing Tricky Dick? Shooting the colonel?"

"Say *what*?"

"What the hell you mean, *treason*?"

"I don't want no part of no *treason*. I ain't no Benadictine Arnold."

"What the hell we even doing down in this goddamn pit?"

"Where you want to go, numb nuts, mess hall?"

"*Who* you calling numb nuts? Anyway, the gooks already blowed up our mess hall. You know, Limerick, you ain't the world's smartest nigger."

"I told you, not to use that word—not even in a joke. We're blacks, now."

"We be black, too, but you ain't as smart as you think, nigger."

"Just sit down and shut up, we're waiting for somebody."

"Who?"

"Ellis."

"ELLIS? That cat's shit's so loose they oughta make him carry a portable toilet."

"Man, are you forgetting? There's a war going on back in the World. I got to talk to *all* the brothers."

"Except Clancy. And Ben."

"Clancy more honky than Snow White. Lifer motherfucker."

"And *Ben*—he worse than a lifer. He don't listen to nobody, he '*middle class*'."

"Shit."

"Check out that radio again."

... your flesh like silk and your face like glass ...

"Oh *man*, that song *still* on?"

The radio clicked off.

Halliday cautiously moved beneath Lam, pressing his finger against her lips. Limerick and his friends wouldn't bust him. He exhaled, kissed her, and ran his hands down her hips. Slowly, still connected, she stretched her legs until she lay flat on top of him in the dark. He rubbed his large hands into her calves, her thighs, her soft bottom, and then he massaged her back all the way up to her neck.

"You 'all down there?" a harsh voice called.

"Come on in, Ellis, don't show no light. Over here."

Ellis clumped down and someone grabbed him.

"Here, sit on this footlocker."

"Where?"

"Right here."

The scent of marijuana swept into the dank bunker.

"Aw, shit, Ellis!"

"Oh *yeah*, man, pass that 'doo' around."

"Don't mean nothing Limerick, no sweat, this here's the herb of liberation."

"A-men, brother."

"You know I'm against that shit. You even know what this meeting's about?"

"Black brothers getting genocided back home after being blowed away in Viet-nam."

"You read that paper?"

"Yeah. Everything cool with me, 'cept for the part about *gooks* being my brother," Ellis said. "I ain't buying that shit. Ain't no gook—dead or alive—got any business being Lester J. Ellis' *brother*, 'specially after he be blasting the shit out of me for weeks with his heavy artillerary."

"Yeah."

"*Artillerary*? What the fuck is *artillerary*, Ellis?"

"You know exactly what the fuck I mean, college boy."

"You can't be blaming the N-V-A for black men not having power back in the world," Limerick said. "White people back home trying to kill us faster than the enemy. Look around—lot more brothers on the line than white people. It's up to us to take power, to take action. Power to the people, black power!"

Halliday heard fists softly knocking in the darkness.

"Yeah. Yeah."

"I can dig that," Ellis said. "Hey Limerick. Where you get that paper on all this Black Power?"

"A friend. In the American."

"I know a door gunner in the 'merical. Pass that doo."

"Here."

"Hey Limerick, what's the name of this bunker?"

"Bunker."

"No man, this bunker got a *name*, I heard it once."

"I heard that something, too."

"Why?"

"Just want to know."

Lam slipped off Halliday, opened her legs, and knelt above him. Her bottom lifted and bucked lightly down, brushing against him, and slowly pulled away until their hips were barely connected. She leaned her hands on his shoulders while lazily circled her hips, nuzzling him, around and around in both directions, while he ran his hands down her silky back and through her silky hair until he grabbed the silky mounds of her round bottom, pulling him deep into her until she bucked involuntarily with tiny high-pitched moans.

"Ahhhhhhhh…"

"Uh, uh, uh, uh, uh, uh, uhhhh!" Halliday panted, unable to keep silent.

"Shhhh," Ellis said. "You hear that?"

Halliday opened his mouth wide to quiet his breath.

"Ellis, you smoke way too much motherfucking dope."

"Medics bunk in here," Limerick said. "Clancy called it the Waiting Room."

"You shitting me?" Ellis said. "The *Waiting Room*? This bunker is number double fucking ten!"

"What?"

"You got any idea what the infantry *use* this bunker for?"

"Medical."

"Medical, my ass. When the shit come down last year, infantry used it for the *dead*. Piled beau coups bodies in here."

Lam slowly bucked her hips against Halliday in the dark, smacked a quick burst of a dozen fast little thrusts, and slowly ground her hips around and into his.

"Haaaaaaaaaaah," Halliday exhaled as quietly as he could.

"Oh yeah," Ellis said. "Two hundred bodies stacked in here for way too motherfucking long, waiting to ship home. Reason they call it the Waiting Room. So many bodies waiting that the medics ran out of room and stacked them in here."

"Aaaaaaaaaaaaaaaahhhhhhhhhhhhh!" Halliday moaned.

"What's that?"

"Maybe rats fucking or some shit."

"Gimme your 45, Limerick."

"Nobody shooting in here."

"You know that medic, Nimmer? He told me he seen a big old King Cobra snake sliding into one of these bunkers to eat rats. Who else got a weapon?"

"I got me a LAW right here," Ellis said.

"Man, you can't use a fucking LAW in here, Ellis, you'd blow us the fuck *up*!"

"Unh unh unh unh unh unh unh unh unh! Unhhhhhh!" Lam throated like a bird.

"Sounds like it *eating* something."

"I'm gonna waste it with my LAW."

"Aaaaaaaaaaaaaaaaaaaaaaaaaaaaaaaaaaaaa," Halliday hissed.

"Fuck this, I'm outa here!"

"Come on man, get the fuck moving!"

"Move!"

Helmets and legs crashed into steel bunks and footlockers, boots stomped up wooden stairs as the bedsprings chimed under Halliday and Lam until the steel frame bunk shook and rattled and skitter-banged against the wooden walls as the metal legs hop-scraped across the rough concrete floor.

Jesusandmomma,jesusandmomma,Jeeeeeeeeeeeeeessssssssssssssuuuuu uuuuussss!

From the top of the stairs, the portable radio blasted:

Sad-eyed Lady of the low-lands, where the sad-eyed prophet says ...

Under the filmy mosquito net, Halliday thrust one last lovely time and collapsed beneath Lam's warm little body. In the darkness, his breath rasped and panted slower and slower as Lam's satin body encircled his skin like a hot wet spirit.

When Halliday finally opened his eyes, dozens of glowing blue specks surrounded him, and he blinked hard to drive them away, cursing the opium flashes.

But faint blue circles still floated all around the bed, a thousand ghostly eyes, raptly absorbing the two naked teen-aged bodies, eyes watching from the immense darkness.

"You see them, Lam?" he whispered.

"See what, G.I.?"

"All the eyes."

"No see no eyes, Howaday."

Halliday shivered and almost panicked until he buried his face in Lam's slender neck and lay very still. When Halliday finally opened his eyes, all the luminous blue circles were gone.

*   *   *

Inside the TOC, Doc and Gabrielle sat before the ashen-faced Colonel Lehr wearing his steel helmet with the black eagle insignia. On the desk was a blue airmail letter, its edges soiled from re-reading.

Outside, artillery pounded. There was a knock on the door.

"Yes?" Lehr said.

Merton stuck in his big round head and grinned.

"Going over to my hootch, sir."

"Oh. Yes," the colonel said, getting up.

The door closed. When the colonel grimaced and paced behind his worn desk, Doc and Gabrielle traded glances. Lehr ran his fingers over a big map under the fluorescent light.

"Sir?" Doc asked.

The colonel turned, glared at Captain Levin and Gabrielle, and leaned over his desk onto his fists.

"Can our troops function drinking beer and soft drinks instead of water?" Lehr said.

"What?"

"We've been running out of water since our purification unit was hit. Now we can't depend on the convoy. Can my troops survive on soft drinks and beer?"

Gabrielle glanced at Doc.

"Soft drinks are sugar water with caffeine," Doc said. "Beer is water and alcohol. Most soldiers don't drink much water."

Gabrielle nodded.

"That's what I thought," Lehr said. "Doctor Marchand, I'd like to speak with Captain Levin."

Gabrielle got up and left.

The colonel sat at his desk and pressed his fingertips together until they turned white.

"I'm having those pains again, Captain."

"Severe?"

"Occasionally."

"I repeat myself. You should go to Saigon."

Lehr laughed.

"How the hell do you think my troops would react?"

Doc looked down.

"Could you examine me?"

Captain Levin exhaled.

Doc opened his bag. He had Lehr sit on his desk and remove his fatigue shirt. He listened to the colonel's heart and lungs and then checked his blood pressure. The colonel stood up and slipped on his shirt.

"So?" Lehr asked.

"Blood pressure's up, as are your pulse and respiration."

"Is that normal?"

Doc exhaled and shrugged.

"It's not so abnormal that I would take you off duty."

"Well, then I suppose, that's all," Lehr said.

"If this gets worse," Doc said in a low, even voice. "Call me. Your troops wouldn't like you having a heart attack."

Lehr nodded. He quickly turned and studied the map.

*   *   *

Merton came into the medical bunker as Halliday walked down the back entrance with Lam, who found a broom and started sweeping.

"Hey, 'cruit? Got a minute?"

"Why?" Halliday asked, narrowing his eyes.

"Show you something. Over in my hootch."

"What?"

"A picture, goddamn it!"

Halliday looked around. Clancy lay dozing on a cot with a big book about army uniforms spread over his face.

"Nimmer," Halliday said. "Be back in a few."

"Like I give a shit?" Nimmer said, behind a *Playboy* magazine, his muddy boots sprawled across the front desk.

Halliday followed Merton up the bunker stairs.

Outside, the mist drifted overhead as they skirted huge puddles with red clay gleaming at the edges and walked down the company street. Near one gutted hootch, a dog snarled, and Merton threw a mud clod.

A thin, exhausted, young soldier in filthy fatigues hurried by. Halliday's body felt heavy, sensitive, and mellow after sleeping with Lam. He remembered how quiet the incoming rockets pops were and tensed. But Daktoum was quiet and deserted. Now, almost all life on the firebase took place entirely underground or in bunkers.

"How many guys we got left, Merton?"

"Four hundred, maybe a hundred artillery."

"That's all?"

"Wounded, dead, malaria, gone back to the World. No replacements. Nobody gives a shit, 'cruit. Fuck the World, fuck those civilians, and especially fuck that fucking fuck Nixon."

They passed a collapsed hootch, a messy drift of wet wood, broken sandbags, and shredded canvas that smelled like cat piss. A torn jungle boot lay in the ruddy water beside a smashed gas mask. A black-and-white Christmas family photograph lay in the mud, smeared with red toothpaste.

Merton's hootch was one of the few untouched on the company street.

Merton flung open the flap of his waterlogged tent and entered a dank semi-darkness crowded with bunks and footlockers. In the back under a dim wedge of light, a huge young soldier hunched over, reading a letter.

Footsteps echoed outside across the mud, and Merton turned to see Ben hurrying by.

"Benjamin!" Merton called.

The medic stopped and looked in.

"What the hell are you two doing?"

"Come 'ere," Merton said. "Show you something."

Ben came into the half-light of the hootch as the clerk took out a manila envelope addressed to Spec Five Jonas Merton.

"Your first name is *Jonas*?" Ben asked.

"Fuck you," Merton said. "And don't say nothing about no goddamn white whale."

"I never knew," Halliday said.

"Why the fuck should you? Who the hell do you think you are anyway?" Merton said, grinning. "Hey, check this shit out!"

Merton showed a photo of a smiling, pink-cheeked woman with straw-colored hair in pigtails.

"My girl," he said, "*Sarah*."

"All *right*, Merton," Ben said. "Give me her address so I can Jody you when I get back to the World."

"In your fucking dreams, you California whore."

"How come you never showed us her picture?"

"Because I'm so goddamn short I look up to midgets. Twelve days and a wake-up in this shit hole! Fucking *'cruits!*"

"She's cute," Halliday said.

Merton rummaged through the footlocker for a tape.

"Want to hear her music?"

"Negative," Ben said. "Come on, Halliday."

"Ten minutes," Merton pleaded. "You guys can stay."

"Sorry. Can't do it."

"Your fucking loss," Merton said, " *'Cruuuuuuuuuits!*"

"Stop calling me a damn 'cruit."

"Hit the fucking trail," Merton said. "Space cowboys."

Ben and Halliday started out the door.

"Hey, 'cruits?"

When they looked back, Merton grinned wildly under a red mop of hair as he flipped them a double bird.

"Gooooooooood luck."

"Yeah, you too, Merton."

Merton snapped the tape in and cranked up the volume. The huge soldier in the back scowled as music flooded the tent.

When the Moon is in the Seventh House
And Jupi-ter ali-gns with Ma-rs,
Then pe-ace will gu-ide the plan-ets
And lo-ve will steer the stars.

*   *   *

Walking back to the medical bunker, Ben asked, "You got any pictures of Jennifer?"

Three incoming rockets popped up on Rocket Ridge, Halliday and Ben ran toward foxholes. As they jumped into the ground, the rockets screamed in close, with deafening howls and explosions that bent the two young men curling and thrusting their hands over their shrieking ears.

Tremendous crashes littered the air with flying debris shot through with screams and whistling shrapnel.

Daktoum firebase grew quiet until a shriek ripped at the silence.

Ben scrambled out of his hole.

"Go get a stretcher!" Ben ordered Halliday.

Ben ran toward a smoking, deflated tent, while Halliday raced to the medical bunker, pumped with fear, and bent over in a crouch, his eyes and ears keen for more incoming.

Halliday ran to the dripping, poncho-draped entrance and grabbed a stretcher off the stack.

Halliday sprinted back, but couldn't find Ben, so he stopped and listened hard. A calming voice spoke over a low moan.

"It's OK, man, all right, you're going back to the World."

Halliday ran towards the voice.

He rounded the corner of a collapsed smoking tent-hootch laced with shrapnel, where Ben knelt above a fallen soldier.

Merton.

Smoke and shredded canvas drifted through the heavy air as Ben pulled fluids from his medical bag. Sprawled on wet green canvas, Merton's ruddy face was pale from blood loss and his arm, flung out. Sarah's photo was crumpled in his hand.

Halliday glanced down. Where Merton's left leg should have been, there was only a bloody mess, and Halliday gagged.

"Hold this I-V, man."

Ben's fierce look stifled Halliday into holding the clear glass bottle, while he tied off Merton's arm, pumped up the vein, and inserted the needle with blood-expanding fluid. Merton's distant look brightened, and his lips moved, recognizing Halliday.

"'cruit," Merton said as softly as a breeze.

Ben put five pressure dressings over the massive wound at the bottom of Merton's torso.

"Let's get him on."

As they carefully maneuvered Merton onto the stretcher, Chaplain Goodby rushed towards them across the red mud. Goodby saw Merton's bloody leg, and his eyes bugged out.

"Oh my God!" Goodby ejaculated.

Ben stood up and pushed Goodby.

"You trying to kill him?" Ben hissed. "Get the fuck outta' here, Sky Pilot!"

Goodby tripped and fell into the mud.

Merton had heard the Chaplain's horror, and his body instantly mirrored the Chaplain's fear. Merton lost hope and confidence, blood pressure and respiration.

Ben and Halliday grabbed the stretcher and hustled away, slipping through the mud a few hundred feet to the bunker.

They careened Merton down the stairs and clattered the heavy stretcher around the corner and onto a sawhorse under the brightest light. The fuming Major Goodby followed.

The stretcher set down, and Gabrielle checked the massive wound. Ben took vital signs—Merton's blood pressure and pulse had dropped, and his breathing was labored. Ben motioned Halliday over with his eyes.

"Talk," Ben whispered.

"About what?"

"*Anything*, you're saving his life!"

Halliday crouched and spoke into Merton's ear.

Nimmer and Clancy hovered close by, assisting Gabrielle. Behind them, Goodby paced, black-assed sullen in front of Doc's office.

"Talk," Ben hissed.

"Merton," Halliday whispered. "You lucky shit, going back to the World, and Sarah'll be there, you free ride, you only got a little old scratch, you'll be home in no time. Man, that Sarah is good-looking, too good looking for your crusty ass."

When Halliday bit his lips to keep tears away, Ben rapped his head, hard.

"You're so damn lucky," Halliday said to Merton. "No more Lehr, no more Daktoum, no more shitty C-rations and crazy fucking lifers. Ohio, Merton, man, I spent a summer there, so damn green my eyes hurt, big puffy white clouds, blue skies, and no rockets, no gooks to worry about, Ohio, man, just you and Sarah, on a picnic in the deep woods, falling asleep near the lake with a fishing pole in your hand, you'll be back before you know it, Merton, no sweat, you're goddamn lucky, man, all you gotta do now is lay back and enjoy the ride."

As Halliday murmured, Gabrielle's fingers flew faster, and Ben hovered over Merton, giving him everything they could.

"Dust-off five minutes out," Clancy said.

Gabrielle checked the dressings. Halliday unhooked Merton's two fluid bottles and carried them as Ben and Nimmer maneuvered the big red-haired soldier across the medical bunker and up the dim staircase.

Outside, under gray light, Gabrielle followed Merton's stretcher through the mud.

On the airstrip, the mist was so low and thick that Clancy popped purple smoke and had to talk Dust-off down.

The helicopter descended in a howling clatter. When they had strapped Merton to the helicopter deck, Halliday gripped his hand, and the fleshy clerk's lip trembled.

"'cruit," he whispered.

The Dust-off medic tapped Halliday, and he scrambled across the aluminum deck. As the Huey lifted, the medic beside Merton gave them a thumbs up.

Clancy headed to the medical bunker with the radio, and the others trotted behind.

When the colonel and the Kid raced up in the command Jeep, Gabrielle pointed to where the helicopter disappeared into the mist. Lehr jumped out and ran onto the airstrip.

The colonel stood on the wet pockmarked tarmac as the unseen helicopter thumped away. Thin drifts of purple smoke still hissed from the metal canister and curled around Lehr.

The colonel turned and marched to the medical bunker, and the Kid followed in the Jeep.

Soft rain fell.

All the medics milled around outside, as if unsure of what to do. Ben went downstairs. Gabrielle sat on the sandbags and lit a cigarette as if the medics weren't there.

The colonel came up to Halliday.

"Bad?

Halliday looked at the ground. Gabrielle glared at Lehr.

"How bad, Halliday?"

"Left leg," Halliday muttered.

"Gone?" Lehr asked.

Halliday nodded.

"Oh Christ."

Gabrielle exhaled.

"He will be lucky to live," she said.

Pain shot down the colonel's arm, so he turned toward the airstrip, trying not to double over.

Finally, Lehr marched to his Jeep.

Gabrielle tried to catch his glance, but Lehr never looked back. The Kid jerked the Jeep into gear and splattered red mud as they disappeared behind the shattered hootches.

Gabrielle dropped her cigarette into a muddy pool and went downstairs.

*   *   *

Halliday looked at the low gray sky above Daktoum, the long, wet airstrip and the ugly sandbagged TOC, with its dozens of antennas sticking into the mist.

Halliday remembered Merton reading *Playboy* at Lehr's desk and falling over, which made him laugh, then fight tears.

Voices shouted, so Halliday ran down the bunker stairs.

As he rounded the corner, Ben and the Chaplain stood nose to nose with Clancy between them.

"Put him up on charges!" Chaplain Goodby shouted.

"If Merton dies," Ben yelled. "I'm charging *you*, Sky Pilot. With murder!"

"Don't raise your damn voice to no officers!" Clancy said.

"Then he should act like one!"

"Stop!" Doc pleaded.

Under the harsh light glaring down from the low ceiling, Goodby, Clancy, Ben, and Doc stood, surrounded by empty olive canvas stretchers.

Gabrielle walked between the men.

"We all did what we could for Merton," Gabrielle said.

She faced Goodby squarely.

"Sometimes you are a very confused man," she said. "Your desire to do something blunts your human feeling."

Goodby went beet red, turned on his heel and stomped upstairs.

Clancy glared at Ben, as he banged scalpels and clamps into an alcohol tray.

Doc and Gabrielle disappeared into the office.

Ben stood under the sickly light, his face slick with rain.

Across the room Nimmer snapped on a radio, blasting:

Get your motor run-ning
Get out on that high-way

Look-ing for adven-ture ....

"Turn that goddamn thing off!" Ben yelled.

The bunker went silent except for the swish of Lam's broom sweeping up the thick red mud that the medics had tracked in on their boots.

*   *   *

Gabrielle sat shuffling cards in Doc's office while he tried to read Time magazine about the upcoming manned flight to the moon, but he couldn't concentrate, and finally, he just threw down the thin international edition.

"Poor Merton," he said.

"Don't," Gabrielle said. "He is no longer in your life."

She pulled out a card and twirled it in her fingers.

"Last night I awoke and heard the lapping of the sea," Gabrielle said. "It sounded so beautiful that I thought I was on Santorini, swimming with my husband."

Doc nodded.

"But mosquitoes started whining," Gabrielle said. "And Donnelly cried out in his sleep, and then I knew that it was not the sea I heard. It was B-52 airplanes bombing."

Doc gently unwrapped the deuce of spades that Gabrielle had bent around her fingers. He put the card back into the desk, held Gabrielle's hand like a teenager, and stared into her liquid black eyes until he began to shake.

"Do you have a cigarette?" she asked.

"Do you want to talk?" Doc asked.

"No," Gabrielle said. "I want to smoke."

*   *   *

Driving the muddy camp road, the Kid's hands shook so hard that he hit a rut and threw Colonel Lehr against the glass.

Pain shot through the colonel like a snakebite, his muscles cramping from his bicep to his heart.

"Goddamnit son, slow down!"

The Kid slowed the Jeep and then parked in the muddy field beside the TOC.

"I'll be in my hootch," Lehr barked. "Tell Merton—Major Ranklin —I'll monitor the net."

The Kid turned away.

"Son," the colonel called. "You have Merton's duties now."

"Yes sir."

Colonel Lehr walked into the dusk and headed down the ruined company street to his hootch.

The Kid stood by the Jeep, his hands still shaking. He heard a single shot, and another and another behind the TOC, followed by laughter.

"Little son of a gun!"

A pistol shot rang out into the darkening sky.

"Your marksmanship leaves much to be desired," a high, thin voice said, laughing.

"Aw, shut up."

The Kid walked around the TOC toward the back entrance, where a giggling Major Sneller stood beside Captain Dunkley with a smoking 45 pistol pointed up.

"Gol-durned monkey!" Dunkley said.

"You had a clear shot."

Dunkley steadied his hands on the sandbags and fired. Red dust showered their fatigues.

"You little so and so!" Dunkley yelled, firing three more wild rounds at the monkey.

He holstered the pistol and rubbed dust from his eyes.

"Damn!"

"Sir?" the Kid asked.

"What?" Dunkley barked.

"Do you know where Major Ranklin is?"

"Try the gook bunker," Dunkley snarled. "Near the river."

"With his par-a-mour," Major Sneller chimed in.

Sneller's grin caught the dim dusk light, which sparkled on his unfortunate tooth.

*   *   *

The Kid approached the squat moldering lump of Ellis's old bunker near the river bluff. The clammy night was shrouded in a low mist.

"How the hell do you gooks eat all that smelly damn food?" a voice drawled from underground.

As the Kid scraped his boots, a round clanged into a rifle chamber.

"Who up there?" a voice called.

"The colonel's driver."

"Colonel ain't here. What the hell you want?"

The Kid crept downstairs past the dull glow from a red, white, and blue Texas flag. He saw a yellow flicker deep in the bunker and Ellis's sullen face.

Behind him, Vietnamese women squatted around a tiny smoking fire. Ellis angled his M-16 toward the Kid.

"You ain't 'posed to be in here! What the hell you want?"

"Major Ranklin."

"He ain't here. Get out. Go try that blowed-up bunker."

The Kid retraced his steps past the glowing Texas flag and up the stairs.

Outside, the Kid heard murmuring and finally traced it to a pair of silhouettes beside a collapsed bunker.

Out on the river bunkers, cigarettes glowed like tiny red lanterns from the guards sitting with their backs to Rocket Ridge, smoking, so snipers couldn't see them. The Kid walked through the mud towards the murmuring.

"Love you, 'lanklin."

The Kid waited while the two bodies came together, and then broke apart.

"Sir?" the Kid finally called out.

"Who's there?" the Major retorted.

"Colonel's driver," the Kid said. "Colonel Lehr's in his bunker."

"Fine. Tell Merton," Major Ranklin said.

"Can't, sir."

"Why the hell not?"

"He was medevacked," the Kid said, his voice cracking.

All at once, Ranklin stood eye to eye with the Kid.

"Merton?"

"Yes, sir."

"What happened?"

"Lost his leg, sir."

"Christ!"

"Yes, sir."

"I'll be in the TOC," Ranklin said. "By the way, PFC—what goes on here, is just between you and me."

*   *   *

Lehr's left foot felt numb as he scraped down the steps into his sleeping bunker. He switched on the desk lamp, which only gave off a dim light. The generator must be phasing, he thought, or else the operators were conserving fuel. Lehr took off his helmet and flak vest and sat on his bed, breathing hard. His lungs shuddered.

After ten minutes, his body quit shaking, and the pain nearly went away. Slightly disoriented, the colonel hoisted himself up. When he reached for his scotch, a man's face appeared in the darkness.

"What the hell?"

The man didn't answer, his mouth just opened, and his lips moved silently. Unshaven, with short disheveled gray hair, the man's hollow, deeply lined face and colorless eyes were alarming.

"What the hell are you doing in my bunker?"

When the man still didn't answer, Lehr unbuttoned his pistol. When the man went for his own pistol, Colonel Lehr fired with a tremendous roar. Glass crashed to the rough concrete floor, and the man held a smoking gun in his hand.

The mirror near Lehr's wall locker had shattered in concentric circles. The colonel dropped the pistol with a metallic thump.

Lehr studied his face in the shattered mirror. He ran his hands through the tangled shock of silver hair and rubbed his grimy face and the deep black circles around his eyes.

Merton, cocky young bastard. Charlie got you. Shit.

Reeling from the broken mirror, Lehr fumbled for a glass and poured a tumbler of Scotch. He held the glass up to the dim light and savored the only immaculate color in the room.

Then Lehr heaved himself to his desk chair and cranked a canvas-covered field telephone.

"Medics," he told the Commo operator.

The field phone's buzzing line echoed.

"Medics," Gabrielle's weary voice answered, as if she were a continent away.

"Ahhhh."

The colonel could not speak.

"Medics," Gabrielle repeated.

"Yes," Lehr managed in a higher register. "PFC Halliday."

"Yes," she said.

The phone line eerie radio drift faded in and out, as if Lehr was talking to another dimension.

"Halliday," the young voice said listlessly.

There was a long silent moment.

"Is anyone there?"

"This is Colonel Lehr. Come over to my sleeping bunker."

"Yes, sir."

Lehr hung up. He stared at the canvas-covered field phone. Gabrielle. The colonel's breath heaved, quick and irregular as he gulped his drink. Dragging himself up, Lehr found another tumbler, polished off the dust with his fatigue shirt, and placed the clean glass on his desk.

A few minutes later, a knock echoed from ground level.

"Come on down, Halliday," Lehr called with a cheery lilt that almost concealed his unsteadiness.

Boot steps descended.

Lehr sat at his desk in rumpled fatigues with disheveled hair. The room stank of gun smoke, cigars, mud, and liquor.

"Sit down, Halliday. Have a drink."

Lehr poured Scotch into a worn tumbler. He toasted, and Halliday sipped the amber liquor. The dim light glimmered on the glass slivers scattered across the shadowy floor.

"Something wrong, sir?"

"Slight mishap."

They stared at the tired lines and weary smoothness of old and young faces.

"Merton …" the colonel began.

Halliday nodded.

"He was a good guy, sir. I mean, *is*…"

"Everyone will miss him."

They gulped their Scotch.

"Really funny …"

They looked down simultaneously, and then at each other.

"He ..."

"Yes, Halliday?"

"Guess it doesn't matter now..." Halliday said. "When you were in Pleiku, I caught Merton reading *Playboy* with his boots up on your desk, so I sneaked in and yelled just like you, and Merton tipped over right on his ass. And then he laughed, that great big stupid laugh of his, which made *me* laugh so hard—until we both had tears in our eyes."

Lehr almost smiled.

"Merton was a funny soldier."

"Yes, sir."

They drank in silence. Lehr felt salt behind his eyes.

"Halliday..." he said, his voice cracking. "I ..."

Halliday gulped his drink. He looked at the broken mirror on the concrete floor.

"How are you?" the colonel asked.

"OK, I guess, sir, everything's fucked, but ...I'm OK."

"Halliday," Lehr said, exhaling as pain rippled through his chest. "You a..."

The colonel pressed his Scotch to his chest so his hand wouldn't shake.

"...played this tape for me one day in the club."

"Yes, sir," Halliday answered.

"Would you—by any chance, could you, sing that song?"

Outside, small arms fire popped and died away. Lehr and Halliday locked eyes.

"You know, sir," Halliday said evenly, staring at the floor. "I wish I could, but I really can't. I..."

Halliday pushed the shattered mirror pieces around with his boot until it was so quiet that they could hear each other breathing. Halliday set down his empty glass and stood up.

"Is that all, sir?"

Lehr didn't look up.

"Yes," Lehr's tired voice said.

"Thank you much for the drink, sir."

"Of course."

Halliday glanced at the colonel, thinking he might look up, but when he didn't, Halliday walked up the stairs.

"Halliday?" the old man's voice echoed up the dark stairwell.

"Yes sir?"

"Good luck."

"You, too, sir," Halliday said to the darkness. "You, too."

*　　　　*　　　　*

Above ground, Halliday waited until his eyes adjusted to the darkness. Maybe Ben would drink a couple beers. Strange old guy. Fuck. Didn't think he had it in him to get broken up over anybody. Merton. Halliday thought about his opium flashback and John Wayne in the dead bunker—what the hell was that? Merton … all those brutal, smart-assed, dead-on funny comments… asking me to sing that song…

Halliday lurched out into the dark ruined company street. He sang softly:

And it's one, two, three, what are we fighting for?
Don't ask me, I don't give a damn,
Next stop is Viet-nam …

*　　　　*　　　　*

That night, Daktoum took no more rockets. There was no incoming artillery fire and no ground attacks. All night long in the jungle hills, the North Vietnamese Army battled Montagnard troops.

Shortly after midnight, the Special Forces camp at Ben Sai suffered a ground attack. Seven soldiers were killed and fourteen wounded.

Rain swept across Daktoum valley and continued until dawn, when helicopters were finally able to land at Ban Sai to evacuate the wounded.

*　　　　*　　　　*

In the gray dawn, the river bunker guards realized that something was missing. The bloated body of the enemy sapper hanging on the Daktoum wire had disappeared.

Under the cover of the mist and the rain, the N-V-A had somehow slipped in through the American Claymore mines, booby traps, and trip wires, untangled the slender, lime-whitened Vietnamese corpse, and carried the body off, right under the noses of the 99th's bunker guards.

18.

At any hour of day or night, in no discernible pattern, rockets, mortars and 152mm heavy artillery shells thundered into the smear of mud, sandbags, wood, metal and flesh that was Daktoum firebase. Because this never-ending roar of furious metal constantly tore at their ears, no one at Daktoum was able to sleep for very long.

The artillery had it the worst because the gun crews were constantly firing and couldn't be underground. Like ragged orphans in muddy green fatigues, the artillerymen hoisted heavy shells into the hot breeches of smoking cannons, bent over, and cupped their shattered ears against the endless shock of outgoing explosions. Again and again and again.

Their huge projectiles roared over a dozen miles of jungle and exploded in the hope that they would kill N-V-A soldiers and gunners and transportation people and women who imitated bird calls in the forest to ease the enemy soldiers' minds as they walked because all the birds had disappeared. They were aiming at the people and the trucks and the wide, muddy network of roads and forest trails and sleeping camps and the thirteen-hundred-bed, thatched-roof hospital on the enemy's Truong Son Strategic Supply Route, hidden deep under a vast triple canopy of tall, unimaginably beautiful tropical trees in Cambodia and Laos.

*   *   *

Gabrielle smoked a cigarette lying in a narrow military metal bed with curly-haired Doctor Levin at her breast, sleeping for the first time in 48 hours. On the concrete floor, the young dog Bacsi shook himself awake and offered his head for petting.

Gabrielle stroked the golden fur until an outgoing explosion reminded her that the eight-inch cannon was firing right behind the medical bunker. This heavy self-propelled gun had clanked into Daktoum and quickly settled into a freshly bulldozed hole in the muddy red ground.

Walls of new, gray-green sandbags shielded the big cannon, where, inside their safety berm, rows of huge projectiles shone with the dull metal glints of color-coded explosive tips for High Explosive, CS Gas, Illumination, Incendiary, and White Phosphorous rounds.

The road south to Kontum had finally fallen—cut off near the burned devastation of Kon Horing village by land mines and fierce ambushes which had cost the 99th six trucks, a new bulldozer, a front loader, and fourteen men. South Vietnamese infantry were supposed to assault, but dense mist had eliminated air support. Because of heavy fighting in the hills, the South Vietnamese refused to reopen the road. Rumors—from intelligence? Muttered curses from Colonel Lehr? An overheard conversation relayed by a helicopter pilot?—had it that the American command in Saigon said the 1st Cav was ready to go if the enemy overran Daktoum. Even if it was true, they were at least thirty miles away. And without helicopters…

The eight-inch gun crew near the medical bunker began round-the-clock fire missions in what was now being called "the siege at Daktoum." Day and night, the big cannon fired and loaded and fired and loaded and fired.

Before long, Gabrielle could not separate the big gun from the thumping of her heart. Pounding, she thought, my body my brain my soul until this unrelenting sound became everything. So, when the pounding of the cannon briefly ceased, the silence became so fearsome that Gabrielle found herself wishing that the gun would begin firing again.

*   *   *

By afternoon, under dull, gray mist, the exhausted crew loaded projectiles like they were sleepwalking.

Inside the medical bunker, the eight-inch gun's outgoing rounds rattled metal trays with scalpels and probes and scissors and clamps soaking in alcohol, while overhead, glass cases of I-V bottles constantly tinkled. Even the massive redwood roof beams shook under the constant pounding of the big gun.

The medics, on call for the next terrible event, smoked and dozed and read. As usual, they tried to keep their minds off the possibility of their own bunker being hit. There was nothing to do, no casualties, no wounded from the hills or firebases. Were choppers even flying? Were there even any air strikes to give them hope? Even Clancy had run out of busywork—and besides, Lam, who was so terrified by the constant artillery that she could hardly speak—kept the bunker immaculate, immediately cleaning every scrap of mud that the young exhausted soldiers tracked in on their worn filthy boots.

Limerick read *Soul On Ice* and only occasionally glanced up when the IV bottles threatened to break. Clancy could only write a single word every few minutes in a long letter that he hadn't been able to finish in a week, because it had become impossible to relate any details that wouldn't frighten his wife and five children back in DC. Donnelly incessantly smoked and bopped his skinny legs in time to a black cassette tape player that he constantly held at his ear.

Halliday watched Lam sweep the bloodstained floor for the tenth time while Nimmer and Cullen argued.

"California ain't really America, Home," Cullen said. "It's the land of the fruits and nuts."

"Blow it out your Okie ass, Cullen."

"I don't need no cuss words to describe you, surfer boy."

"I ain't no goddamn surfer. My parents just moved there. I grew up in New York."

"Right, fairy boy, right."

"SHUT UP CULLEN!" Clancy roared. "I'm sick of this bullshit!"

An outgoing round shook the bunker.

Inside the medical office, Doc and Gabrielle continually played Hearts and rarely spoke. The canvas door flap was pinned open and the busted silver frame of Doc's wife's picture shone on the crude wooden shelf and was visible to everyone.

"Oh man," Halliday said in the main room. "They're trying for that gun again. I hope this fucking bunker is deep enough."

"What if it ain't?" Cullen said. "You ain't ever even gonna know, 'cause you and me and everyone else'll be instant history, poof, meeting your maker ASAP, Home! Gone!"

*   *   *

Donnelly sat on a stretcher gulping his third coffee in an hour, trying to steel his nerves by chain-smoking Pall Mall cigarettes and continually munching tropical chocolate bars from the open Red Cross box of goodies beside the desk.

A strange look crossed Donnelly's face. He jumped off the stretcher and dashed upstairs.

Donnelly ran across the drainage ditch near the airstrip past the smoke pouring off the hot, eight-inch artillery barrel and hovering over the medical bunker in a dark stinking pall. Sweating soldiers in muddy fatigues haunted the big gun like exhausted green flies, loading and firing as fast as they could.

Donnelly opened the slatted latrine door and grimaced.

"Fuuuuuuuuk!" he shouted at the stench, quickly skinning down his fatigues, and easing his butt onto a hole.

The thin latrine walls shook with every outgoing round.

Graffiti laced the soft pine walls—a naked woman sprawled around a knothole, which made Donnelly remember the night they smuggled whores into the compound, and then Markie, his first, the most beautiful woman he had ever seen.

Below the naked woman, someone had scrawled: FUCK THE ARMY

'THE ARMY' was crossed out and replaced with a list of lined-through names:

Nixon
Agnew
Mitchell
Armbruster

Lehr

Donnelly thought a moment, took out a ballpoint pen, crossed out 'Lehr' and wrote 'Clancy' at the end of the list in his uneven, childish hand.

Below, were lyrics from a popular song by The Animals:
We gotta get out of this place
If it's the last thing we ever do …
A rocket popped off the ridge.

Seven seconds later, the rocket exploded in the drainage ditch right beside the two-hole latrine where Donnelly sat.

The huge concussion spewed up a wall of mud that knocked the stinking little shithouse crashing over on its side, with Donnelly still sitting on his throne.

*   *   *

Inside the medical bunker, Clancy put aside his letter.

He listened to all the incoming rockets and the eight-inch blasts until one rocket shrieked in close by. When the eight-inch cannon quit firing, Clancy sprang off the stretcher and hustled up the back staircase.

Outside, Clancy searched the clouds of black smoke around the big gun, which was obscured by a high, sandbagged berm. A scream split the silence.

Clancy ran out.

A recoilless round flashed off Rocket Ridge and smashed into the mud, with a thin cracking wail.

Clancy hit the ground.

The piercing scream repeated, and then another cracking wail blew a second explosion and mud thudded over Clancy.

Recoilless rounds crashed in. The screaming grew louder.

The Duster tank on the river line pounded out forty-millimeter cannon fire.

A desperate cry pierced the smoky silence.

"Oh Gaaaaaaawd, oh Gaaaaaaawd, saaaaaaaaaaaave meeeee!"

Clancy rose, sprinted toward the wailing, scooped up a wounded man, and carried him off.

Dark arterial blood dripped shiny red trails across the mud and down the wooden steps as Clancy carried the soldier in.

Above ground, the Duster and the recoilless rifle up on Rocket Ridge dueled, pounding and cracking rounds at each other.

Sergeant Clancy set the wounded artilleryman on a stretcher and headed upstairs.

The medics scattered books and letters and cigarettes and hustled after Clancy in a furious wake.

The Duster and the recoilless fire died away.

"Help me, Halliday," Doc called.

The young soldier that Clancy had delivered was as wounded as anyone could ever be.

Most of his arms and legs were gone, and his pale jawbone exposed a shocking rip of bone and muscle. Gabrielle and Doc methodically constricted and bandaged and cut and inserted intravenous tubes with terse commands while Halliday assisted.

As Doc worked, bile rose in his throat, but he willed his nausea away, along with a powerful desire to rip off the soldier's dressings and tear out the tubes going into this wreck of a man. Only Gabrielle's swift, steady movements calmed Doc.

Suddenly the young man arched his battered body in spasm and showered the two doctors with blood and sputum.

"Dieu vous garde," Gabrielle whispered.

The young, terribly wounded soldier lay still.

Doc's thin arms shook. Gabrielle wiped off his face and then her own.

"We couldn't do anything," Doc said.

"Bacsi," Gabrielle said softly.

She held his arm, but Doc shook her off, leaned against a stout post and slowly slumped to the floor.

Halliday stared the ruined body.

"Get a bag," Gabrielle said.

Phantom limbs, Halliday thought as he went for a body bag, so many phantom limbs in Vietnam. I'm surprised we're not drowning in them, Jesus.

Lam hummed a sad, barely audible tune as she swept the bunker floors.

"No more wounded, Captain!" Clancy yelled down the staircase. "Seven dead."

"Eight," Doc said.

When Gabrielle reached for Doc, he shook her off. Halliday looked
for a word, an order, comfort, anything, but when Doc finally stood up,
his boyish face was drawn, and his narrowed bloodshot eyes looked very
old.

"Cover him," Doc said. "Take Clancy some body bags."

Under the glaring light, Halliday zipped up what was left of the
young soldier. Then he grabbed an armful of green rubber bags and
raced up the stairs.

"Couldn't do a thing," Doc said to the square lump in the green
bag.

Doc wouldn't look at Gabrielle.

＊   ＊   ＊

Fleeing the doctors and the dead soldier, Halliday hefted the
uneven load of body bags and tried to sidestep the blood trails pooled
on the wooden steps.

Outside, under the awkward weight of the body bags, Halliday
slipped and nearly fell in the mud before he recovered and headed
toward the five medics slowly circling the silent gun. Strange, Halliday
thought, what happened?

"Get the hell out of here!" Clancy yelled.

"Doc said to bring bags."

Under the momentum of the heavy green rubber bags, Halliday
kept coming as Ben approached with something in his hands and
Clancy pointed to green and white piles in the mud.

Halliday looked closer.

Each of the piles was a hot, viscous mound of what had once been a
human being. Now, there was only pale muddy skin, muscle, bone, and
blood mixed with mud, uniform scraps, and leather—a full boot, a
hand, an ear—all massed in odd-shaped, fleshy hunks barely-
recognizable as human.

Halliday dropped the body bags, bent over, and threw up in a
puddle.

"Go back down the bunker," Ben said. "No need to see this shit."

Queasy, Halliday slipped across the muddy ground with his head
hanging, avoiding the other medics. He shuffled down the back

entrance, walked across the main room, passed the desk, and headed up the front stairs.

Outside, he glared at the gray sky and walked into the dead bunker. Slumped in the hidden corner alcove, Halliday trembled when the medics brought in eight, feather-light body bags. Then he was alone again.

Halliday stared into the darkness, desperately hoping that John Wayne would appear and say something, anything, but there was only the dark, sandbagged room with the red dust floor lit by dull gray light leaking in from the entrance.

The silence of the dead chilled Halliday until he felt a hand on his neck.

"You OK, man?" Ben said. "Don't mean nothing."

"Yeah."

Ben squatted down.

"Think about good things, your people back in the World, Lam."

"Yeah," Halliday exhaled.

"She looks a little down. Go do something."

"Yeah."

Ben stood up.

"Come on, man, stand up. Get the fuck out of here."

*   *   *

Doc sat on a stretcher in the main room thinking about the dead soldier. The radio squawked. Dust-off was headed in with a critically wounded V-I-P.

Doc, Gabrielle, Nimmer, and Cullen ran out through heavy mist to the landing pad. A battered helicopter wailed in and settled down with two wounded strapped in the bay.

"Shouldn't even be flying in this crap!" a pale on-board medic muttered, waving at the dense fog. "We'll do our damnedest to come back. Weird shit out there."

Nimmer and Cullen pulled out the barely conscious blond-haired Montagnard adviser, Captain Hardin, eased his stretcher off, and headed back.

The helicopter medic jumped off, grabbed Doc's arm with a meaty hand, and pointed to a slender Vietnamese.

"Take the prisoner, too. Enemy V-I-P."

As soon as Doc and Gabrielle slid out the second stretcher, the medevac chopper lifted, and banked back into the gray-black mist towards Cambodia.

As Doc and the medics hustled away with the stretchers, a dozen mortar rounds cracked in.

Blue-orange blasts exploded across the airstrip near the big dusty olive sprawl of refueling bladders that looked like oversized air mattresses.

*   *   *

Downstairs, under dim yellow-green lights, Doc and Clancy and Ben labored on Hardin. The unconscious Captain took three pints of blood as Doc used suction to clear his broad chest of fluids.

Outside, monsoon rain beat down. The radio squawked.

"No Dust-off until morning," Cullen said.

"God-damnit," Clancy said. "He needs a hospital."

"The prisoner will live," Gabrielle said, wrapping a dressing on the small enemy soldier clad in dark olive khaki.

Cullen leaned over the N-V-A.

"Oughta to smack this little fucker upside his head," Cullen said, brandishing his fist at the unconscious man.

"Shut up, Cullen," Clancy ordered. "Save it. We have to respirate Captain Hardin all night."

Doc and Clancy and Gabrielle traded off with the suction. As soon as the rain stopped, rockets pounded Daktoum. Captain Hardin hovered between two worlds but stabilized around eleven, so his wound only needed suction every hour.

The enemy soldier awoke and with glittering brown eyes took in the wounded Captain beside him.

Doc left Hardin to get a drink of water while Clancy went upstairs for air. The medics sat near the entrance desk smoking cigarettes, talking quietly and pacing.

No one saw the N-V-A soldier lurch up, grab a glass Ringers bottle off a shelf, smash it, and rip the broken glass into Captain Hardin's throat. Hardin gagged and died.

Doc was the first to reach the bandaged N-V-A patient. The thin boyish doctor yanked out his 45, stuck it in the wounded N-V-A's stomach, and pulled the trigger.

Under the deafening concussion, the stunned medics watched with ears ringing.

The gentle doctor stumbled backwards.

Doc looked aghast at the blood on his hands and threw down the pistol, which bounced off a carton of bandages and thudded to the floor.

Doc reeled through the row of stretchers into his office.

Gabrielle found Doc clutching the smashed picture of his wife with his bloody hands.

*   *   *

A few minutes later, Doc opened his eyes.

He was lying in his bunk and looked at Gabrielle like a child after a sweet dream.

"Stay out of there, Major," Clancy bellowed from outside as Ranklin pushed in Doc's canvas door.

"Where's the prisoner?" Major Ranklin asked.

"Dead," Gabrielle said.

"Dead?"

"He killed Cap'n Hardin," Clancy said. "Doc shot him."

Doc looked at Gabrielle.

"I killed the prisoner?"

"Yes," Gabrielle said.

*   *   *

On the radio, Lehr listened to Colonel Trinh rage about the dead prisoner. When Trinh finally finished, Lehr pressed the handset.

"Colonel Trinh," Lehr said. "Go fuck yourself."

Lehr walked out of the TOC and waved the Kid behind him. They drove off with Sergeant Smith to inspect the line.

That night Daktoum was mortared, but there were no ground attacks and no more casualties.

*   *   *

At one in the morning, Donnelly staggered into the medical bunker, his tattered fatigues covered in excrement. The duty medic, Cullen, roared with uncontrollable laughter which woke all the medics up, cursing and then cracking up when they saw Donnelly.

Nimmer put on his boots and led the babbling Donnelly out to the shower, where he made the smaller man strip off his clothes and blue rectangular glasses. Nimmer helped Donnelly scrub himself clean and afterwards, emptied a can of Right Guard deodorant on him. Still, the stink would not go away.

Finally, Cullen put the mumbling Donnelly on a stretcher and gave his pale naked body a full-body alcohol bath. He found clean fatigues for Donnelly and then injected him with a half dose of Thorazine, which immediately knocked out the black-haired teenager.

"Home," Cullen told Donnelly's sleeping face on the stretcher. "I know you're clean, but you still smell like shit."

19.

A week later, under a warm drizzle, Halliday stood beside Lam in a line of soldiers huddled around Ellis's bunker, waiting for the daily Daktoum soft drink and beer ration. Even though it was mid-morning, Halliday dozed off, and when the line began to move, Lam had to shake him.

Halliday found it difficult to speak to Lam. Under the constant rocket and mortar fire, his fear had intensified and being constantly crammed underground with all the medics didn't help. Clancy always slept right beside Lam, to discourage the medics from getting any ideas.

Outside the entrance to Ellis's bunker, Major Ranklin checked the soldiers' rations on a clipboard. After the water purification unit had been hit and the water trailers emptied, each soldier got a six-pack for two days, mixed soda and beer.

Halliday jolted awake.

"Number ten sleepy," Lam said, smiling.

Her black shirt was wrinkled, and the cuffs of her peasant pants were red with mud. Her dark hair hung limp; no one had done laundry or showered for two weeks.

"We check you off," Ellis yelled to the haggard soldiers. "You go inside, get you ration from m' gooks."

The firebase was so silent that it spooked the nervous soldiers, who kept darting glances at green Rocket Ridge under the mist. They strained their ears for any incoming pops, ready to leap because a shelling was long overdue, and everyone could feel it. Too quiet, Halliday thought, smiling—like in the movies when all the Indians are about to attack Fort Apache. Jesus, I'm fucking tired. And I smell like a dog.

A sound like a knock on a faraway door shook Halliday to the bone, and he pushed Lam into Ellis's bunker, with a crush of soldiers shoving from behind. Cracking heavy mortars fell short, exploding on the red clay cliffs of the Dak Poko, where an old bunker still teetered above the water, its sandbags and red soil toppling daily into the river.

The soldiers pressed at Halliday and Lam, but her warmth and breath barely overcame the foul scent of teenage soldiers crowding Ellis's bunker with its thousands of soda cases. Soldiers pressed together in an uneasy tangle of grimy flesh, bad breath and dirty fatigues, but no more rounds came in.

"OK, get your sorry asses out of my bunker," Ellis said. "No sweat, Charlie didn't kill your young ass yet, better luck next time."

The soldiers untangled themselves and filed up the stairs.

"Fucking bull-shit."

"Where's the fucking Cav?"

"They're lying about that goddamn Cav!"

"Fuck that Herd."

"Fucking rain, man."

"Fuck Nixon, his whole goddamn army and all them fucking civilians too."

"You got that, brother."

No one had seen the flashes from the heavy mortar, so the Duster pumped out rounds into Rocket Ridge and ceased fire.

The swirling heavy mist made each soldier feel distant and remote like they were in "the World" back home. Even worse, the silence forced them to think, which they normally avoided.

Ever since the Generals' black-and-white plane had landed at Daktoum, the gray mist hadn't lifted, and sometimes was so thick that the entire camp was covered—usually at night. All over Daktoum valley, defenses were falling, while in the camp, daily, crumbling sandbags spilled onto the red earth.

To the west, the road to Ban Sai and Cambodia had been closed for three days—after a South Vietnamese fuel-tanker truck hit a mine and blew up.

Right outside the Daktoum front gate on Highway 14, a dozen blown-up Army trucks lay mired alongside the road like oversized abandoned toys.

Breezes creaked the doors of these blackened trucks, as if ghosts were opening them. Two-dozen trucks, and thirty men had been lost on the road because of inadequate or nonexistent South Vietnamese security.

Lehr even stopped sending out the 99th mine-sweep team.

Three miles south, below Nhu Canh Du, the road had reopened once, and then closed again. The daily convoys had to return to Kontum with their food and ammunition undelivered.

Standing in line with Lam, Halliday spotted Dodds, a wiry Pathfinders soldier from a pilot rescue team, who had been sleeping on stretchers in the medical bunker.

Dodds hefted an armful of beer and soda cases.

"What's happening, Doddsy?" Halliday asked. "What do you hear?"

"Same shit as you, man. Mostly, you don't want to know. One good thing, though."

"Yeah?" Halliday asked.

"Aerial re-con caught an N-V-A battalion out in the goddamn *open* —an old rice field—shit, that N-V-A has balls as big as shot-puts."

"What happened?"

"Tac-air lit 'em up like a birthday cake," Dodds said. "Napalm. Gunships finished 'em off, rats in a barrel."

"Yeah?" Halliday asked.

"Weird shapes, all them bodies. Lumps in the mud. Supposedly, the 27th Battalion, the best. There it is, man."

Dodds nodded his head like a sage and walked away. Halliday and Lam moved up toward Ellis's bunker entrance.

"I heard the Cav is going to open the road," the Kid said, standing in front of Halliday and Lam. "Or they'll lift us out."

"Don't you believe that shit," Ellis said. "Army letting us rot up here. One day ole Ho Chi Minh gonna stroll right through the front gate, sit his skinny yellow ass down in our mess hall, and chow down on the fish heads and rice special."

"N-V-A blew up the mess hall," the Kid said.

"Well, then ole Ho'll have to have him a little bar-be-que."

Major Ranklin scowled.

Ellis checked off the Kid's soda issue on a clipboard. Tu, eight-and-a-half-months pregnant, watched Ranklin with loving and terrified eyes.

When Halliday entered, Lam caught Tu's glance.

"How is your baby?" Lam asked in Vietnamese.

"Kicks in the morning," Tu replied. "Just like his father."

Downstairs in Ellis's dank fetid bunker, Halliday hefted three cases of drinks, and Lam carried one.

*   *   *

The next morning, Lehr arose from his sleeping bunker and walked over to his crude shaving stand. Despite deep breathing exercises and fifty pushups twice a day, his left arm still felt dull, and the throbbing would not go away. Lehr stared at his face in the mirror.

The pain didn't stop Lehr's mind from spinning—open the road, open the road. Christina, no need to hear your crap again. I can't believe they're caving to that little goddamn warlord prick Trinh, not releasing helicopters—and our command won't even make him open the road. *Priority, Lehr, priority,* and *they'll get to the road soon, we can't bring in the Cav.* Fuck Priority, cut the bullshit, fight the war. Christina, *I'm* burning babies? What does "throwing yourself on their funeral pyre" mean anyway? Daughter, if you could for just one moment, rationalize. Beautiful legs. Goddamn Gabrielle, goddamn women. The Cav could clear this road in two days. Two. *No ground support, Lehr, orders from the top and I do mean the very top.* I'm not going to lose all my armor, *all* my armor, shit, *four* tracks. Ha! Nuts. Surrender. So why haven't the N-V-A tried a large-scale ground attack? Or tunnels? That crazy goddamn Ellis claims they're digging underneath the airstrip at night. I listened for twenty minutes and couldn't hear a damn thing. No way for us to patrol, too many of them, too few of us, too many goddamn vehicles to defend. Goddamn them. Sleep in Daktoum for a week, Armbruster, see the dead and the wounded, write the letters home, you give the orders, goddamn cable.

12 Jul 1969 MSG 094 TOP SECRET
TO: COMDAKTOUM
FROM: COMUSARV
FIRST DAY NO INCLEMENT WEATHER CLEAR HIGHWAY
14 WEST TO BAN SAI STOP

What the hell good will clearing the road to Ban Sai do? As soon as we leave, the N-V-A will just blast the convoys and take the road back. No re-supply. Trinh will never be able to open the road south of Nhu Canh Du on his own. He's still in Kontum—with Ambush Alley a N-V-A free-fire zone, Bridge 39 half blown. *Mission*—just another bullshit line for the press. *Outnumbered Army engineers at Daktoum who attempted to open the Ban Sai road got their asses handed to them in a fucking sling, sin loi, my fellow Americans, sin fucking loi* as the troopers say—that's the copy they ought to write.

Lehr stared at his round shaving mirror nailed on the post. He smoothed his sweat-stained fatigue jacket, scratched at his unshaven chin, and decided the hell with it. He buckled his helmet and headed upstairs toward the TOC to plan the road-clearing mission.

*   *   *

As Lehr stepped outside, he saw dozens of empty cans and upturned helmets filling with rainwater. Good idea, Ranklin—straight out of the Middle Ages, in a week we'll be out of beer and soda. We'll have to rig a pump from the river and use those awful water purification tablets. Who the hell ever started that rumor that helicopters were coming to lift us out? Like we would abandon our trucks and equipment at Daktoum?

*   *   *

The next morning before dawn in Doc's office, Gabrielle slipped out of bed. Putting on her damp black fatigue shirt, she grimaced at her body scent, glanced at Doc's sleeping face, and slipped out the canvas door.

Gabrielle moved through the dim low room filled with the labored breathing of the young medics sleeping on stretchers. She walked up the back stairs without Nimmer, the dozing duty medic—even noticing.

Outside, to the east, gray clouds pressed against black sky. In darkness, she climbed onto the roof and into the parapet.

Bacsi's face has lines that were not there before, she thought. The faces of the dead, her children, the wounded, the dying, all the frightened young soldiers flashed in her mind. After killing that prisoner, he almost crushed me. Is he also cruel? Perhaps. And where has his wife's picture gone? Oh, Bacsi. Perhaps it is time for me to leave.

Gabrielle bent below the crumbling parapet wall and lit her cigarette. She dragged, hiding the glow. As Gabrielle smoked, the dark sky brightened into a thin rim of fire in the east.

Then, a blood-colored sun burst above the haunting green mountain behind Nhu Canh Du.

For the first time in weeks, Daktoum's ruined hootches and crumbling bunkers turned crimson from direct sunlight. Overhead, the immense green wall of Rocket Ridge thrust into a pink sky. All the rugged jungle hills trailed threads of mist, as if the mountains were newly born and still smoking with volcanic fire.

On every horizon, impossibly wild and green jungle hills shimmered, and for the first time in weeks, Gabrielle truly smiled. She inhaled her cigarette with an indulgent pleasure, as she let the first hard sunlight in days warm her face.

*   *   *

Within an hour, the hot blue sky filled with the locust clatter and thump of helicopters—dozens, a hundred—whining, buzzing, whirling through the earsplitting air above Daktoum, carrying food and ammunition and mail and water and replacements—the re-supply finally arrived.

Bedraggled filthy young soldiers emerged from the ground to shake their fists and rifles at Rocket Ridge, proudly cheering the banking, hovering, and descending helicopters, which they raced out to help unload.

On all the green ridges, the screaming, boom-howl of jet fighters swooped down their first sorties in weeks, cracking spectacular napalm bursts across virgin jungle, ripping orange tongues of flame, and exploding starburst fingers of white phosphorus arching through the treetops and tumbling down across the hills.

"All right *Home!*" Cullen screamed, standing on the bunker roof near Gabrielle. "Get them gooks, an' fry 'em up to crispy critters!"

Long lines of helicopters descended on the Daktoum airstrip, dumping pallets of C-rations, medical supplies, water bladders, fuel bladders, and ammunition of all calibers. Big, twin-towered Chinooks lowered heavy pallets of artillery rounds in big cargo nets, which the artillerymen quickly stashed away in bunkers.

On both sides of Highway 14 out to Ben Sai, helicopter gunships exploded the air with rocket and mini-gun fire, strafing tree lines, and firing at secondary explosions.

After the jets finished, artillery batteries blasted Rocket Ridge and all the hill sectors—660, 838, 875, for miles west into Cambodia and Laos out on the Ho Chi Minh Trail. Arc Light B-52 bombs exploded miles away, and the ground constantly shook.

There was little return fire.

Like they are bombing their own ghosts, Gabrielle thought. And just like at Dien Bien Phu, the enemy will remain the same, and all this will mean nothing.

*　　　*　　　*

All morning, the airstrip hummed with helicopter missions, thumping and rattle-whining into Daktoum, rearming and refueling across the airstrip, and charging back out to assault the remote hills and valleys until their machine-gun barrels smoked from firing.

Showing the first pale skin in days, the young soldiers of Daktoum stripped off their dank fatigues and worked bare-chested under the hot sun.

Halliday scored a hundred pounds of ground beef from a supply helicopter along with hamburger rolls, cheese, ketchup, mustard, mayo, and chips.

Ben scrounged a cut-off 55-gallon fuel drum with a crude steel grill, and they broke up artillery pallets for charcoal. Another 55-gallon drum was iced down and filled with beer and soda. For an hour, a hundred, mostly teenaged soldiers of every size, shape and color, along with officers and sergeants, cooked burgers and drank beer and Cokes and laughed and cursed and ate their fill and afterwards, sunned themselves on top of the bunkers in sunglasses and bush hats and bare chests and filthy fatigue pants, lounging amidst rotting sandbags with the fuck-you-what-else-can-you-show-me confidence of a sunny day, a full young belly, overwhelming air power, and plenty of ammunition.

They ignored the rocket craters on the airstrip, the broken hootches, the collapsed bunkers, the muddy red earth littered with fatigues and ripped letters and torn boots and photographs and unfurled recording tapes and the abandoned locks of girlfriends' hair. They tried to forget dead friends and wounded friends, all the lost limbs and lost spirits mired in and hovering all around Daktoum's immense fields of mud.

All afternoon, the guns of Daktoum roared.

Beyond the ruined mess hall, near the river, the 1-7-5mm cannons reared up long barrels and hurled fire and explosives towards Cambodia, Laos, and Ban Sai, rattling every glass in Daktoum. 1-5-5 batteries pounded away high explosive, incendiary, tear gas, and white phosphorus rounds plummeting into the jungle until clouds of gun smoke hung over the Dak Poko riverbank in a fog of war.

This tremendous thumping crashing whining rocketing explosives going out produced a feeling of awe in Halliday as he laid against a sandbag wall, smoking a cigarette, and drinking an icy beer. He closed his eyes and basked in the warm sunlight.

A screaming Chinook landed.

Fifty wounded ARVN soldiers spilled from the back hatch.

Lunch was over.

Doc and Gabrielle and Clancy and all the medics sprang up to haul the wounded into the medical bunker.

Another packed Chinook came in and by then, there were so many wounded that Donnelly and Halliday were sent out to the airstrip to do triage, so only the critically injured went underground to the overwhelmed Doc and Gabrielle and Clancy and the medics.

Halliday worked in a panic, running from stretcher to stretcher. Wounded were scattered everywhere under the hot sun, dazed, walking wounded sprawled on revetment walls and across the shallow ditches. Some even lay on the warm tarmac apron of the airstrip.

Halliday quickly cut through fatigue pants and shirts, searching for wounds and bleeding, speaking pidgin to the wounded Vietnamese soldiers, who mumbled back in shock. The wounded kept coming and coming out of the bellies of grit-swirling Chinooks and Hueys and even battered Korean War Sikorskys that looked like green metal giraffes—all disgorged a steady stream of stunned, bleeding Vietnamese.

Eventually, two hundred South Vietnamese wounded lay beside the airstrip in soiled fatigues and bloody bandages, squatting, lying in groups, smoking, staring into the distance.

The worst cases gathered around the Dust-off pad and on the tarmac apron, until it was carpeted with these small yellow men and boys in miniature US uniforms with oversized weapons and oversized wounds that seemed to bleed very little as they lay suffering in dirty green stretchers.

"Our Dinks got less blood, our Dinks got less blood," Donnelly chimed as he hopped from patient to patient, teetering around deep panic from deciding who should live and who should die. "Our Dinks got less blood."

As the helicopters unloaded the wounded, crew chiefs kicked out their abandoned weapons until a pile of guns rose beside the airstrip— M-16s, M-79s, 45s and even a few M-60 machine guns. Another, smaller heap of weapons lay in the drying mud beside the medical bunker entrance.

Halliday and Donnelly ran furiously back and forth between the med bunker and the airstrip, carrying in the critically wounded, and carrying out the dead, who were dumped on a growing mound beside the discarded weapons.

The Vietnamese walking wounded threw their rifles on the weapon pile with great relief, as if the guns were haunted, and the sole source of their suffering.

Everyone ignored the pile of corpses, except for the camp dogs, lured by the scent of the dead, who scattered when Donnelly and Halliday threw rocks, driving the whining dogs away, noses weaving in scent madness, waiting to sneak back.

Artillery rocketed away, choppers lifted in lines, air strikes cracked a false thunder in the distance.

Halliday and Donnelly yelled over an unceasing rotor wash, cajoling lift ship pilots, and Chinook crew chiefs into evacuating the South Vietnamese wounded.

Underground, Doc and Gabrielle and Clancy and all the medics worked furiously on the critical Vietnamese soldiers, who flowed like blood in and out of the bunker.

Everyone on the firebase was so busy that no one even noticed thin wisps of mist, creeping from the deep jungle valleys until there was a haze in the sky, and faint shadows rippled the muddy red earth.

*   *   *

When the last Vietnamese wounded had been flown out, everyone cleaned up and rested underground. The Chinooks and slicks and gunships flew back to bases sixty miles south.

"US critical, three minutes out," Limerick called, holding the radio mike.

Doc and Gabrielle appeared in the office doorway. Clancy looked around.

"Donnelly and Halliday, run a stretcher to the airstrip!"

Slipping on his flak vest, Halliday shook. With all the gunships gone, the N-V-A would probably shell the airstrip.

Donnelly lit a cigarette and sat on a stretcher beneath a hanging light, his eyes darting until Clancy marched into his tobacco smoke and knocked the bare bulb swinging. Smoky shadows rocked across the dimly lit room.

"Doc, de Doc, de ding dong Doc," Donnelly called across the room, pleading. "I'm way too goddamn humpty-dumpty short to go out there. The gooks'll be rocketing, Doc, I know they will, you know they will."

Clancy batted away Donnelly's smoke with a beefy hand and stuck his face close.

"Short, my ass," Clancy said. "Donnelly, you're going out there if I have to carry you."

Donnelly's eyes darted from side to side.

"Ben," Clancy called over his shoulder. "I need you."

"Four of us?"

"You heard me, we'll do this real quick."

"You're the boss," Ben told Clancy, who still held Donnelly's eyes.

Clancy picked up a folded stretcher and threw it at Donnelly, who had to drop his cigarette to catch it. Clancy scowled and herded the three medics upstairs.

Out of the west from Cambodia, came a hesitant whir of a faltering Huey helicopter. The four medics ran across the bridge, past the discarded weapons pile and the heap of Vietnamese dead, circled by the camp dogs.

The helicopter grew larger, stuttered in the air, and dropped too fast.

"He ain't gonna make it!" Clancy yelled, shoving the three medics running across the pockmarked airstrip.

The sweating four ran hard for two hundred meters, breath-burning, flak vests flapping as the helicopter struggled to stay airborne.

The chopper lurched toward the ground, careening through the air like a dying hawk. Grit slapped their faces as the crippled helicopter clattered down, crashing the asphalt, and rocking into a hard settle.

The screaming turbine died away as the cutting blades wound down.

The pilot slumped behind the Plexiglas, like he was asleep.

Petrified Vietnamese soldiers streamed out of the bay and streaked across the airstrip. Co-pilot Long, red in the face, threw off his seat harness, and roared around to the pilot's side.

"Fuck," Ben said. "It's Stubbsy."

Clancy and Long broke the jammed door and fumbled at Stubbsy's harness.

Mortars crashed into a hootch across the airstrip.

Ben shoved Halliday into a crouch and held onto Donnelly's shirt collar.

"I ain't going nowhere," Donnelly said, struggling.

Ben's eyes blazed mean.

"You sure as hell ain't."

Long unbuckled the seat harness, as Clancy cradled the wounded pilot and inched him out of the bucket seat.

Stubbsy's head dropped limply against Clancy's chest.

"Where's he hit, Chief?"

"Couldn't get no sense out of him," Long said, lifting Stubbsy's legs.

Halliday and Donnelly hustled over with the stretcher and the five men gingerly lowered Stubbs onto the green canvas.

"Jesus," Donnelly whispered. "Mary and Joseph."

"What the fu...?" Halliday began.

"Shut up," Ben said.

The distant, black and orange flashes of mortar rounds hit the Nhu Canh Du end of the airstrip.

"Grab his head, Halliday."

Halliday cupped Stubbsy's head.

As they eased the pilot down, Halliday felt a hole in Stubbsy's helmet and looked down. Wet gray chunks glistened his fingers—Stubbsy's brains. Halliday stiffened.

Mortars cracked closer.

"Let's get the hell going."

Stubbsy slumped on the stretcher.

Ben and Halliday took the rear posts, and Long and Clancy grabbed the front.

"Go tell Doc what we got!" Clancy said, shoving Donnelly toward the airstrip. "Run!"

Donnelly stumbled.

A mortar shell cracked in. Donnelly froze on the ground.

Clancy lunged at Donnelly until the skinny black-haired medic darted away.

Mortars crashed closer. The four hit the dirt beside the stretcher.

A hundred feet ahead, Donnelly flattened on the tarmac.

Orange-yellow bursts kept hitting closer and metal fragments shrilled the air.

"LET'S GO!" Clancy yelled, scrambling up. "GO, DONNELLY, GO!"

The four ran hard with the stretcher, and Donnelly scrambled before them.

Behind the racing stretcher, the helicopter blades slowly wound down with a dull whine and whooshes.

The four soldiers ran at full speed, bucking toward the bunker two hundred meters away. Halliday's lungs burned. Half conscious, Stubbsy hummed a tuneless childhood song from deep in his throat. His singing grew louder until it even drowned out the bearers' heavy panting.

"*Wheeeeeeeeeeee, Wheeeeeeeeeeee, Wheeeeeeeeeee!*"

What was left of Stubbsy sang out a chilling, childhood bliss that Halliday fought not to hear. From deep inside Stubbsy's brain or soul or inert neurons, the free, innocent murmuring of a three-year-old rang out across the pockmarked Daktoum airstrip, as if his father had thrown baby Stubbsy, bounding up from his strong arms, high into the sky.

Ben, Clancy, Long, and Halliday shivered under this intimate eerie recall of childhood.

One hundred fifty meters.

"*Wheeeeeeeeeeee, Wheeeeeeeeeeee, Wheeeeeeeeeee.*"

Stubbsy's strange joy pierced the soldier's hearts carrying his rocking stretcher, pierced their hot hard breath as their boots pounded the asphalt.

The mortars stopped.

Stubbsy's arms fluttered out from the sides of the stretcher.

A hundred meters to go, with a big man on a sailing stretcher at a full run, burning breath and burning lungs, the four men aching from the strain.

Wheeeeeeeeeeee, Wheeeeeeeeeeee, Wheeeeeeeeeee.

Fifty meters.

Stubbsy's hands flapped like wings as shrieks of joy bubbled out of him.

They reached the edge of the airstrip, skirted the Vietnamese bodies and the pile of weapons.

Boot steps cracked across the narrow wooden bridge like horses' hooves.

At the medical bunker, Stubbsy's *Wheeeeeeeeeee* expelled in a final gurgling cry.

The beating wing flutter of his arms fell limp.

Behind them, an incoming 122mm rocket hit the crippled helicopter with a huge orange flash.

As the bearers lurched Stubbsy's stretcher into the bunker entrance, a violent fireball mushroomed up into a thick column of black smoke.

The concussion from the exploding helicopter shook the bunker walls.

The bearers turned the last corner, and swiftly set Stubbsy's lifeless body on stretcher stands under the fluorescent lights.

Doc and Gabrielle set to Stubbsy with deft hands while Clancy and Ben and Halliday circled the stretcher, assisting.

For ten full minutes, Doc pounded Stubbsy's chest, and Gabrielle gave the pilot oxygen.

Finally, Gabrielle switched off the oxygen and gently crossed Stubbsy's arms over his chest. Doc looked away.

"Tag him," Doc said in a child's voice.

"Cause?" Halliday asked in a hoarse voice.

"Massive cranial gunshot wound, posterior."

Across the bunker, Co-pilot Long—wild-eyed and red in the face, huffing with the desperate belief that his friend could be saved—ripped off his flying helmet and slammed it on a post, shattering the face piece.

Gabrielle reached for the chunky officer's shoulder, but Long lurched away, collapsed, and blubbered.

Boots ran down the stairs—the crew—swarthy Eye-talian and skinny Gunner—with wild-animal stares and the hope of a miracle still on their faces until they saw Long, sobbing. Gunner fiercely set his lips, and involuntarily rocked his head in slight nods. Eye-talian kicked a flak jacket into the wall.

Clancy reached up into the low-hanging eaves and wearily tossed a body bag to Halliday.

Under a dim pool of light, Halliday rolled Stubbsy on his side to tuck the rubber bag underneath.

"Gimme that!" Long yelled, charging over and grabbing the long green bag.

Long threw the body bag on the ground.

No one moved. Gunner took something from Eye-talian, and then touched a flash of silver on Long's wrist.

"Come on, man," Gunner pleaded. "You know the promise."

Long removed a silver bracelet and grabbed the others from Gunner. With tears running down his red cheeks, Long took Stubbsy's limp left hand and tenderly held his dead friend's strong fingers.

Long slipped the three silver bracelets onto dead Stubbsy's wrist so the ring of silver on silver chimed across the bunker.

"Oh, Jimmy ..." Long said, staring into Stubbs's lifeless blue eyes.

For a moment, everyone in the bunker froze, honoring James Homer Stubbs, lying young and dead under green, fluorescent light on a filthy canvas stretcher twenty feet below ground and ten thousand miles from home.

Long bent down, tossed the body bag over his shoulders, and turned to Doc.

"I'll see that he gets home," Long whispered. "OK, Doc?"

Long motioned Eye-talian over.

The two men draped the fallen pilot's arms over their shoulders and headed up the stairs. Stubbsy's lifeless feet thumped the wooden risers as they carried him up into what was left of the day's light.

Gunner stood on the reception stair landing, shifting his feet like he was a lost child.

"Montagnard chief give us those bracelets," Gunner said. "For lifting his sick wife out."

Then the diminutive teenager in the oversized fatigues and the big flying helmet trudged up the stairs.

The wet red stain of Stubbsy's blood on the empty green stretcher gathered all the light in the room.

"I didn't tag him, Doc," Halliday said.

"Not important," Gabrielle said, turning towards Doc's office.

Halliday started up the stairs.

"Don't go getting yourself lost, troop," Clancy called. "We got us a Hercules coming in for those Vietnamese dead."

Halliday trudged up the stairs, fumbling for a cigarette. Lam followed, her flowing pants and long tunic stained with blood and mud.

*   *   *

Outside, Lam nestled into Halliday on the sandbags.

"Beau coups sad, Howaday," Lam said.

Halliday stared at Lam like she was a stranger, shook his head, and looked at the mud. Lam tugged his sleeve.

"Goddamnit, Lam!" he said.

Lam slipped her arms around him.

"Please," Halliday said. "Just go the hell away."

Lam turned and slowly walked downstairs. Halliday lit his cigarette with shaking hands.

Across the airstrip, Stubbsy's helicopter burned with pale blue flames licking the twisted hulk. Thick black smoke ran up into the hazy sky, adding to the eeriness of the mist.

The artillery was quiet. Not a single helicopter cut the air.

Ben came out and lit a cigarette.

"Daktoum," he said. "Sorry-ass shit."

Out on the Dust-off pad, Long, Gunner and Eye-talian surrounded Stubbsy lying in the green body bag, waiting for a lift ship near the pile of Vietnamese bodies and the smaller pile of American dead waiting for the Hercules.

Ben stared at Halliday until he looked up.

"Ain't no reason to take this out on Lam," Ben said.

Halliday studied his muddy boots.

"She doesn't treat *you* like a gook, Halliday."

When Halliday looked up, Ben's eyes were on him.

"That's what it's all about, man. Nobody wants to be treated like a gook."

Halliday flipped his cigarette into a muddy red pool and dug his hands into his pants pockets.

Ben stared at Halliday and slowly shook his head. When Halliday didn't look up, Ben went back underground.

Halliday walked to the dead bunker and disappeared.

The bunker was empty—the bodies were all out on the airstrip beside the Vietnamese dead.

Halliday sat on the low sandbagged wall in the dark where John Wayne had appeared. Under the dim light, bits of Stubbsy's brain still shone on his hands.

Trembling, Halliday wiped the drying gray matter on his jungle fatigues.

Outside, the big 1-7-5 gun started up.

Rounds boomed into the hills. Halliday thought he saw a flash of John Wayne and jumped. When he looked closer, it was only an uneven sandbag in the narrow bunker with the faint odors of death.

Clancy stuck his head in.

"Hercules ain't coming tonight," he said. "Haul them bodies back."

Halliday nodded and followed.

Outside, artillery pounded Rocket Ridge and Cambodia. Outgoing shells fluttered away through the mist into the steep jungle mountains and valleys.

*   *   *

The next morning—the second straight day of sunlight—an hour after first light, complying with Saigon's orders, Colonel Lehr sent a team out to open the road west to Ban Sai, followed by two security platoons of ARVN soldiers in clanking armored personnel carriers.

The blackened jungle still smoldered from when the previous day's helicopter gunships had blasted the road. All along Highway 14, burned-out trucks and tanks lay broken and rusting at odd angles beside the cleared strips of red earth that ran out to the tree lines.

The 99th mine-sweep team—a half-dozen men from D Company, swept the dirt road with metal detectors, slowly advancing toward Ban Sai. Three trucks followed at a walking pace, trailed by rumbling ARVN armored personnel carriers, which sporadically blasted machine gun fire at the jungle.

For an hour, the sun baked the skin of the soldiers. Helicopters occasionally crossed the sky at treetop. The team found no mines and took no enemy fire. Everyone joked that "Charlie had up and gone home back to mamasan."

On the west side of Bridge Eleven, Roadkill's Duster hit a mine, which knocked off a track. Then an American truck was hit by a rocket-propelled grenade, which killed four soldiers. Simultaneously, the lead ARVN armored personnel carrier took an RPG hit. Vietnamese soldiers abandoned the carrier as a black column of smoke rose into the air.

The rest of the ARVN security rumbled away so the 99th mine-sweep soldiers got stuck between the two disabled vehicles. Then, withering machine-gun fire from both enemy flanks opened up and pinned down the soldiers in a crossfire.

Jonesy, in a mine-sweep truck, tried to avoid the ambush, but bogged down in the mud. He grabbed the machine gun off the truck and fired—not at the N-V-A in the tree line—but at the retreating ARVNs.

*   *   *

At three thousand feet, Colonel Lehr rode in a helicopter flying back from Ban Sai to Daktoum. Clouds drifted by, and mist was already dimming the sunny morning.

Far below, the red-brown road cut through the green jungle. When smoke and flashes of fire appeared from two stalled trucks, Lehr grabbed a headset.

"Take me down!" Lehr ordered.

The helicopter banked over where ARVN soldiers hunkered down in the ditch around the 99th mine-sweep team. The chopper tried to radio but got no answer.

"Goddamnit," Lehr said. "Left the radios on the trucks."

As the helicopter circled, the colonel radioed Daktoum.

"Brandywine to Ranklin," Lehr said over the chopper noise and the rushing wind, "D Company mine sweep is pinned down three clicks east of the ARVN outpost near bridge eleven. No radio contact. Bring out the reaction force. Over."

"On our way," Ranklin said, "Get me on your net. Out."

Lehr studied the mine-sweep team scattered flat on the red earth in the ditch. Smoke trails rose from small arms fire.

"Put me down," Lehr told the pilot.

"Sir?" the pilot asked.

"On that road. Just get me close."

The co-pilot glanced back.

Lehr nodded. The helicopter hovered down fifty yards past the halted trucks, and an N-V-A machine gun opened-up.

Bullets ripped across the air and into the helicopter with a shatter of metal and Plexiglas.

Lehr got out on the helicopter skids with cries and moans behind him.

"Getting the hell out, sir!" the pilot yelled.

"So am I," Lehr yelled and jumped.

Pulling up, the chopper threw Lehr off balance. Trailing smoke, the helicopter banked up and away.

"Shit!"

Lehr landed a hundred feet from the mine-sweep team and twisted his knee hitting the ditch. Machine-gun fire zinged overhead toward the fleeing helicopter.

The N-V-A machine gun raked a burst over the stalled American trucks and went silent. A soldier's head poked up from the ditch.

"It's the colonel!" someone yelled.

Voices echoed down the muddy ditch.

N-V-A spider holes on both sides of the road opened up with a barrage of fire. The trapped Americans sunk deeper into the ditch until the shooting died away.

The Americans returned fire and rolled grenades towards the tree line and across the road, aiming for enemy spider holes. The air smoked with shooting and grenade blasts.

Under the covering fire, three Americans low-crawled towards the isolated Lehr, who inched toward them. With withering enemy fire zinging overhead, it seemed like hours before the three men signaled the colonel.

"Come on, sir," a scruffy soldier yelled. "Follow us."

Two men led Lehr, and another young soldier followed, crawling under the barrage of machine-gun and AK-47 fire.

"God-*damn!*" the last soldier yelled as he was hit.

Lehr and the scruffy soldier dragged the wounded man down the ditch under fire.

Bullets zinged across the damp muddy road. Finally, the three crawled into the ditch with the half-dozen soldiers.

Beyond the Americans, two-dozen ARVN soldiers lay huddled in the deepest part of the ditch, not firing.

A tall, skinny photographer with black-rimmed glasses lay between the two groups, shooting pictures whenever he could.

Lehr rolled over, gasping under the overwhelming din. Finally, Lehr breathed easier and rolled onto his side. Another soldier had been hit in the thigh, and two men were tying on pressure dressings.

During a lull, the scruffy soldier crawled over to Lehr.

"What the hell happened?" Lehr asked.

"ARVNs abandoned us and hauled ass," the scruffy soldier said. "Their armor won't come back."

"Reaction force's coming," Lehr said. "Where's the radio?"

"On the truck, sir. Two guys got killed trying to get it. Four more still out there."

"Dead?" Lehr asked.

The soldier shrugged.

"We just have to hang on," Lehr said.

Bursts of N-V-A fire came in so fast and thick and furious that Lehr thought a ground attack would follow.

Whenever the enemy fire faded, the Americans opened up. Again, they skipped and lobbed grenades towards the spider holes on both sides, trying to blast the N-V-A—whose faces were clearly visible when they fired—out of their holes. The firing went on until Lehr decided they just might die before the reaction force arrived. He just hoped that the helicopter pilot wasn't so badly wounded that he forgot to radio their position.

"UHHHHHHHHHHHHHHHHH!" a man screamed.

"I thought they were all dead," Lehr said.

"Thought they were too, sir."

The scruffy soldier dragged himself out of the ditch and crawled to the screaming man.

"Oh God, nooooooooooooo!"

The wounded man began to cry in terrible sobs. Under bursts of enemy fire, the medic Cullen scuttled over and then dragged the screaming man back. It was Roadkill.

"Ohhhhhhh nooooooo, my ballllllllllls," he wailed.

A red stain filled Roadkill's lap.

Cullen thrust a morphine syrette in Roadkill's right leg, found an arm vein, and inserted a needle with a fluids pack.

"Dust-off!" Cullen hissed to Lehr.

The enemy fire intensified.

A sleek Cobra gunship appeared at treetop and strafed both tree lines with red tracer bullets. The overpowering mini-gun fire splintered the jungle and thudded into the earth.

The Cobra swiftly banked up and immediately drew fire from the enemy machine guns along the road.

The pinned-down American mine-sweep team went quiet. The wounded murmured, and the soldiers rested as the gunship circled high overhead.

N-V-A machine guns fired controlled bursts at the gunship.

With remarkable speed, the thin Cobra swooped out of the sky, again thundering mini-gun fire into the tree line.

Just as the Cobra looked like it would hit the ground, the ship shot two rockets and pulled steeply up.

Explosions engulfed the green jungle tree line as red-yellow flames billowed, shattering branches bursting with black smoke. There was no return fire.

"All fucking *right!*" somebody yelled.

"Took that sucka right out, Jim!"

"Check out them apples Papasan! *Fuck you.*"

The Cobra circled high overhead.

Again, the Cobra dove toward the treetops, blasting rockets. As the knifelike helicopter neared the ground, the air exploded with orange fireballs.

The Cobra quickly pulled up.

Bursts of N-V-A fire exploded all around. One flaming ball hit a skid and the helicopter hesitated. Another burning fireball smashed into the Cobra gunship below the cockpit, exploding tongues of flame that enveloped the helicopter.

The flaming Cobra hung suspended in the air and then swiftly arced down as if the pilot were flying it into the earth.

The long sleek Cobra hit the ground with a sickening metallic thud and exploded fire all across the green jungle.

The N-V-A machine guns started up again.

The Americans put out return fire during lulls.

N-V-A soldiers moved boldly in plain sight, while the Americans tried to forget how little ammunition they had left.

The N-V-A rushed the ditch, the Americans fired back. Lehr shot an N-V-A soldier who came so close that the man fell on him, and the colonel had to shove his body away.

The N-V-A kept rushing and firing, rushing, and firing—from spider holes so near they could see the whites of the enemy's eyes.

Just as Lehr decided they couldn't take another assault, whining explosions blasted from the east.

"Beehives," one young soldier said.

"The reaction force," Lehr muttered.

Shotgun rounds from an American tank smashed at the tree line as the other Duster clanked up, firing 40mm rounds into the trees. Dump trucks filled with engineer riflemen put out M-14 fire. At first, the N-V-A gunfire intensified, then quickly faltered, and died away.

Fifty? A hundred? N-V-A soldiers in dark green uniforms slipped out of holes and bunkers and gun positions and bolted into the scrubby tree lines along the road, their pith helmets dancing with branches.

The blasting clanking roaring column of the 99th reaction force drove right up to the ditches, where the tankers and American engineers rolled off their trucks and fired at the tree lines for maybe five minutes.

When there had been no return fire for several minutes, Lehr yelled "Cease fire!"

The Americans stood up and smiled the stupid, child-carnival grins of those who have survived certain death.

Ben, on the lead truck with Smitty, checked the dead Americans lying in the road. Five teenage soldiers lay so still that Ben didn't even move fast.

The tall, skinny photographer with thick, black-rimmed glasses circled them like a friendly ghost, shooting pictures.

As Ben gazed at a dead black soldier, he sat up.

"Son of a bitch!" Ben yelled, jumping.

"OK, man, it's OK," the soldier told Ben. "I ain't dead."

"What the fuck?" Smitty asked. "You scared us."

"You ain't got no idea what scared is, Jim," the black soldier said. "I can't believe I ain't dead."

"What's your name?"

"Jeffries."

"What happened?" Ben asked. "You want to sit down?"

"No, man. I never thought I'd stand up again. I was already dead, man, the only question was when."

Jeffries shook his head and shuffled around on the road. Someone lit him a cigarette and when he finally spoke, it was like he was figuring out a dream.

"After Burfrey and Delarosa and Matt got it, I ran over to help, but they were dead and the firefight go so heavy that after I ran out of ammo, all I could do was get flat," Jeffries said. "Couldn't make it to the ditch, so I just lay there trying not to get hit. During a lull, three N-V-As crawled out of their holes to check the bodies for loot. I knew I was fucked, 'cause Annie Mae's silver ring was way too tight, and I'd surely scream when they cut off my finger, so I just figured that I was gonna die. But when they got to me and yanked my finger, her ring just slipped right off—like it was three sizes too big."

His bloodshot eyes teared up as he held out his hand.

"Wow," Jeffries said. "Jesus *was* in the ditch with me."

Ben and Smitty felt the deep ring indentation around Jeffries' finger.

"Man, you a walking miracle," Ben said. "Go climb on that dump truck and get yourself a beer—some fool brought some, figuring you guys might need it."

"Move out!" Lehr called.

"Saddle up!"

The 99th trucks turned around on the muddy road and loaded up the living and the wounded and the dead. They left the gun truck and the two tanks behind firing bursts at the green tree lines, mopping up, but the N-V-A were gone.

As they left, the ARVN tanks returned.

The engineers' small reaction force convoy sped down the long red road through the dark brooding jungle past ghostly blown-up trucks and burned-out tanks.

As they reached the Daktoum gate, the green hills sank back under the gray mist. To the west, the last patch of sunlight in the valley clouded over.

*   *   *

Colonel Lehr—riding back with the Kid, who had driven out with the reaction force—sped to the front of the convoy and stopped his Jeep just inside the front gate.

The colonel climbed up the Daktoum gate tower and stood in the parapet watching the reaction force straggle in.

Under the swirling mist, Lehr studied the road through binoculars. Below him, exhausted young soldiers climbed off the mud-spattered trucks and smoked cigarettes.

"Half-assed operation ..."

"Fucking ARVNs."

"Fucking lifers, man, they're the ones who'll get you killed..."

"Bull-shit, you weren't scared, man. Everybody was scared shitless, every swinging Richard."

"Fuck it, don't mean nothing. Six more days of this shit I'm back in the World."

The mist chilled the colonel.

The radio in Lehr's Jeep crackled up into the tower—Ban Sai Control came on the net with curt wild messages for air support, Dust-off, artillery. Enemy tunnels and ditches had finally encircled the Ban Sai perimeter. The smaller camp to the west had been probed every night and constantly took incoming fire.

Goddamn half-assed operation, Lehr thought. How the hell can you keep a road open with ARVN security and no air support? *Priority, Colonel, Priority.* Jesus! That Cobra just dropped right out of the sky. If it hadn't taken out that N-V-A machine gun, they would have overrun us.

The colonel's left side ached, and the muscles around his heart felt cramped.

The last mine-sweep truck with all the dead soldiers, rolled in and slowly headed to the medical bunker.

The gate guards dragged barbed-wire barricades across the entrance road, sealing the perimeter. Then, they reset the CS gas and Claymore mines below the tower.

The reaction force soldiers climbed onto their trucks and drove back to their company areas.

A big Hercules transport plane appeared out of the clouds above Nhu Canh Du and banked steeply down.

"Everyone's in, sir!" the Kid called up to the tower.

Lehr nodded.

The big transport plane corkscrewed down and landed with a squeal of tires on the Nhu Canh Du end. The Hercules's engines roared and braked, heading fast toward Lehr, atop the gate-tower at the Cambodia end of the strip.

A hundred meters away, the fat, cigar-shaped, camouflaged plane slowed with a blast of engines and quickly swung around.

Eight big pallets skidded out of the rear lift gate and clattered onto the runway.

The transport fast-taxied toward the Dust-off pad.

The green hills lay under mist so thick that the Hercules appeared to be covered with gauze.

Bodies, Lehr figured. Trinh sent the plane for the ARVN bodies. Christ.

A tremendous roar echoed above Daktoum, and the colonel searched the low gray ceiling. Helicopters—headed back to Pleiku and Kontum, with the loss of visibility. And Trinh sends this goddamn plane, *now?*

Lehr scoffed so loud that the Kid glanced up from the Jeep.

A rocket thundered in. The helicopter noise had drowned out the warning pop.

Instinctively, Lehr ducked, and then peered over the tower walls. The rocket hit the end of the airstrip with a tumbling red-yellow explosion that cracked his ears.

Rockets walked down the airstrip toward the transport plane, which screamed its engines up into a desperate hum. The engines howled, the pilot let off the brakes, and the big, squat plane shot forward.

Just as the front wheels lifted, a 122-millimeter Russian Katyusha rocket hit the transport's tail.

A cone of flame erupted.

The Hercules careened sideways and sheared off the landing gear. As the plane bounced down the Daktoum runway, sparks shot out from the belly with screams of tearing metal. Black smoke flooded the gray air as the burning plane lurched to a halt at the Ban Sai end of the airstrip.

Lehr scrambled down the tower ladder and ran to his Jeep.

The Kid sped them towards the burning plane and got as close as they could to the flaming transport, but no one escaped. Lehr sat in his Jeep, sweating under the immense heat.

"Medical bunker," Lehr said.

*   *   *

All the medics watched the Hercules transport blow up.

On the bunker roof, Clancy radioed for departing helicopters to take out the American bodies.

Then the mine-sweep trucks came into the muddy medical lot, followed by a dump truck carrying the reaction force.

Clancy yelled to Halliday and tossed him a fistful of death tags. Ben and Halliday climbed up into the deuce-and-a-half truck bed, found the dead soldiers' dog tags, and wrote down causes of death, while the reaction force soldiers milled around.

The skinny photographer with the black glasses shot pictures from a dump truck and then climbed down and moved around, shooting as the medics bagged the dead.

When a helicopter thumped in the mist, Clancy ran out to the airstrip and popped purple haze. The helicopter descended through the lavender smoke near the Vietnamese bodies and the pile of weapons.

Ben, Clancy, Halliday, and Cullen—who had ridden in with the dead—carried out the four American bodies to the chopper. The crews's faces were drawn as the medics hustled up and loaded the dead.

The South Vietnamese bodies were still heaped beside the runway.

Beyond the corpses, smoke from the burning Hercules billowed into the dimming mist.

*   *   *

Inside the medical bunker, Lehr walked past a wounded man on a stretcher, knocked on Doc's closed canvas door and stepped inside.

The slender Doctor sat beside Gabrielle.

Pain stabbed at Lehr, so he jammed his fist into his throbbing pectoral muscle. The colonel's unshaven face was ashen, and his eyes clouded as he leaned on the doorframe.

"Colonel?"

Lehr bit his tongue so hard that he tasted blood. Only then did his chest pain stop.

The colonel straightened up, nodded curtly, and then pushed his way out of the small room. He skirted along the stretcher rows and went up the back stairs.

Lehr stood outside, watching the black smoke billow from the plane at the end of the airstrip.

*   *   *

The medics lifted the last body into the helicopter.

"Where's that ambulatory?" Clancy yelled to Halliday.

"Ambulatory?"

"Go down and get him!"

Halliday ran back with Cullen and Ben.

Clancy held onto his bush hat, dashed under the spinning blades, and banged on the pilot's Plexiglas window.

"Two minutes," Clancy said. "Got a walking wounded."

The pilot nodded and pointed at the dead soldiers.

"Long as they don't mind," he yelled.

Clancy turned away. The turbine held at lift speed.

When Halliday didn't appear, Clancy set his jaw and ran across the bridge to the medical bunker.

Halliday came out from the back stairs, helping a disheveled wounded soldier in muddy fatigues, whose dirty young face was creased with deep lines and looked familiar.

"Leggo, man," the soldier said, trembling.

The helicopter vibrated at lift speed, and the gunner waved them on. Halliday recognized the wounded man. Jonesy.

"Come on, Jonesy, your bird's waiting."

Jonesy's face was sallow, gray, and caked with mud.

"I been hit," he said.

"I know, Jonesy," Halliday replied.

Fresh blood seeped through the dirty-brown bandages.

"I'm scared, man," Jonesy roared, contorting his pale face.

Halliday prodded him across the gray bridge.

"Just get on the chopper."

"You're that crazy fucker we tied to the back of my truck."

"Yeah, come on, Jonesy, they're waiting."

The helicopter's skids rocked back and forth, ready to lift.

"I don't know," Jonesy said, turning away.

Halliday grabbed Jonesy and gently turned him around.

"I don't want to go."

"Just get on the bird, man."

"I seen a Cobra blown out of the sky!"

Jonesy stared into the mist with a mad grin, and Halliday looked around for help. Clancy was leaning into the colonel's Jeep talking to the Kid.

Jonesy broke away in a stiff, unearthly run, flapping his bad arm. Halliday caught him and steered him to the airstrip.

"It's a perfectly good chopper," Halliday said. "Get you back to the World didimau.

Jonesy beamed as Halliday maneuvered him under the helicopter rotors, but when he spotted the bodies, Jonesy threw off Halliday's arms with superhuman strength.

"Number fucking ten bad luck to ride with the dead!"

Jonesy planted himself like a steel stake and Halliday couldn't move him. He waved for help, but Jonesy broke away in a weird, goose-step.

Halliday chased Jonesy down as the helicopter crew gestured wildly.

Two hundred meters away, a mortar round exploded.

The pilot grimaced. He waited thirty seconds and then lifted the helicopter.

Grit sandblasted Halliday and whipped Jonesy's muddy fatigues like a tattered flag. The helicopter whined away, into the mist.

Another mortar screamed in, and Halliday hit the dirt.

"Get the fuck down, Jonesy!"

Jonesy shuffled around like a ghost.

Halliday, flat on the runway, crawled towards Jonesy and tried to tackle him, but the wounded man reeled away with a wild grin on his mud-caked face.

"Down, you stupid fucker, *down*!"

Jonesy froze like a deer on a highway.

A blast of metal, smoke, and fire ripped at Halliday, and he fought panic at the near hit but kept his eyes on Jonesy.

The wounded man clutched his chest with both fists, as if to prevent something from leaving his body.

Finally, interminably, Jonesy toppled over, taking, what seemed to Halliday, minutes to hit the runway in a collapsing heap of bandages, muddy fatigues, and cooling flesh.

Halliday crawled over, but there was no life left in Jonesy.

*   *   *

An hour later, inside the TOC, a mud-stained, disheveled Colonel Lehr grabbed a Flash Precedence cable from Ranklin.

Lehr marched into his office, closed the door, and unfolded the cable.

SECRET 03613 19 JUL 69
SUBJECT: DAKTOUM REDEPLOY

TO: COMUS DAKTOUM
REDEPLOY ALL US PERSONNEL/EQUIP KONTUM NLT
1AUG 69
JOINT COMUS ARVN KONTUM

Finally, Lehr thought. How in hell do they expect me to *redeploy?* Now? Road closed, can't even count on gunships in this mist. Christ, just lead my two-hundred-and-fifty vehicles plus artillery down Highway 14 with two Dusters and no Tac-air? Who the hell are they kidding? How can I leave Daktoum—unless Charlie gives up?

The Kid knocked and brought in heated C-ration beans and franks, cheddar-cheese crackers, and coffee. Colonel Lehr picked at the food while he leafed through cables, reading the Flash Precedence's and the Priorities and bundling the rest.

The radio squawked out terse messages from the bunker line. Outside, artillery pounded in a constant rolling thunder.

In the corner, a small, furry nose peeked out of a hole in the floor. When Lehr threw a C-ration can at the rat, pain throbbed in his chest, and the rat ducked back in the hole.

Pull out, now? We'd be lunchmeat, just like today.

Lehr cranked the field telephone line, but no one answered. He yelled for the Kid and walked outside.

Except for artillery flashes, the night was black. A red tracer shot streaked over the bunker line as the Kid hustled up. Lehr sank into the Jeep seat and massaged his aching chest.

Sandbagged walls and bunkers appeared and disappeared under the mist that muffled the artillery and small arms fire. The Jeep whined and bumped on the long slow ride around Daktoum perimeter, and the murmuring of young soldiers followed the colonel everywhere.

"Medical bunker," Lehr said.

They parked in the muddy lot beside the ambulance. The colonel got out and went downstairs.

Clancy stood alone atop the medical bunker. When he saw the Kid, Clancy slipped off the low rooftop and walked to the colonel's Jeep.

"Kid," he whispered.

"Sergeant Clancy."

His warm hand covered the Kid's on the steering wheel.

"You OK?"

"Yeah," the Kid said.

Clancy squeezed the Kid's leg in the darkness and briefly wrapped his big arm around the Kid's shoulders, hugging him. The Kid leaned his cheek against Clancy's warm neck, scented with aftershave.

"You take care, hear?"

"Yes, Sergeant Clancy."

Clancy's bulky warmth disappeared into the dark night.

*   *   *

Lehr came down the medical bunker stairs into the big dim room where medics lay dozing on stretchers.

"PFC Halliday?" Lehr asked a small curly-haired medic at the front desk.

"Upstairs—he hangs out in that shitty old Graves bunker," Donnelly replied with an unsettling lilt. "Sir."

The colonel nodded.

*   *   *

Gabrielle watched Lehr leave through a slit in Doc's door.

"What is it?" Doc asked from behind a medical book.

"Nothing," Gabrielle said. "A soldier, for Halliday."

"Oh," Doc said.

*   *   *

Outside, Lehr dismissed the Kid and watched the Jeep drive away. He found the entrance to the dead bunker and went inside.

A propped-up flashlight cast jagged shadows across the sandbag walls where Halliday sat before a muddy body on a stretcher. Lehr recognized the dead battalion courier. Halliday glanced at Lehr and turned back to Jonesy's corpse in an unzipped green bag.

The colonel's chest cramped, and he gritted his teeth.

"First friend to get it?" the colonel asked.

"No sir," Halliday said. "Merton was my friend."

"Merton made it," the colonel said. "Got word from 71st Evac. He's in Japan."

Halliday nodded and turned back to the body. The maze entrance flashed silver as a low, pervasive rumbling sounded like an immense waterfall far away.

Lehr laid his hand on Halliday's shoulder.

"No one forgets when first friend was killed," Lehr rasped.

Halliday fought back tears.

"I didn't really know him," Halliday said. "Except drunk in Saigon. I didn't even like him. Jonesy was mean—bad mean sometimes. Why does *his* dying get to me? Because he wouldn't save himself? Goddamn fool."

Lehr shook his head.

"Why don't you goddamn do something," Halliday said. "You're in charge."

Lehr cracked a laugh, which was lost in the sandbags.

"*I'm in charge?*"

"Yeah," Halliday challenged. "Do something!"

"Such as?"

"Tell Saigon we're leaving."

Oh Christ. Lehr bit his tongue. His hand felt dead on Halliday's shoulder. He thought about the cable and Eagleton saying, "*command couldn't provide helicopters for a few days.*" *Couldn't?* Some "*big operation forty clicks south.*"

"Can't," Lehr murmured. "Not yet anyway."

"Why not?" Halliday yelled, twisting away from Lehr.

"We'd never make it," the colonel said. "Without armor or air, we wouldn't get half an hour down that road before Charlie wiped us out. We have to wait for enough air."

Jonesy's dead face gave off a frozen grin.

Lehr's steely glint focused beyond the room. As his hand rested on Halliday's shoulder, a peaceful smile formed on his lips.

Halliday could barely see the old man's face, though his shadow loomed high on the bunker walls.

"Why not, sir?" Halliday said quietly. "The infantry pulled out. They're talking peace. We can't even fight them, really. We're just sitting ducks. Why?"

The colonel stiffened and then he exhaled.

"I don't know, Halliday."

The Colonel's mind raced—*REDEPLOY ALL PERSONNEL AND EQUIPMENT.* The burning helicopter thudded into the earth, Merton laughed, smoke swirled above Gabrielle's hospital, the baby made of ashes collapsed and blew away, ashes, *ashes, ashes we all fall down, you're killing children, Daddy, you trust your country too much, someone has to take responsibility, John,* Monique and Gabrielle, naked, whispering with short red stabs of their cigarettes in the dark, the night, the goddamned night, the senselessness, the pain, the night, duty for God and country, *oh say can you see,* see fucking *what?*

"Why not, sir?" Halliday said. "Why don't you know?"

Lehr shook his head.

"I just don't, Halliday. My first tour I fought for freedom, my second tour—for ... duty. Now, I don't know..."

The colonel turned and a dim flash of light caught his eyes.

"Maybe this tour is for ... me."

"For you?"

"Yes," Lehr said.

"What do you mean?"

"I really wish I could believe in *not* killing the enemy, but I don't," Lehr said. "But I also don't know if we're doing any goddamn good here at all."

The colonel patted Halliday's shoulder and walked out of the bunker of the dead. Halliday ran after him.

Outside, monsoon rain fell so lightly that it felt like it could rain forever. Halliday barely made out the big, dark, muddy lot crisscrossed by wooden pallets, the ambulances, and the few sagging canvas tents.

Ghosts of electricity pulsed at the clouds; small arms fire crackled from no discernible direction. Somewhere far off, grenades exploded, and artillery rocketed out and fell to earth.

Halliday caught up with the colonel on a wooden pallet half-sunk in the mud. He grabbed Lehr and turned him around in the rain.

Lightning flashed. Lehr's pale face was wet and shining.

"Are we gonna get out of here, sir?"

"I don't know."

Halliday held onto Lehr's shoulder.

"What do you mean you don't *know?*"

Lehr's eyes gleamed with terror and strength and an overpowering sadness.

"I don't think we *want* to leave."

"What?"

Lehr stared at distant lightning. His wet face, his gray eyes looked almost dead.

"You could lead us out," Halliday said. "Sir, march the whole battalion right down Highway 14, no weapons, no vehicles, just us, marching out. That *Life* photographer's still here. When the country sees us on the news marching out unarmed, the whole fucking war would be over. All of us, every soldier in Vietnam, everybody back in the World would know that this goddamn war was finally over, and you were the one who started the whole thing."

Lehr gripped Halliday's shoulders.

"I wish I could," Lehr said. "But I can't help anyone."

The two men, old and young, stood in the pouring rain lit by dim flashes of lightning.

"I can't even help myself."

Lehr took Halliday's hand off his shoulder and placed it back at the young man's side.

Lehr looked deep into Halliday's eyes and turned away.

"Wait, sir!" Halliday called. "I'll drive you back!"

"No," the colonel said, stepping across the mud in his dripping fatigues.

Halliday watched the colonel walk through flashes of light and into the dark rainy mist.

"Good luck, sir!" Halliday yelled.

"Good luck," Lehr echoed.

*   *   *

The colonel marched through pools of water and stopped at the end of the company street near the airstrip.

"You!" Lehr yelled at the low mist, shaking his fist. "Yes, *you*, you tired old son of a bitch!"

Under a flash of lightning, the colonel saw two dripping rags overhead—the red, white, and blue American flag, and the yellow Vietnamese banner, which some soldier had forgotten to take down off the flagpoles.

"Yes, you son of a bitch! I'm staying!" Lehr yelled at the drizzling night. "You hear me? I'm *staying*! I won't let you kill us out on the road like you did the French at Mang Yang!"

The colonel's chest pounded as Lehr slipped to his knees in the mud.

A flash of artillery caught a shapeless rain poncho slogging through the wet darkness.

"Colonel?" Chaplain Goodby asked, coming up.

"What?" Lehr said harshly.

"Are you all right?"

On his knees in the mud, Lehr stared at Goodby's pale, pie-shaped face surrounded by a slick rain poncho.

"Of course," Lehr said.

Lehr stood up and glared at Goodby.

The colonel walked briskly through the rain past the ruined tents on the company street and disappeared.

Trying to catch the colonel, Chaplain Goodby slipped. He wavered back and forth in the mud, trying to keep his balance. When lightning flashed, the Chaplain saw a sandbagged wall, caught it, and steadied himself. Goodby grinned, pleased that he had not gone down in the mud like the colonel.

*   *   *

Gabrielle sat up in bed with sweat running down her face.

Across the small room in the other bed, Doc murmured. He leaned up on his elbow and saw Gabrielle's face in the dim slash of light from the canvas flap.

"What?" he whispered.

"Nothing." Gabrielle said. "A bad dream."

"Do you want to talk about it?"

"Why?" Gabrielle said. "It is only a dream."

"You don't believe in dreams?"

"All my life, Vietnam has been at war. How could a dream make anything different? What could a dream mean? All I can do is help people when they get hurt. I can't stop the hurting."

"But you have to believe," Doc whispered.

"*Believe*? In what?"

"I don't know," Doc said. "Hope?"

"Hope?"

"Yes," Doc said.

"And do you, Bacsi?" Gabrielle said in the darkness. "Do *you* believe in the hope?"

"I ...."

Doc couldn't finish his sentence.

*   *   *

Halliday went back into the bunker of the dead to retrieve his flashlight. The bulb had gone out, and he felt a slight almost electrical sensation in the dank air. Something heavy grazed his foot, and in the darkness, Halliday thought it was an overhanging sandbag, so he kept feeling around on the dirt floor until he found the flashlight.

When it wouldn't work, Halliday banged the cylinder on his palm until a weak yellow beam lit the sandbag walls.

Halliday froze in horror.

An immense King Cobra slithered over his boots—black and as thick as his calf. The snake coiled around Jonesy's body and then slowly reared up to Halliday's eye level.

When the Cobra spread its hood, the tiny yellow eyes and flickering forked tongue paralyzed Halliday. As the great serpent swayed back and forth, Halliday swayed with it, desperately trying to think of how to get away.

Finally, he threw his flashlight at the snake, and dove towards the entrance, in a cloud of dust. Halliday rolled outside and ran down the bunker stairs.

He grabbed his M-14 rifle from behind the entrance desk and hurried back upstairs.

Jamming a round in the chamber, and holding his rifle out, Halliday slowly entered the dead bunker, ready to shoot.

His flashlight lay on the ground, dimly illuminating Jonesy's body. Halliday searched the bunker, but the giant black snake was no longer there.

He stood alone in the morgue bunker beside Jonesy's pale, smiling dead face in a half-zipped rubber bag on a muddy green stretcher on the red Daktoum dust.

20.

After the rain, Halliday sat atop the medical bunker sipping bourbon with Donnelly, Ben, and Nimmer. Explosions vibrated the humid air along with the tremendous dull ground rumblings of B-52 bombs.

"Nobody can find shit in this mist," Ben said.

"Except your own ASS!" Donnelly said with a shriek.

Cullen appeared out of the front entrance.

"Gooks in the streets of Nhu Canh Du, N-V-A hitting the ARVN camp," Cullen called across the sandbagged roof. "Ban Sai got beau coups probes, Home."

After Cullen left, the bottle went around again.

"No more," Ben said getting up. "Later."

"I'll have some," Halliday slurred.

"Don't be a dumbshit," Ben said, slapping Halliday's shoulder.

Halliday threw his hand off. Ben shook his head and left.

"OK," Donnelly said, offering the bottle. "Clancy'll just break it if he sees it."

Nimmer lit a joint, and passed it around, but only Halliday smoked. Donnelly drummed on the wet sandbags.

Small arms fire crackled from the bunker line. Then came a strange high-pitched scream.

"Know what that is?" Nimmer said.

No one answered.

"Tiger," Nimmer said.

"Bullshit," Donnelly said.

"Wrong. I heard it before once, in the Ho Bo Woods."

"Where the fuck is that?"

"Iron Triangle. It's all gone now."

"Gone? What's gone?"

"The Ho Bo Woods. It's famous. Big V-C stronghold, so we burned it down, the entire fucking forest. Then we defoliated it, so it ain't even there no more. Ho Bo Woods, nothing but burned stumps. Sin loi, motherfucker."

An M-60 machine gun spat out a long hard burst.

"Stupid fuck!" Nimmer yelled. "Burn up the barrel, *dumbshit*, firing like that!"

"Can't see anything anyway," Halliday said.

A green AK-47 tracer zinged high over the medical bunker, but only Halliday saw it. He stood up, mock saluted Nimmer and Donnelly, and then swayed across the bunker roof.

When he eased himself onto the ground, Ben was waiting.

"I need to talk," Ben said.

"Hey, I quit drinking."

"About Lam," Ben said.

"Yeah," Halliday said. "You *like* her, right?"

"I do," Ben said.

"Go for it," Halliday said exhaling.

"*Yeah?*"

"Hell yes. I never did her any good. I tried but couldn't."

Ben nodded.

"Guess I'm a dumbshit. And a chickenshit. Take her back to the World. That's what she wants."

"Thanks, man," Ben said, gripping Halliday's shoulder for a long moment, before disappearing across the dark firebase.

"Good luck," Halliday whispered like a song.

As Halliday descended the bunker stairs and tapped on each wooden step like a childish game.

The big main room was quiet except for murmuring in Doc's office.

In the pool of light around the entrance desk, screeches and moans came out of the tiny speakers on the two radios that the grim-faced

Cullen monitored. Clancy lay face down on a stretcher, writing a letter under a dim hanging bulb.

Tiptoeing through the dark, Halliday hit his knee on a sawhorse.

"DAMN!"

Halliday flopped onto a waist-high stretcher and unlaced his boots.

"Halliday," Clancy commanded. "Come here, trooper."

Halliday exhaled. He slid off the stretcher, scuffed across the concrete in his unlaced boots, and sat down two stretchers away from Clancy, almost in darkness.

"Sergeant Clancy," he declared.

With a quick lithe motion, the burly Clancy shifted up into a sitting position.

"You've been drinking," Clancy said. "With all those other fuck-ups."

Halliday's mouth tightened.

"Yeah."

"Halliday, you know you ain't ever really off-duty as a medic. Now, you all screwed up," Clancy went on. "If I had my way—none a' you would be drinking around this bunker, but that young doctor just won't back me up."

"I'm not that fucked up. *Gotta* drink," Halliday said. "Only way to fly. 'Specially after your friends get blown away."

Clancy glared.

"I know what you're going to say, Sergeant Clancy. *Fighting for Freedom*," Halliday said. "Whose freedom? Not *ours*. Some fat-assed politician too chickenshit to serve? That's a good reason for Merton to get his leg blown off."

Halliday slipped off his boot. He waved it at Clancy.

"His *leg*, his fucking *leg*—no more softball, running hiking, girlfriend, nothing but a Phantom-fucking-Limb—so some military-industrial-complex dickhead can get rich making artillery rounds. Man, just the thought of that ought to make even *you* want to get drunk. What did those people ever do for you? You think they even *like* black people?"

A single bulb shone on Clancy's bare scalp and shadowed his powerful round face.

"Ain't really your job to think about that, is it, Halliday?"

Halliday dropped a muddy boot.

"What do you mean?"

"Your job is to *drive* the ambulance, *help* the Doc, *treat* the wounded. And now you're all *fucked up.*"

"I'm OK."

Clancy snorted and folded his big arms.

"Halliday, just remember, if you *hurt* anybody when you're drunk —*you* got to live with it."

"I know," Halliday said, scowling.

He dropped his other boot on the floor.

"I don't want to see you drunk anymore," Clancy said in a low even voice.

"What?"

"I'm holding you personally responsible."

"*What?*" Halliday said. "OK, then I'm holding *you* personally responsible."

"Me?" Clancy laughed. "What the hell are you holding me responsible for?"

Halliday stood up. His face flushed and twisted into rage as he flung out his arms.

"For *this!* All of it!"

Halliday knocked over an M-16 rifle with a clatter. Instinctively, they both jumped—but the rifle didn't discharge.

Clancy's thick forearms bulged, and his fingers clasped and unclasped.

"You might think a little different, Halliday," Clancy said slowly. "If you saw what the Communists did in Ko-rea."

"I don't give a shit if they ate burned babies with chocolate sauce! This ain't Korea or Iwo Jima or Tippy-fucking-canoe, it's *Vietnam.* We're cutting our own throats, eating our children, can't you see? Can't you?"

"Shut the hell up!" Cullen groaned across the darkness. "Knock off all that peacenik crap, Halliday, you sound like god-damn Limerick. I got fifty days left, and I don't care who started it, or who ends it, I just want to do my duty and go home, Home, so shut it up."

Donnelly skipped down the stairs, muttering, and stepped into the pool of light beside Cullen.

Across the room, Clancy pointed at Halliday.

"Halliday, I *mean* it. I don't want to see you drunk again—or you either, Donnelly," Clancy said, pointing at the Irishman. "Both of you are gonna have to answer to me."

Clancy puffed up his chest.

Nimmer came in, and then all the medics settled down on stretchers.

Clancy turned off his light and the underground room went dark except for the soft glow around Cullen's desk near the entrance landing.

They lay for a long time in the darkness, listening to the war outside muffled by tons of earth all around them. They listened to the hushed moans and pops of the radios, and the rats scurrying overhead in the rafters, and the ever-deepening sounds of their own breathing until they fell asleep.

*   *   *

Gabrielle ran her fingers down Doc's slender back as he stared at the rough pine wall at the thin strip of light falling through the canvas doorway.

The radio spat out veiled panic in curt messages.

"Nhu Canh Du?" Doc whispered. "Ban Sai. Are they lost?"

Gabrielle lowered her body so her breasts touched Captain Levin's soft skin.

"You know what that means?" he said.

"Yes," she whispered.

"They'll try a ground attack."

He eased her away and sat up.

"What did you think that they would do?" she whispered, rummaging through her bag. "Let you *be*? It's *their* country."

Gabrielle struck a match to a cigarette.

In the brief flame, Doc saw the shining darkness between her legs, her curved shoulders, her breasts, her long, tangled, black hair, and flashing eyes. Doc looked away to his wife's picture. Even the dusty, cracked glass and the dried blood couldn't mask her beauty.

The match burned out and Gabrielle's cigarette was the only light in the room. She sat on the opposing bunk.

"It's childish," she said.

"Childish?"

"All of us, here in Daktoum."

"How can you say that?" Doc said. "You're saving people."

Doc flew off the bed toward her, but he stepped on Bacsi, asleep on the floor, and the dog nipped at Doc's right calf.

"All we can do is save a few lives," Gabrielle said.

"That's something," Doc said.

He sat down beside her and rubbed the bite on his leg. Doc lay beside her and tried not to think of anything, but he couldn't get past her breathing and his beating heart.

Finally, the moving glow of her cigarette dimmed.

"I learned one thing," she said. "From our war."

"What?" Doc asked.

"No one can save their country from itself."

"Are we supposed to?"

Gabrielle shrugged.

"Who knows? It is hard enough to save yourself."

Gabrielle stubbed out her cigarette and the small room went dark. The tinny radio voices outside became shrill, and finally died away in a low buzz of static.

*　　　　　*　　　　　*

Ben slipped across the muddy firebase to the river line.

To the east, flames from Nhu Canh Du made the mist red with flashes and rumbles and muffled explosions. The dense, wet air stank of rotting canvas, gunpowder, and mud.

By the misty firelight of cannons, Ben skirted large shining puddles and hurried past shattered hootches sinking into the red mud. In a flash of an explosion, a hulking truck loomed up, mired in the muddy camp road.

Ben's boots made sucking sounds as he came to the thicket of barbed wire on the river bunker line. Something moved, and he raised his M-16 rifle.

A soldier hurried past.

"Don't fucking shoot me," the man said.

Artillery thundered out blue-yellow flames, so Ben was able to follow the river line by the flashes. A flare above Nhu Canh Du turned the mist briefly silver.

A tower bunker had collapsed, and tons of red earth had slid down a deep gully into the river. A hasty tangle of barbed wire, sandbags, and metal stakes linked this fallen bunker to the Daktoum perimeter and was strewn with dozens of Claymore mines and a maze of trip wires.

Ben turned away from the river perimeter.

He scraped the mud off his boots and descended into Ellis's bunker.

At the bottom of the stairs, Ben banged his M-16.

"Who goes?"

"Medics."

"OK, come on in, brother."

Ben stepped down the mud-slick steps towards a dim yellow light. His eyes and nose smarted at the pall of smoke and the stink of unwashed bodies.

In the back of the shadowy bunker, Lam huddled with four Vietnamese women over Ranklin's girlfriend on a stretcher beside the tiny blue flames of burning C-4 on the floor.

"Over here, man," Ellis said.

Lanky, slow-moving Ellis sat cross-legged inside low jagged walls of blue Pabst Blue Ribbon beer cases. A big Texas flag was gathered on a wall of green Seven-Up cases. An oiled M-60 machine gun lay on glossy Playmate centerfolds spread across the dank concrete floor.

Crates of M-79 grenades were stacked along the blue and red beer-case walls, along with three freshly oiled launchers. Dozens of LAW rockets were piled atop the dull olive shine of ammo cans.

Ellis grinned, a joint hanging from his mouth.

"Shit coming down, baby," Ellis said, offering the joint.

Ben held out his fist. Ellis knocked it up and down and finished the dap by bumping elbows and shoulders.

"You dig you a Coke, brother? *It's the Real Thing.*"

"No thanks, brother," Ben said.

"Hey man—ever seen Jennifer Jackson? Miss March, '65."

"Just because I'm from the suburbs, Ellis, you think I live under a fucking rock?"

Ellis pointed at the *Playboy* centerfold taped on the blue Pabst cases where a smiling black woman with spectacular breasts smiled from the glossy paper.

"Now *she* one magnificent bitch," Ellis said, grinning.

"Looks just like my girl back in the World," Ben said. "Where'd you get all this ordnance, Ellis?"

Ellis picked up a grenade launcher, cracked open the breech, and examined the wide barrel.

"Big pile out near the airstrip," Ellis said. "ARVNs tossed 'em 'fore they dee-dee'd. Major had my gooks throw lye all over them bodies near the Dust-off pad to keep off the stink, so we scored ourselves some weapons. And beau coups ammo."

Ben nodded.

"Shhhhhhh," Ellis said, freezing and then intently listening. "Hear that?"

"Artillery?"

"No, man. *Digging*. Hear it? Shhh, listen," Ellis said. "I told that colonel, but like everybody else, he thinks I'm batshit crazy. Shit, them gooks is *coming* tee-tee time, Benjamin man—every way they can—sappers, human wave, digging tunnels, maybe even on tanks, shit. I heard they even got choppers and Chinese fighter jets out there on old Ho's Trail."

Ellis's eyes blazed red as he checked the M-79s clean. He picked up the M-60 machine gun and stared down the barrel.

"You're certainly prepared, Ellis," Ben said, looking over the weapons, the ammo, the stacks of Pabst beer and C-rations—all held together stylistically by the naked pinups on the walls. "You're ready for World War Three."

"Bring it on, Jim," Ellis said. "And then, we be bringing it back home to the block."

"You been talking to Limerick."

"I'm down, baby. Dig it."

Ben nodded. He looked over the Pabst Blue Ribbon wall to the Vietnamese women squatting near Tu on the stretcher.

"I need to talk to our dispensary girl," Ben said.

"Do what you need, brother, ain't got no use for that bitch," Ellis laughed. "So *now* you be taking her *back*, after Clancy just dumped her *here*?"

"I need to talk to her."

"Well, then go-od luck to you, my brother," Ellis said as they knocked fists.

Ben walked to the back of the bunker and stood over Lam, sitting on her haunches holding the pregnant Tu's hand. The sharp-faced woman frowned at Ben.

"Ranklin come?" said the pregnant girl on the stretcher.

The sharp-faced woman shook her head "no" and glared at Lam, who let go of Tu's hand.

Lam made an uncomfortable smile and faced Ben.

"Benhamin."

"Hey, Lam. Can we go outside? Talk?"

"OK, G.I.," she said.

Lam followed Ben past the tied-back Texas flag and Ellis cleaning his machine gun on the floor.

They stepped up the dozen muddy steps and went out into the night.

As Ben guided Lam over to a wall teetering above the river, an artillery flash revealed their silhouettes.

Weapons rattled from the tower bunkers, and rifle safeties clicked off.

"MEDICS!" Ben shouted to the bunker guards.

Lam sat down.

A flare popped overhead, but Lam didn't even flinch as it zigzagged across the sky. Ben leaned his rifle on the sandbags. Artillery fired on the bluff.

"You love Halliday, Lam?" Ben asked.

The flare lit up her long black hair, but her face was in shadow. Ben held his breath.

"No know, G.I.," she whispered. "Howaday make Lam beau coups sad."

"That's just how he is," Ben said. "He tries, but he just can't help himself. You like me, Lam?"

"Yeah, G.I."

"Well, I like you. A *lot*. Ever since I saw you. A *beau coups* lot."

Lam turned in the flare light and tried to smile.

"How come you no say before, G.I.?"

Ben fumbled in his fatigue pocket and pressed something into Lam's hand.

"For you, Lam."

The flare light revealed a red apple. Out on the barbed wire were black shreds of cloth from the dead N-V-A soldier.

Lam's hand shook.

The little parachute faltered, plummeting the burning magnesium into the mud with a sizzle, and flashing their twin shadows onto the collapsed bunker wall.

"No like apple so much no more," Lam whispered.

"It's OK, Lam," Ben said.

Ben squeezed her hand over the apple and laid his cheek against hers.

"Lam, I love you," Ben said.

Her hand went limp.

The shreds of the dead N-V-A's peasant pants danced on the wire as the flare burst into an eerie glow and flamed out.

Ben gripped her hands in the dark.

"It's OK. Take your time," Ben whispered. "There's nothing we couldn't do back in the World, you'd love California, Lam, I know you would."

Lam sighed.

"Too much now, G.I."

"Right," Ben said, exhaling and getting up. "We're still in Daktoum."

Lam leaned over and kissed Ben's cheek.

"We talk-talk, G.I."

The apple dropped to the mud. Ben retrieved it and wiped it clean.

"I'll keep it," he said, slipping the apple into his pocket. "In case you change your mind."

Ben held her hand as they walked back.

When they walked into the dim yellow bunker light, Ellis flashed a lewd grin at Ben.

In the shadowy back of the bunker, Tu's huge, frightened eyes stared up from the floor.

Lam nodded to Benjamin, ran over to Tu's stretcher, and spoke Vietnamese.

Ben turned and cocked an imaginary pistol at the grinning Ellis, still cleaning his machine gun. Ben headed upstairs.

*   *   *

Major Ranklin rushed through the dark night and went down the stairs into Ellis's bunker.

He nodded at the lanky black man behind the uneven beer-case walls. Tu slept peacefully on a stretcher in back with the medics' girl holding her hand. The sharp-faced woman glared.

Ranklin knelt, and when he ran his hand across Tu's forehead, the sharp-faced woman frowned.

Tu opened her eyes and smiled.

"'lanklin," she whispered.

Ranklin kissed Tu and held her small hands.

"Baby come soon," he said. "Go back to sleep."

"OK, 'lanklin."

Ranklin tried to leave, but she gripped his hands.

"Lo' you, 'lanklin."

"I love you, Tu."

Ranklin slipped his hands loose, smiled, and got up.

At the entrance, Ranklin glanced back, but Tu had already closed her eyes. The sharp-faced woman glowered.

As Major Ranklin rushed across the dark camp back to the TOC, all the artillery batteries fired a steady stream of projectiles roaring out into the night.

*   *   *

Colonel Lehr lay on his bed in the dark in full battle dress. When something slipped down his bunker steps, Lehr drew his pistol, and eased back the cocking mechanism. A match flared, filling the doorway with light, and Lehr nearly fired.

Gabrielle's long hair undulated in shiny black waves, and her deep-set eyes flickered under the brief light.

Colonel Lehr threw his arms around Gabrielle.

"Stop," she said.

Lehr eased Gabrielle over to his bed, lit a candle, laid her down, and held her until she slept, under the hissing static of the radio on the floor.

*   *   *

Later, Gabrielle awoke to a candle dripping wax on the floor. She slipped from Lehr's arms and gathered her clothes off the concrete floor.

Lehr awoke and watched her dressing in the candlelight.

"It is over," she said.

"What?"

"Everything."

Gabrielle laced a muddy boot.

The pain—which had subsided as he dozed—tore at Lehr's side.

Gabrielle bent over to lace her other boot.

"I cannot stay," she said.

"What?"

Gabrielle shrugged.

"I cannot be here anymore, Colonel," she said.

"Where will you go?"

"I don't know," she said. "Anywhere but here."

"You can't go out on the road," he said. "That's an order."

"You're *ordering* me to stay, Colonel?"

"Yes," he said.

She stared and then slowly shook her head.

Lehr studied the gentle arc of her nose, the dark circles around her eyes, the sensuous lips, the tangle of black hair.

The colonel waited for her to speak, but Gabrielle just turned around, and walked slowly up the bunker steps.

Only the warm scent of her lingered in the dank air.

*   *   *

Outside, Gabrielle stood beneath the massive, crossed timbers above the entrance portal of Lehr's bunker.

The scudding mist over Daktoum suddenly swept away under a red-orange glow of flame from Nhu Canh Du, burning.

To the west, artillery flashed yellow-blue flames onto the mist, and beneath Gabrielle's muddy boots, the earth rumbled from bombing.

She stared at Lehr's uneven bunker timbers lit by artillery and then looked down the colonel's black staircase.

"Au revoir," she called into the darkness.

There was no answer.

Gabrielle clutched at her fatigues like she was shivering, and then she rushed into the night.

*   *   *

Halliday awoke, sputtering water. Ben stood over him with a dripping towel.

"Get up, damn it—we're getting hit."

Halliday yanked on his boots and quick-tied the laces around his ankles.

Across the bunker, radios howled with panic.

"Sappers in the wire!" Cullen yelled.

The medics scrambled off the stretchers, grabbed their weapons, and readied supplies. Doc's dog whined.

"Bacsi, shut up!" Clancy yelled. "Get them I-Vs out and prepped. Halliday, you and Donnelly grab that sixty and get on top the back entrance. Get me some whole blood, Limerick, then go guard the front stairs. Shoot anything that ain't G.I."

*   *   *

Halliday huddled beside Donnelly, whose body shook as he clutched his rifle. Halliday gripped the cold machine gun and pointed it at the darkness.

Red American tracers and green N-V-A bullets ricocheted over Daktoum. A mortar popped, going out, and flares lit the black mist. Rifle fire chattered all around.

Someone charged through the blackness.

Halliday fired a high burst. Red tracers shot over the TOC.

"Hold fire, goddamnit!" a voice yelled.

A stretcher ran out of the dark.

"Sorry," Halliday called out. "Thought you were sappers."

Two young soldiers appeared from the dark, carrying a man without a foot.

"Ain't no more sappers," one soldier said. "This dude blew them away."

Boots scuffled up the back entrance stairs.

"Halliday, Donnelly, downstairs!" Cullen yelled. "Now!"

*   *   *

The medical bunker filled with waves of wounded. Stretchers creaked and thumped downstairs, young men screamed and moaned for their mothers and lay mumbling in shock with distant eyes. All the medics and the two doctors worked under the dim phasing light—dressings, splints, morphine, plasma, tourniquets, fluids, suction—treating oozing, broken soldiers.

Blood dripped onto concrete and lay drying in dull, shining red pools. Limbs tumbled into garbage cans, soiled dressings heaped up, skin clung to the wet canvas stretchers.

Rockets, mortars, and machine guns crashed overhead.

The radios spat out panic amidst shrieks and moans of frequency drift and curt, hopeful lies about luck and the promise of safety. Ceaseless B-52 strikes shook the bunker timbers, the ceilings, the rough floor, and the good red earth.

So many wounded dragged in and filled the stairwells so even Halliday treated them, working in dim corners with a flashlight because Doc and Gabrielle and Clancy and the others only had time to look at the very worst.

The medics worked all night until their arms were bloodstained up to their elbows, soothing the suffering young men with first aid and softly-spoken lies.

*   *   *

Before dawn, sixty miles south in Kontum, Colonel Lehr's friend, Colonel Alexander Eagleton argued with Major Ky, Colonel Trinh's duty officer, to release a helicopter to evacuate wounded from Daktoum. Only after Eagleton threatened to wake up the notoriously short-tempered General Armbruster, did Major Ky agree to divert a single Chinook helicopter for a dawn mission, though he refused to wake up Colonel Trinh.

Eagleton was so furious that he stomped back to his air-conditioned trailer and drank a double scotch to calm his nerves, something he had never done in his military career.

*   *   *

Just before daybreak, with enemy mortars intermittently falling on Daktoum's artillery batteries along the river, Sergeant Clancy talked the Chinook helicopter down through the gray mist, nearly landing on the Vietnamese corpses.

Forty-two American wounded and thirteen bodies were quickly loaded onto the big helicopter that howled so loud that the medics couldn't hear themselves think.

Limerick walked out of the darkness wearing a clean uniform and carrying two olive duffle bags. He shook hands with all the medics and dapped Ben.

"Where you going?" Ben asked Limerick.

"Philly," Limerick said.

"To fight the good fight?"

Limerick nodded.

"Don't get your ass killed," Ben said. "Especially after surviving all this bullshit."

Limerick got on the Chinook and never looked back.

"Didn't even know he was short," Halliday said.

"Man plays his cards close," Ben said.

As the medics turned to leave, Clancy glanced into the Chinook. He spotted Donnelly, lying between two wounded men, trying to sneak out on the helicopter.

Clancy yanked Donnelly up and flung him out of the rear hatch onto the asphalt. The short medic landed on his butt beside the heap of dead men.

The waist-high perfect tangle of dead South Vietnamese bodies looked like ghostly sculpture, the small rigid figures whitened by lime, which couldn't quite quell the retching smell.

As Donnelly picked himself up, the Chinook helicopter closed its hatch and lifted into the mist.

The medics staggered across the mud, shuffled down into their bunker, and collapsed on bloody stretchers.

*   *   *

Colonel Lehr watched the Chinook disappearing into the cloud cover from the parapet atop the TOC.

After the mortars stopped, Lehr took Ranklin into his office and shut the door. The major's elegant hands nervously twitched and dark bags encircled his eyes. When Lehr offered a chair, Ranklin sat.

"Major," Lehr began. "Could we leave Daktoum today?"

"What, sir?"

Lehr threw him the redeployment cable.

REDEPLOY....

Ranklin read the cable.

"Is it possible to leave Daktoum?" Lehr repeated. "Today."

Ranklin closed his eyes.

"Major?"

Ranklin stood. His eyes darted from side to side and back toward the river bluff, where artillery was firing, and his jaw stiffened.

"Major?" Lehr asked.

Ranklin looked nervously around and paced.

"Today? It's possible. But I … wouldn't … redeploy yet. No, not today, sir," Ranklin said, his blue eyes darting.

Ranklin shook the cable clasped in his hands.

"Definitely not today. We'd have to leave behind… too much equipment."

Lehr nodded.

"I agree. We'd probably get chewed up on Highway 14," Lehr said. "A couple more days—the mist could lift, maybe we could blackmail USAR-V into kicking the South Viet's ass to releasing some Tac-Air and choppers to escort our convoy."

"Yes, sir."

"Of course, this is classified, Ranklin," Lehr said, watching the Major's fumbling hands. "Overall, is morale holding up?"

"I believe, yes, sir."

Lehr tugged the cable out of Ranklin's hands, carefully folded the rough yellow paper, and slipped it into his breast pocket. Lehr watched the Major's shifting blue eyes.

"How are you holding up? Personally."

"Oh, fine, sir, fine."

"Good," Lehr said. "Just a few more days…"

As Lehr ushered Ranklin out, pain ripped down his left shoulder.

"Good luck, Major."
"Good luck, sir."

              *   *   *

After a round of deep breathing, the colonel's pain passed. Lehr slipped on his flak jacket and grabbed his M-16 to examine the damage from the night's attacks.

At the back entrance, Lehr turned around and glanced into the command bunker.

The Kid grinned sheepishly; his pale delicate face bent over a grimy stack of papers. Sergeant Loudermilk bustled out of the Commo shack, chewing gum, and allowed the colonel a quick respectful nod of his lumpy, close-cropped skull. Sergeant Major Bricker ambled his strong, lanky body out of his office beside the colonel's. Bricker's deceptively sleepy eyes looked wise, but Lehr smelled alcohol.

"Shall I accompany you, sir?"

Lehr shook his head at the tall, ruddy thirty-year veteran.

"No thank you, Sergeant Major. Need to stretch my legs. Carry on."

Lehr scanned the huge redwood beams and columns, the rough-cut pine walls, the battered gray chairs, the bulletin boards brimming with yellowing notices, the dusty clip boards, the big green maps of Daktoum marked up with grease pencil. On the posts were taped soldiers' photos of wives and mothers and girlfriends, crossed off short-timer's calendars and naked Playmate pinups tucked into little corners. Big blue plastic fans spun and rotated on the worn gray desks.

The colonel smiled and glanced down at the wooden floor stained with red mud. Every army ends up in the mud.

Lehr turned sharply.

As he hurried out through the maze entrance, the monkey screamed. Goddamn monkey, Lehr thought, smiling. How the hell has he avoided getting killed? Maybe it's all that good N-V-A training.

By the time the colonel crossed the muddy camp road past a burned-out truck hulk, mist wet his face. He passed ruined bunkers and wrecked hootches with torn heaps of canvas, twisted screens, and smashed waterlogged wood.

As Lehr neared the river bunker line, a rocket roared in two hundred meters away.

The rocket exploded between the twin flagpoles.

The colonel ran to the river command bunker and hustled inside, surprising Sergeant Smith and Chaplain Goodby, looking out through the gun slots. The cramped bunker stank of mold and dust and unwashed soldiers.

"Where the hell's Dunkley?" the colonel yelled.

"In the TOC, sir."

"Get him on the horn. He should be out here."

"Yes, sir," Smitty said.

The rocket bombardment was disciplined. A 122 fell roughly every minute on Daktoum, each landing with a terrible roar and a devastating explosion.

Sergeant Smith monitored the sniper fire, which had increased steadily, as N-V-A trenches and spider holes steadily crept down Rocket Ridge toward the river.

Lehr turned to the Chaplain.

"Why are you here, Padre?" Lehr asked.

"A soldier wanted to see me, sir."

"For confession, Padre?"

"Sir, you know I'm a Baptist."

A chunky young soldier raced in, banging his flak jacket and rifle on the wooden doorframe. Smith loaded him up with steel ammo boxes and dispatched him.

Rockets pounded closer, hit-by-hit, steadily walking down the company street from the airstrip toward the TOC. The radio chattered, marking each hit.

The chaplain looked pained.

"What, Goodby?" Lehr asked.

Goodby's small black eyes shone like raisins in the cheesecake of his soft face.

"Nothing," Goodby answered, until Lehr's eyes bore into him. "The soldier's wife went off with another man, sir."

"Jody," Lehr sighed.

"Sir?"

"What did you tell him?" Lehr asked, remembering that rainy day in Laguna Beach when Monique told him to leave.

Pain throbbed in Lehr's wrist.

"*God works in mysterious ways?*" Lehr said, instantly regretting being so nasty.

The chaplain's round mouth opened.

"Sir, that's ..."

An exploding rocket drowned out Goodby's reply.

Lehr studied the eager, lumpy chaplain. He wanted to be kind, but he just couldn't.

"Do you really *believe* all that?" Lehr asked, as he looked out a firing port at the TOC. "I mean, the mystery of faith?"

The chaplain didn't answer.

*   *   *

As Sergeant Loudermilk hustled his thick body across the TOC, successive rocket concussions shook the bunker walls so hard that dust seeped down overhead in a powdery red rain that coated all the paper and blueprints and maps and yellow legal pads scattered across the desks.

Loudermilk stuck his head into the colonel's office, where the Kid pecked away on Merton's old typewriter.

"Dunkley?" Loudermilk asked.

The Kid shrugged.

Loudermilk found the hulking Captain Dunkley in the S-2 Intelligence section, going over Teletype messages and plotting suspected enemy positions on a big map of Daktoum.

"Colonel wants you," Loudermilk said, savoring the words. "Out on the line."

Under thick black glasses, Dunkley's face stiffened as he followed Loudermilk out into the main TOC room.

"Perimeter command bunker," Loudermilk said.

A rocket crashed in close.

Lieutenant Fairbanks ran out of Intelligence, tugging his black ascot. Dust covered Fairbanks in a faint red powder, and he laughed, brushing it off his head and shoulders.

Everyone in the command bunker froze, stunned by the magnitude and the closeness of the barrage.

Major Sneller sat at his desk, rocking back and forth, and making odd chuckling sounds as blueprints shook in his trembling hands.

"Where are you going?" the Kid shouted to Dunkley.

Dunkley glared at Major Sneller.

Major Ranklin walked out of his office, his chin stubble as gray as his hair.

The sergeant major ambled toward Ranklin.

Loudermilk glanced over his shoulder just as the rocking Sneller looked up.

Fairbanks' black scarf froze in the doorway.

Loudermilk disappeared into the Commo section.

"Captain, I need to see you!" Ranklin shouted across the suddenly silent TOC.

All at once, the barrage seemed to cease.

The dour sergeant-major's long jaw fell.

A horrible sound drowned the bunker with a roar like ice picks stabbing their ears.

A white-hot flash detonated.

Chunks of shrapnel blew out the front half of the TOC.

A millisecond later, Ranklin, Sneller, the Kid, Fairbanks, Dunkley, and Sergeant Major Bricker's bodies were roasted by a gigantic flame that curled all around their filthy fatigues.

Sergeant Loudermilk had disappeared, along with the Commo section, most of Intelligence, and a few enlisted men from the 15th Engineers equipment company who were standing by as a reaction force.

The TOC's sandbagged ceiling collapsed; the entire front wall gone, so the mist drifted in, mixing with smoke and flames and the red dust from a thousand vaporized sandbags.

In an awful madness of panic, Ranklin led the moaning Sergeant Major Bricker by the hand in a crazed race through the wreckage of men and bunker, rushing blindly into the gray dimness, where he stumbled onto Lehr's muddy Jeep.

$$*\qquad\qquad*\qquad\qquad*$$

Colonel Lehr watched the 122-millimeter rocket hit the TOC from his firing hole in the perimeter command bunker.

"Jesus Christ!" Lehr yelled. "The TOC took a direct!"

The colonel charged out and ran towards the collapsed command bunker.

Black smoke billowed out of the TOC's broken walls, where dust and debris still hung in the air.

The rocket fire and bursts of small arms died away.

*   *   *

Ranklin stumbled out of the smoke and helped Sergeant Major Bricker into Lehr's Jeep and sat down to drive away.

"For God's sakes, wait, man!" Lehr screamed.

Ranklin froze with his bloody, peeling hands stiffly gripping the black steering wheel.

Lehr and Smitty ran into the smoking ruins of the TOC and returned with dazed lurching soldiers. The chaplain shepherded the Kid, Sneller, Fairbanks and Dunkley toward the Jeep.

Dunkley fell over backwards, and lay, face up in the mud. Stripped of his thick glasses, Dunkley's nearsighted brown eyes seemed naked, as his deeply burned face reflected the gray sky.

When the Colonel bent down, Dunkley pulled Lehr close.

"Get them," Dunkley whispered.

"I will," Lehr assured the large captain.

Lehr hoisted up Dunkley and settled him in the Jeep.

"Go, man!" Lehr said, hitting Ranklin's shoulder.

Ranklin drove the overloaded Jeep away, slipping through the mud.

The colonel and Smitty and a dozen enlisted men, who had run up, combed the smoking ruins of the TOC for wounded.

They piled the survivors into Recon's small gun truck, which the colonel drove to the medical bunker.

*   *   *

Dark clouds hung so low over the medical bunker, it seemed as if the mist was pressing the huge mound down into the red mud.

The first Jeep approached, whining hard in low gear as Clancy, Halliday, and Ben ran out.

The soldiers clinging to the bouncing Jeep resembled ghosts—
hollow men shrouded in loose green skins of tattered jungle fatigues. A
shocked, vacant pallor coated their scorched faces and dulled eyes as
they rode toward the medical bunker with a seemingly regal disinterest.

"Burns," Clancy said.

The Jeep halted.

Sergeant Major Bricker slowly uncoiled his lanky body from the
Jeep's front seat and walked off, unaided. Bricker passed Donnelly and
Cullen running up, but no one stopped the tall sergeant major. Ranklin
shook off help, so Clancy went to the back seat.

Clancy peeled Captain Dunkley off the laps of three men sprawled
across the small back seat. Ranklin got out, tilted the passenger seat
forward, and helped out Major Sneller and Lieutenant Fairbanks, whose
black hair was burnt dull gray and fell off in locks, smudging his collar.
Sneller and Fairbanks swayed off, holding each other, and refusing help.

Clancy faced the last soldier in the back seat of the Jeep.

"Make it on your own, trooper?" he asked.

The flushed, flaking face was so still that Clancy had to lean his
head to the man's heart to see if it was beating.

The Recon truck, filled with wounded, bounced, slid across the
mud field, and halted right beside Clancy.

Lehr jumped out of the driver's seat as medics ran out from the
staircase tunnel. All around Clancy, medics yelled and grabbed
stretchers and carried wounded from the truck bed down into the
dispensary.

The last man sitting in the Jeep had no heartbeat.

Clancy searched his eyes for life, but a dull glaze was frozen in the
shining pupils. Suddenly, the ashen, flaking features of the badly burned
man screamed at the sergeant.

"Kid?" Clancy said, finally recognizing him. "Kid?"

Clancy lifted the Kid out of the Jeep and laid him down on an
open stretcher on the muddy ground.

No one paid attention to Ranklin, who stood leaning against the
Jeep, staring at the airstrip. Ranklin eased himself back into the driver's
seat, gripped the steering wheel, and looked through the mud-spattered
windshield as if he were watching the road.

Nearby on the muddy ground, Clancy pounded the Kid with
closed-chest massage.

"Come on, Kid, come on, Kid, you can do it, Kid, start beating it, Kid, gimme just a little beat, a little one, come on Kid, come on, Kid, come on, I'm right here!"

The pale youth's glazed stare reflected the dull gray clouds.

Tears ran down the sergeant's face until shining channels cut through the grime on Clancy's strong cheekbones and wet the front of his faded green fatigues.

Finally, Clancy stopped.

He laid his big head on the Kid's chest and sobbed when he heard no heartbeat. Everyone else had gone underground.

Sergeant Clancy cradled the Kid's limp young body into his big arms and gently lifted him.

Clancy stood, not knowing where to go.

Finally, he just stopped moving, with the Kid's body draped in his burly arms.

Clancy turned his back to the medical bunker and faced the gray wall of mist obscuring Rocket Ridge.

Behind Sergeant Clancy and the dead Kid, Major Ranklin sat in the driver's seat of Lehr's Jeep, staring straight ahead.

*   *   *

Downstairs, the entire medical bunker vibrated with tense energy as the medics tried to ease the moaning and the cries of the wounded. Even Lehr tended the injured. Only the immense lie of the tanned, peeling skin, which resembled a common sunburn, betrayed the terrible conditions of the wounded. The stink of charred tissue and burnt hair from so many bodies choked the air.

"Help me, I'm cold, I'm cold, I'm sooo cold, Doc," a man lying on a stretcher near Halliday cried. "Help me, Doc!"

"Fluids," Doc announced calmly to the room. "No morphine unless I say."

Halliday grabbed a plastic intravenous tube, ripped off the seal, and searched for a vein on a tall, raw-boned man, whose skin was pink and flaking off.

"Sergeant Major?" Halliday asked.

The long rawboned man nodded.

"You're going to be OK, Top."

The soldier on the next stretcher moaned.

"Dooooooooooooc, pleeeeeeeeeeeeeeeaaaaaase, you gotta gimme something, pleeeeeeeeeeeeaaaaaaase, Doc."

Halliday abandoned the sergeant major.

He fumbled at the moaning man's arm, cut off the fatigue shirt, and pierced the soldier's arm twice with the I-V needle, missing the vein. Because of all the burned tissue, it was hard to find the tiny veins beneath the flaking burned skin.

"Pleeeeeeeeeeeeeeeeeeaaaaaase Doc!"

Searching frantically for the vein, the overpowering smell of burning flesh made Halliday gag, so he turned away, grabbed an alcohol sponge, and jammed it in his nose.

Finally, Halliday found the vein, and inserted the needle just as the harried Doc rushed up to check the man's eyes, heart, and breathing.

"OK," Doc whispered. "Morphine."

Halliday squeezed a small metal syrette into the I-V bottle, sending morphine directly into the bloodstream, and soon the man's terrible moans gave way to a faint sighing.

Halliday looked at the soldier's name tag: Dunkley.

"I didn't even recognize him," Halliday whispered.

"Leave him," Doc said. "Go help someone else."

Doc quickly surveyed the dispensary.

Rushed grimacing medics tended the wounded under the phasing fluorescent light. Halliday ran from table to table, stretcher to stretcher, helping wherever he could.

In the back of the shadowy room, the sergeant major hoisted up off his stretcher and lurched toward the stairs. Halliday spotted him and caught up.

"Out," the old soldier muttered.

Halliday guided Bricker up the long staircase.

Outside, under gray light, the sergeant major stumbled toward the artillery shell piss tube sticking out of the ground. Bricker fumbled at his trousers and urinated.

Halliday looked away and saw Ranklin, sitting in the colonel's Jeep, staring straight ahead.

Clancy stood nearby, holding a soldier in his strong arms.

When the sergeant major finished, Halliday helped him down the long stairway into the dim medical bunker filled with wounded and the whispered commands of rushing medics.

Halliday eased the sergeant major onto an olive-green canvas stretcher in a dark corner.

"Ahhhh," Bricker sighed almost pleasantly.

When Bricker grew very still, Halliday knelt and frantically examined the sergeant-major's long body, taking his pulse, and pounding on his heart.

"Top?" Halliday called, then louder. "Top! Top!"

Doc appeared.

"Shhhhh Halliday," Doc said, sliding the sergeant-major's eyelids down with an expert gesture. "He's dead. Find another patient."

Halliday bolted up and ran into Lehr, whose grim mouth was set as he went stretcher to stretcher, trying to identify the wounded.

"Have you seen Major Ranklin?" Lehr asked.

Halliday eyes widened, and he took off up the stairs, followed by Lehr.

Though the light was fading, the gray mist hurt their eyes.

Halliday ran to the Jeep where Ranklin gripped the steering wheel and stared out.

Sergeant Clancy was silhouetted against roiling gray clouds covering the hills, but for a thin green slash beneath Rocket Ridge. Lehr studied the slim body in Clancy's arms.

"Jamison?" Lehr mumbled, stopping. "Is that my driver?"

Clancy turned to the Colonel as if he was offering the Kid's body.

Lehr staggered and turned away.

Leaning over the Jeep, Halliday held his hand to Major Ranklin's throat, searching for a pulse.

As Lehr walked up, Halliday stood up and shook his head.

Major Ranklin sat very still in the faded canvas driver's seat of Lehr's mud-spattered Jeep, his pale blue eyes staring through the muddy glass up at the hills. A wry smile graced his lips. His pale, angular face was pleasantly pink, with only the skin on his chin and forehead peeling a little.

Major Ranklin's bloody hands still gripped the black Jeep steering wheel, even though he was unmistakably dead from the immense body shock from massive third-degree burns, which colored his face like a bad childhood sunburn.

Neither Halliday nor Lehr spoke.

Behind them, Clancy towered beside the medical bunker, his strong arms cradling the Kid's lifeless body up to the darkening gray sky.

21.

As night approached, Colonel Lehr monitored Daktoum Net from atop a machine-gun parapet in his new command post, Ellis's bunker.

Mist flooded the darkening sky.

Wavering columns of black smoke and falling aerial flares fed into the low ceiling.

The western horizon thundered with explosions from besieged Ban Sai, astride the low pass into Cambodia.

To the east, all around Nhu Canh Du, sporadic fires burst up in red-green flashes of jungle.

Sniper fire split open the night like a blister, from hidden positions on Rocket Ridge above the river bunker line.

Rockets fell randomly—so many, it was as if the N-V-A weren't even aiming anymore.

The Daktoum defenders wildly returned fire into the night, but under the heavy mist and enveloping darkness, few enemy flashes were visible up on Rocket Ridge.

*   *   *

At twilight, a Chinook helicopter throbbed down through the mist to evacuate Lehr's burned men.

Anti-aircraft fire from the old French camp, recently abandoned by the South Vietnamese, pounded at the helicopter. Burning orange balls rose over the Daktoum airstrip; luckily, the rounds went high.

The twin-towered Chinook lifted into the mist with only the wounded; there was no room for the dead.

*   *   *

The mist chilled Lehr atop Ellis's bunker behind a hastily erected parapet built around the wide airshaft.

Below Lehr, a crude wooden ladder led down into the bunker. The Teletype had been obliterated, so the last garbled message that Lehr had received from command was that a reaction force was "*standing by.*" Sixty kilometers away.

"That's all we need," Ellis said from below.

"What?" the colonel asked.

"A tiger just came through the wire."

"A tiger?"

"Yes, sir."

Ellis grabbed an M-16 rifle from the weapon pile in his room and walked over to Chaplain Goodby sitting near the Vietnamese women at the back of the bunker.

"Major Preacher?" Ellis said. "You know how to use this?"

Goodby nodded, and Ellis handed him the M-16.

"You see that tiger, you light him up," Ellis said. "I ain't scared of no gooks, but *tigers?*"

The chaplain climbed the stairs with the M-16.

Up in the parapet, Lehr scanned the fires burning to the east and the west.

The thirteen remaining artillery cannons pounded away and suddenly went silent.

Then there was such an immense rumbling that Lehr jumped. B-52 strikes—closer than ever before, less than a mile away. Edgy, he thought, for the first time I feel edgy, like too much coffee. Dull little pains shot through his arm, his wrist, his elbow, his armpit, and his heart. The colonel scanned his watch. Pain every 55 minutes, Christ, what does that mean, besides stress? Gee, I wonder where my stress comes from?

Lehr laughed.

Ellis glanced at him, and across a pool of darkness, their eyes locked. A long burst of automatic weapon fire lit up the bunker line, and a man screamed.

"Hold fire!" a weak voice yelled.

The radio squawked.

"Oh man," Ellis called up to Lehr. "Some numb nuts tried to grease Sergeant Smith. Thinking *he* was the damn tiger."

*   *   *

Down in the medical bunker, Doc drank instant coffee and paced. The room was littered with medical trash, which the medics slowly cleaned up. A man in a stretcher with a high fever moaned, probably malaria. Halliday and Donnelly bathed the naked man with slushy ice made from beer.

"The ice machine still works?" Halliday asked.

Doc shook his head.

The smell of hops and grain cloaked the bunker's stale air, which added to the underlying stink of bad sweat, urine, blood, and death that seemed permanently imbedded in the timbers.

After the medics finished cleaning, they flopped on stretchers, but tensed at every sound and their eyes darted across the dim room whenever deep sporadic rumblings echoed down the stairway. Radio traffic was subdued, mostly drifting static and erratic squelches broken by short messages of barely concealed panic.

Clancy lay on a stretcher in a fitful daze, mumbling.

Doc sought refuge in his room.

The worn black playing cards with the Death's Head lay scattered across Doc's bed, desk, and concrete floor. The Queen of Spades had fallen into his open desk drawer and landed on the cracked photograph of Doc's wife. Doc picked up the queen and absently stuck the card into his breast pocket behind his stethoscope.

Doc tried to rest but could not sleep because Gabrielle's scent was everywhere.

In the dispensary, restless medics engaged in pointless arguments. Rats ran back and forth in the ceilings; mosquitoes buzzed the medics and stung their necks and arms and ankles.

Doc's dog, Bacsi, lay under his bed whining.

*   *   *

Walking across his ravaged firebase, Lehr wondered why Gabrielle wasn't there to treat the wounded. Lehr kept seeing his headquarters exploding, and the scorched faces of his dead staff. He thought of what Eagleton said when he had arranged the Chinook. *You're authorized one Spooky mission tonight, Lehr. Unfortunately, there's a new battle tonight in the south with Priority—they really stepped into it. Lucky for you the Cav is standing by...*

The colonel passed beneath the ugly beams framing his sleeping bunker and went downstairs. At the bottom he held the post to steady himself.

His desk lamp had fallen, spilling a dim cone of light onto the floor. A foul smell assaulted him.

A dog growled in the darkness, dropped something with a dull thud, and ran past Lehr. He chased the dog up the stairs, where it stood, silhouetted in the skittering flare light.

At the top of the stairs, the long hard canine head was thrown back, with its mouth wide open. Sharp yellow teeth flashed, dripping something. The flare went out. Lehr turned to his dim room and drew back, startled.

Behind the dim cone of light on the bunker floor, Gabrielle's eyes shone as if disembodied as she stepped out of the darkness with her black-leather medical bag.

"We've been ordered ... to ... re-deploy," Lehr said. "I'm just waiting..."

"Waiting?" she said. "For what, Colonel?"

Pain split Lehr's chest, and he slumped against a post.

"We can't go down that road," Lehr whispered. "Not tonight."

Gabrielle became a blur until the pain faded.

"They *ordered* you to leave Daktoum?"

Lehr opened his hands to the darkness.

A rocket screamed in and crashed into the airstrip. The explosion resounded and echoed away.

The generator died, and the lamp on the floor went out.

"I can't help anymore, Colonel," Gabrielle said.

Lehr held onto the rough timber, feeling his way to her.

"Do something," she said, moving away. "For me."

"What?" Lehr asked.

"Tell the gate to let me out."

"No," Lehr said.

Gabrielle inhaled deeply.

"Please."

The generator restarted, and the lamp flickered back on. Gabrielle's face appeared in shadow. Lehr shook his head.

"No," Lehr said, starting up the stairs. "There's no security out there."

"There's no security here," she said.

"Maybe," Lehr said. "I have to try."

"Why?" she said.

The colonel's footsteps drifted up toward the crashing of artillery and were gone.

*   *   *

Doc found Gabrielle in the colonel's sleeping bunker, dressed in an oversized pair of Lehr's fatigues. Her face shone, and her thick black hair was pulled back into a ponytail. A fresh orange smell masked her dense scent, and Gabrielle smiled like a girl on a first date.

"Despite everything, it is beautiful tonight," she said. "I have always loved summer monsoon."

Light from the colonel's desk lamp on the floor shadowed Gabrielle's face.

She walked over and took the young doctor's shoulders. Gabrielle hugged Doc, and then kissed his cheeks twice.

"Adieu, Bacsi."

Doc tried to kiss her back, but she broke off.

Gabrielle snatched up her black medical bag and bounded up the stairs.

"Wait!" Doc called. "Where are you going?"

"Away!" she called at the top of the stairs.

Doc ran up after her.

Outside in the darkness, Doc couldn't see where Gabrielle had gone. He broke light discipline and scanned the company street with his flashlight, but all he saw were collapsed sandbags, broken hootches, and the shine of mud in the dark night. Doc thought he heard a Jeep start up, but the roaring artillery drowned it out.

When the big guns finally stopped, Doc couldn't hear the Jeep, so he walked back to the medical bunker.

$*$ $*$ $*$

Inside Ellis's bunker, the sharp-faced woman and Lam tended the jittery, pregnant Tu. All the other Vietnamese had fled earlier that afternoon when Lehr ordered them to leave.

"'lanklin?" Tu repeated. "Wheah 'lanklin?"

No one told her that Ranklin was dead. Goodby couldn't bear to complicate Tu's hope and pain, so he just turned to the sandbagged wall, switched on his pen flashlight, and read his pocket Bible.

$*$ $*$ $*$

Halliday lay in the medical bunker on a stretcher, trying not to obsess about the tiger and the King Cobra that were loose inside the camp. Flashing orange stripes and the huge black snake haunted him—he kept imagining the great cat bounding across the airstrip, joining the snake, and both of coming down into the medical bunker to get him.

Around eleven, the worst rocket bombardment yet fell on Daktoum.

Halliday lay on a stretcher, clutching a death grip on the wooden rails. He gritted his teeth at all the horrible crashing that cut and slashed his ears like broken glass. He imagined the night sky bursting with fire and metal and suffering and death.

Above him, the scaly claws of highly agitated rats scurried above the ceiling boards. Death rained down from the sky, horrible terrible death imagined as a child. Death haunted Halliday, flailing limbs and screams and fire and crushing suffocation and torture, a desperate rain of hell and death spilling out of the mouths of priests and nuns and parent shaming, death, falling on his bunker, thunder and lightning and shrapnel—the piercing knife-roar of exploding metal stabbing Halliday's heart and pinning him to the stretcher with bloody visions of his own flesh, cut into bleeding ribbons.

*   *   *

On and on the shelling crashed down, ripping Daktoum apart with the dullness of an hour-long beating where the flesh stops aching and the thought of being beaten becomes worse than the actual sensations. What the hell do they want? Halliday wondered, staring up at the massive ceiling beams. Why would they even want Daktoum? It's a shithole. And now it's trashed.

Exhausted medics lay all around him like living corpses on bloody, sweat-stained stretchers—Cullen, unwashed, Nimmer, unshaven, Donnelly's food-stained flak vest layered with bandoliers of ammunition. Their hands were never further than three feet from a weapon. The medical bunker stank of stale cigarette smoke and bad body funk flooded with the terrible indefinable smells of too many wounded and dead.

The barrage went on until Halliday's shell-hammered head danced with crazy, white-knuckled panic. For what seemed like days, rounds continued to fall on bunkers and buildings and into the red mud and into soldiers, crackling explosions pounding the airstrip, crashing timbers, disintegrating canvas, ripping metal into junk and flesh into slime with terrible noises.

*   *   *

Fear haunted the medics like poison in the liver. Cullen imagined his arms blown off, Ben visualized his heart torn out, Doc saw his skilled hands as stumps without fingers, Clancy—no right arm, Nimmer could not speak because of the hole in his throat, Halliday watched himself roll down the sidewalk in a wheelchair, and Donnelly constantly shook, transfixed by an image that taunted every young soldier—his sex blown completely off.

Donnelly hummed and when the rockets would not cease, sang out: "Dak-toum Bridge is fall-ing down, fall-ing down, fall-ing down, Dak-toum Bridge is fall-ing down, my fair la-dy."

"Shut the fuck up!" Nimmer shouted.

Nimmer hovered over the radio, trying to make out messages over the chaos of shelling and radio static. So far, there were no ambulance calls, no wounded—yet—nothing to call the medics outside into the rain of death.

*   *   *

So many rockets fell that eventually the barrage became a helplessness that covered Halliday like artillery, like the relief of the first blow in a fight, ripping away the imagined cyst of tension so when his breath finally deepened and came faster, he felt that all the waiting was over and now death or whatever would come soon.

*   *   *

Later, the radio cracked with three curt calls.

Three times, Nimmer shouted into the radio, and three times Halliday felt the hand of death.

"KIAs?" Nimmer asked. "Roger that, pick 'em up later. Lifesaver out."

Donnelly and Halliday had ambulance duty, but so long as the soldiers were dead, ambulance pickup could wait. The medics waited: mad, long finger tapping, fist clenching, frustrating minutes, hours, until panic bore into them as Nimmer repeated messages from the command net.

"Lost contact with Ban Sai," Nimmer yelled.

They waited while the sky continually roared, both sides raining as much death as they could upon each other.

To the west, Ban Sai grew silent; to the east, Nhu Canh Du burned with a dull roar.

Finally, the barrage ceased and gave way to an unearthly silence.

Though the explosions still crashed in the medics' minds, the silence seemed worse and produced an unrelenting tension that boiled their brains.

"Bastards!" Cullen screamed.

He grabbed a bottle of fluids off a shelf and threw it. When the glass shattered on the plank walls and saline fluid exploded and scattered gouts of shining liquid and sharp slivers of glass across the mud-stained concrete floor, it felt good.

Clancy lay on his stretcher, transfixed, as Cullen wound up like a fastball pitcher and quickly smashed three more bottles against the walls. Finally, Clancy jumped up and caught the larger Cullen in a headlock.

"OK troop, enough! That's enough! Calm down."

Cullen struggled hard, but Clancy dragged him to a stretcher, both men heaving with hot breath. When Clancy finally let go, Cullen just stood there, his big, close-cropped head hung down, his pale skin bursting with sweat.

The burly black sergeant turned to the medics circling like cattle.

"Get some god-damned sleep—all of you! Ben, get up on the roof with your weapon in case that tiger still around. Halliday and Donnelly, go get them bodies. Bad for morale to have bodies lying around. You know where they are—two at the mortar pit, one at the front gate, four in the one-five-five area. Bring 'em back, tag 'em, put 'em away, and get some sleep!"

*   *   *

After the barrage ended, Lam and Tu couldn't stop crying, so lanky Ellis turned from his machine-gun portal and hustled across the main room. As Ellis came close, he slipped on a mud clod, and fell against the sharp-faced woman's chest, where he felt something metallic.

The sharp-faced woman forced a smile and quickly retreated behind Lam.

"What the hell you got in there, girl?"

Ellis grabbed the sharp-faced woman.

"Colonel!" Ellis yelled. "This gook got something in her blouse!"

"No got nawthing, G.I.!"

"Take care of it!" Lehr yelled from the parapet.

"Oh yeah? Let's check out that nothing!"

The sharp-faced woman's face went rigid as Ellis ripped her blouse open and revealed a large white brassiere.

"Hold your rifle on her, Major Preacher!" Ellis said.

Goodby came over and pointed his M-16 as Ellis wrestled with the sharp-faced woman until her brassiere ripped away tearing the cloth.

"FUCKYOU NUMBAH TEN G.I.!" the woman hissed.

The woman covered her breasts as Ellis peeled off the torn bra and squeezed it until he found a small metal box sewn into the cloth under one cup.

"What the fuck?"

Ellis ripped out the metal box and held it near the dim light. Lehr finished a radio call and climbed down inside.

"Looks like a transmitter, Colonel—a god-damn radio!"

Ellis shoved the woman so hard that she fell down.

"Number ten V-C whore!"

Ellis spat in the woman's face, and her lips clenched in a thin line. Ellis yanked Lam up to her feet.

"Me no V-C," Lam pleaded. "Me no number ten, G.I.!"

"Girl, I don't give a shit what you say, shut the fuck up."

"I no do nothing, G.I., ask Howaday G.I., ask Benhamin G.I.," Lam pleaded with Ellis, "Me number one medic girl!"

"You number one *shit*!" Ellis said.

Ellis ripped open Lam's blouse and groped her body with a rough hand while Colonel Lehr examined the transmitter.

"Little one ain't got nothing, Colonel! What do I do?"

"No do nothing, G.I.!"

"Shut the fuck up! What do I do with 'em, Colonel?"

Colonel Lehr's face set in hard lines. Merton, the Kid, Ranklin, the sergeant major—all their faces flew by, and when Lehr closed his eyes, he could still smell burning flesh.

"Take them outside and tie them up," Lehr told Ellis. "Goodby, you watch the pregnant one."

Ellis snorted. He found a roll of Commo wire, bound their hands, and then wired their feet in a crude hobble.

"Better to die as a martyr than be enslaved by imperialist aggressors," the sharp-faced woman said to Lam in Vietnamese.

"Shut the fuck up all that gook talk!" Ellis said.

Ellis tore a dirty olive T-shirt and gagged the two women.

Ellis shuffled the sharp-faced woman outside to the river bunker line and securely wired her to a wooden post between coils of barbed wire leading to the collapsed bunker.

The night spat out small arms fire and popping flares. Artillery boomed, flashing the low clouds.

Mortars hit the Nhu Canh Du end of the airstrip, falling short and bursting red-yellow explosions.

The sharp-faced woman stood calmly, bound to her post, while Ellis dragged out the struggling Lam. Ellis lashed Lam's feet and arms and body to another splintery post, and then the lanky black soldier stood back.

Flare light reflected off the mist, and cordite smoke drifted past the two women tied in tangles of barbed wire.

"Mamasan, babysan, you just like Solomon and the baby," Ellis said. "If your gook buddies choose *not* to rocket us no more, maybe you get to live, so then we can turn your skinny butts over to *our* sorry-assed gooks for interrogation, bic?"

Ellis laughed in the faces of the two women tied to the posts and walked away from the wire. He held his weapon overhead and shook it at Lehr, barely visible on the bunker roof, talking on the radio.

Ellis disappeared underground.

*   *   *

Ben sat in the parapet above the back entrance of the medical bunker holding his M-14 rifle. Mortars exploded near Nhu Canh Du, and illumination flares careened through the mist. Ben felt Lam's apple in his pocket and smiled.

Ben heard a clatter and turned.

In full battle gear, Halliday rushed out the front entrance, cringed at all the mortars and small arms fire, bolted to the ambulance, and yanked open the driver's door.

Something caught Ben's eye in the shadows—Donnelly, hiding near the front entrance. When Halliday started up the ambulance, Donnelly sprinted across the dark lot, and ducked into the Waiting Room bunker.

Halliday opened the ambulance door and stood out on the running board.

"Donnelly!" Halliday yelled. "DONNELLY! Where the fuck are you! Let's go!"

Halliday waited for a long moment and then climbed into the ambulance.

Ben stood up.

"He's in the Waiting Room!" Ben yelled.

Exploding mortars on the airstrip drowned out Ben's voice, as he ducked beneath the sandbagged wall.

When Ben looked again, the ambulance door slammed.

"Halliday!" Ben yelled. "Wait!"

Halliday drove the ambulance rattling off into the night.

*   *   *

Halliday wheeled the boxy ambulance, acutely aware of its large red cross on the roof, swaying along the slick Daktoum camp road.

Bursts of mortar and artillery fire lit the shadowy road. Overhead on Rocket Ridge, ghostly tree hulks flashed under the flares lighting the mist.

Hundreds of flare parachutes were scattered across Daktoum, in broken trees, fluttering atop the hootches, and the barbed wire like the tiny cloaks of departing spirits.

The ambulance crept through the night, churning across the slippery roads.

Halliday steered the top-heavy ambulance by the dull glow of blackout lights and sporadic flares rocking across the low clouds down into the mud and sputtering out.

Small fires burned all over Daktoum.

Smoke and mist drifted over the crumbling sandbagged walls where the rain-soaked possessions of the dead and wounded lay buried in the mud, torn fatigues and boots, audio cassettes, and photographs of lovers, of mothers, pale blue airmail letters.

Halliday stopped beside the mortar pit and shut off the engine.

"Medics?" an exhausted voice called from the dark.

"Yeah."

"Over here."

A hand guided Halliday into the foul-smelling mortar pit inside a crude circle of sandbags. Two teenagers hefted slippery bodies and dumped the corpses onto the ambulance floor.

"Sorry," Halliday explained as he roughly shoved the bodies inside. "No room for stretchers."

"Don't reckon they'll much care."

Halliday slammed the double doors.

"Good luck," the voice whispered.

"You, too, man," Halliday said. "Good luck."

Halliday cranked the starter and wheeled the ambulance around the TOC, where a fallen flare flickered shadows on the massive collapsed walls.

Artillery thundered out—barrels aimed horizontal as the big guns pounded Rocket Ridge point blank with beehive shotgun rounds, which exploded so near that the concussions shook the boxy ambulance.

The hot, viscous scent of fresh bodies wafted through the ambulance as Halliday held the muddy steering wheel, his hands sticky with their blood.

The ambulance swayed through shadows and firelight until wide frightened eyes peered from the bunker at the front gate, and a short chunky soldier in helmet and flak vest crisscrossed with ammo bandoliers confronted Halliday.

In the middle of the camp road, a slight young soldier—maybe a hundred-twenty pounds—lay flat on his back, dead in the mud, with his mouth open, as if in surprise.

Halliday got out and with the guard's help, pulled up the dead man, and swung him inside atop the two corpses.

Halliday banged the rear doors shut.

The guard stood on the camp road under the dim carnival of flare light. He looked at the camp and shook his head.

"She just drove out, man," the guard said, awestruck. "Right out. I couldn't get the colonel on the horn, so when she asked real nice, of course, I let her go, why the fuck not? She just up and fucken *left*, man. Drove right out of here. Fuck, how could I stop anybody leaving this shithole. That French broad got her some kind of balls. I mean, where's she gonna fucking *go*? Nhu Canh Du? Ban Sai? *Where?*"

Halliday had no idea what the guard was talking about.

"Good luck," Halliday whispered.

"Fat fucken chance," the guard replied. "I shoulda gone with her, I shoulda. Any place is better than this jugfuck."

Halliday climbed in.

As he circled the ambulance across the shallow airfield drainage ditch, the bodies in back shifted and banged.

"Good luuuuck, motherfucker," the guard called out.

To the north, what looked like a string of giant firecrackers blew across the misty ridge line.

The steep crest flamed with huge red tumbles, bursting with billows of smoke blacker than the night, and on such an immense scale, that the entire world might just be obliterated.

"Jesus," Halliday whispered.

Overpowering concussions thumped and jangled and rattled the ambulance.

On the Daktoum riverside, a bunker exploded.

A headless torso flew up like a broken doll, the flailing arms and legs briefly silhouetted in a hot orange flash.

Then the night went black.

*   *   *

"Jesus Christ, probe!" Lehr yelled to Ellis.

Chaplain Goodby answered the buzzing field phones, while Ellis poured mad machine-gun fire out the firing portal, and brass shells clattered across the concrete floor.

"They're in the fucking wire!" Ellis screamed.

"Kontum Control," Lehr radioed. "Delta Tango Lifeline. Request Spooky ASAP, Over."

"Roger that," the radio said. "Delta-Tango, Spooky's rolling, bring him up on your net. Good luck, Control. Out."

*   *   *

As Halliday drove, six Daktoum river bunkers lit up—all flares and red tracers and explosions, as a hundred rifles blasted the perimeter wire and the steep hillside.

On the river line, silhouetted by the flashes, two slender Vietnamese soldiers sprinted through a roil of gun smoke.

"Jesus Christ!" Halliday whispered. "They're inside."

A machine gun whirled around and fired *into* the camp. Red tracers sprayed Daktoum like flashes of neon, rounds zinging over Halliday's ambulance.

Shifting flare light froze everything into stark, black-and-white cutouts of ruined tents, sandbagged walls, and lumpy bunkers.

Halliday sped the ambulance out of the flare light, following the curving road to the darkened artillery area on the highest river palisade facing Rocket Ridge.

Under smoking flares swaying down through the mist, the ambulance bounced toward the low ugly sprawl of an artillery bunker that Halliday half-remembered.

A rocket had destroyed one end of the bunker.

Timbers and red earth collapsed in a smoldering heap. The flares burned out, so Halliday slowed to a crawl.

A hand reached from the blackness into his window.

"Stop," a voice ordered. "Get your ass out!"

Halliday slammed on the brakes, pushed open the ambulance door, and jumped out. The hand yanked him toward a half-collapsed overhang.

"Spooky," the voice said.

A hundred feet overhead, a big propeller airplane roared by with an overpowering light flooding the camp.

A terrible blaze of red pounded down as thousands of bullets thudded into the earth with the primal guttural roar of a killer hailstorm.

"Get your ass in here!" the voice yelled, shoving Halliday down a few stairs into darkness.

Halliday stumbled into a sandbagged chamber with an overwhelming stench of blood, sweat, urine, defecation, and death. He gagged and threw up on the dirt.

So many bullets snapped into the bunker top that it sounded like a giant shovel smacking dirt on a grave.

"Piss on 'em, Spooky!" someone snarled. "Fucken piss on 'em!"

Hundreds of red tracer slashes pierced the narrow gunport, glittering crimson streaks on the soldier's face.

Halliday looked over his shoulder.

Under an eerie light smoking with gunfire and mist, the old 1930s propeller plane swooped a hundred feet overhead.

A flash lit up two Vietnamese tied on a post near the wire.

The big plane spat out another flesh-tearing roar of bullets, showering the battered camp with thin red tracer lines.

The black airplane roared by so close that Halliday instinctively jerked back and banged his helmet on a timber.

"Fuck!"

The plane disappeared into the mist.

*   *   *

Spooky swooped over and over Daktoum, working every corner of the camp.

"Any more sappers?" Lehr yelled at Ellis from atop the new command bunker.

"Not yet, sir!"

Lehr confirmed with the bunker line and radioed Spooky.

"Concentrate fire outside the wire. Over," Lehr said.

"Roger that, Delta Tango Lifeline. Out."

"Much obliged, Spooky."

Neither Lehr nor Ellis nor Goodby noticed that the pregnant woman had disappeared.

*   *   *

"OK, we're clear," the voice inside the foul artillery bunker told Halliday. "Bodies are over here."

The big hard hand led Halliday to a pungent, knee-high pile of inert flesh in the center of the bunker.

Under the dim battle light, Halliday had thought they were sandbags. The voice and Halliday lifted the bodies one by one and hauled them out to the ambulance.

As they piled the dead into the ambulance, the bodies settled into a perfect tangle of arms and legs and twisted torsos, blood-smeared faces and hands and muddy boots and fatigues.

A foul sweat crowned Halliday's forehead as he closed the ambulance doors.

Spooky thundered overhead.

Halliday jumped.

The big plane roared off, firing a long burst beyond the front gate.

"What happened?" Halliday asked.

"Gun took a direct," the unseen voice said.

The voice disappeared into darkness.

Explosions, tongues of fire, and the constant *kakak, kakak, kakak, kakak* of small arms and rattling machine guns tore at Halliday, standing beside his ambulance.

Spooky roared back out of nowhere, banking over sideways, and blasting the river bunker line with the huge spotlight.

Red tracers ran in sheets down the steep, stump-scarred palisades and pounded into the shiny black river. Bellowing an electronic roar, the bat-like airplane disappeared into the mist.

Halliday exhaled and climbed into the ambulance filled with dead soldiers.

The ambulance—top-heavy with seven bodies—was hard to control, swaying and slipping on the mud slick camp road past the collapsed TOC bunker.

Spooky's bullets jangled sparks flying off the barbed wire.

Halliday tightened his grip, jerking the steering wheel so much that the top-heavy ambulance lost traction and drifted across the mud so gradually that Halliday barely noticed the until the big box slid off into a ditch.

The old ambulance ever so slowly tipped over until Halliday's door sank into the side of the ditch and gravity pressed him against the window as it filled with mud.

Claustrophobic, trapped with seven dead men, Halliday squealed, and smashed his helmet against the windshield, which somehow calmed him.

Gunfire zinged overhead in random shots.

Halliday forced himself to take deep breaths, carefully twisted himself around, and struggled through the open passenger window, swung his legs out, and jumped down.

Halliday walked around the tipped-over ambulance.

Didn't look like too bad—thank God, the rear doors didn't open, Halliday shuddered—if he had lost a body....

Standing in the mud, he peered through the crescent-shaped back windows.

The seven bodies were a nasty tangle of arms, legs, and heads.

"Shit," he said. "Clancy's gonna have my ass."

When Spooky roared over, Halliday dove into the mud and red tracers blasted all along the river perimeter.

A flare popped and again, harsh white light see-sawed through the mist.

When Halliday turned back, the ambulance exhaust sputtered, so he leaned in the passenger window and switched off the engine, then fished around inside, and dug out his rifle and ammo bandoliers.

Crouching and jumpy, Halliday hustled towards the medical bunker.

Under shifting flare light, he slogged past ruined hootches and blown-up bunkers. Behind him, the artillery fired beehive rounds at Rocket Ridge.

Fearful, Halliday ran down the muddy road just as Spooky swooped in, so the great white searchlight fell right on him.

Halliday froze.

The black plane roared by close overhead, banking so steeply that its wing nearly touched the riverside bunkers. The big engines strained, while another electronic roar zapped immense red sheets of tracer bullets down on the river line.

Halliday hurried away into the darkness of the Daktoum Company Street—a ragged loneliness of smashed wood and torn canvas.

Somewhere, a dog barked viciously.

Halliday spotted a flash of orange.

Orange? Shit!

The jittery, nine-foot-long tiger prowled the company street, snarling at the gunfire, the explosions, and the shifting flare light. The tiger turned toward Halliday.

"Lordy Lordy," Halliday whispered.

He sucked in his breath and ran away.

When a mortar illumination round flashed on the colonel's sleeping bunker, Halliday ducked inside as a recoilless round crashed into a nearby tent.

Pitch black. Feeling the wooden sides, he hurtled down the steep stairs with breath burning until the concrete floor hit his boots and nearly dropped him.

Struggling, Halliday felt something extremely strong and lithe brush his leg. Fear cut off his air so he began to hyperventilate, paralyzed by the tiger. Finally, he slowed his breath. Blood and air returned, the pounding in his throat slowly ceased, his hands unclenched.

Halliday let out a ragged exhalation.

The tiger growled so close that Halliday violently shook. He gasped and lurched into a bunker timber so hard that he saw stars.

Everything went black as he slumped and slid down the thick wooden column.

*   *   *

Halliday awoke alone in the darkness, mind racing, body twitching, and heart shuddering.

A match and then a cigarette flared on John Wayne's shadowed face.

Stinking like rotting death, Wayne took a long drag, glared at Halliday, and pointed up the stairway. Then the burning match went out.

Halliday opened his eyes and slowly stood up.

He lit a match. He was alone in Lehr's dank bunker—no John Wayne and no tiger.

Halliday rubbed his aching head and headed upstairs to the war.

*   *   *

Tu sat panting, huddled in the doorway of an abandoned bunker, her eyes wild at the fiery, smoke-filled sky above Daktoum. Her cheeks streaked with tears and her hands curled around her swollen belly.

Somewhere in the darkness, a dog growled.

*   *   *

Chaplain Goodby, perched atop a stack of metal ammo boxes in Ellis's bunker, monitored three field telephones attached to hastily strung wires gathered in big loops around a thick beam. Ever since the generators had been hit, only a weak kerosene lamp lit the bunker.

Outside, the firing slowly died away.

Goodby fingered Colonel Lehr's daughter's letter in his fatigue pocket, pulled out the airmail letter, and ran his fingers across its striped, blue edge. The colonel needs all his strength now. He doesn't have time to be distracted by the death of a loved one. But the man is a failure—what else was a father whose daughter writes how much she hates what he's doing, and then she jumps off the Golden Gate Bridge?

*   *   *

Ever since Daktoum came under fire, Colonel Lehr couldn't feel any pain. The intense shelling spurred his mind and body into the clean precise actions of command. Reaction force, fields of fire, commo to the artillery, conserving ammo, illumination, the bunker line, Duster control, quad fifties.

Spooky, shit, her sister ship crashed into a ridge above Ban Sai, bad luck, Ranklin. Gabrielle. Wonder where she is?

When the incoming stopped, Lehr climbed down the bunker ladder, grabbed the radio, and monitored the net from the parapet atop of Ellis's bunker.

Spooky droned overhead.

The plane's brilliant light sprayed through gaps in the clouds and cast huge shadows across the camp tents. Lehr glanced at the low clouds tinted orange from the fires.

A lull settled over Daktoum; small arms fire died away. Lehr radioed Spooky.

"Go ahead, Delta Tango Lifeline."

"How's your visibility? Over."

"Ahh ... almost zip. Getting a bit hairy—you still got Indians? Over."

"Negative," Lehr replied. "Request you recon by fire down 14 toward Ban Sai? Over."

"Ahhh ... sorry about that, Lifeline," the radio crackled. "Besides the low visibility, we're running on empty. Got to refuel and get back to you, Over."

"Thank you much, Spooky. Delta Tango Lifeline Out."

"Ahh ... Lifeline? Control says ahh ...we can return your ten twenty for Route one-four mission at ahh approximately oh-four-four-five, to oh-five-two zero hours, Over."

The colonel eased himself off the parapet and slipped down the ladder into the bunker.

Underground, Lehr leaned against the sandbagged wall and exhaled. Instantly pain returned, and when Goodby caught his glance, the colonel scowled.

Over in a shadowy corner, Ellis grinned over a hot machine-gun barrel, and Lehr nodded back.

"Hey Colonel?" Ellis said, looking around. "You seen that pregnant V-C bitch ennywhere?"

Lehr shook his head.

"Shit!" Ellis said. "Should I go look for her?"

"Forget it," Lehr said.

A whirring sound tore across the night and exploded, followed by another and another and another.

Recoilless rounds blasted the camp with piercing cracks like a giant whip.

The colonel bounded up the ladder into the parapet.

The Duster tank at the Nhu Canh Du end of the airstrip burst into flames.

"God damn it!" Lehr cursed.

When the big bunker beside the Duster blew up, Lehr grabbed the radio handset.

"Reaction Force, bunker one-zero!"

"Stay put," Lehr yelled to Goodby.

The colonel grabbed his M-16 and ran outside.

Ellis strapped on a half-dozen LAWs and followed Lehr.

*   *   *

Halliday hunkered on the stairs right below the doorframe of Lehr's sleeping bunker.

A dozen soldiers ran by, but it was so dark, and they went by so fast that Halliday couldn't tell whether the pounding boots were friendly or enemy.

*   *   *

The machine-gun truck's four fifty-caliber machine guns pumped out withering fire all around the burning Duster and the bunker. Illumination rounds arched up from the mortar tube and streak-lit the smoky mist. Small arms popped and crackled; Claymores boomed on the wire; 1-5-5s lowered their barrels and smashed point-blank rounds at the perimeter wire, the river, the smoky palisades, and all the skeletal tree trunks looming out of the mist on the defoliated hillside.

*   *   *

Cullen and Nimmer met underground on the landing inside the medical bunker. Hefting big black medical packs and wearing flak vests and helmets, the two tall young men readied to head out, Cullen to the reaction force, Nimmer to the casualties on the river bunker line.

They struck a stance like opposing football lineman with their elbows held wide.

"AH-CHA-CHA-CHA-CHA!" they chanted.

Cullen and Nimmer made crazy wild grins, knocked shoulders hard, and then headed upstairs.

*   *   *

Colonel Lehr and Ellis—carrying the radio—joined the dozen-man reaction force, leapfrogging from wall to sandbagged wall through the camp of smashed tents, moving toward the burning fighting positions on the bunker line near Nhu Canh Du.

The mortar tube kept careening up a steady stream of illumination rounds through the smoke and mist, but still, Lehr could see no shadowy sapper teams, no half-naked enemy soldiers running by with explosives taped to their legs.

As the reaction force approached the burning Duster beside a smoking bunker, Lehr ordered a halt.

No enemy soldiers were visible. There was no rifle fire.

Another bunker blew up in the artillery area on the bluffs, a half-mile away.

*   *   *

After the reaction force ran past Halliday, hiding in the colonel's bunker stairway, a huge explosion rocked Daktoum, followed by another and another and another.

When Halliday peeked out, the mist was shot through with silver flashes and a wildly burning bunker silhouetted the big artillery guns. Halliday gripped his rifle like death and thought, we're fucked now, we're completely fucked.

*   *   *

"Satchel charges in the artillery," Ellis yelled at Lehr.

The exhausted reaction force left the smoking Duster and followed the colonel back across the muddy camp towards the burning artillery bunker on the river.

*   *   *

Under the haze of flashes and shadowy light, seven N-V-A sappers ran through the Daktoum wire beside the blown-up bunker near the 1-5-5-gun battery. Four sappers burst into the camp, and three got caught in the barbed wire by machine-gun fire.

"You diiiiiiiiiiiiiiiiiiiie G.I., you diiiiiiiiiiiiiiiiiiiiiiiiiie!" a Vietnamese voice screamed.

The three dying N-V-A soldiers flashed in and out of view on the wire, their thin, grease-blackened bodies lumpy with taped-on explosives.

Two N-V-A sappers assaulted the corner river bunker with grenades.

The two enemy soldiers climbed atop the bunker, turned the fifty-caliber machine gun on the artillery pieces, and shot at the running shadows of American soldiers.

*   *   *

After the bunkers blew up, Halliday aimed his rifle toward the burning explosions but couldn't see anything to shoot.

"It's fucking over," he said, his heart pounding and sinking at the same time.

*   *   *

The two N-V-A sappers darted through the camp, trailing explosions, fires, and screaming wounded.

Dull, smashing detonations echoed from the tents and bunkers as soldiers, ammo, grenades, and gasoline exploded.

*   *   *

Lehr split the reaction force up. Half went after the N-V-A sappers, and the other half assaulted the turncoat 50-caliber machine gun atop the hostile river bunker.

Ellis fired a LAW rocket at the bunker, but the round sailed high, burning a long rope of fire up over the river, and detonating out in the stunted trees on the steep hillside.

Firing short effective bursts, the turncoat machine gun pinned down the reaction force into fighting holes and behind sandbagged walls.

Ellis aimed another LAW rocket from his shoulder and blew the turncoat machine gun apart.

The reaction force hunted down and killed the two remaining sappers.

Americans lay dead and wounded, and the living dragged themselves into the remaining bunkers.

Daktoum—and the hundred-odd American soldiers left in it—lay in chaos. Half the artillery pieces were damaged.

Fires, artillery, and explosions smoked across the mist, while random red American tracers and green N-V-A bullets ricocheted overhead.

An N-V-A machine gun, dug in across the river in a spider hole, pounded out streams of fire into the camp and dueled bursts with Bunker 14's M-60.

*   *   *

Clancy dispatched medics to the wounded scattered across the camp and then waited downstairs with Doc and Ben.

"What should we do?" Doc said.

"Stay here," Clancy said. "Can't have you out getting shot, Captain. What if somebody needs you?"

The three prepped surgical kits and fluids and bandages and oxygen and prepared the suction machine.

*   *   *

Donnelly, hit by shrapnel from a sapper's charge, lay alone and bleeding at the top of the scarred pine steps of the Waiting Room, falling in and out of consciousness and mumbling: *Jack fell down and broke his crown ...*

*   *   *

Then they came, they really came.

N-V-A sappers erupted from a muddy hole tunneled under the airstrip—six, eight, ten, twenty grease-blackened sappers all carrying explosive charges. They fanned out to the isolated bunkers along Highway 14.

Dozens of whining B-40 rockets and hollowed-out bamboo canisters filled with napalm blew up the northern Daktoum bunker line, which exploded with a cracking sound like a bullwhip.

*   *   *

Colonel Lehr watched his northern line of defense blow up into a fiery horizon. When the fuel dump went up, a hundred-foot-high wall of flame flashed Daktoum bright with false daylight roaring through the mist and sucking all the oxygen out of the air with a huge concussion that knocked soldiers off their feet.

"We fucked," Ellis whispered.

Crouching next to Ellis, Lehr's pain so dazzled him that it almost seemed like a comfort.

"Back to the bunkers," Lehr ordered, getting to his feet.

The remains of the reaction force followed the colonel.

As they ran through the mud, weapons and bandoliers and flak vests flapping at their sides, past broken hootches and bunkers—from the west came a distant rumbling, clanking of metal, and dull roaring engines rising into a terrifying noise that throbbed toward Daktoum.

"Armor," Lehr said, awestruck.

Ellis and Lehr led the way back to the temporary command bunker.

The reaction force peeled off and scattered into muddy fighting holes.

Ellis ran inside the chaos of his bunker.

The lanky black soldier worked as fast as he had ever had in his life, moving stacks of LAW rockets up the ladder and onto the rooftop parapet with the help of Chaplain Goodby.

As the first N-V-A light tank wrecked the front gate bunker, Ellis stunned the enemy with a direct hit—the lead N-V-A tank blew up in a shower of flame.

As N-V-A tanks wheeled around the burning leader, Ellis kept firing LAW's.

Lehr directed the artillery to aim point-blank canister rounds at the front gate, while Chaplain Goodby tried to raise the remaining highway bunkers on land telephone lines—only four responded, all of them yelling incoherently.

Ellis blasted another tank and scored partial hits, knocking off the tracks on two more, but N-V-A tanks just kept driving around the burning hulks and over the crushed barbed wire barricade into Daktoum camp.

*   *   *

After the first armored wave, the N-V-A tanks were shadowed by infantry in pith helmets and black web gear, wearing good boots and putting out bursts of AK-47 fire.

Daktoum's machine guns and M-16s and M-14s fired long bursts and short bursts, clanging rounds that flashed and zinged off the tank metal.

Ellis's LAW rounds streaked out lines of fire toward the enemy.

As enemy infantry poured into the breached Daktoum perimeter line, the North Vietnamese tanks returned fire from turret guns, systematically moving from bunker to hole to bunker at every flash of fire, finally zeroing in on Ellis's bunker.

Most of the rounds went high and exploded across the river on the steep ridge. The air roared with scarlet-black explosions as tanks cracked duels with the remaining Daktoum machine guns and the big artillery guns.

Soldiers yelled and screamed.

Grenades burst beneath the smoky sky.

Sappers ran crazy, dropping charges in every camp fortification and bunker. North Vietnamese riflemen sniped at any American above ground, methodically moving from the edges toward the center of the big American camp.

*   *   *

Chaplain Goodby moved as fast as he ever had, tearing ammo boxes open, scattering wadding on the floor, and feeding belts of M-60 ammunition up to Ellis.

"Kontum Control, this is Daktoum Lifeline," Colonel Lehr radioed. "Condition Red, Condition Red."

*   *   *

When the sky caught fire, Tu panicked and blindly ran outside, her pregnant belly swaying down the camp road.

*   *   *

In the fog of battle, Halliday hunkered in the entrance to Lehr's bunker, until he saw a pregnant Vietnamese woman running, Ranklin's girlfriend. Jesus, she's gonna get killed.

All around Halliday, explosions and fires raged; rounds zinged overhead.

Tanks and black-clad N-V-A soldiers streamed through the gate. The cries of the wounded were everywhere, and there was so much firing and so many explosions that Halliday couldn't decide what to do. Shit, he thought, I'm staying here. To hell with that pregnant woman, she's not my problem.

A flare burst overhead.

The woman froze on the camp road under the harsh light. Tracer rounds zinged all around her until the flare dropped and flashed out.

Halliday cursed. He exhaled hard, stood up, and stumbled out of the shadows. Crouching low, Halliday ran to the woman and yanked her along behind him.

The American soldier led the pregnant Vietnamese girl scuttling along the camp road through smoke and bright explosions and small arms fire zinging overhead.

Under sputtering flare light, the red cross on Halliday's ambulance blazed ahead just as the first wave of N-V-A foot soldiers hit the hootches closest to the airstrip. The N-V-A threw grenades and shot up the American tents, the explosions setting fires.

R-P-G rounds whirred overhead and exploded.

Halliday stopped in the middle of the muddy camp road, paralyzed. The crying woman tugged at his arm.

Firelight and flare light flickered their faces as the slick road flashed red and white, red and white.

After a mortar flare rocketed overhead, Halliday dragged the woman to his ambulance, tilted over in the ditch. He fumbled at the back doors and eventually pulled them open. With a surge of adrenalin, Halliday pushed in the hysterical Vietnamese woman, and then hoisted himself atop the bodies.

When Halliday slammed the door shut, Tu started screaming at the dead all around her.

"Shut up!" he yelled. "Shut the fuck up!"

The woman quieted.

Somehow, Halliday managed to pull two corpses around her as she lay panting. Then Halliday wrangled the arms and legs of corpses around himself.

His heart beat hard and wild under the warm, stinking dead as his overpowering fear nearly took him into panic. The young soldier and the younger Vietnamese woman carrying Ranklin's child, lay entwined, uncontrollably shaking, the certainty of death haunting them as close as the warm corpses wrapped all around them.

*   *   *

Lehr manned an M-60 machine gun through the firing portal as Goodby fed him belts of ammo.

Up on the rooftop parapet, Ellis fired rocket after rocket at the N-V-A onslaught pouring through the gate.

Zinging small arms and artillery and machine-gun fire and grenades shredded all around the bunker with a tremendous earsplitting howl.

"Get some!" Ellis screamed.

The whine of a rocket-propelled grenade cut off his voice as a shower of mud from a near hit sprayed the parapet wall with cracking shrapnel.

At his gun portal facing the front gate, Lehr methodically fired his last machine-gun belts.

Ellis shot off his last LAW, jumped down the ladder, grabbed a grenade launcher, slipped on bandoliers and a big sack of magazines, took his M-16, and raced outside.

Lehr dropped the empty machine gun forward on its mount and hefted his M-16 and an ammo bag with a dozen grenades and clips. Lehr ran out, yelling to Goodby:

"Come on, Padre!"

Chaplain Goodby followed Lehr, but halfway up the bunker steps, the overwhelming din bewildered the chaplain.

Goodby turned around and slipped back down the stairs.

He collapsed amidst the dull piles of spent brass, cardboard wadding, and empty ammo boxes scattered across Ellis's bunker. Goodby leaned against the jagged wall of Coca Cola cases and rested his head on the drooping Texas flag.

Outside, the battle howled.

Through a film of red dust, a Playmate centerfold scotch-taped to the Coca Cola wall dangled before the exhausted Goodby. Miss July's head had been torn off, so the Chaplain's eyes rested on the shiny photograph of a naked young woman's body climbing out of a swimming pool.

Goodby smiled and sighed.

He pulled out Lehr's daughter's letter and tossed onto the pile of firefight junk.

Chaplain Goodby felt in his shirt pocket, took out his steel-covered Bible, and found his favorite verse, the 23rd Psalm—*Ye, I walk through the valley of the shadow of death*—as Ellis's bunker blew up in a hard rain of fire and metal.

*   *   *

Ellis saw the RPG round heading right for him.

For a bright, endless moment, the round seemed to hang in the air on its golden rope—until the flash lit up, and he saw his name in big red neon letters—LESTER JEWEL ELLIS.

*   *   *

"Something's wrong," Clancy told Doc and Ben as they waited in the empty medical bunker. "Bad wrong."

Clancy squeezed the radio handset.

"Can't raise nobody—not Bunker line, Lifeline, nobody."

Outside, the roar of the battle dimmed.

Doc reached into his fatigue jacket pocket and took out the photograph of his blonde wife and thought about his child growing inside her, which flooded him with feeling.

When Ben saw the photograph, it made him think of Lam and how maybe his mother could help her learn English—maybe she might even go to school.

"You OK, Doc?" Ben said.

"Yes," Doc said, nodding. "You?"

"Me?" Ben said, laughing. "I'm having a fine old time."

Clancy stared at them like they were insane.

From outside came a tremendous roar, followed by silence.

Then there was the sound of running boots.

Someone started down the front stairs.

Clancy dropped the radio. The footsteps retreated.

"Ben, see what's out back. I'll take the front, Doc, get you a rifle—not that god-damned worthless forty-five."

A bamboo canister filled with napalm tumbled down the front stairs.

Then, it was as if the entire Daktoum medical bunker took a dive right into the sun.

*   *   *

Colonel Lehr crept from shadow to shadow, hugging sandbagged walls as he crossed Daktoum. Something in his muscles, his blood, recalled the all-night street fighting in Italy when he was very young. His lungs ached, and his nose burned from cordite as thick as coal dust in the air, but Lehr felt good and strong and alive. He stood up, fired, moved, stayed still, got up, moved low, then froze for three seconds, picking off enemy soldiers with single shots and lobbing grenades at waves of N-V-A soldiers.

From bunker to ruined bunker, Colonel Lehr moved and fired like a training movie with a pumping glow that coldly and efficiently propelled him with a full, hearty, and strange passion that brought back the feeling he had upon seeing his first naked woman. He squeezed the woman away in a fleeting burst from his M-16 trigger, and then he moved again. By the book, by the book, fire, run, hide, fire, run, hide. That's what it's all about, Lehr thought. Goddamn you, Armbruster, if you could only see me now.

The colonel heaved himself up.

He ran past a tangle of dead men to another shadowy wall, knelt, and fired a burst that clicked his M-16 empty.

Lehr reached for a bandolier, but the canvas bag and his fatigue pockets were empty, so he took refuge behind a heap of sandbags, unknowingly right in the middle of the ruined officer's club.

Lehr searched a dead soldier for ammo, but there wasn't any, so he tossed his M-16 aside with a clatter, unbuttoned his forty-five pistol, and cocked it.

A massive shaking convulsed his left side.

Lehr's body shuddered, his chest heaved, and he gasped for breath.

It's like my heart has burst, he thought.

Though his body twitched and jerked, he felt strangely removed and distant. The pistol tumbled out of his hand and cracked onto the concrete floor of the ruined Officer's Club. A wet feeling throbbed across his chest, like his heart had exploded and was dripping inside.

All around Lehr, mortar flares blazed out in the sky.

The continual roar of the battle separated itself into isolated explosions, sporadic gunfire, and finally, single shots.

Lehr heard screams and crying, hoarse breathing and shouts and running footsteps and everywhere, the dull roar of fires. The cries of wounded soldiers fell away with the single shots and finally, the night went quiet and exhaled.

Colonel John Lehr rested on the sandbagged wall, unknowingly facing Rocket Ridge. A dying heart fluttered in his chest. The darkness before his eyes grew dim and then very bright. Lehr felt something metal and square in his left pants pocket, and he clutched at it.

Out of the blackness beyond the ruined Officer's Club, Gabrielle briefly appeared, then his wife, kissing him when they were first married, and his daughter Christina, laughing as they played Frisbee on Thousand Steps Beach in South Laguna, racing across the shining sand beside the endless blue Pacific. Lehr struggled to catch their eyes, but then everything faded, and the night returned, black and as misty as the trails of smoke drifting by above him.

In an instant, Lehr saw the faces of every man at Daktoum. Tears that felt like blood ran down his cheeks.

"Yes," Colonel John Lehr whispered.

Lehr felt his heart stop beating.

A moment later, an AK-47 round shattered his dead chest.

*   *   *

A sweating young North Vietnamese soldier in black ran up and saw the eagle insignia on Lehr's helmet.

"Dai uy! Dai uy!" he called excitedly for his captain. "Lai day, lai day!

The young soldier withdrew his long knife and stabbed at Colonel Lehr's body until his captain ran up and dragged him off. A political officer came over.

"This is a great victory over the imperialist aggressors!" the political officer declared, "I have never heard of a full American colonel being killed in ground combat!"

*   *   *

The back door of Halliday's ambulance swung open.

Two slender, hard-breathing N-V-A soldiers surveyed the dark ambulance cabin. One soldier took out his long bayonet and kicked at the bodies. He stabbed the body beside Halliday and had a hard time pulling out the knife.

The other soldier laughed, spoke in Vietnamese, and then shot his AK-47 into the ambulance, with a terrible roar that startled the first soldier, who yelled, and shoved him.

Under the ringing roar of concussion, Halliday slipped his hand over the woman's mouth and held it so hard that he thought she might choke. Halliday shook uncontrollably at the thought of his death and tried so hard to avoid crying out that he moaned.

The N-V-A soldiers' sudden laughter covered his moan.

Ears ringing, Halliday thought that he heard footsteps walking down the muddy camp road.

The big ambulance lay almost on its side.

The rear door revealed a corpse's arm that had slipped out.

*   *   *

As soon as the rout of Daktoum was certain, the North Vietnamese infantry and armor immediately retreated, piling their dead and wounded atop the light Russian attack tanks. The first wave of ten sped off toward Ban Sai.

The last tank bore the bodies of Lam and the sharp-faced woman, whom the soldiers had found hanging on the Daktoum wire near two dead sappers.

A small mop-up team of N-V-A infantry soldiers quickly combed the big American camp, shooting and throwing grenades in the remaining bunkers and tents.

To the west, the ghostly buzzing of a helicopter at treetop echoed in the mist. The last soldiers took cover until a radio operator waved.

A small helicopter—one of the few used by the North Vietnamese army—boomed closer, flew very low under the thick mist. The helicopter skimmed over the Daktoum gate and the burning N-V-A tanks and circled the destroyed camp. The helicopter was painted black and showed no running lights as it set down near two marker flares close to the flagpoles where Lehr had first landed, months before.

A thin, granite-faced general of middle age—who reported directly to the legendary Vietnamese General Vo Nguyen Giap—stepped from the helicopter. He spoke briefly to the tank commander and then to the political officer.

All across Daktoum, fires burned.

The general studied the American camp for a few moments without expression, then he climbed aboard the black helicopter, which immediately took off.

Flying without lights close to the ground, the helicopter soon overtook the tank column. The North Vietnamese helicopter followed the road to Ban Sai and then disappeared across the border into the dark jungles of Laos.

As soon as the general's helicopter was out of sight, the withdrawal order was given.

*　　　　*　　　　*

For a very long time, Halliday and the woman Tu lay unmoving beneath the ripe bodies. Rifle shots and explosions still stung their ringing ears when they heard the beating of a helicopter come and go.

Sometime later, a propeller plane circled high above and flew droning off into the distance.

Later, snarls and growls split the quiet night.

Halliday cautiously peered out the rear window.

A red streak on the eastern horizon bathed Daktoum firebase in dim crimson light. The snarling dogs grew fierce.

Halliday watched through the smeared window until the crimson light paled.

He squirmed out from under the dead men and tugged on the bodies covering the pregnant woman.

Their eyes burned.

A breeze swayed the ambulance door creaking as Halliday freed the woman. When she lay clear, atop the dead men, he slowly pushed open the rear door, put his finger to pursed lips, and signaled the pregnant woman to stay.

Halliday slipped off the dead bodies and slid out of the ambulance with his rifle, which had somehow remained inside.

Soft light shimmered over Daktoum.

Halliday crouched, ready and cautious—even though he sensed that there was no one alive in Daktoum except dogs.

He passed the ruined mess hall, the rubble of the officer's club, and scores of blown-up and burned bunkers and tents. Soldiers were sprawled everywhere in the perfect postures of the dead. After Halliday saw the astonished face of the dead mess sergeant, he refused to look at any soldier, afraid that if he saw a friend, he might come unhinged.

He climbed the walls of the shattered TOC bunker and stood amidst the tangle of antennas surveying Daktoum.

The dark hills still lay in shadow.

The broken, smoke-black fuselage of the transport plane was piled at the end of the airstrip near the hulks of helicopters—twisted aluminum and plastic melted into puddles.

On Daktoum's low western palisades, artillery gun barrels were black silhouettes against the sky.

On the Nhu Canh Du end, a smoking, burned-out Duster tank haunted the skyline.

All along the flattened company street, soldiers' bodies were strewn randomly, like victims after a flood.

Halliday's feelings and bones and mind went foggy under all the devastation and a night spent beneath ripening corpses. He wandered in a daze through the pale pre-dawn light.

Barely able to move in his stunned trance, Halliday trudged on, so consumed that he missed pregnant young Tu slipping out of the ambulance.

Tu followed him at a distance, cradling her swaying belly.

Among the ruins of ghostly sandbagged bunkers and charred jungle buildings, dead soldiers lay sprawled in the mud beside pale, freshly smashed wood.

Halliday walked past fire-blackened bunker entrances and large shell craters.

Wisps of smoke and flickering flames lit his way.

The sound of dogs grew louder.

Mumbling and shivering in the dawn Highland chill, Halliday came to Lehr's big bunker.

Snarling ripped his still-ringing ears as a pack of dogs raced by chasing a yellow mongrel.

The pack viciously snapped at something in the yellow dog's mouth as he bolted around the misshapen bunker with the pack following.

Halliday stumbled after the yipping dogs.

He walked right into the pack, canine fur brushing his legs, kicking his way through the nipping and snarling.

Halliday lunged at the yellow dog, which bolted away.

In the yellow dog's jaw was a severed hand, clutched in a tight fist.

Halliday raised his rifle. As the yellow dog veered around the mound of Lehr's bunker, he shot it in the head with a single crack of his M-14.

The shot broke the silence of the firebase.

The yellow dog flipped over, dead in the mud.

The yelping pack scattered out into the pale light.

Halliday knelt and pried the severed hand out of the dead dog's mouth. When he unclasped the bloody fingers, he found a chrome Zippo, the one that Ben had loaned him in the officer's club bar, so long ago.

Wiping the blood off his hands, Halliday remembered that Lehr had kept it. Lehr. He slipped the lighter in his pocket and slung the rifle over his shoulder.

Carrying the severed hand, he walked around Lehr's bunker.

Across the valley, the sun came up like thunder above the still-smoking Nhu Canh Du and then the steep brilliant wall of Rocket Ridge emerged, trailing strands of mist.

As Halliday rounded the bunker corner, the deep blue sky silhouetted a hanging man.

From the heavy crossed entrance timbers, a naked man hung upside down, slowly swaying from commo wire, twisted around his bare ankles.

The man's eyes were gouged out, and his hands cut off. Trails of dried blood ran down the corpse, filling the eye sockets and staining the short gray hair.

Halliday gasped, trying to recall Lehr. The colonel's bloody arms pointed at the steep green hills. Unable to take his eyes away, Halliday heard a sharp guttural cry and turned.

Tu slumped against a sandbagged wall, her mouth wide open, and her hands clutched to her large belly. Her black pants were soaked, and water pooled in the red mud around her feet.

Halliday dropped Lehr's hand and ran over.

Tu gripped Halliday with such a fury that all he could do was ease her onto the wooden landing step beneath the hanging Lehr. Her legs contracted, and she screamed as Halliday struggled to pull off her black silk pants and underwear.

Tu shuddered and let out a piercing cry.

Moments, minutes, an hour passed until inch-by-inch, the bloody top of a baby's head appeared.

Halliday wiped his hands on his fatigues, ready to catch the child.

The baby came with remarkable speed until strong sunlight sparkled the wet, blood-streaked little body. Halliday stared at the tiny new life in his hands and using his knife, gingerly cut the twisted cord near the child's belly.

But the infant would not breathe, so Halliday, remembering a movie, held the baby girl upside down by her feet and then smacked her lightly on the bottom, causing her to howl.

The newborn girl opened tiny, blinking round eyes to the hard early morning light of Daktoum.

*   *   *

In his Kontum trailer, Colonel Eagleton was awakened by telephone.

"O-I-C, sir," a voice said. "Lost contact with Daktoum Lifeline. They called in a Condition Red."

"What?"

"Last contact was 0400 hours. A Spooky low on fuel. Daktoum took boo-coo fire and probes, but everything seemed OK. Spooky couldn't get back 'til now. Visibility was minus zip up there, sir."

"Goddamnit man, why didn't you wake me?"

"Sir, been trying to raise Control for an hour, Spooky said they were OK when he left. We've had pretty sketchy radio contact with Daktoum since their Teletype went down."

Eagleton slammed down the phone.

In two minutes, he was out the door in a new flak vest and helmet cover, clean jungle fatigues, and polished jungle boots. He jumped into his Jeep and drove through the dark to the helicopter staging area.

A platoon of soldiers huddled together in the darkness, resting on their rucksacks, while the helicopters completed pre-flight.

Colonel Eagleton braked the Jeep and jumped out.

A husky, battle-dressed Captain walked up.

"Hawkins?"

"Sir."

"Change of mission. I need your Combat assault team, ASAP—Daktoum."

"I thought that was the Viet's op, sir."

"We still have support there. Condition Red. Cancel your insertion and get me two gunships."

*   *   *

Within ten minutes, a Command-and-Control ship led a string of ten Hueys and two Cobra gunships toward Daktoum. Eagleton stared out at dark jungle.

"Could just be a commo problem," Eagleton said.

The chopper pilot cut in on his headset.

"Sir, Spooky made a high pass over Daktoum. Couldn't raise anybody. Too dark for a look-see, but no enemy fire."

Below the line of helicopters, virgin jungle poked through the dark mist, the long ridges like great ships, thick and dim as night. After twenty minutes of flying, the choppers descended to treetop. The gray-black sky dissolved into strands of mist.

"Here's our visibility, sir."

The red slash of Highway 14 appeared below in the silver half-light, littered with abandoned trucks and Jeeps.

Beneath the green, triangular-shaped mountain, Nhu Canh Du lay smoking. Green tracer bullets angled in at the last helicopter, but the ground fire went wide and streaked toward the massive black wall of Rocket Ridge.

The tail gunship returned a burst of fire.

The dawn light struck Rocket Ridge into a dazzle of green, and as the sun came up behind the line of helicopters, pillars of smoke rose from Daktoum firebase. The helicopters banked around in a line above the ruined firebase.

"Jesus!" Eagleton said, "What happened?"

Captain Hawkins, grimaced, set his jaw, and shook his head.

"Somebody down there, sir," a voice said over the headset.

The chopper banked.

Beneath the helicopter, a naked dead man hung upside down from a bunker entrance frame.

Beneath the dead man, a disheveled American soldier held a newborn baby by its heels above a Vietnamese woman lying on the bunker steps.

"Jesus H. Christ!" Eagleton said.

*   *   *

They had gone.

Back into the hills and the forest, following an extensive network of trails hidden beneath the triple-canopy jungle and back into tunnels dug so far beneath the earth that even B-52 bombs couldn't reach them, back to where they needed to rest, because Bac Ho had said that to win independence, they might have to fight for a thousand years.

*   *   *

"Lehr?" General Armbruster asked on the radio.

"No," Eagleton said. "Only one man survived."

Ghostly echoes and static bled through the radio transmission.

"I'm damn sorry, Eagleton—you two were close."

"Yes, sir."

Armbruster's breath rasped.

"Damn sorry, Colonel. I know it's no consolation, but heat-seeking and Intel confirmed that the main N-V-A force turned south. Colonel Trinh's claiming victory—and I'm not so sure he's completely wrong. The N-V-A didn't break the ARVN. And no American will ever die at Daktoum again."

"What?"

"Redeployment, Colonel—that order stands. From now on, Daktoum is Vietnamese. I'm thinking that it would be an act of great good faith for me to fly up there this morning with General Linh and congratulate Colonel Trinh. For the Vietnamization policy. We can be up there, by, say, noon."

Howls of radio traffic whispered over the line.

"Yes, sir," Colonel Eagleton said hollowly. "Of course."

*   *   *

Captain Hawkins' platoon drew the grisly task of bagging the American bodies and laying them out near the airstrip. The Vietnamese woman and her infant daughter were dusted off to Pat Smith's hospital in Kontum.

Two Cobra gunships, joined by the slicks, reconnoitered Rocket Ridge, Daktoum valley, the Badlands, and out to the tri-border area beyond Ban Sai.

None of the slicks or gunships drew fire.

Once again, full regiments of the North Vietnamese Army had vanished into the triple-canopy jungle.

*   *   *

After the medics checked out Halliday, Colonel Eagleton took charge of him. The two walked along the cratered airstrip towards Ban Sai, with long lines of bodies at their back.

"Halliday," Eagleton said. "I know how you must feel."

Halliday turned and reached out to choke the colonel, but Eagleton caught his arms. He stared into Halliday's eyes.

"Colonel Lehr was my friend," Eagleton said.

The young soldier in the bloodstained fatigues glared at the colonel in the pressed uniform and shook his head.

Behind them, Hawkins' men cut loose Colonel Lehr's body and eased it to the ground.

Halliday laughed a harsh bitter scoff.

"You think I've never seen combat, soldier?" Eagleton said.

Halliday walked away toward Rocket Ridge and fought crying, but tears cut across his dirty cheeks. Eagleton saw them and looked down.

Behind them, the line of body bags grew longer.

Eagleton took a deep breath and grabbed Halliday.

"I am not just a callous rear-echelon bastard."

Halliday's face twisted in hate.

"Listen, son," Eagleton said. "In an hour, a four-star general will be up here. To give you a medal. Personally, I think you've been through enough."

Eagleton's grip eased, but he kept his hands on Halliday's shoulders, and the young soldier did not take them off.

*   *   *

At noon, Halliday, Colonel Eagleton, and a short stout South Vietnamese colonel faced General Armbruster and six staff officers beneath the flagpoles on the Daktoum airstrip. Bright new American and South Vietnamese flags had been flown in and ceremoniously run up the two tall poles that loomed over the ruined camp. Halliday wore new jungle fatigues, which had been brought in with the generals.

As a Vietnamese colonel pinned a medal on him, Halliday glared, but he couldn't tell if Armbruster even noticed. Colonel Eagleton was given the same Vietnamese medal.

I get one for hiding under bodies, Halliday thought, and he gets one for hiding in Kontum.

*   *   *

That afternoon, after the generals and the colonels had flown away, mists swept across Daktoum, bringing back the low ceilings with a touch of rain.

Water gathered in depressions on the pockmarked airfield until the large puddles mirrored the low gray sky, the red earth, and flashes of the green misty hills.

On the airstrip, Captain Hawkins' soldiers humped the rain-slick body bags into a transport plane.

A lone American infantryman trudged through a rain shower—a scout or a LURP who had straggled in with the Montagnard troops temporarily taking over Daktoum.

The soldier's M-16 was slung downward, and his body bent under a heavy rucksack. He stepped warily, trailing wisps of smoke from a dangling cigarette. As he exhaled, a cloud of smoke drifted into the mist.

Halliday sitting on a sandbagged wall beside Lehr's body, barely noticed the infantryman walking through the light rain. Lehr's body lay in a green rubber bag atop a new olive-green stretcher like the ones Halliday had carried a thousand times. Lehr was going home. Armbruster had authorized a helicopter.

I should be happy, Halliday thought, getting out of this fucking place. A flash of Ben and beautiful little Lam brought salt to his eyes.

He looked at Lehr's body bag and then up at the steep green hills swollen with rain.

Halliday stared at the misty valleys and tried to imagine Lehr in Heaven, which almost made him laugh. The old man—gone, along with Ben and Clancy and Doc and all the medics. Everybody, gone. Goddamn, the Ridge looks like its glowing—maybe all that fresh green is just the mountain, laughing at the American army, at every goddamn army. All our guns and planes and choppers and soldiers couldn't do shit against those hills.

The soldier approached. His helmet cover and fatigues were nearly colorless, and his flak vest was stained with more stories than anyone would want to hear.

Halliday stared at the green hills.

When the soldier spotted the body beside Halliday, he silently slipped onto a sandbag wall.

The soldier watched the bodies being carried into the transport and looked at Lehr's green bag lying before Halliday.

"A brother?" the man said.

Lehr?

"Yep," Halliday said.

"Lost beau coups brothers here," the infantryman said.

He reached into his fatigue pocket for a crushed pack and shook out two cigarettes. He handed one to Halliday, cupped his hands, struck a match, and extended it. Halliday bent over and inhaled.

The infantryman laid a filthy hand on Halliday's shoulder.

Like a wave, Halliday broke, until everything had come out in great rasps, and tears ran down his cheeks in wet lines. All the while, the hand rested on his shoulder.

As quickly as the tears had come, they were gone.

The rain stopped.

The mist lifted and all the evanescent vapors of the Annamese Cordillera drifted back into the deep jungle valleys.

"You need a bird?" Halliday asked the infantryman in a new voice. "If you don't mind riding with me and Lehr."

"I'd be honored," the soldier said.

Halliday nodded. He ran across the airstrip to the transport plane and then returned to the infantryman sitting on the sandbag wall above Lehr's body.

"It's up to us, now," the soldier said, sweeping his hand over the hills, the firebase, and Lehr's body. "We're the ones bringing it all back home."

He dragged on his cigarette and snuffed it out.

Halliday wasn't sure what he meant.

Twenty minutes later, a helicopter thumped in.

When the lift ship dropped towards Daktoum, Halliday bent to pick up Lehr's stretcher; the stranger shouldered his heavy rucksack and picked up the back posts.

They stepped slowly across the mud beside the airstrip. They set Colonel Lehr's body down on the faded Red Cross near the burned-out hulk of the medical bunker.

The helicopter boomed in with a rainbow of mist that rattled the olive-green body bag. Halliday and the stranger slid Lehr's stretcher inside and strapped it to the aluminum deck.

Halliday nodded at a vaguely familiar pilot and co-pilot, who nodded back. The infantryman tossed in his rucksack, and Halliday sat down in the jump seat beside him.

The turbines whined, the bird lifted, hovered a moment, dipped its round nose toward the ground and tail high, shot forward up into the air, gaining speed and altitude.

At the end of the Daktoum airstrip, the chopper rose and banked over the burned-out hulk of the transport plane.

They headed east toward a long line of puffy clouds over the coast, where the turquoise horizon of the South China Sea was lost in a shimmer of light.

*   *   *

Three months later, Halliday stood, sweating beside a hundred veterans on the Bien Hoa Airbase tarmac.

A long silver airliner taxied up with a roar and stopped, the engines wound down, and a stairway ramp was rolled up.

The cabin door of the Boeing 707 opened.

A hundred fresh-faced young soldiers in pressed khaki uniforms walked down the aluminum ramp into the heat.

Halliday and all the veteran soldiers looked right past the shocked and confused new faces.

All the veterans could see was the vibrating silver airplane, shining through waves of heat.

*   *   *

High above the Pacific, Halliday closed his eyes. He leaned back in the airline seat and dozed until a rustle of nylon woke him. He opened his eyes to a smiling blonde stewardess in a pale blue skirt who handed him Coca-Cola in a glass with ice. As Halliday sipped the sweet bubbly drink, the pilot announced that they would land in Seattle in fifteen hours. Raucous cheers broke out, and he was flooded with relief.

Halliday set the glass on the tray table and took out Ben's chrome Zippo. He turned the lighter over and stared at the mirrored surface: *Daktoum 1969.*

An unfamiliar face stared back—deeply tanned skin, grim lips, badly cut hair—and wild eyes he barely recognized as his own. He clicked the lighter open, hit the thumbwheel, and the spark burst into flame. He shook out a cigarette and lit it.

Halliday exhaled and stared out the window as great ships of clouds rushed by.

The World, he thought, I'm really going back to the World. But what was back there? Would anyone understand? Would they care? Did they have any idea of what they've done?

The clouds parted.

Far below, the blue Pacific shimmered, flowing endlessly like soldiers sailing back and forth to every war in history, carrying every terror and every dream, rocking like the sea below, limitless, indifferent, and always shining with hope fulfilled and hope shattered.